BURNING

RED

TRINITY SLAIN

Black Rose Writing | Texas

The author grants the final approval for this literary material.

First printing

This is a work of fiction. Names, characters, businesses, places, events, and incidents are either the products of the author's imagination or used in a fictitious manner. Any resemblance to actual persons, living or dead, or actual events is purely coincidental.

ISBN: 978-1-68513-389-4
LIBRARY OF CONGRESS CONTROL NUMBER: 2023948142
PUBLISHED BY BLACK ROSE WRITING
www.blackrosewriting.com

Printed in the United States of America
Suggested Retail Price (SRP) $22.95

Burning Red is printed in Garamond Premier Pro

*As a planet-friendly publisher, Black Rose Writing does its best to eliminate unnecessary waste to reduce paper usage and energy costs, while never compromising the reading experience. As a result, the final word count vs. page count may not meet common expectations.

BURNING

THE RED LEGACIES

RED

Burning Red is a work of fiction. With that said, this dark paranormal thriller has content that may make some readers uncomfortable. Situations are very dark and may be triggering to some. Everyone deserves to enjoy stories. And if pushing your limits causes stress to your mental health, please stop. Please take note of the listed potential triggers below:

-Violence
-Blood
-Gore
-On page sex/ nudity
-Kidnapping/ captivity
-Reference to suicide attempts
-Sexual Assault
-Torture
-Death

Now, if you've made it this far and want to keep reading, go for it! But don't say I didn't warn you. No seriously, you've been warned. And if you enjoy the story, please feel free to follow me on social media, drop a review where you can, and sign up for my newsletter.

Chapter 1

Garron

A whisper came from the vent in my cell wall. It was amazing that I could clearly hear his voice over the thumping pulse of my heart, but I couldn't respond. My throat was raw and dry, my tongue felt thick and as if it were glued to the roof of my mouth.

"Hey, Garron, you OK?"

I wished he'd quit asking. He knew the answer. I squeezed my eyes shut, pressing the palms of my hands to my temples, wishing I hadn't told him my name. I moved and the cot below me creaked, too small for my large frame. I pressed my palms harder and stilled my movement as shallow breaths panted through my nose. Acid in my stomach rolled at the offensive stench and I quickly changed gears, gasping between my now parted, chapped lips. The common smells of damp wet earth mingling with an undercurrent of sick decaying flesh were always more discernible when I returned from a treatment. Even the antiseptic cleaning products they had down here couldn't cover up the stench from my heightened senses. It made me want to gag, but I knew that would just make my head pound harder. The black out coming, just wasn't enveloping me fast enough. I hoped the darkness that swallowed me up each and every time would finally keep me, but I always recovered. And today would sadly be no different.

My body thrummed with pain. It overwhelmed the hate and rage, for now. Rolling onto my side, I gripped my head as I coughed harshly, wondering if it might explode. Curling up as tight as I could, the cot creaked with an almost high pitched squeal. Brain matter would leak out of my ears at any second from the now sharp, throbbing pangs. This last round of torture was a bitch. It seemed they were always getting more creative with my daily doses. The pain wouldn't last. Just long enough to make me wish I was dead. Could be minutes, hours, days. Who fucking knew? I could never tell time since we had no windows or clocks. But right now, I didn't care, the pain filled my vision with black dots that swam around, making it harder to hold back the vomit that was burning up my throat.

"It's OK, talk to me when you can. Hang in there man." It was the last thing I heard as it all went black.

. . .

A few weeks had gone by, at least I thought it had been weeks. The man in the cell next to me said his name was Jaxon. I tried not to listen to his ramblings; he was in denial that he was stuck here forever, like the rest of us. But I knew better. We were all going to die down here.

Shortly after he arrived, I had started the new injections, we both had. My years here were a monotonous, tortuous nightmare, filled with poking, prodding and pain. It was clear he hadn't had enough time in this hell to accept his fate. Aside from the physical training and tests required to prove their continued studies, I just sat here, rotting away. I was a fucking lab rat. And now he was too. Our bodies were put through constant horrors. But I'd grown to expect the pain, almost welcome it, and he would too over time. It was the only thing we were allowed to feel.

Jax continued trying to talk to me, almost every day. He was a relentless bastard. I had no intention of interacting– ever. But I couldn't help paying attention. What choice did I have when he never shut up. It had taken what could have been weeks before I even responded. Why would I when most of my neighbors usually died within a few days. But oddly, not this one.

He'd told me about how he and the three others ended up here. The three young adults that had tragically found the broken and infected man in the woods and summoned his help. How those three students of the local school had the unfortunate timing to wander off the hiking trail. The horror of the man's pale flesh, elongated limbs, blood red eyes and nearly unhinged jaw still had Jax reeling with questions. But not me. I knew what he was. Or better, what he was becoming. And this poor soul had no idea. He was oblivious to the realization that the same fate would most likely be his. Soon, he would be a shell of a man. Just another monster. Like the rest of us. But I did wonder if the man had escaped this hell or if he'd managed to become infected elsewhere. How had either of those options been possible? It surprisingly gave me hope. Hope of escape. Hope of destroying this place and the evil within it.

Eventually, I'd given him my name. I don't know what possessed me to do so, and some days I completely regretted the decision. But slowly, we became...friends? I hadn't had a friend in so long, I wasn't sure if that was what I should call him. We talked quietly using the small air vents located near the ceilings of our containment areas almost every night. Mainly Jaxon would talk—I truly didn't have much to say. How could I when this hell was all I could remember?

Some stories were humorous or adventurous, of days enjoyed with family and friends. On occasion I actually laughed. It was more of a quiet chuckle, but it still surprised me every time. I didn't even know I could still do that. It made me feel...human. Even if I wasn't any more. I had missed so much. It was so strange hearing stories of the outside. Outside. I frowned. I couldn't remember the last time I had seen daylight or even smelled fresh air. I didn't even know how long I'd been here. Maybe it was best I didn't know. The years all blended together. The constant new drugs made my memories fuzzy. I snorted to myself. *Fuzzy?* Hell, I couldn't even remember my last name or how old I was. I tried not to feel sorry for myself and to hold my anger at that. My anger always made Jax go quiet. Sometimes I just couldn't control the rage that boiled within me. I'd get so angry I'd black out. I'd wake up with my scrubs in shreds, cracks and claw marks in various spots in the concrete walls. There was never a scratch on me though, even with the blood I had noticed on my destroyed clothing and smeared on the walls. I think the rage worried him. Maybe it made him finally realize what his future held—just darkness filled with monsters. What the hell were they turning us into?

A woman named Sierra frequently featured in his stories; it was clear he had a strong affection for her. But it was when he spoke of his sister that I found myself clinging to each and every word. I'd fabricated a picture of her in my head, and she was perfect, from her sassy wit to her darkened past. I'd wished I could meet her. But I wasn't a dreamer, and knew it would never happen. Besides, I was too much of a monster now. My chance at a normal existence was over. But it wasn't too late for Jax, and I would do what I could for my new friend.

On nights when Jaxon wasn't retching from the 'treatments', we'd started discussing a plan to escape this place. It was kind of exhilarating. A total fucking long shot, but exciting none the less. I was used to most of the medicines by now. 'Treatment' days were the same, usually leaving me weak or unconscious, until recently. But Jax's body was new to this. He'd spent hours shaking with fever and vomiting each time he returned. I could barely remember those early days. So many years had passed since then. I didn't believe in God anymore, but I found myself wanting to pray for him. How could a God allow this place to exist? It was a work of pure evil that convinced me only the Devil reigned here. But maybe, if there was one, he was listening now. And if he wouldn't help me, maybe he'd help Jax. But really, who was I kidding? The only help we were going to get was from ourselves.

Each time we came back to these rooms, these cages, I hoped that he wouldn't die. I found that I actually enjoyed having someone to talk to, a friend...I had forgotten what that was like. It had been so long since someone even spoke to me instead of ordering me around. And since Jax had begun telling his stories, I started to dream. I'd escape this hell, dreaming of simple things, peaceful things like walking through forests, fishing in rivers or even just admiring the sky. The way the colors would change from the rise of the sun in the early morning to the breath stealing sunsets in the evening. And once in a while, she'd be there with me. She was perfect, even though I couldn't see her face. I could feel her presence and she radiated a warmth that drew me closer, calling to me and taming the monster beneath my skin.

I'd try not to feel destroyed when I opened my eyes to the dank cold walls of my prison, realizing it had all just been a dream. A life and freedom I could never have. Anger quickly replaced the sadness. I didn't know how, but someday I'd kill every one of the motherfuckers who kept me here and burn this place to the ground.

Jax was adamant that we needed to get out of here. I listened to his crazy plans and offered input where I could. I'd been down here long enough to know my way around a bit. Not that I had ever traveled without a guard. When alone, we'd discuss the different hallways and conversations we'd overheard from the guards. We were trying to map a way out, getting any information we could. Jaxon had even spotted a fire escape route card near the entrance of one of the testing areas. At night, we'd each tried to scratch halls, doorways and routes into a makeshift map into the wall under our cots. Adding to it each day, we hoped the guards wouldn't notice. We'd decided only one of us would make it, as the other created a diversion. The plan was set. Next week, I was going to help Jax get out of here, and he'd come back for me. If he didn't, I just needed to know that someone had gotten out of this hell—even if it wasn't me. But the one thing I wouldn't budge on, one thing I made him promise, somehow, someway, this place would burn. Even if I was in it.

Ken, one of our regular security guards, tapped the reinforced glass front of my cell with his ASP and barked for me to get up. I had been so lost in my thoughts, I hadn't heard him approach. Dammit. His reddened round face with sunken, beady eyes, stared impatiently at me from the doorway. I lifted my lip in a disgusted sneer. He was clearly not healthy, usually having wet pits visible through his shirt and an odor smelling like cat piss that followed him. Today, his short sleeve button down was saturated again and his forehead was beaded with sweat. He slid his key card over the door release; it opened with a click, followed by the light grinding noise of the metal frame sliding open.

I leapt up with a quick movement and his body stiffened. "You're looking a little stressed today. Not starting to feel bad for treating people worse than animals, are ya?" I poked. I knew agitating the guards was a bad idea from experience. But talking with Jax had renewed some of my snarky wit. I was glad to have a little part of myself back, briefly wondering what I had been like before being stripped of my humanity.

"Shut the fuck up and move it." He snapped his wrist, extending his retractable ASP back open. My lip curled back, exposing some teeth and I held back a growl. Mark, another guard I hadn't immediately noticed, moved in behind him, hand on his gun attached at his hip. Well, my observation skills were just shit today. Mark's eyes narrowed and he jerked his chin forward as his grip on the gun tightened. These guys were on edge. Maybe today was a bad day to poke the bear. I kept the disgust on my face, but relaxed my shoulders and stance a bit. Allowing them to recognize their dominance...for now.

I did what I was told as they shoved and prodded me down the hallway. My head down, I stared at the stains surrounding the bottom of my scrubs, frowning. They never seemed to reach my feet due to my long legs and swished, making a barely noticeable scuffing noise as I walked. I had the route memorized even though I always just stared at my bare feet, briefly wondering why I was never given shoes. The thoughts raised my anger and a heat sizzled beneath my skin. They probably thought it was a deterrent to run. Like that would be the deciding factor. I rolled my eyes. I had more energy today, and my renewed defiance had me lifting my head. Sick of cowering to these pieces of shit.

I tried to pay more attention, mentally cataloging the multiple doors lining each hallway, some with windows. One of the rooms contained a bunch of monkeys and rabbits in cages. The animals were devoid of hair, with gray skin and small red veins just barely visible underneath. Scars lined various parts of their little bodies and my anger began to rise once more. I shuffled closer to the window, ignoring the guards demands and prods to my spine. Blood red eyes of a monkey shot up, connecting with mine and a small shock rolled through me. The heat beneath my skin flared hotter and a feeling of helplessness overwhelmed my mind. I stumbled back a step in confusion.

My knees buckled from sharp pain as Ken smacked the ASP across the middle of my back. I was immediately hauled back to my feet by the two men. Lowering my chin, I turned my face toward Mark and growled low in my throat, the pain already forgotten. His eyes widened with fear and he took a step sideways. Ken's taser was inches from my face as he smiled, daring me to fight. He shoved my shoulder, spinning me around. And I let him.

"You'd better behave, Rat." He spit out, then planted his boot against my tailbone, giving me a shove. I took the hint, barely containing my rage, knowing now was not the time. I had to be patient and that took all my effort. I knew I could tear their limbs from their bodies with ease. Hell, I craved it. My strength was growing or maybe it was just the fog they'd held over me for so long was lifting. But why? Was it the new injections? It had to be. I let out a deep sigh, clenching and unclenching my fists, trying to calm myself. Breathe. It wouldn't be long before Jax and I would put our plan into action. And I'd make sure all these fuckers would die.

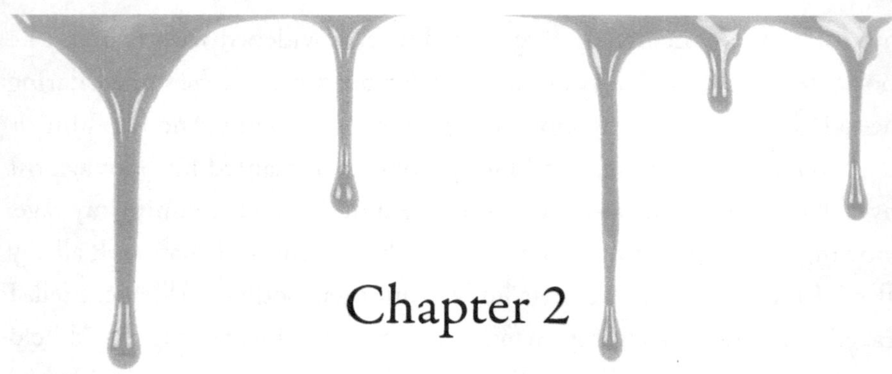

Chapter 2

Maxine Devins

"Where the hell are my keys?" I growled out loud. I wove back and forth, stomping across the sticky, half dried mud of the Wilderness Sportsman's shop parking lot. My feet alternated between crunching, slapping and sucking noises that I tried to ignore. And it wasn't hard. I was constantly distracted. Worrying about my missing brother was boiling over into every aspect of my life. Jaxon had been missing for two months. Two whole months. And I was what, going to work? I wanted to be out there, searching. But I'd made a promise. He made me promise. We both knew his plan was going to take time. I just wish he'd filled me in on more. I hated being in the dark, even if he thought it was for my own good. My big brother, always trying to be my protector. I wondered if he'd ever realize I was a grownup.

My head was down as I dug through my bag, continuing to bitch at myself for not putting my keys in my coat pocket—clearly, I carted around too much crap. Frank would be pissed if I'd lost them again. My boss was usually tolerant on most levels, but I didn't want to push my luck. Slamming into a wall, I gasped as I stumbled backward and lost my balance. Big hands grabbed my arms and stopped my descent. Startled, I yelped and shoved both palms out as I hopped backward and regained my footing. My eyes struggled to focus straight ahead, then I saw the broad chest of the human wall I'd run into. "God, I'm so sorry, I was looking for my keys and–" The wall interrupted me.

"Maxine, nice to see you again." A dark voice purred.

Blinking a few times, recognition slowly started to sink in as I followed the thickly muscled chest up to the face towering over me. The hairs on my neck rose and I stiffened briefly before automatically widened my stance. "Mr. Blasco, I wasn't aware we were on a first name basis." I stated evenly, proud there was no shake in my voice as my skin began to crawl. Mr. Blasco stood well over six feet tall; his black hair was trimmed military style, and his matching eyebrows furrowed over his deep-set, dark brown eyes. He always had dark circles under them, matching what I imagined his soul looked like. I watched his jaw muscle flex, and a small grin grew across his thin lips.

"I told you to call me Eddie," he drawled.

"Well, Eddie," I said, straightening out my stance and green fatigue army jacket, "we don't open for another thirty minutes. You could come back then?" Clearly making a statement instead of a question, as I raised one eyebrow, jutting my chin forward. Moving around him, done with the conversation, his hand reached out to stop me. I sidestepped and spun with my back now to the store. "DON'T touch me," I growled, taking a defensive position, with my hands raised in fists.

"Ooh, I like feisty." Eddie's eyebrows rose at the challenge. His grin grew, and he raised his own hands, palms facing out, a dark chuckle leaving his lips. My eyes widened and I immediately took another step backward, panic building in my chest. My defensive behavior just challenged him, and it looked like it was exactly what he was hoping for.

"Easy there," he purred, as he started advancing on me, a smirk curving his lips and excitement glittering in his eyes. I thought I saw a sparkle of red in them. *What the...* My eyes widened further and I swallowed thickly, a chill running up my spine and tightening my scalp. I took another step backward.

A loud bang ricocheted behind me, causing me to jump, a small squeak bursting from my mouth. The door to the store slammed shut with force.

"Max, what the hell is going on?" Frank barked in his deep and raspy timbre. I took a breath to speak, but Eddie answered first.

"Just stopping in to pick up my order," he feigned innocence, "but I think I may have startled your employee here," and he gestured toward me.

"Mr. Blasco, we open at nine a.m." Frank crossed his arms over his chest and looked Eddie up and down. "But since you're here, we'll grab that shipment for ya. No need for you to come back." Frank narrowed his eyes, staring at him for a moment. It almost seemed like a standoff, and I started fidgeting when Frank cleared his throat. He looked toward me, then pivoted as he stepped forward, opening the door and waving us both in. "Max, grab his order out of the stock room and mark it delivered, will ya?" He held my eyes as I passed him and gave me a knowing nod.

"Uh, yes sir," I muttered, and quickly moved through the store. Stopping briefly to throw my bag in the employees' lounge, I looked around. Frank had made his thick-as-mud morning coffee again using the ten-plus-year old Mr. Coffee pot and had managed to consume half of it already. The daily newspaper was scattered over the square card table, and all the folding chairs were up against the wall but one. I sighed, wondering how long he'd been here already or if he'd ever even gone home last night. Turning on my heel, I hurried to our stockroom and grabbed the case of 9mm shells with 'Gregori' written in Sharpie on the side.

Carrying the case of ammo back to the counter, I slowed my steps, trying to catch the murmur of voices. I couldn't make out any words, but the tones seem short and clipped, as if they were disagreeing. Moving quietly, I tried to listen, straining my ears.

"You tell him to get that shit under control. They're getting out. And I won't cover for them much longer." Frank's low tone was barely audible, but clearly angry.

"You'll do as you're told, old man. Or you might end up in a hole with them. And you know I'm not talkin' about the six-foot deep one." A dark chuckle followed Eddie's threat. As I rounded the corner, they became silent— they must have heard my approach. *What the hell were they arguing about?* Stepping around a clothing rack stocked with flannels, a stream of morning sun shining through one of the windows brought my attention to the M9A1 Beretta strapped to Eddie's waist. Working here further contributed to my once basic knowledge of firearms. So, I was firmly aware it was a military issued tactical pistol— mainly issued to US Marines. I scowled, staring at the pistol as multiple questions ran through my head. I raised my eyes, meeting Eddie's glare, and tried to straighten my features. The small corner of his mouth lifted...and I realized he'd caught me looking. Demented piece of shit probably thought I was checking him out. My stomach rolled at the thought, and my scowl fell back into place.

Frank cleared his throat, drawing both of our attention.

"Your order is all set, and the receipt was emailed to the Gregoris when they paid online."

I slid the box down the counter and quickly made my way back through the saloon-type door separating the business side. Frank reached for the box and passed the purchase the rest of the way over. Eddie snatched it from the counter and turned, thanking him for the supplies.

As he reached the door, Frank barked out, "Don't forget we open at 9 a.m., Mr. Blasco."

"See you next time, Mr. Stark." He smiled as he turned back toward us. His gaze skipped right past Frank and locked on me. "Later, Sweets." He winked as he exited.

Shaking off a chill, I looked at Frank.

"There is something really off about that guy. He's got a serious creep factor. And what the hell does he need a case of nines for every week?" Seeming to ignore my question, Frank scowled at the door, lost in thought.

"I'm gonna grab some more coffee, wanna cup?" he asked, finally glancing in my direction. I froze for a brief second before I could answer.

"Uh, sure," I stammered out, throwing him a weak smile. I stared at Frank's back as he made his way toward the staff lounge, the familiar suspenders holding up his baggy jeans, the regular limp in his step. Frank had NEVER offered to make me a cup of coffee before.

Still rooted in the same spot, trying to figure out what the hell just happened between Eddie and him, Frank's holler from the back lounge caused me to jump. Still in shock that he offered to make me coffee, I shuffled down the darkened hallway. Old hunting photos and sharpshooter awards lined the wood-paneled walls, and I slowed to look at one in particular. Pulling my sleeve down over my palm, I wiped the thin layer of dust out of the way. Two men stood with their arms around each other's shoulders, each gripping a pistol in the opposite hand, a shooting team trophy on the ground between them. A slow smile made its way across my face. My dad and Frank were not only great friends but had been teammates for several years. Traveling together and winning tournaments across the country. It was one reason this store was so popular. The owner wasn't just some store clerk; he was a national sharp-shooting champion. It made people frequently seek his advice. Hell, the two of them taught Jax and me to shoot. We had even won a few state youth shooting competitions. Frank still had me practice on the regular. Said I needed to keep up my skills; employees not only needed to be knowledgeable, but competent as well. Dad and Frank were pretty tight before my dad had been incarcerated, and I guess Frank was doing him a favor by letting me work here. I was thankful. And aside from my brother Jax, and my best friend Cory, he was the closest thing to family I had left. A sour feeling filled my stomach at the thought of my brother and a sadness glassed over my eyes. I missed him something awful. *Where the hell are you, Jax?*

Frank Stark, the owner of Wilderness Sportsman's, had always been lenient with me, treating me kind of like a daughter and not just an employee. I'd always secretly wanted to ask if Tony Stark was a relative, but he wasn't really the joking kind of guy, even with me. And I imagined the Ironman comment wouldn't be received as funny if spoken out loud. But the thought always made me smirk a bit anyway.

Frank, as he preferred to be called, was in his early sixties. He had around a five-foot ten frame, a graying skull trim, a growing belly and a slight limp that showed from years of physical abuse. It was clear he hadn't led an easy life. If you looked close enough, you could see his left foot pointed outward at a strange angle. A long scar ran from the middle of his right cheek all the way to the missing top portion of his right ear. Being retired from the Army had left him with physical as well as mental scars. He was a serious, no bullshit kind of guy. He always looked to be teetering on the edge of an anger explosion, but he'd never been anything but respectful toward me. We didn't have personal discussions, but I'd always had the feeling he was seeing more than a conversation could say anyway. His shrewd eyes seem to soak in everything. Dad had said Frank had done several tours with his platoon, earning a purple heart and several medals of honor. He'd saved hundreds of lives, only to finally retire and have his beloved wife die from cancer soon thereafter. Although I'd never seen him drink alcohol while at the shop, it was clear most of his lonely dinners were of the liquid variety.

The store didn't open 'til nine most days, but he was always there, usually having the place up and running by seven. Today I was more than thankful he'd been here. I'd often wondered if he made that schedule for me, since he was here anyway. After his wife passed away years ago, this store seemed to be the only thing keeping him going. My dad was probably one of his only true friends and considered a frequent flier to this store, being an avid hunter, fisherman and gun aficionado. Frank had done him a solid by offering me this job about four years ago. I had been bouncing around between jobs. I'd struggled through college and decided after I graduated and had a year or so on the job, I wanted nothing to do with my associate degree. Frank had one of the most popular stores within several counties and actually needed my help. Besides, his inventory and bookkeeping skills were less than desirable.

Being in a small rural upstate New York city, most everything from here to Canada was prime locations for hunting, fishing and camping. There wasn't much else to do around here. Bradington had once been a flourishing mining community, which was unusual for our area of the globe. But it had been about two centuries since the mines had closed, give or take. I guess they just dried up. I'd never put much thought into it. Other than my mom telling us stories of generations of her family settling here, when Jax and I were little.

Clanking noises down the hall brought my focus back, and I continued my shuffle toward the coffee. Reaching the break room, I glanced down at the outstretched hand holding the steaming cup. Bringing the rim to my lips, I blew away the steam and took a sip. My eyes widened as I looked across my cup and stared at Frank.

"What, coffee suck?" he asked, his eyebrows pulled together.

"Uh, no. I just... it's good. That's all." I smiled, lowering my eyes to the ground, stunned that my coffee was made just the way I like it. Damn, the man was observant.

"Max, I've gotta talk to you and Cory about something. When he gets in today, come get me. I'll be in the basement. Got some things to do down there." Frank stated and headed out of the room.

"Um, Frank?"

"Yeah?" he responded, turning back toward me.

"I uh... I thought... I thought it was off limits. And that you didn't want anyone down there?" Frank ran a hand through his hair and turned toward me fully. Looking me in my eyes, his face was serious when he nodded.

"Yup, but I do now. So quit screwin' around back here and get ta work. I'll see ya down there in a bit, with Cory." With that, he turned and headed down the hallway. I stood there for another minute, staring down the now empty hallway toward the basement stairs. A loud ding from the shop door opening pulled me back to attention, and I hustled to the front of the shop to do my job.

Quite a few customers came and went. Oddly, most bought rifles and lots of ammo, and we sold out our animal traps. Some stocked up on outdoor survival supplies, but none of our usual fishing and camping gear. Strange, since fishing season was starting within the next week. My morning flew by with no time to think about creepy Eddie, and it was finally time for lunch.

As I headed over to lock the door and turn around our 'out to lunch' sign, Cory barreled through. I let out a high-pitched squeal, stumbling backward.

"Geez, Cory! You scared the life out of me!" Apparently, my nerves were still a little frazzled from this morning.

"Sorry," he said between breaths. "I got a message on my voicemail. Frank said to get my ass down here early today. Said he needed to talk to us both. Do you know what's up? I'm not getting fired, am I? I've only been late a few ti — Oh shit! Did he say anything about the paintball course? God, do you think he's firing me!?" he rambled on at top speed.

"Jesus! Take it down a notch. For crying out loud." I huffed out, rolling my eyes. "He's been a little weird today." I explained, lowering my voice and leaning forward a bit. "He made me a cup of coffee and said he wanted to see both of us down in the basement when you got here."

Cory's eyes went wide, and he gaped at me. He stood quiet and shocked for a moment longer, then leaned forward. "He wants to see us, downstairs? I thought that was off limits?"

I shrugged my shoulders. "Not sure what's up, but we'd better get going. Uh, you wanna go first?" I asked with a sly grin and raised my eyebrows.

"Fuck no!" Cory blurted out immediately. "He's still pissed that I let my friends into the paintball range with beer last weekend. You first." He showed a toothy grin. I snickered and shook my head. He still looked like the kid I grew up with when he did that.

Cory was the closest thing I had to a little brother. The lanky little kid I'd known had grown up into a handsome young man. Now he was just under six feet tall, still lean, but with a muscular build, and sandy blonde hair parted on the side that flopped over one of his blue eyes. His cocky attitude and smart-ass wit didn't quite match the pretty boy appearance.

He worked at the shop part-time on the days he wasn't running the paintball range that Frank also owned. Twice a week, I swung by his apartment and got his ass out of bed early enough for a run. Most of the other days, he nursed a hangover from hanging with his buddies and trolling for college girls. I hated to admit it, but I feared the day he'd wake up and decide to move on. I was quite positive he could be making an amazing salary using his Geology and Environmental Sciences degree. A person would never guess, but he was actually quite brilliant. I was torn between wanting him to go and accomplish great things and staying in this shitty little city to be closer to me. He was like family, and I was seriously running low on members. God, everything was falling apart.

I shook myself out of what would have been a depressing spiral of thoughts, and finished locking the door, then turned the sign around in the window.

"Well, let's get going. The suspense is killing me." Cory demanded, practically bouncing. We both turned and headed down the dimly lit hallway. I reached for the doorknob to the basement but paused and looked over my shoulder. Biting my bottom lip nervously, I whispered, "Think we should knock?" Cory shrugged his shoulders, and I did the same. I let out a nervous breath and knocked three times.

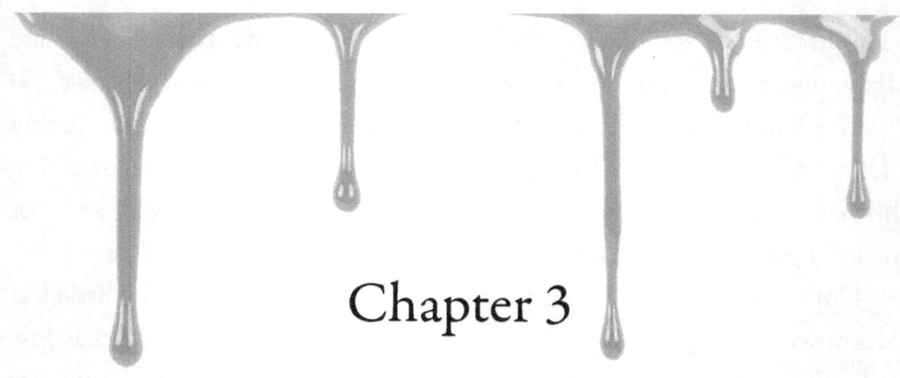

Chapter 3

Maxine

Frank answered with a muffled, "Yeah!"

Turning the knob, the dingy wooden door swung wide as it creaked on old hinges. I looked back at Cory and raised my eyebrows. I didn't wait for his response but swiveled my head back around and yelled down the darkened stairwell.

"Frank, Cory's here. Want us to come down?"

"Well, I'm not gettin' any younger down here."

Dusty 2x4 slats of wood for steps and a few support beams lined our way as we slowly descended the stairs. I could barely hear the low hum of the fluorescent lights over the light drone of our local radio station as it played in a distant area of the basement. Some clanks and the scuffing noise of feet as it slid over a gritty surface sounded as Frank headed our way.

Frank met us at the bottom of the stairs.

"Follow me," he said in greeting. Turning around without waiting, he went back to where he'd come. We silently followed him, weaving around and between stacks of boxes from different sporting goods companies. The smell of mold, cardboard boxes and dust tickled my nose.

"It's a lot larger down here than I thought it would be," I said aloud.

Frank huffed. "Just wait here a minute," he commanded, stopping at a solid- looking door. Turning around to face us completely, his face was grave, and his lips were pulled down into a scowl that tugged on the scar lining the side of his face. Running a hand over his face and pushing it through his short, trimmed hair, he cleared his throat.

"Look, you guys have been with me for a while. I... Well, I think of ya both like family. Sometimes annoying family." He paused and glanced at Cory, and the deadpan look Frank gave him almost made me giggle. "But still, family. You guys are all I've really got since my wife died. It's this business, and you two and Jax." I frowned, my previous humor now gone, replaced by an uncomfortable tug in my chest. My eyes darted back and forth between the two men. Cory's eyebrows drew together, echoing the worry trying to take place in my thoughts.

"What's going on Frank?" We asked in unison.

"Jinx!" Cory yelled, slamming a hand into the air and a giggle slipped past my lips. Frank just shook his head at us.

"Listen, I need you two to see something. Weird shit is goin' on around here." He paused, looking at our quizzical expressions. "Have either of you even noticed?" Frank's brows drew in toward each other as his mouth turned down again. My lips flattened at his disappointed stare, and I shrugged one shoulder. Frank shook his head. "So, as I was sayin', there's some weird shit goin' on. I've had a couple of calls from locals. Thought people were just being freaks. Turns out, I've got my own proof."

"Frank," I barked, as I flung both arms out and slapped my hands against my thighs, "what on earth are you talking about?" His odd behavior was wearing on my patience.

"I'm goin' to show ya both something, but ya gotta keep quiet about it, ya hear?" Frank looked at us both sternly, holding up his index finger like he was going to scold a child. My eyes widened in surprise, and we nodded. As he turned back around, my stomach tightened in a knot, and I wrapped one arm around my middle. Cory was dead silent at my back as we waited for Frank to open the door. The beeps from the door code he entered sounded like an alarm clock in the small, quiet space. Each beep made my pulse race faster.

Opening the door, we followed him through — the brightly lit room was huge. My eyes first tracked along the two opposing walls lined with mesh cages. It wasn't so much the cages that attracted my interest, but the insane number of weapons neatly organized within them. This room was nothing like the rest of the basement. It was completely devoid of dust and moisture. There were no scattered boxes, advertising signs or store overflow — no clutter at all. Just clean, gray cement floors and rows of fluorescent lights overhead to illuminate the immaculate space. A few tables with books, maps, notepads, and various other items on them were neatly arranged in the distance. A few coffee cups sat to the side of the clearly used workspace indicating much time spent there. "Holy shit," I muttered, barely audible.

"What the fuck?!" Cory blurted out, loud and clear. Frank turned, making a tsking noise.

"This is my... hobby." He said, waving a hand outward at the shelves.

"Hobby?" I croaked and made a squeaking noise.

"Now, don't go getting those crazy ideas. I'm no serial killer. So, stop lookin' at me like that." Frank grinned widely and walked over to a tall, thin, vertical cabinet, pulling it out. It looked like a spice rack I'd seen in some kitchens. But this rack did not contain spices. I was utterly speechless. I wasn't sure if my brain was working at all; it had completely stalled. I wasn't even sure if I'd even closed my mouth yet, or if it was still hanging open. The sliding cabinet contained a few rows of knives of various shapes and sizes. The black background of the cabinet made the knives seem incredibly sharp as they glinted in the light. My eyes moved to the sword hanging above them, its intricate detail drawing my eyes like a magnet. As I walked closer, rounding to the opposite side that Frank was standing on, I was shocked again. Different boxes of ammo, some calibers I'd never seen before filled three quarters of the cabinet.

Frank leaned forward and reached up to a few keys dangling from hooks above the ammo. Grabbing one, he turned and walked along another set of cabinets attached to the wall. Trailing his hand down the length of the countertop, he stopped next to a door. Using the key, the door opened, and he started to step through. Pausing, as he realized we weren't moving, he turned to us, "Well, come on. It's in here."

Before even stepping over the threshold, a low growl like that of an angry cat reached my ears. As I made my way inside, my eyes swung around the room, landing on a medium-sized metal dog crate. Fluorescent lights brightened the space, making the crate and its contents easily visible. The biggest, angriest red squirrel I'd ever seen was crouched inside. It had to be at least three times the normal size of an indigenous squirrel. Its once beautiful, auburn fur was matted to its body, and the previously fluffy tail looked like it had been used as a chew toy. Several patches of fur were missing. Gray flesh was exposed beneath the bare patches and visible, bright red veins spider-webbed under the skin.

"Wh — What the hell is it?!" I shifted my frozen stance, and the squirrel tracked my movement, increasing the volume of its growl. The squirrel crouched down as if to spring at me, and its lips peeled back to show sharp, jagged teeth with saliva dripping from its mouth. It's normally dark, beady eyes were enlarged and rimmed with red. And the feral growl turned to a sharp hiss as it launched itself at me. Stumbling back against the wall I used it to hold myself up. The squirrel continued to slam into the cage, denting it outward, trying to get at us? Or...me? Frank grabbed my arm and started pulling me around the side of the table toward the exit. Pushing a stunned Cory back to the doorway, he all but shoved us out. I couldn't take my eyes off the little monster as spittle flew from its mouth while it howled and continued to thrash.

The door slammed shut and Frank gripped both of my arms. Refocusing on his face, not the door behind him, I realized he'd said something. "Wh — What?" I asked shakily.

"I said, he doesn't like you." Frank paused, waiting for me to blink, then let go of my arms and continued. "I trapped that freaky little shit in one of my coyote traps about five days ago. It's been nasty and aggressive, but not that bad," he pointed at me.

"Wh — Why's it so big?! I've never seen a squirrel that size. Jesus, Frank, it's the size of a small dog!" My voice rose with each word.

"Not quite sure yet. But I've got some ideas. I caught him in a trap on the side of Bear Trail Mountain. It was eating a possum. I assumed it got snagged in the trap while trying to drag it somewhere."

"That fucking squirrel was eating a possum!?" Cory's voice went up two octaves. "They're supposed to eat nuts and berries and shit! Is it rabid? I've never seen a squirrel that big. And what the hell was wrong with its eyes?! Jesus Christ, Frank, WHAT IS IT!?"

"Simmer down kid, that's what I wanted to talk to you two about. More and more reports of animals 'not quite right' keep coming in." Frank said calmly, as he turned away from us, gathering up some scattered papers. "Amongst other things." He mumbled so low I could barely hear him. Turning back with the stack of papers held to his chest, his eyebrows pinched. "Seriously, you two haven't heard anything?" Cory and I just stood there dumbly, shaking our heads almost imperceptibly. Frank sighed and abruptly changed the subject. "Either of you heard any stories about the old mines?"

"The ones shut down over a hundred years ago??" I asked, completely confused by the direction of Frank's question. "What does that have to do with that rabid squirrel?!"

"It's not rabid. God dammit. He should have told you." Frank paced the small space. "He was supposed to tell you. With the increase in activity, they have found a way out." He muttered angrily, tossing the papers back on the counter.

Throwing my train of thought through another loop, Frank's voice softened as he turned toward me once more and asked, "Have ya talked to Jax recently?" I shook my head, eyebrows drawn tightly together. Frank's gaze stayed on me as a look of compassion took over his features. Anxiety began to make my fingers tremble, and I clenched my fists, hoping to hold them still. I hadn't been able to reach my brother in over two months. But how did Frank know that? I hadn't mentioned anything, not wanting to worry him. Jax had been working on gathering condemning information about the Gregoris. The spark of disdain I harbored toward that family began to bubble with just the thought, and I clenched my fists for a different reason. They'd murdered my mother, and we planned to prove it. We both knew it was dangerous, and he'd made me promise not to say anything. I shook my head again as I tried to swallow, unable to answer verbally, my thoughts spinning. A buzzing noise from the store doorbell broke through my confusion, signaling our time down here was up. Frank rubbed his hand back and forth over his forehead.

"We'll pick this up later. Customers are waiting." He sighed and pointed us toward the exit.

Swallowing hard, I recognized the dismissal but still didn't move. Frank's shrewd gaze stayed on me. His lips formed a grim line as Cory grabbed my arm and led me out of the storage space, my feet practically dragging. I couldn't put these pieces together. I knew what my brother had been working on; we'd planned some of it together. It was supposed to be our secret. A horrible feeling settled in the pit of my stomach. If Frank knew something was wrong, then Jax was truly in trouble. And I had a pretty good idea who was responsible for his absence.

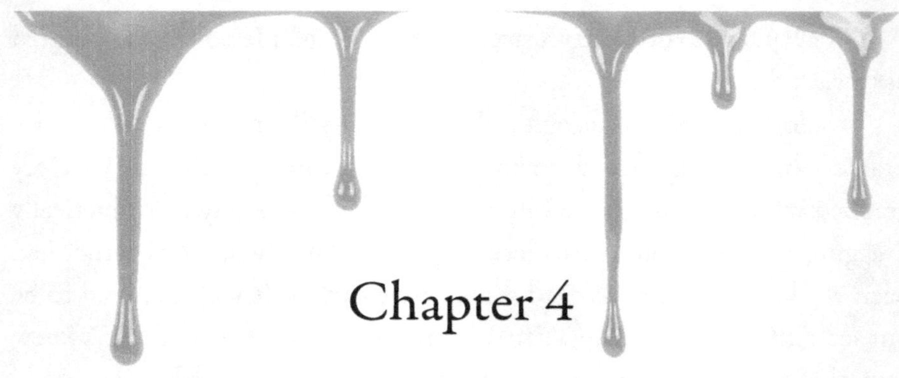

Chapter 4

Maxine

"Hey, I'm done with today. You ready to head out?" I hollered at Cory from the opposite side of the store, more than ready to get the hell out of here.

"Yup, I'm down in the break room, gonna sign out now."

Dragging my tired ass down the hall and into the break room, I dropped into one of the folding chairs that sat around the card table. The conversation with Frank weighed heavy on my shoulders. Frank's cryptic comments and questions left me feeling anxious and more worried about Jax than before. And now I had even more confusion. Trying to piece together the scene in the basement and my missing brother. The Gregoris had something to do with all of it, I was certain. But I had no proof. Jax wanted to gather information on his own, thinking it was too dangerous for me. Damn him for always trying to shelter me. I could handle it. I wasn't the fifteen-year-old disaster I'd once been. The loss of my mother and incarceration of my father had hardened me. My jaw muscle flexed with the pressure as I clenched my teeth and stared down at the table.

Cory turned from collecting his things and took one look at me, then sat down across the table. He slid his things to the side, propped his elbows on the table, and clasped his hands together.

"Spit it out girl, what's eatin' ya? I know it's not that squirrel." He snickered, trying to lighten my stressed mood.

Leaning forward, resting my elbows on the table, I mirrored his movement, before dropping my head in my hands.

"Something's wrong," I muttered. "Jax hasn't spoken to me in eight weeks. And Frank's weird ass questions freaked me out, I guess. I'm driving to his place on my way home to check if he's been there. We've never gone this long without talking. I'm worried. He got a job working for those pieces of shit...I knew it was a bad idea." I hated the Gregoris. If it weren't for them, my dad wouldn't be in jail, and my mom would still be alive. "Jesus, what if he's lying in a ditch somewhere? What if THEY put him in a ditch somewhere?!" I started rambling, nerves getting the better of me. I wouldn't put any kind of criminal activity past them. They'd always thought they were above the law. With that much money, maybe they were.

"Hey, Max, he's OK. You know Jax, I'm sure he's working some angle or got a new chick he doesn't want you to meet yet."

"Sierra would cut off his balls." Cory's eyes widened, and I laughed because it was true. "Besides, he loves her. He's just afraid to let her know. She probably wants babies, and he's scared to death of babies." I laughed again, Cory joining in.

"Everyone is scared of babies. They look like creepy old men and scream like little banshees from hell." He grimaced and shook his head. "Your bro's got big balls to date that one. She's a tough cookie. I took a few of her kickboxing classes at the gym. Damn, the girl's got moves." He wiggled his eyebrows and made me laugh again. "Thinking it through, I might be willing to put up with babies for some of that." He smiled slyly while nodding.

"You're obnoxious." I rolled my eyes. "I took a few years of those and the self-defense classes with the other instructor, Paige. That routine whipped my ass, but I loved it. Umm...you know, it's usually a girls' class. Why were you..." My brain started rolling through his reasoning and the smirk on his face sealed my conclusion. "Ohhhh, girls." I rolled my eyes. He was such a player. "Anyway," I continued, "I'm good. You've probably got a date tonight, so you better go get ready. It's gonna take you forever to fix that fucked up hair of yours." I burst out laughing at the distraught look on his face. "Seriously, have a good night and weekend. If you feel like going for a run, shoot me a text." Standing, I grabbed my jacket and started for the door.

"Seriously yourself. If you need me, call. You know I'd help you with anything. Stop worrying, I'm sure he's fine." He shot me a wide smile. "Oh, and Max," he paused dramatically, his eyes shifting back and forth as if looking for someone listening in, "be careful... watch out for those rabid squirrels." He gestured with his fingers in front of his mouth like fangs and made growly noises. I snorted.

"You're a dick, but I love ya." I said, shaking my head as I reached the doorway. "See ya when I see ya!" Throwing a wave over my shoulder as I headed out. Next stop, Jax's place, and I sent a small prayer that he'd be there.

Tires crunched over the gravel as I pulled into my brother's driveway. No lights lit the interior of the house, and his Jeep wasn't there either. I frowned. Sliding out of my car, I left the keys in the ignition, not worried about anyone stealing it; we both lived in the middle of nowhere. Tapping the flashlight app on my phone, I navigated toward the house. The automatic porch light turned on as I bounded up the steps. Tucking my phone in my pocket, I cupped my hands against the glass as I peeked in the windows, but there was no movement inside. Already knowing the door was locked, I went over to the wooden rocking chair next to the far side of the railing. Jax had a magnetic strip and a spare key under the seat. Reaching down, I popped the key free and opened the door.

The stench that hit my face made me gag. "Jesus Christ," I swore as my eyes teared, and I pressed my forearm against my nose. Struggling to swallow the saliva that pooled from gagging, I pushed through the smell and turned on the kitchen light. Clearly, it had been a while since Jax had taken out the garbage. Pulling my t-shirt up over my nose and grabbing the garbage bag, I tied it closed as quickly as possible and ran it outside. Leaving the door open, hoping the fresh air would clear out the stink, I began looking around. Everything was there, nothing missing. I dug through his desk, hoping to find anything. He had a few pictures in an envelope labeled 'Frank' stuffed all the way in the back of one drawer. I flipped through them. An elevator key lock; a panel open below the regular building floor buttons; hallways so long I couldn't see the end; some sort of laboratory; a field of plants in what looked like an endless room... *What the hell were these?* One photo was blurry. As if it had been taken through one of those windows with inlaid mesh. It looked like a person on a metal table, but I couldn't be sure. *What the fuck ARE these!?* I slid the photos back into the envelope and rubbed my thumb over Frank's name. Why was his name on this? I put the envelope back where I'd found it. More questions burned in my head. Walking back through the living room, I paused at a scratching noise coming from the kitchen.

As I rounded the corner, the scratching got louder. *Great, now something is getting into the garbage.* Picking up my pace, I stomped my feet, hoping to scare the little scavenger. But the scratching didn't stop. Slowing my steps a little, now getting curious, a nervousness tingled in the back of my mind. The scratching had turned loud and frantic. My heart started to race, and the low throb of my pulse grew in my ears. Reaching the edge of the kitchen, I rose up on tiptoes, but couldn't see over the counter yet. My gaze darted around, landing on the butcher's block. I crept closer and tried to stay low as I reached for one of the knives.

Gripping a carving knife, I steeled myself. The scratching suddenly stopped as I rounded the countertop and froze. Breath caught in my lungs in a soundless gasp. It was the biggest, mangiest fox I had ever seen. It had to be almost as big as a German Shepherd. There were sporadic patches of missing hair among the matted fur. Grayish, translucent skin shone through the empty patches, a plethora of red veins underneath. I watched its eyes widen, rimmed with red, and locked on mine. Images of the squirrel in Frank's basement flashed through my thoughts. Shit. I didn't dare move; all the hair on the back of my neck stood at attention as I fought to not let out the trapped breath with a scream. The fox had been scratching through the floor where the garbage bag had leaked on the way out. The smell must have attracted it. And now it was growling at me.

Its hind legs dropped, readying itself to spring. The moment it launched; I darted right. It missed me by an inch. The coarse fur from its mangey tail brushed the skin on my arm as it flew past. Scrambling for traction, it skidded across the floor, its nails making manic clicking noises on the old tan linoleum. My hiking boots gripped the smooth floor a little too good for what my body anticipated, and I pitched sideways. Swinging my arms out and regaining my balance, I twisted and pushed myself toward the door. If I could get out and close the door behind me…a sharp pain radiated through my calf muscle. A cry burst out as my knees buckled, and I caught myself on my hands. Still gripping the knife, I tried to crawl forward, but the fox countered. Tugging me back by my leg, it continued to growl. I rolled my body with as much force as possible, trying to ignore the burning pain as my skin tore with the movement and kicked the fox in the head with the opposite foot. It let go of my leg and I immediately started pulling myself backward. Blood soaked through my pants and began to smear a trail across the floor in my wake. An earsplitting howl exited the crazed animal, and it readied itself to spring once more. Remembering the knife in my hand, I punched my fist forward as the animal lunged. The blade pierced its chest as it knocked me flat on my back. I grabbed the animal's throat with my other hand, holding the snapping jaws inches from me as my arm shook with effort. Its breath was rancid and drops of saliva splattered on my face. Twisting the knife, the fox let out an ear-piercing shriek and went limp. Shoving it to the side, I scooted out from underneath the now lifeless animal. Climbing to my feet, I ran to the door as fast as I could with my injured leg, and slammed it shut behind me.

Delirious from shock, the adrenaline from the attack must have brought me home, because I didn't even remember the drive. Stumbling into my house, I fell through the door. Shaking with full body tremors, my limbs felt like overcooked spaghetti, and my vision blurred. The wound in my leg throbbed to the beat of my heart and blood coating my pants had them sticking like a second skin. But I was so out of sorts I didn't care. Too weak to stand as the room spun, I crawled on my hands and knees, climbing directly into bed. Without one coherent thought, the world went dark.

Nightmares plagued my restless sleep. I searched for Jax, and monsters chased me through the darkness. Human-like beasts with glowing red eyes, huge muscles, elongated arms and hands that stretched into claws reached for me.

I felt myself go in and out of a twilight-like sleep as I thrashed. It was so hot, too hot. I sweated through my clothes and soaked my bed. Bouts of stomach cramps had me curling in on myself as I faded in and out. Suddenly, jerking upright to a sitting position, I threw myself to the side as I purged whatever I had eaten that afternoon into a small wastebasket next to my bed. Collapsing back and shaking, I faded out once more. This time, however, I slept like the dead.

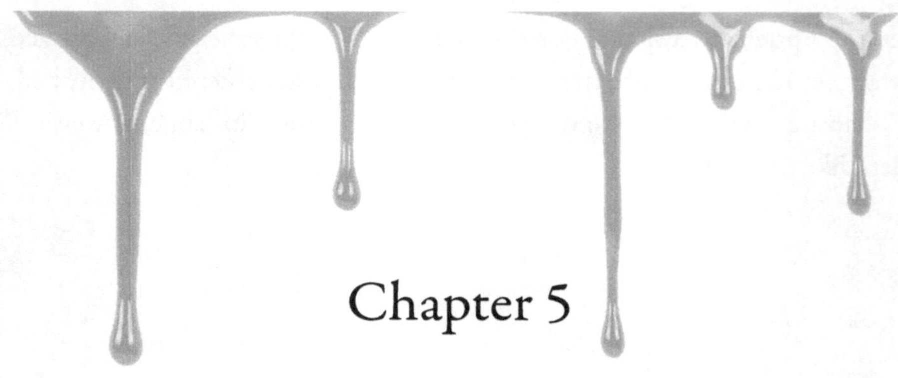

Chapter 5

Maxine

Advil, I needed Advil…like a hundred of them. Shielding my eyes from the sun streaming through my window, I forced myself to sit up. Never in my life had light been so offensive. I stumbled to the kitchen, turned on the sink, and shoved my head under the faucet. Drinking as if I'd been in the desert, I gulped. The cool water felt glorious as it sluiced past my lips and over my face. I wasn't sure how long I'd been drinking, but my stomach began to cramp, making me stop. Sliding down to the floor, I swiped the back of my hand across my mouth and sat with my head between my knees, breathing heavily. My stomach tightened again, and this time a pang of hunger hit like nothing I'd ever felt before. I literally crawled toward the refrigerator. The cold linoleum against my hands and knees made me want to rest my face on the floor, but my hunger overrode my desire to do so.

Ripping open the door, I squinted against the harsh light shining out of the fridge. I scanned the contents. Snatching the bag of deli sandwich ham, not bothering with the zipper lock top, I tore into it and shoved half the wad of meat in my mouth. Barely chewing, I swallowed as quickly as I could and then stuffed in the other half. *Still hungry.* I clawed open a leftover KFC box holding a chicken thigh. A light moan sounded as I chewed through the salty, crispy breading and into the tender meat below. Devouring it in seconds, I threw the empty box to the floor behind me. Breadcrumbs littered the area and clung to my clothing. *More.* Digging like a badger, I continued my pillage, throwing bags of salad mix, yogurts, a container of steamed vegetables... A growl ripped past my lips as my eyes landed on a package of raw hamburger. The clear cellophane wrap had no chance as my fingers clawed through, grabbing a handful of the cold red meat. It was the most amazing tangy smell to ever hit my nose. My mouth watered. Somewhere in the back of my mind, I knew eating raw meat like this was NOT normal. But I couldn't resist. Finishing off the 2.39-pound package, I licked my fingers, wishing there was more and wondered why the stores never packaged even pounds. Finally, feeling a little sated, I sat back on my ass and leaned against the refrigerator, taking deep breaths. Turning my head to the side at the sound of small feet padding across the floor, my kitty Cleo approached with caution.

Sitting back on her haunches, cocking her head to the side, she watched me from a few feet away. I met her stare and thought I heard a voice. I jumped to my feet in an instant, scanning the area. In seconds, I had visuals on all the doors and windows within sight, then relaxed a bit at seeing them all still locked. My ears strained for any other voices or noises. The water pump ran, a clock ticked from the other room, and a bird squawked outside. I let out a breath and completely relaxed my stance, chiding myself for my paranoia. Realizing my headache was finally gone but still in a bit of a haze, I looked at the mess I'd created. *Jesus. What the hell? What was wrong with me?* I muttered aloud, cursing to myself as I began cleaning up the mess.

After tidying up the kitchen, sort of, I glanced down and realized I still had yesterday's clothes on. My sluggish mind didn't really care that my shirt was crusty and stiff and that my pants were shredded. In that moment, I crinkled my nose at a foul, offensive odor. Tilting my nose toward my underarm, lifting it slightly, I jerked my head in the opposite direction. *Damn.* Scrunching my face, I tried to turn off my senses. It was me. I smelled horrible. Stripping my clothes off as I lumbered my way to the bathroom, I couldn't wait to shower. Hoping it would help relieve this fog and the ripe stink, I cranked the water as hot as I could stand and stepped under the spray.

My memory of last night was even more fuzzy than today, and pieces were missing. Closing my eyes, I let the hot water run down my back, relaxing my muscles. I tried to recall the previous day's events... work, then Jax's house, the stank-ass garbage, and... my eyes popped open. Oh my God, the rabid fox. Vivid images flooded back to me. Its enlarged frame and its patchy gnarled pelt. The deranged look in its red eyes as its jaws snapped at me. *Holy shit.* I froze. It had bitten me. I frantically searched my body for injuries... nothing. I should've at least had puncture wounds where it sunk its teeth into my leg, using me like a rag doll... but my flesh was only a bright pink where the bite should have been. *Maybe it didn't break the skin?* I knew I was lying to myself, remembering the blood coating my skin and pants, but I just couldn't make sense of it. Holding the wall to keep myself upright, I pulled in long, deep breaths, trying to calm down. *How did I even make it home?! Jesus Christ!* I couldn't remember the ride home. I vaguely remembered stumbling through the door, then falling into bed...

My brain side-tracked from that thought and shifted to the photos I'd seen in Jax's drawer. Where were the pictures? I'd put them back. *Dammit.* Jaxon was still missing, and I'd left the only clues I'd found. Frank's name was on the envelope, and I couldn't understand why. What did he have to do with anything? And what the hell was going on at the shop? Frank had rambled about the squirrel and had had all those weird questions about the area's history. The frigging mines had been closed for almost a century. No one had even given them a thought in ages! I braced my hands against the shower wall and let the hot water punish the back of my neck as my head hung loose. None of the pieces made any sense. But something in the back of my mind kept screaming that the Gregoris had something to do with all of it. All my thoughts jumbled together, and my heart pounded in my ears. My breathing came in short gasps. I clutched harder at the wall, my legs feeling weak as I tried to remain upright.

What was I going to do? Who could I go to for help? I couldn't get Frank or Cory involved. The Gregoris were dangerous, and I had a pretty good idea what they would do to someone if they caused any kind of friction. They'd make them disappear, one way or another. Just like my mom. Just like my dad. Just like Jax. I ground my teeth together. I knew without a doubt that they had something to do with this. They knew where Jax was. I had to find him before he disappeared forever. I couldn't lose another family member. A sheen of sweat broke out across my forehead. I pushed my fear and anxiety down. I wasn't going to lose Jax. I would get answers from those bastards. And I was going there right now. Well, as soon as I got out of the shower anyway.

Forming a quick plan in my head as I dressed, I made the only decision I thought could possibly work. I had to speak with Elias. He'd always had a soft spot for me. I knew that and had used it before. We were friends once — before they killed my mother and destroyed my family.

Guilt ate at me. I was the reason Jax got the job. I had purposely found a way to 'accidentally' run into Elias. I'd made light conversation and indirectly begged for employment for my brother. It had worked, just like we'd planned. Now Jax was missing, and it was my fault. I should have never helped him get that job. We both knew it was a bad idea, but Jax insisted it was the only way to find out what truly happened to our mother and to free our father from prison. We were doing this for them.

I pressed my eyes tight, letting out another slow breath. Opening them, I refocused on the girl in the mirror. God, I looked pale. An almost gray hue colored my skin. I sighed, doubting makeup would even help. Hoping I could pull off a little charm with Elias once more, I put on some mascara and lip gloss. And prayed by the time I got there; I wouldn't look as frazzled as I felt.

Pulling into the parking lot behind the Second Wind Medical Facility, I finally found a parking space in the upper lot above the school. The grounds resembled that of a college campus, with the school and medical facility connected. Swiftly crossing the large parking lot, I headed toward the school entrance. Elias lived on the fifth floor of the school. It was still early, but all the parking spots were already full directly in front of the ominous-looking school. The Gregoris owned all of this, the school, the hospital, and the entire mountain. Running both institutions, it made them look like the perfect, rich, sympathetic givers to the community. But I knew better. Something was seriously wrong here. My mother died because of their dirty secrets, and I'd be goddamned if I lost my brother too.

Fisting my hands inside my hoodie's pockets, I headed through the lobby toward the elevators, keeping my pace swift and my head down. Not making any eye contact, I tried to avoid any conversations—I wasn't sure if I'd be able to contain my anxious energy if I had to make small talk. Some very large combat boots found their way into my line of sight as they moved directly in front of me. Stopping, my gaze traveled up and up to the eyes of a ginormous, tree trunk of a man. His arms were crossed over his chest and he had a perma-scowl in place. Jonas silently looked down at me, blocking my way.

"Good morning, Jonas," I said as I looked up, smiling sweetly, attempting to keep my bubbling anxiety under wraps.

"Max," was the only reply I got, along with a nod.

"How are you? It's been a bit since I've seen you." I wanted to smack myself for the generic small talk. Then my brain stalled out for a second as I looked him up and down again. I felt my brows draw together as I took in his massive frame. "Is it my imagination or are you bigger?" *Jesus, super tactful.*

"Been working out. What do you want?" he asked flatly.

"I want to see Elias. Is he here?" I asked, already knowing he was. He hardly went anywhere unless his dad sent him. When we were kids, my mom used to talk about Nico sending the boys to special clinics across the globe. Nothing fun, I was sure.

I started to shift uncomfortably when I got no response. "So, what do ya say, big guy? Send me up?" I tried to brighten my smile. Jonas grunted and stayed silent, staring at me. I fought the urge to fidget under his scrutinizing gaze, and kept my sweet smile in place, pretending to be patient. Finally, he answered. "Alright, I'll take you up. He knows you're coming?"

"Nope, just thought I'd swing by, say hello, see how you guys were doing." I clenched my fists in my pockets and shrugged my shoulders while keeping my smile wide, hoping it looked genuine and not totally deranged. Jonas turned and headed to the elevator, and I followed.

The doors closed and he reached out, pressing number five. My gaze followed the movement and settled on the panel below the keypad — there was a key lock. A small gasp escaped me at the memory and realization — it was the same as the picture I'd found at Jax's house. Jonas swung his head toward me and his questioning stare pinned me in place. Swallowing thickly,

I schooled my features into a tight smile and dropped my eyes, praying I didn't cause any suspicion. My mind raced as I tried to remember the other photos. I glanced sideways as he opened his mouth to say something, but the elevator chimed and the doors began to open. I quickly stepped around Jonas and took a left down the hall. I had been here to deliver supplies from the store before, so I knew right where Elias' office was.

I tried to keep my pace casual, but wasn't sure if I accomplished my goal. Making my way down the brightly lit and lengthy hallway, I worked on collecting my thoughts. Trying to piece together the photo and elevator key connection, I wished I'd paid more attention to those pictures. My heart raced and I quickly swept away a small bead of sweat from my upper lip.

Rounding the corner, I stopped at the threshold of Elias Gregori's office. Jonas grunted as he gently placed a hand on my shoulder, startling me as he guided me to the right, so he'd have enough room to enter around me. Elias was sitting at his polished and pristine desk, but his chair was spun around, and he faced the windows overlooking the school grounds. I shoved my now sweaty palms back into my pockets and my throat tightened. *What the hell was I going to say?! Did you kill my brother? Just like your father did my mother?! Fuck!* I hadn't thought this through enough. *Don't freeze, don't freeze!* I swallowed hard. Maybe I could just turn around. I mentally slapped myself. Nothing suspicious about a person running out as if they were on fire after asking to see you. It was too late; I was already here. Jonas spoke, breaking my insane inner dialog, and lightly pushed me forward a step. His hand trailed down my back, leaving a tingle of warmth before disappearing. "Elias, Maxine Devins is here to see you."

"Good morning, brother." Elias spoke with a smile in his voice as he slowly turned his chair.

Dressed in a navy-blue suit, his dark brown hair was parted and slicked to the sides. His elbows rested on the arms of his chair and his fingers were steepled together at the base of his thin, pale lips. The shrewd, icy blue stare that met mine as his lips slowly turned up in the corners said it all. He had been expecting me.

"Good morning, Max. It's been quite a while. How have you been?"

"Hello Elias. I've been well, and you?" I pasted, what I hoped was a pleasant smile on my face, trying to hide the panic I felt welling up inside as my palms grew damp again.

"Max, small talk was never your strong suit, and Eddie picked up my last order from the shop. What is it that I can do for you today? Is it you who's now looking for employment? I have plenty of positions that would fit you perfectly." His grin widened and he lifted an eyebrow as his eyes locked on mine. Anger flared to life for a brief moment, then an odd tingling in the back of my mind registered, and I swayed slightly.

"Please, have a seat, Max." He pointed to a chair without breaking eye contact. My head felt foggy and my mind sluggish. I sat without hesitation. My legs practically buckled underneath me. I thought the blue stare started to swirl, and I was mesmerized, being sucked down the whirlpooling depths. I tried to think... of anything. But it was just blank as Elias' gaze bore into mine.

The chime from the elevator broke my haze, and I swung my gaze to Jonas as he monotonously stated their father had arrived. *Fuck, I did NOT want to see that man.* My heart rate picked up, as did all the hair on the back of my neck. Abruptly standing, both brothers' attention immediately turned back to me. I cleared my throat. "I'm sorry, Elias, I'm suddenly not feeling well. We'll have to catch up later." I said in a rush as I made my way toward the exit. Reaching the archway, I skidded to a stop.

"Well, Maxine Devins." My name was drawled out nice and long; it made me want to gag. I surreptitiously rubbed my sweaty palms on my pant legs, trying to keep my face neutral. "What a lovely surprise. And..." he paused, making a small humming noise. "What a lovely young lady you've become. You look so much like your mother." His eyes traveled from my face to my knees and back. I shivered and my stomach twisted. "What brings you to see my boys today? A playdate perhaps?" It wasn't so much a smile as a sneer that took over his face. He reached out and rested a meaty hand on my shoulder, steering me back into the office. "Don't leave on my account."

"Max was just saying hello, Father," Elias said tightly.

"Is that so? I had guessed she was looking for a job. Employing you and your brother is the least we could do. We owe your mother that much." At the mention of my brother and mother, my focus snapped back along with my rage. Vicious retorts swirled in my head. *Owed my mother!? You'll pay in blood for that, one day very soon.*

"Actually, Mr. Gregori," I said through gritted teeth, "I'm looking for my brother. He's been missing for over two months. You wouldn't know anything about that, would you?" I said in an accusatory tone, knowing I probably shouldn't have, but he just pissed me off, hitting a nerve with the mention of my mother. "I mean, it wouldn't be the first time an employee of yours has... gone missing." His glare met mine and tension filled the air.

Elias abruptly stood and moved around his desk, briefly breaking our escalating stand-off. My eyes widened and my lips parted as a small breath whooshed out. He wasn't using crutches. I hadn't seen him walk without assistance from appliances, ever. Even when we were kids, his disability prevented any normal activity. Jonas remained still, arms crossed over his chest, as if nothing out of the ordinary was happening. My gaze shot back to Nico, and I watched his initial amusement as he glanced at Elias. The distraction was short-lived as a sneer curled his upper lip, and his brows lowered and pulled together, his attention coming back to me.

"You. Little. Bitch. Who do you think you are talking to?" Nico spat.

"I know EXACTLY who YOU are." My voice dropped, becoming low and menacing. "And I'm going to find my brother." Stepping backward, I turned, stomping to the elevator at a high speed. I wanted to scream. Anger built like a raging storm, but a hint of terror trickled in... I had probably just numbered my days. No one talked to the Gregoris like that.

"Max, wait!" I heard Elias yell.

Standing in front of the elevator, I punched the button with my index and middle fingers in rapid succession, hoping the doors would open quickly. *Open goddamnit!* Footsteps pounded down the hallway and I glanced back. Nico was coming at me like a freight train. *Fuck!* My heartbeat slammed in my ears like a drum solo and my breathing sawed in and out like I'd run a marathon. I frantically looked around. The stairwell door. Running for the door, I grabbed the handle. Locked. *Who locks a fucking fire escape!!* Slamming the handle up and down in my panic, it gave way, and I yanked it open.

I scurried over the platform and grabbed the banister for my descent. That same meaty hand landed on my arm, spinning me around. "Where do you think you're going?" Nico growled out, grabbing both of my arms harshly.

"Don't touch me!" I howled. Placing my palms against his chest, I tried to push myself free. Still gripping my arms, he slammed my back against the brick lined stairwell.

"You Devins. Think you know everything!" SLAM. "You know nothing!" SLAM. Sparkles surrounded my vision. "I own your mother!" SLAM. "I own this city!" SLAM. "And I own you!" The air whooshed from my lungs—I saw red. Literally. My vision was a crisp red and the hate I felt for this man exploded. My body felt like it was burning, and a growl rumbled low in my throat. Nico stopped cold. His eyes widened as he looked at me, then shoved me back, this time letting me go and stumbling backward as though he couldn't get away from me fast enough.

"What the fuck?! She didn't..." he whispered, reaching back for something to support him.

"You will never own me, and you will pay for what you did to my mother." I growled in a low, menacing tone, cutting him off. I moved toward him, chin lowered, chest heaving and arms out to my sides with my fingers curled into stiff claws. "Where is Jax?" My voice didn't even sound like me. It was low and dark, filled with promises of violence.

He actually screamed. Tripping over his own feet, moving backward, his lower back slammed into the railing and his top-heavy form flipped over. His arms pinwheeled for balance, but they were no help. I leapt forward, grabbing hold of his suit jacket. It barely bought him an extra second as his weight tore the material free and he fell. I was leaning over the rail, unable to move as I watched in horror as his body descended, still clutching the piece of fabric. Ricocheting like a ping-pong ball, his body cracked, bent and twisted. He fell five floors, landing in a broken heap at the bottom.

Harsh breathing had me looking over my shoulder to the doorway. Jonas was standing there, all unmoving and tree-like, supporting Elias, whose breaths sawed in and out of his chest. "Wha—" Elias started to speak, but froze, his eyes growing wide.

"I... I tried to help him," I held up my hand, still holding the piece of material as a sob broke free. Slowly opening my palm, I watched the piece of fabric drift to the ground through blurry tears. "Oh my God, Elias, he's... dead. I'm so sorry." I hiccupped, then covered my mouth as another sob broke loose. Elias and Jonas did not move. They did not speak. They both stood there, eyes wide and frozen in shock. My eyes darted between them as I panicked, my heartbeat drumming in my ears. Not knowing what else to do, I turned and ran. As fast as I could, I sped down the stairs. A pool of blood was expanding around the heap of twisted limbs as I passed. Shoving the exit door open, I literally bumped into Eddie who was in a dead run toward the accident. Neither of us made apologies. My breathing came in rapid pants as I kept my head down, not meeting his eyes, and just kept going, not looking back. I had a feeling in my gut that he'd turned to watch me. But I didn't care. My sole focus was to just get away.

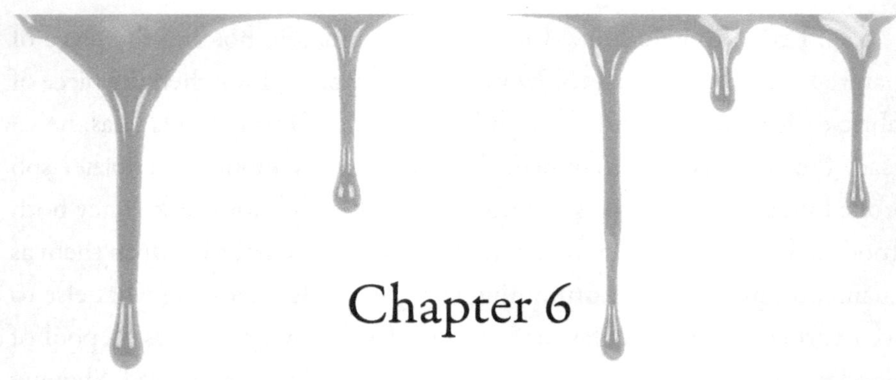

Chapter 6

Elias Gregori

I watched Maxine's panicked face leech of color. My mind tripped and sputtered at the cold realization. My father was dead. She clearly hadn't meant to kill him. Even if she'd despised the ground he walked on, she wasn't a killer. But I couldn't move. I wanted to go to her, wrap my arms around her shaking shoulders, and console her. But I couldn't move. My limbs felt as if they had turned to stone. I watched her, the tears that streamed over her beautiful cheeks and her delicate hands as they covered her mouth to contain her wails. And I still couldn't move. Jonas was just as still at my back, his hand roughly gripping my arm. And I wondered for a brief moment what he was thinking. Was this real? Our father was dead. He was dead... And I was... what? Sad, angry... happy. Yes, maybe all of those.

My father owned half of the city and the Second Wind Children's Home that sat midway up his mountain, where I resided. Below, I could see most of the eastern landscape of the small, pathetic city from my fifth story office windows. They extended across the entire length of my private space, providing a coveted view. The entire floor was a small gift from my father to encourage independence. Or rather, rid himself of a nuisance. The open floor plan, aside from this business space, provided easy maneuverability when I had to use my wheelchair, which had been seventy-five percent of the time, until recently.

I had resigned myself to the fact that my entire life would be spent feeling weak in this body. I could never do any of the things I truly wanted. The diagnosis given had been metabolic bone disease... which wasn't an actual diagnosis. Rather, it was an umbrella term that applied to 'Osteogenisis Imprefecta'—better known as Brittle Bone Disease, or Rickets. It's usually an inherited condition causing stunted growth or gravely affecting one's lifespan. Doctors had both of my parents tested, in hopes of finding a cure. But they were negative for anything that could have housed the defective gene. Over time, I continued to grow, my body advancing at a normal rate. However, my bones remained fragile, and I could never run, jump or hike. Even playing with other children was nearly impossible. One wrong move or even a touch could cause bone fractures, leaving me immobile and in orthopedic casts for months at a time. I had become accustomed to limited contact with others.

But our new doctor was a top Harvard graduate, specializing in genetic research and we'd recently had a major breakthrough. The previous treatments, thanks to Dr. Devins, were maintaining my situation, keeping my bones from degenerating further as well as having a few other unexpected improvements. But the recent discovery had truly been life changing. The amazing advancements and my...abilities were progressing at a staggering rate.

Then she arrived, making today the best day yet. I hadn't been face to face with Maxine in so long. My body reacted with renewed energy the moment she stepped out of that elevator. I had seen her on the security cameras as she stomped across my parking lot, and knew she was coming here. I had heard rumors about her missing brother. The next logical step would have been for her to come here. She would never ask to speak with my father, so I knew she would come to me. It was just a matter of time. And I could be patient. So patient.

Excitement I hadn't felt in forever sparked to life, and I wanted to jump up and down. Too bad the day ended up taking a sour turn.

After the chaos that ensued following my father's traumatic death, I finally had a few minutes of peace to think. The staff had all come running. Nurses and doctors had worked to revive a man that would clearly never be waking up. His body had contorted in nauseating directions. Jonas had been emotionless as always, staying by my side. I imagined he had felt similar, that there was no true love lost, even though it was our father. 'Father' being used as a biological term and not one of endearment. I sat at my desk, trying to sort through my feelings... what was I feeling? Sifting through the plethora of common emotions, I was slightly shocked at the realization that it was relief I felt. Relief. That bastard was dead. No more of the belittling, shaming and verbal bashing I'd received my entire life. No more hearing how I would never be a man and what a disappointment I was. Anger rose inside me. Not because he was dead, but because I hadn't been strong enough to take care of him myself. I had wanted to be the last face he looked at. For years, I had made plans in my head, imagining his death. Poisoning, shooting, car accident... I'd even thought about making him simply walk off the roof of the clinic building using my emerging abilities. I'd dreamt of making him do horrible things. Like cutting and peeling his own skin from his bones as I watched him bleed to death in a puddle of his own flesh. A small smile shaped my lips with the thought, but then it fell as I remembered how Max had taken that small bit of potential pleasure. Even if it was unintentional, she had stolen my satisfaction of watching the life drain from his eyes. I felt robbed.

Jonas was stoic as usual— not much could change his monotone demeanor. The only emotions he'd ever really expressed were indifference and rage. I knew there had been no love lost between him and my father either. I'd made it clear that I'd listen if he decided to talk about it. But he'd only grunted and given a nod. I didn't expect much else. I would always be available for my brother, always. It's only been him and me for so long, since our mother passed from cancer.

The police had arrived on the scene, asking questions and filing reports. I made it very clear it was an accident and omitted Maxine's name from any of the discussions. The local authorities were of no concern to me or my family. We have been lining their pockets for decades, and if they wanted our continued support, they'd do as I said. But just for good measure, I used a little mental suggestion, making sure Maxine wasn't even a consideration.

I wanted to deal with her myself, and those bumbling idiots were not going to get in my way.

Eddie Blasco, my father's primary security guard and confidant, had seen Max running from the scene. He was chomping at the bit to go get her. He was an annoyance I tolerated, having the feeling he may be useful. But I didn't like him. His eagerness volunteering for pick-ups at the sports store was what first alerted me to his little obsession. I've seen Eddie interact with Max on occasion. And I've watched him watching her, wanting her. With one of my awakened abilities, I couldn't tell exact thoughts, but I could sense emotion, and there was darkness within him. Just because I wasn't physically able to do the pick-ups myself, didn't mean I was oblivious to his interest in her. And that made me dislike him even more.

Having been trapped inside most of my life, until recently, had given me plenty of time to work on my technology skills. I had multiple drones at my disposal and could bypass the necessary firewalls to tap into any wireless security camera feed I wished. Most people had no idea how easy it was to access something as basic as a video doorbell. I could hack into almost anything that had web access. Watching Eddie when I'd sent him on errands had proved useful. Not that I wanted him anywhere near Max, but it had given me an opportunity to see her. On a few occasions I'd simply watch her. My silent drones tracked her without noticing.

Watching her leave her workouts, her hair piled on her head with sweat glistening off her skin, was one of my favorite hobbies. I'd imagined myself, slowly untying her blonde locks to let them fall down her back. And how I'd run my hands over her heated skin and curves, slippery from sweating. As she heaved from exertion, how my fingertips would caress her breasts and her perfect, pink nipples until she begged for more. I swallowed, hard, knowing her body would be the most amazing thing I could lay eyes and hands on. I could barely wait. My cock was straining against my zipper, thinking of the things I would do to her. What I'd have her do to me. I've had plenty of women. They could easily be bought. Money, and spending it, had been without restrictions or limits, so I had picked and chosen whatever, or rather whoever, tickled my fancy. Not surprisingly, most of my requests were of the curly blonde variety. But they had never compared.

Rubbing my palms against my eyes, I refocused my thoughts on my father. They quickly twisted to include how he had treated Eddie better than his own sons. The spicy warmth I'd felt just moments ago, chilled with my new mood. I seethed as the dark thoughts swirled. Why couldn't he just have... I shook my head and unclenched my hands.

All in the past now. I'd never have a chance to measure up to him. As much as I despised him, I couldn't help but wish for his approval. Wishing he'd be as proud of me as he was of Eddie. But it didn't matter anymore. I was done living under Eddie's shadow. My father wasn't here to keep the golden boy on his pedestal any longer. He had always been allowed to do whatever he wanted if the job got done. He'd had the most flexibility of our staff, because he had proven his loyalty and commitment to the family time and time again. My father had trusted Eddie to harbor his secrets and tie up his loose ends or eliminate them. He was a machine. A controllable machine. Doing whatever was asked of him without question. I would expect the same. And he'd damn well better step up to my command.

It was about time I got filled in on all the Gregori secrets. Especially what was transpiring in the depths of this facility. I had only been privy to basic intel with my father in charge, with just being sent to the lower lab for my most recent 'treatments.' My father's research and the several doctors' progression in the direction to 'improve' both of his sons had been slow but working. I now knew there was more, so much more. And it was finally time. I had waited so long. Now that my body was growing stronger and my father was finally out of my way, I would know all I was entitled to know. I needed to act fast; power waited for no one. And I was ready. I'd have a nice chat with Eddie. He would be serving me now. They all would. And he would stay away from Max. My lips curled into a smile. I had plans for her.

My entire life, she'd been the object of my desire. The cute cherub face of the girl who played with me as a child, grew into the beautiful angelic features she had today. I'd never had enough confidence to pursue her or even say anything. I had been weak and fragile. But that was changing. These last few weeks of treatments had been working beyond what I could've ever hoped. My body was filling out, and I was getting stronger by the day. I hadn't wanted my father to know, so I'd continued acting the same, hiding my improvement by leaning on Jonas or my crutches. And the strange side effects of previous treatments, my abilities to manipulate thoughts and sense emotions, was growing as well. I tried to manipulate Max today before my father arrived. I've had nothing but successful attempts so far, and it had been a shock that I could not change her train of thought. It was as if there had been a block between us, or a wall? Maybe it was just me, my nerves? She'd always made me feel... spirited, and at odds with my normal self. We may have never been close, but I'd always kept tabs on her.

Maxine was almost the spitting image of her mother, Dr. Jane Devins—a shame, that one. I had never forgotten the kindness she showed me as a child. It must have been hell working for my sadistic father; I recalled several arguments between them. She had been unwilling to complete some tasks he had asked of her, and when she failed to find a cure for my mother's cancer using unethical methods, she disappeared shortly after. Thought to be dead now. I knew my father had had something to do with it. Everyone knew. Her husband, Clint, had stormed into our home after her disappearance. That man was one brave and crazy redneck. To think he could have ever gotten away with the accusations he spewed at my father... He'd been lucky he'd involved the authorities. But they would never have helped him, with all of them being on my father's payroll. It had been smart. Involving the police had kept him alive. A long-term sentence in prison may not have been ideal, but at least his kids could still visit him and not a tombstone.

Now that Nico Gregori was dead, I would be the head of the Gregori legacy. Things around here were going to change. We were going to be doing things my way. And I was going to start with that new doctor today. No more waiting. I was going to be a better man than my father could have ever dreamed of me becoming. I was going to make history. My life would start right now. Max would be mine. She'd grow to love me; I'd make her if necessary. And if anyone tried to touch her or take her from me... my fists tightened on my chair arms and my body tensed. I took a deep, cleansing breath and tried to calm myself. God help anyone who tried to get in my way or stop me.

Chapter 7

Garron

As I was being prodded down one of the many hallways once again, when my ears perked at some noise in the distance. The doorway to an office must have been open as I could hear voices drifting out. Two people were having a heated discussion. Some woman named Maxine was causing trouble at the clinic and was trying to find her brother. And it sounded like the man leading the conversation was highly agitated.

"YOU will try harder! And if you can't... Well, let's not be negative." His voice took on a cool tone. "Dr. Brindle, my father is dead. I will be giving the orders from now on. The woman will be brought here. And that's final."

"But, Mr. Gregori, I'm sorry. I'm just not comfortable with this. It's kidnapping." That shaky voice I recognized; it was the doctor who administered my 'treatments.'

"The sedatives you've been giving the others has made them compliant, yes? Just keep her quiet, modify the dosage, and make her... more susceptible to suggestion. My suggestion. She's mine. I'm getting stronger, it's working. We are moving forward with this experiment. DO. YOU. UNDERSTAND?" The male's voice rose.

"But, the others, I was told that they're volunteers and inmates. People without other options or lifetime sentences. She's not willing!"

"You are truly, not as smart as I gave you credit for." He laughed without humor and the dark, cool tone returned. "You will help me! Did you really think they were volunteers? Would anyone volunteer to become a monster? I want you to think hard about the direction you will be heading in from here on out, Dr. Brindle. By the way, how are your children?" There was a long beat of silence, then he continued, and I swore I heard a smile in his voice. "Bet your healthy little ones enjoyed their play date at Golden Park today. They're so adorable, look just like you." He made a tsking noise. "But that husband of yours...He's got a temper. Is he still jealous of your long hours spent working here? Don't feel bad, he's been busy fucking the nanny." His voice dropped an octave. "You know, I can fix that problem for you too." I heard the doctor gasp.

"You— Stay away from my family." The shake in her voice intensified along with the fear and the anger. "Stay away from them. Please. And... I'll do what you ask."

"Make her mine, and we won't have a problem. I'll have my men bring her to you within a few days. That should give you time to make her... stay, more comfortable." The smile I heard in his voice made me scowl. "Pleasure doing business." The clicking of his shoes retreated further away.

I hadn't realized how far we'd gone, or that I'd slowed my steps. But we passed another two long hallways before rounding the corner and I saw the doctor bent over her desk, head in her hands, sobbing. My brows furrowed once again. *How the hell did I hear them so clearly that far away?* Her head jerked up at the sound of our footsteps. Brown hair pulled up into a bun was now sticking out in different directions. She swiped at her eyes, slightly puffy and red-rimmed with running mascara. Clearing her throat, she ran her hands down her lab coat, collecting herself.

"Ken, please take the next subject to room three. You know what to do. I'll be right there." She stood, turning away from her desk and headed through a doorway marked 'Ladies' room.'

Following the new injection and usual review of daily samples like blood, urine and saliva, the doctor came back in. She never came back in. At least, I didn't think so. Curiosity sparked as I watched her move into the room. Her feet dragged a bit, and her shoulders slumped. Usually, this was the point where the goons would drag me back to my cell. But today I was still conscious, and that was new as well.

"Subject's tests and ultrasounds of internal organs appear healthy. Today's MRI shows heightened function of the frontal lobe, and the hypothalamus has now doubled in size. Unknown hormones have been detected, but only appear when patient is under duress." She set down a small recording device and moved toward me.

Walking up to my chair, she knelt and looked into my eyes with a small penlight. After a long moment, she let out a small sigh.

"You're not here because you chose this." I didn't respond, just watched her. Why was she talking to me? She never spoke to me directly, or I to her. Her brows furrowed and she shook her head slightly. "Were you ever even in prison?" Again, I didn't respond. It wasn't because I didn't want to, I just couldn't remember. "It's OK, I wouldn't talk to me either. I'm...God, I'm so sorry," she whispered, sounding defeated. She stood on another sigh and turned toward the door. My mind raced.

"What..." I croaked, not used to speaking until recently. Spinning back toward me, eyes wide, her mouth dropped open. I tried again, clearing my dry throat. "What's happening to me?"

"Oh God." She covered her mouth, clearly not used to me responding. "I should've known, but the money was so good, and the Gregoris made so many promises..." She shook her head. "We were supposed to be doing tests to help people heal, be stronger, and be better. Cure and build immunity to diseases. The advanced minerals here are unlike anything on this earth. But this, you, the others... I never wanted..." A choked sob sounded, but I had no pity. "I don't know what to do." She covered her face with her hands, then pushed them up her face and over her hair. "That poor woman, they'll bring her here. Make her like you and the others...no, like a submissive zombie for that freak. And it's all my fault." She hiccupped. "I don't know how to undo this. He'll control everyone... everywhere. He's changing and we're all in danger."

"Help..." She jumped slightly at the sound of my voice, and I cleared my dry throat again. "You can help. Stop this... from continuing. Stop... letting them hurt us. Let us... go. Please." Struggling to keep my voice soft, I didn't know if my attempt at begging was working. Jax was the only person I'd talked to in so long, let alone begged. I learned a long time ago that it didn't help. No one here cared what one of us prisoners said– ever. So using her emotional distress as an advantage might be our only chance.

"I can't. There is nothing I can do now. He'll hurt my family." She began pacing, muttering to herself. I was growing anxious. She looked like a caged animal... and I knew exactly what that felt like. I needed to convince her to help, but how? Conversation was not my strong suit. This could be my only shot and I was blowing it!

"There was a reason Dr. Heller moved you up here from the lower-level confinement. Your body has responded to... 'The Red' and your MRI shows increased brain activity. Your cellular response is unique. No other has adapted like you. Except for the newest male, he has shown the closest results with similar tissue regeneration and mutation. Your body has reacted... positively. You're not even feeling the effects of the sedative anymore, are you?" She wasn't really talking to me, more like she was thinking aloud. Her fingers tapped on her closed mouth, and she nodded her head up and down. "OK, I... I need time to think..." She paused for a moment. "Guards!" she barked.

"No wait..." I barely got that out on a hoarse whisper when Ken and Mark pushed through the door.

"Take him back to his room, we're done for today. Tomorrow, we start again. Up his protein intake for morning meal. And make sure he eats it." She directed the guards to unlock my bindings and they hauled me to my feet. My brain reeled from all the information. I had a bad feeling stir in my gut. Something... worse than usual, was going to happen, and soon.

Mr. Cat Piss pushed and prodded me down the hall. The smell was so bad it almost made my eyes tear. That, combined with the nacho cheese stink rolling off Mark, fanned my anger. I couldn't tell if my sense of smell was growing stronger, like my hearing, or if they were just really fucking disgusting. And they were going to drag another innocent woman down here. I knew what they did to the women down here. Most of them didn't last a year. Their rancid stench, combined with this situation had a heat flare in my chest as my anger rose.

Rounding the last corner toward my prison, Nacho gave me a shove. I whirled around so fast their eyes couldn't even track me. My hand darted out and contacted the side of Mark's head. He flew into the wall, a cracking noise sounded from the impact, and he slumped to the floor. I stared, not even breathing hard. *Bastard deserved it.* Electric pain exploded through my body, my limbs spasmed and I crumpled in a heap. Stunned and shaking uncontrollably, I rolled my eyes to see Ken, arms extended, pointing his stun gun directly at me. *Fucker.* Then all went black.

Chapter 8

Jaxon

I could hear the commotion but couldn't see a damn thing. I was fucking helpless in this cage. Panic and rage warred within me, and heat raced up my spine.

"Garron!" I roared. "What's going on? Answer me!" I saw three more guards run past my cell as an alarm rang and red lights flashed from the ceiling. I slammed my fist on the thick, clear glass separating me from everything else. A small spider web fracture appeared where my fist hit and I gaped. This was bullet-proof grade glass. Supposed to be unbreakable. What the actual fuck? I looked at my hands — not a scratch. Red, angry skin, but not a scratch. By the time my outburst and the shock at my strength registered, the guards were walking away. All but Mark, who was being held up and stumbling. Blood was smeared and streaked across his face from his temple down to his chin as his eyes rolled around in their sockets. They didn't even glance in my direction, just kept going.

I tried to get Garron to respond, but nothing. Unable to sit still, I paced back and forth in my small space. Calling Garron's name on and off for hours left me feeling helpless. I could vaguely hear his harsh breaths, so I knew he was alive. But I had no idea what kind of shape he was in. Finally laying on my cot, sleep completely evaded me. It was still dark, or as dark as it ever got down here. Not quite morning yet, as the hall lights were dimly lit during down-time hours. Finally, I heard a cough and groan. Abruptly sitting upright, I waited.

"Jax, you there?" Garron croaked.

"Yeah, man, glad you're alive! You OK?"

"Rough fuckin' day. Something is going on, and it's not good. We've gotta get out of here. Soon. Our bad days are about to get worse."

"Tell me about it. What happened today?" I asked calmly, then just waited. The suspense ate at me, and I clenched my hands into fists, trying not to be impatient. My knee bounced rapidly as I struggled to remain seated. The urge to jump up and down while screaming for him to just spit it out was barely contained. When he finally spoke, I was shocked. The doctors' explanations were only mere fragments of a much larger story. And what was transpiring here... was nothing less than a nightmare.

"WAIT! What?!" I interrupted him. My breath caught on a lump in my throat and a knot formed in my stomach. "Did you say Maxine?" *Maxine was not a common name. Please God, no. Let it be somebody else.* I just held my breath.

"Yeah, I did. Whoever she is, she certainly pissed someone off. I think they said she's looking for her brother. Caused a big ruckus. And I think someone died. The uh, man, the doctor was talking to, said his father was dead. I'm not sure, but I think the guy they were talking about was the boss of this operation. I've heard a few names over the years, and I've put some pieces together. I think it was probably one of those Gregori bastards. I don't know any first names though. Sorry."

I was frozen. I didn't even think I was breathing. *Holy shit. Ho-ly SHIT! Goddamnit Max! She's looking for me? Oh God. They'd kill her. What the hell was I going to do now!? How could I even help her from here?* I ran my shaking hands through my hair and gripped the ends as I let my head hang.

"You hearing me, brother?" Garron asked, interrupting my inner dialog when I didn't respond.

"Holy fuck," I finally muttered.

"What?"

"That's my sister." My voice was only a hollow whisper. "My sister's name is Maxine. Who was the man talking? Did you hear a name? Come on, man, did you hear a name?" The questions grew louder as they raced out of me in a panic.

"Jesus, Jax! You'd never told me her name! Um, I think the doc called him Mr. Gregori. So, it must have been one of his sons. Simple deduction here. But, like I said, no first names. No one's ever told me a name... except maybe you and a few others stuck down here. And Jax, he said he'd have her in the lab within the next few days. They're planning to do the same shit to her that they're doing to us." Garron's voice was grave.

"That motherfucker!" I roared, rage taking control. My body shook with the need to be violent as my veins threatened to burst into flame. Every inch of my body felt like it was going to combust.

"Breathe, Jax, breathe. We gotta get out of here. We'll stop them. Stay with me. Don't lose it." Garron pleaded. "If you lose it, they'll dose you up real good, and we'll never get out. You hearing me? Answer me, Jax!"

Breathing heavily, I slid down the wall and put my head between my knees, linking my fingers behind my head. Red hazed my vision, and I could feel my muscles growing, changing. Panic was flooding in. *Breathe. Breathe. Get control of yourself!* I willed myself to calm down. Then memories of Elias burst through my thoughts—he'd always had this strange obsession with Max. Even when we were little kids, he was always staring at her. Like she was a shiny toy, just out of reach. I needed out, then I was going to kill the weaselly little fucker. *Breathe. Come on Jax, get it together!* I rocked back and forth, slamming my back into the wall with force as I gripped my head, digging my nails into the back of my skull. I needed to focus on the pain.

"Talk to me, Jax. Tell me about her. Then we're gonna figure out how to get outta here," Garron demanded.

I loosened the grip on my head and pushed myself flush against the wall, and slowly opened my eyes. Blood coated my fingertips, but my hands otherwise looked normal. *Thank God.* I let out a shuddering breath, swallowed thickly, and started talking. I told him everything. How an unbelievable job offer for my mother brought us back to the city of her family origin. But led to her murder, and my father being imprisoned. And how I had to get guardianship of my sister at the age of eighteen so the state wouldn't separate us. God, over twelve years and it seemed like forever ago.

I told him about how I'd had to keep a closer eye on her after my dad was convicted for life. She'd sunk into a depression and had attempted suicide. She had no idea I knew. But after that, how she seemed to make the decision to grow from the pain of my parents being gone. She was strong-willed and determined, and had sunk herself into her studies, graduating high school with honors. Friends were kept at arm's length; instead of socializing, she worked a part-time job through school and helped cover bills. Never complaining. She even managed to work out, taking up running and kickboxing classes to take the edge off her anger. I really noticed a difference in her after that. A sort of confidence. She had a soft spot for animals, and even graduated from our local SUNY college with a Veterinary Technician degree. I had been so proud of her.

I told him about the Gregoris and our theories. That they owned the school, the medical clinic, half the city and this entire mountain we were currently imprisoned under. I'd been trying to get information to incriminate them and prove that they murdered my mother. And now I knew there were probably dozens of others. How I'd stumbled onto information about unethical experiments in this very facility. Sadly, Garron was all too aware of the unethical portion of my story.

There was something very special about the mountain itself—information I'd found went back almost one hundred years; it seemed a type of radiation was in the ground here. It was the reason the mines had been closed down so long ago. Almost every single mine worker had died of some type of blood poisoning. Documentation of the sickness that closed the mines was extremely hard to find. I'd had to piece it together with scraps of information. Somehow, the local headlines surrounding all the deaths had vanished.

I'd even managed to dig up information on some of the school residents that had 'gone missing or left the program.' They'd all been orphans with no family to claim them upon release. They simply disappeared. I'd uncovered at least five cases so far... there had to be more. Oh, and the almost dead guy the students found, that got me locked up down here. And how I was worried and wondered if they were imprisoned down here like us. I must have rambled on for hours. It was a lot to hear, and I hoped he was listening because now that I was saying it all aloud, all the puzzle pieces were coming together. At least, I thought they were.

After I finished, Garron was silent. I waited for him to say something for so long; I thought he'd fallen asleep. When he finally spoke, his voice was rough.

"You've gotta go, Jax. Get your sister and get out of here. Leave. Start over somewhere else. If what you're saying is true…" There was a long pause. "God, Jax. They've made a secret facility! And we are in it, underground, where no one knows about us." There was a pause, and his voice quieted as he began again. "I am all too aware that I'm some sort of experiment. They have made it perfectly clear that I and the rest of the poor souls trapped here are nothing." I heard a thump like he kicked something. "I gave up trying to get out. Until you, I had forgotten there was even an outside. I'll help you, I don't know how, but I'll get you out."

"Hey. I'm not leaving without you." I protested.

"Listen, you get her and run. Don't come back here. They'll kill you, or worse. They've been doing this for God knows how long, and they've been getting away with it. I don't have any family. At least, I don't think I do. Fuck, I can't even remember my life before ending up here at all. I don't even know how long I've been here… where I'm from…" He trailed off. "Jesus, I am probably one of those missing kids." His voice grew solemn.

I hadn't thought about how he'd ended up here. Now I felt like an utter ass. He couldn't remember because they'd been fucking with him for so long, and I just poured salt in an open wound.

"Look, WE are getting out of here. I'm not leaving you to rot in this place," I said with conviction, and I meant it.

Chapter 9

Maxine

I had to be in shock. This couldn't be normal. But who would I ask? I didn't know any other people, aside from the Gregoris, that had killed anyone. Killed. A manic laugh broke loose, and I squeezed my fist to my mouth. *Shit, I was losing it. What had I done!? Oh god. It was an accident, right?* I squeezed my burning eyes shut as I shoved the mop back into the closet. Not knowing what else to do as I waited for the police to come take me away, I cleaned my house. It was a nervous tick. If your life was in utter chaos, clean it up. So, I scrubbed every inch. I didn't want to sit still. Because when I slowed down, I had time to think. And I did not want to think.

But mental and physical exhaustion was winning, and I finally crawled into bed and curled up in a fetal position. My stomach twisted in a tight knot and the lump in my throat seemed fixed in place after seeing Nico die. His image flashed behind my lids, and I curled my body tighter, hoping I wouldn't vomit. The sight of his limbs twisted in all directions as he lay in a growing puddle of his own blood haunted me. Not the fact that he was dead; I'd been wishing that man was dead for as long as I could remember. No; it haunted me because he was still a person, a human being. Was I a murderer now? I hadn't shoved him over the banister, but I did... something.

Elias and Jonas were there... I was unsure about how much they had seen. Did they realize it was an accident? Maybe that's why the police hadn't arrived yet. I wished Jax was here. My mom, my dad... anybody. I turned my face and sobbed into my pillow, gripping the soft material that quickly grew wet from tears. What was I going to do? Was I supposed to go on like nothing happened? Could I?

I reached over to my nightstand and picked up the phone, then set it down. Who was I going to call? And what the hell would I say? *Hi, I think I accidentally killed Nico Gregori after I accused him of killing my mother and brother- Wanna stop by for coffee?!* I hiccupped and slammed my face back into my pillow as more sobs racked my body.

A thought popped into my head. If the police hadn't come yet, my days were probably numbered. They'd send someone to get rid of me...like they had done with the rest of my family. Oh my God. What was I going to do? Now on alert, I sat up and wiped my puffy eyes, then pushed the damp, unruly curls out of my face. Looking around my room, I tried to come up with a plan. God, where should I even start?

I picked up the phone again, staring at it for a long moment; I scrolled through my contacts for the one friend who'd always been there for me— Cory. He picked up on the second ring.

"Hey chick! Why you calling me? You never call. You break your texting finger?" He chuckled.

"Hey. Umm, listen... can I ask a favor?" I sniffed.

"Girl, you sound like shit. Do you have a hangover? Or— Have you been crying?" His voice pitched higher on the last word. "OMG, you have been crying!? You don't cry! Why the hell are you crying!? I'm coming over right now."

"Jesus, Cory, wait—" But he'd already hung up. Fucking great. At least my house was clean. Should I shower? I had about twenty minutes before he'd get here if he left his place right away.

I scrubbed my hands down my face and dragged myself out of bed. Splashing water on my face and pulling my hair in a messy bun was all he was going to get. I shuffled out to the kitchen and made a pot of coffee, then filled Cleo's bowl. She must be out prowling; I hadn't seen her today.

Waiting for Cory, I paced. I grabbed my phone again, found who I was looking for, and hit the call button. Sierra picked up after a few rings.

"Hey, Max, how's it going?" Her usually melodic voice was a little rough.

"Hi, Sierra. Sorry to bother you, but I was just curious if you've heard from Jax?" I mentally crossed my fingers and knew it was a long shot, but I had to try.

"Oh sorry, Hon, it's been a few weeks. We had a fight, so I was guessing he'd had enough. I haven't tried to reach him. I kind of... left the ball in his court, so to speak. I think we're done. He hasn't even texted me." She sounded sad and sick.

"Hey, you feeling OK? You're not sounding so great."

"I've got a little fever, must be some kind of virus. At least, I hope that's all it is. I was running on a trail through the park with Paige yesterday. We must have pissed off a couple of squirrels, cause I had to smack one off of Paige with a stick. It managed to nip me. I just hope it's not rabies. If I'm not feeling better tomorrow, I'll go to the clinic."

"You got bit?" My voice went up and so did the hair on the back of my neck.

"Gosh, I don't think it even broke the skin. The spot where I thought I was bit is just an angry pink mark. Probably just a scratch. No worries, Hon. Hey, I'm gonna go lay down, I'm pretty wiped out. If you see Jax... just tell him... never mind." Her voice trailed off, sorrowful.

"Hey, Sierra? He loves you; you know."

"Yeah, well. It's been weeks. Maybe he decided he doesn't anymore. You take care of yourself, Max. And if you need something, anything, you ask. You are still family to me, even if your brother and I go our separate ways."

"Thanks, you too," she hung up. She was such a beautiful soul. Goddammit. I prayed Jax was OK. He needed to fix that situation— or I might kick his ass myself. But I knew something was very wrong. I could feel it. Acid rolled in the pit of my stomach. All the pieces were slowly coming together. I refused to let the dark thoughts continue.

I poured myself a coffee, added a little cream, and headed out to my back porch just as Cory came tearing down my driveway. I sat down in my folding canvas camping chair and pulled my knees up. Cory bounced across the yard and up the steps, taking a seat next to me. "Nice chairs. Looks like we shop at the same store," he chuckled. I gave him a tight smile. He smiled back, watching me, waiting for me to start. I wasn't sure I should involve him. I'd never forgive myself if I got him hurt.

"Want a cup?" I waved my coffee mug at him.

"Yeah, I'll grab it. Mugs in the same spot?" he asked. I nodded. After a few minutes, Cory returned with a steaming mug of coffee and sat quietly, looking out toward the mountain.

"So," he broke the silence, "you gonna tell me what's going on? Somebody hurt you?" I glanced sideways and watched his knuckles whiten as he tightened the grip on his mug. I breathed out slowly, pondering what to say.

"No... but I've gotta talk to someone. It's... umm, it's a lot. You think you're up for it?" He nodded without hesitation, his face serious. His blue eyes looked back and forth between mine. I knew I could trust him. So, I took a deep, shaky breath and told him everything. And he listened. It felt so good to talk to someone about the whirlwind that had been going on. I prayed my need to talk didn't put him in any danger. The Gregoris were a malicious family, even with Nico dead. Elias and Jonas were unstable, each in their own way. And that was very scary. I needed to find Jax, soon. I had a horrible feeling something very bad was happening, and I might have just made it worse.

Chapter 10

Jaxon

We hadn't slept. We had been going over plans to get out of here and we only had one more day to make it happen. Garron and I both decided to use any last bit of information we could gather from our 'treatment sessions' today. And maybe with any luck, sway the doctor to help us. Garron was certain she was having a change of heart... now that she had some truths exposed. I prayed he was right.

Hearing the guards' boots stomp down the hall, I quickly laid back on my cot, pretending to be asleep. At the beep of the key card and the 'shhhhup' noise of the door sliding open, I cracked my eyelids. The same moment my eyes registered Eddie, his boot kicked my foot.

"Get the fuck up, pretty boy. Time for your medicine." He sneered. I rolled to my side and sat up.

"What's the matter, Blasco, get demoted? Now you're in the dungeon too, huh?" I quipped. We never had gotten along. The pompous asshole had been a constant thorn in my side during my training session to work for the Gregoris. I'd always had to bite my tongue; afraid my mouth would get me fired. I'd needed that job if I was ever going to get the information I desperately wanted.

He grabbed the shoulder of my issued scrub top and tried yanking me to my feet. Reacting without thinking, I jerked out of his grip and slammed my palm into his chest. Eddie flew backward into the wall of my cell, grunting from the impact, his eyes wide with surprise.

Holy shit, that was me! And it felt like I had exerted no effort at all!

Eddie recovered quickly, pulling his retractable ASP from his belt as he moved toward me. The second guard, Ken, stood in the doorway, blocking the exit. There was a look of panic on his face as he glanced between us. I focused back on Eddie, readying myself for the fight.

"Why fight?" Eddie sneered. "You and the rest of these fuckers are tainted. No way you're ever getting out of here. As a matter of fact, I think someone you know will be joining you shortly." He smiled, showing teeth. "Not that you'll ever see her down here. She gets the 'deluxe accommodations,' if ya know what I mean." He wiggled his eyebrows and nodded. I let out a roar and took one step forward. A sharp pain flared through my side and my body convulsed, dropping to the ground. Shifting my eyes to the side, Ken was wide eyed and holding an outstretched taser. *Fucking tasers. We're going to have to do something about those*, I thought to myself as my body spasmed.

I was still limp, unable to regain my muscle control as the two goons dragged me down the hall. But at least I was alert. My head lolled to the side as I tried to take in all the adjacent hallways and doors. We stopped at a door I'd never paid much attention to. Eddie dropped me like a dead weight, nearly making Ken topple over me.

"He so much as twitches, zap his ass. I've gotta grab the new serum for the doctor. Wait here." Eddie swiped his key card and shoved the door wide. Cages lined the walls, filled with all sorts of animals. Rabbits, monkeys, a fox, a few squirrels... they all looked... wrong. Larger than normal and mangy, with bald spots showing sickly gray skin that was visible underneath their matted pelts. Most of them were now going ape shit that someone had come in. Growls echoed and cages rattled as various animals slammed into them.

An intercom buzzed from inside the room and Eddie picked up the receiver.

"Yes, we're on our way." He paused, listening. "But that is in the western corridor, why... no ma'am. Yes, we'll be right there." He slammed the receiver down. Stomping back to us, Eddie looked down at me. "I hope she melts your skin off," his lip curled in disgust, and he punched me in the gut. Air whooshed out on a grunt and my body curled inward. "Get his arm, let's go. We're going through the lab to the western corridor." Eddie barked, and Ken responded with a quick, "Yes, sir."

As we passed through the lab, I saw several metal tables organized in rows. Carts with trays covered in paper and surgical napkins sat next to them. I could only assume a plethora of instruments laid under those napkins. I tried to take mental notes of supply cabinets and any type of instrument I might use. Not being able to see under those napkins had me guessing— with my luck, it'd probably be a stack of gauze— fucking useless.

Regaining some coordination, I was able to stumble along with my escorts. Two doors, a left, then a straight-away. Trying to catalog my route, I looked around. "Move it, fucker," Eddie ground out as he gave me a shove. I growled and Ken's hand moved back to his taser. Taking a deep breath, I focused on moving forward. A banging noise had me turning my head to the right. If I hadn't heard the noise, I would have never noticed. Tinted glass panes somehow made the walls seem solid. Forcing my eyes to look harder, I sucked in a sharp breath and an icy dread ran down my spine. My mind stuttered. The entire length of hall was lined with cells. Cages. Filled with people!

I could barely hear anything within them, they must've also been soundproofed to an extent. I squinted at some movement, a girl pounding on the glass, calling my name... Bella. *Oh my God.* I lunged forward without thinking, putting my hand on the glass.

"Bella!" Pain ripped through the back of my neck as Eddie tried to regain my attention with the use of his favorite wand. Spinning around, I barely kept myself from surging forward. Rage bubbled from my gut. Eddie held up his ASP, ready to use it again, and Ken's taser was out.

"She's a kid, Eddie. You have a fucking kid down here!" I growled.

"She's fucking contaminated. You all are. You're all on borrowed time. So, get fucking moving. I've got a schedule to keep." He moved the asp to his left hand and rested his right on the butt of his pistol strapped to his side. "Now, MOVE!" The command was firm as he nodded to the left.

My eyes dropped to the gun and back to his face, meeting his eyes. Wishing I could shoot daggers or laser beams, I knew the hate on my face was clear. Reluctantly, I moved. I had no choice, no leverage right now. But one of these days, I was going to kill that fucker. He gave me a shove and it was all I could do not to rip him to pieces right there. But I knew I needed to wait. We had to get out of here...all of us, together. And now was not the time. This was going to be harder than I thought. Things just got more complicated.

Continuing down the hallway, now aware of the shaded glass, I was horrified by the number of people I saw locked down here. Some were banging on the glass, begging to get out, while others were just staring into space, as if they were watching the most fascinating movie— but there was no movie. Clearly broken by whatever was being done to them down here. Several of the occupants appeared to be nearly dead, not moving, with a red foam leaking from their mouths, eyes and ears. *Jesus Christ. What have they done?* My heart dropped when I recognized a female huddled in a corner of a cell.

Sierra's best friend looked as if she'd been dragged through the dirt. She was filthy, with sticks and leaves protruding from her hair, and she still had workout clothes on. "Oh my God, Paige," I whispered. Her head immediately jerked upward, and she leapt up, darting toward the glass. Placing her palms against the glass, she whispered my name back as red tears ran down her face. *How the hell had she heard me?*

Eddie shoved me again to get me moving. He was ranting obscenities, but I was too lost in my thoughts to listen. I clenched my jaw and swallowed back the bile that rose in my throat. Fear ripped through my mind and my chest tightened as I realized Sierra might be down here somewhere. She and Paige shared an apartment— they were always together, unless she was with me. But I'd been MIA for... I didn't even know how long. If they did anything to her. God help me. I'd tear every— my dark thoughts ground to a halt as we entered a room I hadn't been in before.

This room looked similar to the animal lab we had passed through... but everything was human-sized. Several metal tables with carts of covered surprises waited along one wall. Countertops with computers, microscopes and lab equipment I'd never seen before filled the opposite space. It was all cold and sterile and smelled of antiseptic.

"So, Dr. Brindle, where do you want him?" Eddie asked as he threw the box he had collected from the animal lab on the counter just as the doctor walked in.

"You imbecile! You can't just throw those down! You'll ruin months of progress! I have a mind to report this to Mr. Gregori."

"Apologies, ma'am." He held up his hands. "Where would you like Mr. Devins?" The doctor's head swiveled around; eyes wide.

"Devins?" she questioned, her brows now drawn together and a scowl lining her mouth.

"Yes, ma'am. My apologies again." Eddie cleared his throat and corrected, "Patient RX5." She schooled her features, before she nodded at him and pointed to the furthest table. Eddie and Ken roughly shoved me onto the cold metal slab and locked the cuffs.

"Make sure those cuffs are secure." She barked as she lifted and inspected the contents of the poorly treated box. Dr. Brindle spun around, holding the vials of red liquid. "You two are extremely lucky. They're not damaged. Now, get out of here so I can get to work. And have the next subject ready to go. Mr. Gregori does not tolerate delays." The two guards left the room, and the door swung shut. Dr. Brindle turned her assessing gaze to me. The dark circles under her eyes were prominent, and a frown marred her lips. She broke eye contact and began shuffling around the room, grabbing various items. "Devins... Do you have a sister?" She asked quietly with her back to me.

"I do..." I swallowed. "Maxine." The doctor nodded and continued moving around the room, collecting more items. She brought a few syringes and vials back to the little cart next to me. We were both quiet while she gathered her things. After a few moments, she let out a shaky breath.

"He's going to bring her here. I'm not sure what he wants... He's getting stronger, you know." It wasn't a question, so I remained silent, waiting for an opportunity to plead our case. "The same element I've been working with, for you and the others, was given to him as well. His father forced me to modify a strain, hoping it would help his condition. And it has, he's changing… like you… and the others. But different." She let out a choked noise. "I never signed on for this. I wanted to help people. To make a difference." Clearing her throat, she continued with visible effort. "He's keeping tabs on my family," she whispered through a soft sob, covering her face with her hands. "I don't know what to do. I can't let my family get hurt." She wiped a tear away from her reddening eyes.

"Help me… help us get out of here. I have to save her. And I'll do what I can for your family." My mind raced as I watched her shake her head. *How could I possibly help her family? Think, Jax! Think! How the hell could I make good on a promise like that?!* An idea flared to life as a face popped into my mind. Frank. I'd been working with him to get my father out. To get proof of the Gregoris' misdeeds and prove his innocence. But if that didn't work, we had been preparing to break him out if necessary. He had connections and resources that could help. "I can get help, get them to safety. I promise you, please… don't let him continue this… this brutality."

"I… I can't. If he finds out… they'll be killed… or worse. You don't understand. He's becoming capable of things I never could have imagined. His previous treatments, they were…unheard of. I tried to follow up on the previous doctor's charts and notes but haven't had much success. Dr. Heller and his team worked on these modifications for decades. And some residents have been here since the beginning. Elias has been progressing at an alarming rate with disturbing results. He's able to manipulate thoughts… other people's thoughts!" she whispered harshly. "The Red has not only made his body stronger, but his mind as well. I can barely think for myself when he's here. He's becoming mad." She sobbed, wiping her sleeve under her nose. Walking over to the lab equipment and grabbing a small glass slide and another vial filled with red liquid, she returned with her head hanging low.

"She's the only family I have left. I can't let Elias hurt her. Please. I'll do anything," I begged.

"I just can't. I don't want to see anyone else hurt… and Elias is planning something… big. I'm scared for my family." She hesitantly made eye contact.

"I can try to help them. Get me out and I'll do everything I can to keep your family safe. I… have a friend." I blurted. "He's got connections. He served in the armed forces and knows people all over the world. He can help. We can protect them. I just have to get to him." I watched her silently as she thought over my words... and my fate. It felt like hours as I anxiously waited for her reply. My hands were literally tied. If I couldn't convince her to trust me, we'd be stuck here, and Max... Swallowing hard, I tried to shut down my train of thought. I didn't want to think about what Elias was planning to do to her.

"You can help my family?" She paced, rubbing her hand over her mouth. "If I can figure out how to get you out... Promise me. Promise you'll help them. Get them a message to get out of here, get far away, another country. My husband has family in Cuba. Tell them..." Her breath stuttered, "tell them to go there." I met her desperate stare.

"Yes," I answered without hesitation. "I will do whatever I can. I promise you. Please help us get out of here." Burgeoning hope filled my chest.

"Us?... Jesus." She kept her voice low and rubbed a hand up her forehead, pushing her hair back. "I can't promise. I think I can get you a key card. The rest will be up to you. That idiot Ken, or maybe Mark. You'll never make it out of the main halls. They're all guarded. And the elevators. This is impossible!" She paced back and forth. Then abruptly stopped and spun toward me. "The unfinished caves and tunnels. I've read the construction plan to expand the lab and containment areas. There looks to be an unfinished exit on the other side of the mountain. I have no idea what shape it's in. I'm not even sure if it's connected. I've heard there are small mining accesses from almost one hundred years ago." She paused, sucking in a breath, slapping a hand over her mouth. Her wide, red-rimmed eyes bore into mine. "Oh God, the failed..." she choked, then swallowed hard, collecting herself. "The subjects on which the experiments were unsuccessful... they... they have been disposed of down there. I heard that they were dumping them in the caves." The doctor covered her face with her hands, a sob escaping as her shoulders shook. "How did I ever get here? I'm going to hell." She muttered through her hands.

"Doc, hey!" I interrupted her not-so-internal debate. She pulled her hands away from her face, wiped her eyes, and looked at me. "Listen, they're coming, I can hear them." Her eyes darted up and around the room toward the door.

"You can hear—"

"If this goes sideways, for you and me, tell Garron. Get Garron the card and information about the tunnels. We'll do this together. And I'm getting those kids out of here too."

"I—"

"Doc, we don't have time." I interrupted. "Get him the key card and directions to the tunnel, then we'll—"Ken and Mark stopped my dialog by dragging a barely conscious Garron through the doorway. I let my head loll to the side, feigning incoherence.

Dr. Brindle cleared her throat. "Put the next patient over there," she pointed to the next steel table. Without a word, the guards hefted Garron's weight onto the table with a grunt and started latching the restraints, not even glancing at the two of us.

"You idiots! I told you he needed to be awake!" She stomped over toward Garron's bedside and tripped, knocking into the instrument cart and careening downward. It tipped over and all sorts of metal instruments clanked across the floor. Ken bent down to assist Dr. Brindle up off the ground. As she clutched onto his arms while rising to her feet, she smoothly released his key card and slid it into her lab coat pocket. *Clever girl.* "Send in my assistant to get this cleaned up. I can't get behind schedule. Mr. Gregori will be down later today for his progress reports." She dropped her head and moved back toward the computers on the opposite side of the room. "I'll be done with RX5 in twenty minutes. You can return him to containment then." The guards left the room.

Garron's head rolled to meet my stare.

"Nice to see you, brother," he rumbled in a deep voice. I smiled and nodded. The doctor turned back to us both.

"Whatever you two have been working on, we have about nineteen minutes left." She slid the key card into the waistband of my scrubs. "I'll try to explain the unfinished tunnels; I've only seen the construction plan, never been there." She launched into directions and descriptions to the best of her ability. "Just... don't forget my family. I don't know if I'll ever get out of here to see them again." She swiped a tear from her cheek and straightened. Collecting herself, she turned back toward us. "You're both–" she cleared her throat as her eyebrows drew together, "changing. You're different now. The Red is mutating, and your bodies are adjusting. Not everyone's progress has been favorable. I don't even know what to expect next. Your type of advancement is so new, we only have a few years of data with direct usage of Red. RX—" she paused, "uh, Garron's data is much more substantial."

Her voice dropped to a mutter as she began rambling to herself as she paced. I swore I heard her say something about decades. Before I could ask; she stopped pacing, whirling back toward us. "I'll try to explain quickly. We won't get this opportunity again." She swallowed audibly and pushed her shaking hands up her face and over her hair. Taking a deep breath, she cleared her throat and launched into a 'CliffsNotes' version. "OK, so your cells are mutating, changing. Most mutations in the genes controlling cell division lead to different types of cancer. We were trying to reverse that. Both of you have been successful. Garron's progress of regeneration is beyond anything we've seen." She resumed her frantic pacing, twisting her hands and mumbling to herself. It sounded like she said, *'Probably because he's been here since the beginning.'*

I opened my mouth in confusion, ready to ask what the hell she was talking about. But she spun around and kept speaking, not even pausing. "And yours is increasing as well. Your healing, pain tolerance, and muscle tissue have advanced. We've been able to track your biology. It's incredible. But there are consequences. You now require different proteins to stabilize. And I haven't figured out why, but an increase of hormones through heightened emotion usually results in a physical change. Both of you have been able to return to normal, but not all subjects have been able to recover." Her voice lowered to a trembling whisper. "I am so sorry, for everything."

The door clicked open as the guards came back in.

Chapter 11

Garron

We were basically trying to escape by sheer luck, no truly laid out plan. I had a horrible feeling we were totally screwed, but I wasn't going to squander the opportunity. Jax waited until lights-out, the both of us pretending to be passed out from our extensive treatments of the day. Dr. Brindle had told the guards we were probably going to sleep through the evening feeding due to the excessive number of tranquilizers she gave us. So, they wouldn't be coming by anytime soon. It was a decent enough cover and should buy us some time.

I heard the soft beep of the key card, and my door slid open. We nodded to each other and silently snuck down the hall. Staying close to the walls, we moved as quickly as possible. Sweat beaded over my brow and my palms were damp as I waited for the alarms to sound. Nothing but the soft slaps of our bare feet reached my ears. We made our way down two hallways, took two right turns and came to the animal portion of the lab. It was the only route we knew, and we were sticking to it. Sliding the key card, we entered swiftly and closed the door behind us. The animals all jumped to attention and started screeching.

"Holy Shit! What do we do? This is going to bring every guard in our direction!" Jax whispered. I panicked, eyes wide, looking around for... anything.

"Jesus, just go. We need to get out of here." I turned to the cages, anger and panic warring within me, spiking my pulse and a heat up my spine. "Just shut up! Before we get massacred!" I barked at the animals. Silence. They immediately stopped. My mouth fell open as I tried to process what just happened. I looked at Jax. He stared at me in shock, his mouth agape. "What the fuck?" I muttered.

Jax shook off the startled look.

"No time, man. Later. Let's go!" He grabbed the sleeve of my scrub top and tugged me into motion. We picked up the pace and made our way around two more corners and another left. Our feet padding over the cold floor was the only noise. The shaded wall with the other captives was just up ahead. The first door had barely slid open when copper-colored locks of hair flashed by as a petite young lady launched herself into Jax's arms. He covered her mouth with his hand and shook his head before she could make a sound. She nodded and he released her. Looking up at me, I saw a weak smile with tear-filled eyes light up her face.

"We're getting you out of here," I assured her. She took a shaky breath and nodded again.

Jax continued sliding the key card past three other doors, holding a finger against his lips to hush the inhabitants. Two young men, guessing they were late teens-early twenties by their size, joined us and a woman looking terrified and sick stumbled out of the last cell. Her face was ashen, and red stains tracked down her cheeks.

"Paige, we're getting you home." She gave him a quick hug. "Is Sierra here? Have you seen her?" Jax' rushed out the hushed questions.

"No." The woman sniffed. "I went to the clinic alone. But last time I saw her, she was getting sick. Like me." Jax's jaw flexed as he nodded. Not wasting another second, he signaled the group by swirling his finger in the air and pointing forward.

Jax took the lead, weaving our small crew through a maze of halls and a field of hydroponic plants; I held the rear. Checking over my shoulder every other minute, my senses were on high alert. I couldn't believe we'd made it this far. My pulse was racing from nerves and excitement. At the end of the field, we huddled down. Jax bringing everyone up to speed.

"Listen, from here on out, it's going to get bumpy. I'm not sure how to make it through the tunnels. If we get separated, just keep heading east. There is an exit... of sorts, I think. Old and unfinished mining tunnels, as well as natural caves, are scattered under this mountain and the city. Once we make it out and into the forest, my dad has a hunting cabin about three miles northwest of the reservoir. Follow the river and you'll run into it. It's off the grid. No power, but there will be some provisions. We'll have to lay low until we can come up with a more solid plan. Garron and I need to contact Dr. Brindle's family and instruct them to safety."

"Fuck her. She did this to us." One of the young men growled. I grabbed his shirt, yanking him forward and his eyes went wide.

"Maybe. But she's the only reason we're getting out of here— we owe her." I let him go and he stumbled backward. His eyes narrowed on me, clearly unhappy with our disagreement, but he kept himself in check. I wasn't interested in a scuffle with this guy; we had more important things to worry about right now.

"Not the time, Trent. We'll deal with everything when we make it out of here." Jax said in a tone laced with finality.

The sick woman grabbed Jax's hand, and his head jerked toward her.

"Jax, I don't know if I can make it. I feel so weak. I need to tell you..." She panted, trying to catch her breath. "Sierra and I... we were... attacked by squirrels, I think?" She sounded confused. Jax scowled, his eyebrows pulling together in confusion.

"I don't understand, squirrels?" He gave her a sympathetic look. "Let's just keep moving. We'll get you some help as soon as we get out of here." He looked at me and I shrugged. *Maybe she was delusional?*

"We were jogging through the park, the woodsy part of the trail. We got attacked and then we got sick. I went to the clinic, but she stayed home. They said they were moving me in case I was contagious." She sniffed. "Sierra didn't look so good when I left. She had a fever, Jax, like me. But she didn't want to go to the clinic." He drew in a deep breath and blew it out slowly through his nose, scowling. The muscle in his jaw ticking again.

"She'll be OK. She has to be. We'll get out of here and I'll find her," he vowed, then looked at me. Worry lined his face.

"Your Sierra?" I questioned. He nodded. "We'll find her," I grabbed his forearm in a silent promise. He turned and slid the key card over the scanner. The double doors slid open, both in opposite directions, producing a large entryway. The lights turned on, they must have been automated. Plastic sheets hung from the walls, and an array of construction equipment was scattered around. There seemed to be more than half a mile of tunnel, lit with single bulbs about every fifty feet in front of us. I moved to the front of the group. My eyes quickly sharpened, adjusting to the dimmer light, and I stepped over the threshold, waving to the others to follow. Then all hell broke loose.

An alarm started blaring through the facility as the overhead lights began flashing red. Guards started pouring in from the other end of the garden space. They must have seen us before the alarm went off.

"Go!" I barked. And we all took off running. Gunshots rang out behind us.

"Holy shit, they're shooting at us!!" Trent screamed.

The ground was uneven and damp as we pounded down the corridor. Angry shouts echoed around us, yelling at us to stop. We weren't gaining any distance and there was a three-way split coming up. "Should we separate? They're gaining on us!" I yelled to Jax as he dragged the stumbling woman along.

"Take the kids east. We're going west. I'll meet you where we discussed!" he shouted. Another shot ricocheted off the wall next to my head, spraying bits of rock and dust, stopping my protest.

"Move it!" I barked, urging the others to pick up their pace. The guards were close now. I could hear their heavy breathing over the slapping of our feet on the damp stone. The split came up fast, and I shoved the kids to the left as more gunfire went off around us. I stumbled, feeling a sting in my leg at the same time I heard a sharp cry of pain. Paige must have been hit. I turned to see Jax lift her in a firefighter hold over his shoulder and disappear in the opposite direction, guard's right on his heels.

I wanted to turn around. We shouldn't separate. I couldn't leave him here, not after everything we'd been through. We were supposed to get out of here, together.

Goddamnit, he split us on purpose! He knew East was the best direction to get out! I let out a frustrated growl as I kept running, pushing the kids to go faster. He put me in charge of getting these kids out. I put the pieces together too late. He was the diversion to give us a chance. Goddamnit!!

I refocused on moving forward— the lights were further apart now, no longer flashing where we were. I could see the kids clearly in the dim light, running as fast as they could. Up ahead there was an incline, and another split. "Left!" I shouted, just in time for a guard to dive through the air and tackle my legs. I flew forward, my hands hitting the cold, hard ground, catching my fall. Immediately, I rolled onto my back, jerking my right leg out of his grip, and kicking him in the face. His head rocked back so hard I heard a snap, then his body went limp. Two more guards were just feet away and I scrambled to get vertical. The one on the left pulled a taser from his belt as he continued to run forward. With it aimed at my chest, I tried to turn away at the last minute, but failed. The taser prongs pierced the thin layer of cotton and my skin. Electric pain speared through my body; a growl made its way past my gritted teeth. Grabbing the prongs and wires, I yanked them out of my skin, just in time for the other guard to drop his shoulder and ram me in the side. My body was thrown back against the wall, and I used the solid support to push myself back toward my assailants. Landing a punch on the side of the guard's face, he spun and dropped to the ground. Turning toward Mr. Taser, I saw him raise an ASP over his head, and start swinging it like a tomahawk in my direction. I blocked the blow with my forearm and drew my right leg back, thrusting out and snapping his knee in the opposite direction. The high-pitched scream that left his mouth echoed through the halls. He reached back, looking for another weapon, and I grabbed his head. Twisting with a force I didn't know I had, I snapped his neck and let go as he dropped to the ground. The other guard was moving, hands feeling around for something to defend himself with. In the distance, I could hear more footsteps approaching.

"You contaminated freaks are dead," the guard coughed.

"Wrong thing to say, buddy." I stomped my right heel into the side of his skull. Hearing the bone crunch, I knew he wouldn't be chasing us anytime soon. I reached down, grabbed the ASP lying on the ground and Mr. Taser's key card and took off.

I met up with the kids about half a mile later; they were waiting for me at another intersection. We were no longer being followed, by the guards anyway. Something else was down here. There was a smell… and it wasn't the coming from the earth and rock.

"Which way?" Bella panted. No more lights lined our way. It was pitch black. My eyes had adjusted enough to see shapes. I was astounded that that was even a possibility in this darkness. The previous tests had shown crazy results, but I hadn't been through any extensive testing since starting the new regimen. "Can you all see?" I questioned.

"Yeah, a little." A male voice answered. "I'm Mason, by the way."

"Trent here."

"Garron. And we go east. Let's move." I pointed in the direction and moved to the front. They all fell into line behind me. Good. Because I wasn't feeling up to babysitting. I bit back an urge to growl. It should've been Jax taking care of these kids.

"Where are we going?" Bella asked, and my teeth clenched.

"Cabin. About three miles northwest of a reservoir, hopefully. It's near where we're supposed to come out. We're going to be laying low." I cleared my throat and swallowed. "I'm going to try to keep you safe while we wait for Jax to catch up. So, for now, what I say goes, understand?" It wasn't a question. "OK", "yup" and a "yes, sir" chorused behind me.

We walked as quickly as we could over the now wet rocks and dirt. My leg was throbbing, but I pushed down the pain and kept going. The walls and ceiling were getting narrower and lower the further we went. There were several areas where we had to duck or climb over rocks. A few spots were so tight, we had to turn sideways and sidestep our way through. We moved slower now, starting to tire from what felt like hours of walking in silence and darkness. A warning prickled at the back of my nape, and I had a constant feeling of being watched… or hunted. My senses were on alert, but no sounds reached my ears.

A sharp incline had us climbing on our hands and knees over loose stones. Bella slipped and I reached back, catching her arm, and pulled her toward me.

"Thanks," she breathed.

We crawled through another tight stretch of passageway, areas so tight I had to slide on my belly, pulling my body along with my forearms. A soft sob left Bella's lips. I turned my head enough to call back to her. "You OK?"

"I'm scared. I don't think I can go any further. I can't breathe, it's too tight." She admitted in a high, panicked tone. "Just leave me here." Her voice cracked, her breathing was now coming in short, rapid gasps. I briefly thought about doing as she asked. Time was ticking and I didn't think we could afford to move any slower. But if I left her, there was no doubt that whatever was silently stalking us would get her. I clenched my teeth.

"Come on, Bells, you can do this. It can't be much further." one of the boys responded, offering the encouragement that I lacked.

"I know we're close. I can smell the change in the air. Just a little further," I told them. *There, I could do this.* I had no fucking clue where we were, but I had to keep them moving. I pulled my body over a sharp ridge of rock and rolled down a small drop on the opposite side. The cavern opened up and there was enough room to stand. I climbed back to the small opening and reached in. A small cold, clammy hand reached out, grabbing mine and I slowly pulled her toward me. Her body shook and her shoulders heaved from the deep breath she took as she tried to collect herself while clinging to my arms.

"Smell it?" I asked.

"Yes," she replied with a smile in her voice as she stepped back and wrapped her arms around her middle. I turned back to the opening and helped both guys out.

"Come on, this way," I said. We rounded a corner into another larger opening that tunneled straight ahead. A small bit of light reached my eyes from about a quarter mile away. "There." I heard the kids let out deep breaths as we moved forward. We picked up our pace, excited to see light. My steps almost faltered as a nervous energy started to fill me. I hadn't seen daylight in years... decades maybe. I had no idea what time of day it was, or how long we'd been making our way out. It felt like an eternity, but we'd finally made it.

We reached the end of what now looked to be a mining shaft, just as the doctor had described. It had been boarded up from the outside. I pushed on the old beams of wood. They creaked but didn't give way. I stepped back and swiftly moved forward, slamming my shoulder into the wood. Pieces splintered and broke away. I repeated the movement, and the rest of the old beams broke apart. Pushing out the broken wood, I created an opening by pushing and pulling fragments of the rotten planks away, making it big enough to climb through. My pulse raced as I took in the small view of the forest in front of me. I swallowed the hard lump that had lodged in my throat and stepped into the light.

The forest was glowing with a dusky light. I took a deep breath, closing my eyes with my face turned toward the sky. The air was crisp and clean, and a slight breeze caressed my face. I could hear the rustle of leaves from the breeze and birds chirping in the distance. It smelled amazing; it felt amazing; it was amazing. My chest tightened. When was the last time I'd been outside? I truly had no idea, it felt like a century.

The kids moved up next to me, breaking me out of my newfound appreciation of the outdoors. Now that we were in the light, I could see how dirty and disheveled we all were.

"It's gonna be dark soon. Where to now?" Bella asked as she looked around while wiping dirt from her arms.

"We head to the cabin, and we wait for Jax." I watched her nod out of the corner of my eye. "Let's go, who knows if the guards are aware of this exit. They could be trying to find it right now." We took off on a slow jog down the mountain, making our way around rocks, ledges, and trees. We quickly came to an old logging road. The set of tracks looked to be months old, which eased my mind. The training I'd been subjected to seemed to pay off— in this instance anyway.

Pushing the dark memories to the back of my mind, we kept moving. Following the road on bare feet wasn't easy. The kids hadn't complained, but I knew they had to be exhausted and sore. Trent was the only one with shoes, and I didn't waste time wondering why. Just the lucky one, I guessed.

My leg was beginning to ache again, and I didn't want to look. We couldn't stop, not yet. At that thought, I realized I no longer heard footsteps behind me.

I stopped, slowly turning around. The kids stood frozen, watching something with confusion etched on their faces just a few yards from me. I quietly and cautiously made my way back up the road. Only a few feet from them now, I followed their line of sight.

Two squirrels, the size of small dogs, were crouched over something, eating. Their usual shiny and fluffy gray coats were dull and matted. Chunks of fur were missing, exposing sickly gray skin. They started a tug of war, growling at each other over today's food of choice. Bella let out a gasp, as we all realized what the food of choice was at the same time. A leg. The foot attached to the human leg jerked back and forth between them. Well, until Bella's gasp registered. As one, they turned toward the sound. Directing their growl at her, we could clearly see their blood covered faces. Which were beginning to show teeth, their eyes large and rimmed with red.

"What the fuck!" Mason choked. Their attention snapped to him, and they started advancing, like they were stalking prey, their scroungy tails twitching.

"Help," Bella whispered, not taking her eyes from them.

The kids started slowly backing away. Trent's arm went up in front of Bella as he sidestepped, putting himself in front of her. The squirrels made a chattering noise, and their attention darted back and forth between the teens as they inched their way closer, matching their movement. Their growls increased, and their tails waved spastically in the air. Then they dropped their torsos, tails still up, readying themselves to leap. My brain was having a hard time comprehending what I was seeing. Paige had said she was attacked by squirrels. I'd thought she was crazy. But clear as day, they were going to attack those kids! Kids I'd promised Jax I'd get to the cabin. I wouldn't fail. I felt heat spread through me, instinct running my actions.

"Stop!" I commanded, putting my hand out, palm forward, "Stop!" The squirrels immediately froze, sat back, and looked at me.

Chapter 12

Jaxon

Paige was shot. I didn't have time to look at her leg, but I knew it was bad. I could smell blood. It had a coppery tang, as well as something sour... I could only associate the smell with sickness. Her skin was starting to look more pale and gray by the minute— and I swear I could start to see dark red veins, peeking through her thin skin.

"Jax, leave me," she panted. She was seriously slowing us down, and if we didn't keep our pace, we were dead. I set her down at her request, but it wasn't working. She was too slow. I picked her up again, tossing her over my shoulder.

"Not a chance. Besides, Sierra would kill me if I didn't get you out of here."

"Ha, I knew you still loved her," she wheezed over my shoulder. "I told her not to quit on you. Honestly, I don't think she could even if she wanted to." I zig-zagged back and forth down the darkened tunnels, taking random lefts and rights. "She loves you too, Jax. You know that, right?" She coughed and it sounded wet.

"Paige, would you shut up! We can have this conversation once we get out of this literal hell hole." She just grunted in response. I had no clue where we even were at this point. The lights had gotten further apart, then stopped altogether about a hundred feet back. I could still hear the footsteps of others chasing us, so I knew we hadn't lost them yet. Paige was light, but still slowing me down. Sweat trickled down my spine and the hair on the back of my neck stood at attention. I slowed my jog. Something just felt... off. No, it wasn't just a feeling, it smelled wrong too. The damp, mold and dirt smell were still there, but this was something else. Coppery, sickly and an undercurrent of sweet. Like rotten meat. But it wasn't Paige's injury. This was different and it was getting stronger the further we went. There was no time to turn around, however, and I had no idea how close our pursuers were.

I kept my slower pace, jogging down a straight stretch of tunnel. My sight had adjusted enough to see ahead and some basic shapes. As my toe connected with an obstruction, I realized it wasn't as good as I had thought. I stumbled and pitched sideways, trying not to drop Paige. My opposite shoulder bounced off the stone wall, and my body twisted as I tried to keep hold of her. Then we fell through an opening.

I'd completely missed seeing this opening, and briefly thought of how many others we must have passed. Flipping Paige to land on my chest, I grunted with the impact as we slid down a steep, smooth incline. She whimpered as we hit the bottom and bounced on the floor. Leaning forward, I braced one hand on my knee while reaching with the other to help her up. We stood together, trying to catch our breaths as we surveyed our surroundings.

Paige took a breath to speak, and I quickly covered her mouth with a nearly inaudible "shhh" in her ear. I pointed up. She turned toward the doorway we had fallen through just as two guards with flashlights ran past. Apparently, this doorway wasn't obvious, even with better lighting.

"We need to find a way out of here, do you think you can climb?" I asked.

She let out a shaky breath, "I don't know. Jax, my leg really hurts. But I'll try." I could hear her fighting back tears.

"Hey. We're getting out of here. But I need everything you've got. You can do this." I whispered, pulling her back to the steep slope. I tried to climb the incline first. But it was just too steep. With nothing to grab onto, I just kept sliding back down. We'd have to find another way. Standing, I raked both hands through my hair in frustration, then froze. My ears registering an odd noise.

I grabbed her outstretched arm and yanked her behind me with more strength than I thought I had left. A gasp left her lips as I reached behind me. Gripping her hips with both hands, I pushed her backward. Her front was to my back as we moved silently toward the wall. There was something down here with us. The soft scraping noise was coming closer. I couldn't see anything yet, but the shhhhkk, shhhhkk, shhhhkk of something being dragged was getting louder. Paige's hands tightened on my forearms, and I knew she'd heard it too.

Continuing to push her backward, she stumbled and tripped. Her nails dug into my shoulders as she tried to remain upright as bits and pieces crunched under our unsteady feet. I gritted my teeth at the sting of her nails, knowing they had drawn blood. My eyes went to the ground and my brows furrowed. It took a moment to realize Paige had tripped over some scattered and shredded cloth. And now our unsteady feet were atop a small pile of bones. I swallowed hard, hoping Paige hadn't noticed and continued to push her backward.

This stretch of cavern was huge. The middle was open, aside from a few large stalactites and stalagmites scattered around the space. There were a few possible exits on the opposite sides of the cave. God knew where they led. But if I had to take a guess, I would've said nowhere, or whatever was coming at us would have probably gotten out of here.

The scraping noise grew louder. Shhhkkk, shhhkk, shhhkkk. I could feel Paige trembling behind me.

"What the fuck is that?" she whispered in my ear.

"I can't see anything yet, but we need to go." The need to get away from whatever was down here prickled up my spine and tightened my scalp. I frantically looked around for anything we could use to escape. Nothing. Spinning around, I looked up. *There!* A thin ridge, about a foot and a half wide and roughly nine and a half feet up, ran along the cave wall and neared the opening. If we could make it up there, we might be able to slide along the ridge, and jump to the opening in the tunnel. Paige followed my line of sight and shook her head.

"Jax, I can't jump that high, especially with my leg."

The noise of deep inhalations, something scenting the air, pulled my attention around. I could just barely make out an outline now. I narrowed my eyes, trying to see better. It was tall, maybe seven feet, and its head tilted upward as it sniffed the air. Extremely long arms hung by its sides, swinging slightly with each limping step. I couldn't be sure from here, but it looked like its leg was broken, twisted backward. I focused harder. Yes, the limp was because it was stepping directly on the end of its tibia, the foot wasn't even in use. It was just being dragged behind as the creature advanced, making that horrendous noise.

I turned back to Paige. Her eyes were wide, and her face had drained of the last bit of color she had had left. She could see it too. Grabbing her arms, I placed her hands on my shoulders. "Give me your good foot. I'm boosting you up. Cling tight to the wall and start making your way toward the opening." She nodded as I laced my fingers together and stepped her right foot up. "One, two..." I tossed her up. She pulled herself onto her knees, clutching the wall, and slowly got to her feet. There was barely enough space for her to hang on. *Shit, this is gonna suck. I am a lot bigger than she is.*

I stepped back a few feet to get a running start. Taking a quick look over my shoulder was a mistake. It was close enough for me to see clearly now. Pale gray, nearly white skin was stretched tight over muscle and sinew. A plethora of red veins visible under the creepy skin. The head appeared more oval and larger than a regular person. Its huge mouth hung wide open as if it couldn't hinge closed. It's jagged and sharp looking teeth on full display. And the eyes were red, all red. No whites, no irises, or pupils, just red, like the color of fresh blood. The arms looked as though someone had stretched them. Huge, claw tipped hands hanging next to its knees. A shiver ran up my spine. *Fuck that!* I ran forward, using my adrenaline, and pushed off the ground as hard as I could.

I flew in an arc. My body slammed against the wall with a thud, knocking the air out of my lungs. My toes rocked back on the edge of the ledge as I started to lose balance. Leaning forward as hard as I could, an arm reached out and helped steady me against the wall. *Holy fuck, did I just make a nine foot vertical jump?* No time to think as the creature was almost close enough to touch us now.

"Thanks," I breathed. "Now go, Paige, go!" I yelled in a whisper. She started her sidestep shuffle along the wall and I followed, both of us gripping the wall of damp stone the best we could, trying to keep our balance. Creeping, at what felt like a snail's pace, we made our way to the opening. It was a good four or five feet jump to our exit.

"Paige, you've got to jump."

"It's too far. I'll never make it," she whimpered.

"We're running out of time! Go, now!" She turned, trying to put her back against the wall, and slipped. My hand darted out without thinking, grabbing her forearm on her descent. She swung backward, slamming her side against the ridge we were climbing across and let out a grunt. A squeal and thrashing quickly followed.

"It's got my leg!" she shrieked.

I was losing my grip. *Fuck!* I tightened my hold as much as possible and yanked, swinging her backward like a pendulum and out of that thing's grip. On the return swing, I grunted with effort as I threw her up and over the threshold. She bounced and rolled across the ground, landing gracelessly in a heap. She crawled back to the doorway, peering down at me.

"Jaxon! Hurry!" She whispered.

I sidestepped a little closer and readied myself to jump.

"Jaaackssssson," a garbled voice said as sharp claws on pale gray hands lined with red veins reached for me. My eyes widened as I tried to look down at the creature. Moving my feet out of reach, I kept shuffling to the side as I tried to get a better look. The remains of the tattered clothing hanging from the creature began to register as familiar. The shredded scrubs were the same color as the ones I now wore. And I'd seen the tattoo on its forearm before. The skull smoking a cigarette was original and etched in my mind. And the only time I'd even seen that was from the guy I'd found all twisted and broken in the woods with the students. The same guy that ended us all down here. Flashes of memory spun through my head. Oh my god. It was also the same Clay that was in prison with my dad. How did he get here? *What the fuck was happening?* Cold dread coursed down my spine.

"What are you?" I whispered, horrified.

Not waiting for an answer, I jumped, pushing off the ledge, my arms extended as I leapt. *Oh shit, I wasn't going to make it.* My upper body slammed onto the ground, my lower half not quite making it. The impact knocked the wind from my lungs, and I kicked my lower body in the air trying to push myself up. Paige grabbed my arms and started pulling. As soon as I could take a breath, I wiggled myself up enough to swing my right leg up over the edge and rolled onto my back. I just lay there for a moment, panting.

"Jax, I can hear someone coming! Get up!" She whispered, tugging at my arm. I turned on my hands and knees and climbed to my feet. Nodding toward the left, we started heading back in the direction we'd come from. I was hoping to get past the guards and catch up with Garron.

As we jogged around another corner, I was lost in thought, trying to remember which way to go. An arm shot out, clothes lining me. My head snapped back as my feet flew up in the air in front of me. I landed hard on my back and Eddie's face came into view as he straddled me.

"Howdy fucker," he said with a smirk, "miss me?"

Paige screamed as a few more guards rounded the corner. I kicked my leg straight up, nailing Eddie right in his balls. As he bent over me to cup himself, I slammed my fist into his face. Grabbing his shoulders, I tossed him to the side and stood. Moving toward Paige, I grabbed one of the guards' heads and bashed it off the stone wall. He dropped lifelessly to the ground. I turned as another guard kicked Paige in her wounded leg, eliciting a scream as she crumpled down. She had her hands wrapped around the wound as fresh blood seeped between her fingers. Whimpering, she scooted backward on her ass, using her good leg to push away from the guards.

I crept up behind the guard who was stalking toward her. Grabbing his head with both hands, I twisted until I heard a pop and crunch. The noise briefly reminded me of breaking celery. I watched as he slumped to the ground, his unblinking eyes staring at nothing. Turning back toward another scream, I saw another guard dragging Paige down the corridor by her hair. As I moved forward, a sharp pain jolted through me. My body spasmed and I dropped to my knees, unable to move. Eddie came into my line of sight, spit blood on the floor at my feet and looked me straight in the eye as he wiped his mouth. I raised my hands toward him, agonizingly slow, as my body did not want to respond.

"Sucks, doesn't it? This is the upgraded taser. You and that waste, Garron, were showing resistance. How ya like it?" he asked, showing all of his teeth.

"I'm gonna wipe that fucking smile off your face." I ground out, looking up at him.

"I never did like you; you know." He kicked dirt at me, a small humorless laugh leaving him. I coughed and my eyes watered from the invasion. "But I hear I may get a chance to get to know your sister. I bet I'll enjoy her company soooo much more than yours." He wiggled his eyebrows and his lip curled up.

"You fucking touch her and I'll kill you!" I roared, channeling my energy into moving. It felt like my body was being electrocuted while stuck in glue, but I managed to rise to my feet. Eddie pulled his arm back, slamming his fist into my face with brutal force. I flipped backward off my feet and hit the ground.

"I've been getting a little 'boost' from the good doctor myself lately. I'm impressed," he smiled, looking at his fist. "Not a scratch. And don't you worry, I'll take real good care of that pretty sister of yours before I hand her over. I've been waiting a long time for this." He grinned and I roared so loud I thought the walls shook. The last thing I saw was the bottom of Eddie's boot as it connected with my face, and everything went black.

Chapter 13

Maxine

What a fucking mess. I felt so confused, scared, and hopeless. The pit of my stomach churned with bile as I bit back a sob— crying never helped anything. The police still hadn't come, and the Gregoris hadn't sent anyone to kill me, yet. *Jesus, I can't believe I'm even thinking that.* I needed to find Jax. But how was I supposed to do that? Especially after accidentally murdering the father of the one person who could help me?!

"Fuck!!" I screamed into my pillow, squeezing it against my face.

Depression was sinking in. I had managed to overcome deep depression years ago, but the feelings were coming back two-fold with the recent trauma. I wasn't sure I wouldn't slip down that slope again with the dark thoughts swirling in my head. My cat took that moment to jump into my lap, and the tears started pouring from my eyes. She was a strange angel. I rubbed my fingers through her fur and around her ears, probably comforting me more than her as memories assaulted me of the last time she'd saved my life.

Jax was working one of his two jobs, and I was home alone. After another shitty day of high school, I had been feeling pretty hopeless. A darkness festered within me, and I was sick and tired of feeling worthless. It was a dark cloud that chased away any sunshine. I'd pushed away any friends I had, severing any connections. I had decided not to bother with the struggle of life anymore. I didn't want to be a burden to my brother and just wanted to see my mom again.

The state had yet to confiscate my dad's extensive gun collection. His best friend, Frank, had some pull with the local law enforcement and was helping with the paperwork to keep all of dad's things. He'd helped Jax fill out all the necessary applications, and now we were just playing another round of the waiting game.

Grabbing my dad's hidden keys to his gun cabinet, I grabbed his favorite .44 Magnum. Heading out the back door, I sat on our porch and just stared at the gun in my lap, my finger dancing over the cold steel. I opened the chamber, just like dad used to show me, to see if it was loaded. One bullet. I spun the chamber and closed it. The cold tip against my temple wasn't the only reason goose bumps broke over my skin. I squeezed my eyes shut. My palm slightly sweaty as I gripped the handle. Click.

I sighed, not sure how I felt about the empty chamber. With trembling hands, I brought the gun to rest across my lap once again and opened my eyes. Popping the chamber back open, I let my gaze drift across the backyard, seeing nothing. Not bothering to look back down, I spun and snapped it closed again. The lump in my throat made it almost impossible to swallow. "I miss you so much mom," I whispered as a small series of sobs broke from my lips. Closing my eyes as tears dripped down my face, I placed the barrel against my temple once again.

A firm weight landed on my lap, scaring the shit out of me. My eyes popped open as I squealed and dropped the gun. The gun clattered to the floor and went off. The noise echoing through the space was almost deafening. My surprised gaze darted back and forth between the cat on my lap and the large hole shot through the garbage can next to me.

Shaking off the dark memories, I decided a cup of coffee couldn't hurt. Maybe downing some of the warm liquid might heat me from the inside out. Making sure the liquid was hot enough to practically scorch my mouth, I sucked down the cup, and dragged my feet to the bathroom. What was I going to do? Looking up, I startled at the reflection staring back at me. My skin was pale, almost gray; I leaned forward, wide-eyed and rubbed my hands over my face. Pulling my long blonde locks away from my face, I secured them in an effortless ponytail. I had to get it together.

Anger at myself flared in my chest. *Come on, think! What would Mom or Dad do? I imagined they'd be disappointed if they could see me right now.* Splashing some water on my face, I looked back in the mirror and gasped, stumbling backward, and falling on my ass. I slowly reached up, grabbing the edge of the sink to steady myself. Hesitantly, I leaned forward, looking into my eyes again. Unremarkable hazel eyes stared back. I could've sworn my eyes had flashed red. *Jesus; I was losing it.* Shaking my head, I dried my face, then headed to my room.

A run would help clear my head. Before I could change my mind, I quickly called the store. The answering machine picked up and I left Frank a quick message that I'd be late. I hoped he didn't freak out; I was never late. I'd explain all of it later... or as much as I could anyway. A nervous energy was making me feel twitchy. It was probably the coffee. It felt like my blood was vibrating through my veins. God, I wished Jax was here. I sent Cory a quick text also, as he'd probably be called in to cover for me. I'd apologize in person later.

I dressed quickly and grabbed my iPhone and ear buds as I headed for the door. Bounding off my back deck, I headed down the road in a fast walk. Shoving the earbuds in, I cranked up some Powerman 5000, trying to drown out my thoughts.

Starting at a slow pace to warm up, I breathed in the crisp morning air. The sun was not quite breaking the ridge of the mountain yet, but it was still enough light for me. My eyes had always adjusted easily, even in the dimmest of light. Being out like this was a balm to my soul. A light fog rolled across the fields. Combined with the morning dew, it made everything appear to have a whitish hue. Feeling my muscles loosening up and my energy rising, I decided to head down a lesser traveled road. Even though my cabin sat far enough away from the county road that it was private, it was still regularly traveled, even this early in the morning. And I didn't feel like running into anyone I knew.

Veering from my normal route, I took a left and jogged down a quiet, single lane road that headed through the woods. My body almost pushing me in the direction. The trees leaning over the twisting road looked beautiful, with the first rays of sun beginning to shine through their branches.

Picking up my stride, I broke into an easy run. Enjoying the wind rushing through my hair, my thoughts and worries temporarily disappeared. A small rabbit darted out of the brush from alongside the road. My eyes tracked the rabbit and my stomach let out a growl as my mouth watered. Without thinking, I picked up speed, trailing just behind it as it ran along the road. A strange but pleasant scent tickled my nose, and my body started to warm— warmer than usual from an ordinary run. Momentarily distracted, I realized only one side of my body felt hot. As if I'd turned just my left side into the rays of the sun. Before I had time to register another thought, I was knocked off my feet, the air whooshing from my lungs.

Tumbling off the side of the road, I pulled in my arms, and head as I rolled. My body slammed into the ground, yet the pain I anticipated from the fall didn't come. Something cushioned most of my impact, and the tumbling world finally came to a stop. Strong arms wrapped around me as sparkles crowded my vision, and I tried to catch my breath.

Panic surged through my limbs, and I threw an elbow, trying to buy myself some space. The grip loosened and I staggered to my feet, stunned and dizzy. My dazed vision wouldn't focus, but I readied myself to defend as a huge figure loomed in front of me. A man countered my movement and lunged without warning. I was immediately tugged back down. The chance to suck in a shocked breath didn't happen as a hand slapped over my mouth and another wrapped around my waist. The weight of the man pulled me backward. Running on adrenaline, I shoved my feet into the ground as hard as I could and used the momentum to roll backward over my attacker. Not expecting my resistance, my attacker's grip loosened, and I rolled to a crouch behind him. As I scrambled to gain balance, the man slammed into me again, knocking me back down. His large hand covered my mouth once more and his body pressed me into the ground.

I tried to scream as I bucked, attempting to wiggle out from under him. His face neared my ear as an angry hiss left his lips.

"Shhhh!!! Settle down, be still!" He whispered harshly. *Yeah, right. Did he think that would work!?*

I continued to struggle, terror flooding my veins. Elias. He'd actually sent someone to kill me. A pang of hurt stabbed at my chest. I'd truly thought we were friends, and maybe he'd believed what happened to his father was an accident. I didn't want to die out here.

Vaguely, I heard the roar of a motor getting closer. Hope stirred in me. If I could just break free, and get back to the road, I might be able to get help. I redoubled my efforts, thrashing below my attacker.

"Shhh! You blasted woman! Quiet! I'm trying to help you!" He whispered again, pressing me harder into the ground with frustration. "If they see us, we're dead!"

I froze for a moment, scowling and trying to suck in deep breaths through my nose. The engine noise was getting closer. I was going to miss my chance. Taking rasping breaths, I tried to calm myself. *Think! Panic would not help me.*

My heart was pounding in my chest to a painful rhythm. Clearly, my efforts were near hopeless, he was too strong. I channeled my self-defense classes, trying to remember anything useful. *If I can get him to loosen his grip, I might make it.* I slowed my struggle and nodded, or tried to as much as I could in his iron-like grip. My mind reeled. I had no idea who this was, his head was turned away from me, his dark hair and voice not familiar. *Some fucking psycho is attacking me in the woods! And he thinks I'll just lie here?* I couldn't help myself and flailed as panic renewed, bucking my hips, and trying to move. But his body's weight was still pressing me against the cold, damp ground. I wasn't ready to die here.

My heart was thumping painfully in my chest and the strange heat from earlier started to spread. It was so hot it stole my attention, adding to my confusion. He leaned toward my ear.

"They're looking for me and you. If they find us, we're both dead, or worse." He said grimly. *I wondered for a quick second, what could be worse than death?* "They are NOT help, Max." I stilled at his deep growl of words; my breath caught in my chest. *How does he know my name?* Finally, he pulled back enough to look at me. Seeing the surprise in my wide eyes, he continued, "Your brother sent me. He helped me escape."

Shocked beyond belief, I laid frozen. My eyes must have been the size of saucers. That was the last thing I expected to hear. *Jax? He's alive!* A million thoughts ran through my head.

"Don't move," he whispered, pressing his body over mine, not budging, his hand still over my mouth and our faces just inches apart. My heart had restarted from the shock and was once again slamming against my ribcage. I wanted to scream, to ask a million questions, to understand what the hell was happening right now. I shook my head, trying to dislodge his hand.

"What the fuck is going on?" I tried to yell. But it was completely incomprehensible, muffled, from his big hand covering the lower half of my face. I tried to breathe slowly through my nose and pleaded with my eyes for him to let me go.

"Shhhh!" he growled. Brilliant green eyes, the color of spring leaves, stared into mine as thick brows pulled together. Then the barest shake of his head, as his eyes pleaded for me to listen. It was suddenly easy to notice the contrast of heat radiating from his body and of the cold ground at my back. He was so hot! It almost burned where our bodies touched. A faint buzzing noise grabbed my attention, and I realized it was music. My ear buds were lying on the ground somewhere among the foliage.

Another noise registered, and my eyes widened with hope. Bucking, I tried to turn my head, but my attacker held me immobile. My eyes darted to the side, and I watched helplessly through the shrubbery as a black Hummer blew past us. Dust flew behind in its wake. A slightly defeated breath whooshed out of my nose past the man's large hand. My help had just disappeared down the otherwise deserted road. *Fuck.*

"Please don't scream. Our lives depend on it." The stranger pleaded.

Slowly, he removed his hand from my mouth and relented. Pushing with my hands and feet, I scrambled out from under him, backing up in a crab walk.

Catching my breath, I wheezed, then began firing off questions.

"Where is Jaxon? How do you know my brother? Who the fuck are you? What do you mean he helped you escape? How did you find me here? Did the Gregoris send you?" They just kept pouring out, like rapid fire. He lowered his head and held up a hand in a stopping gesture, dropping to his knees in front of me.

"I have so much to tell you, but it's not safe here." He shook his bowed head. Breaths heaved in and out through his nose, his chest straining against the fabric as a muscle ticked along his jaw. Pushing both hands through his hair, his huge biceps flexed and the shirt he wore made an audible tearing noise. If I wasn't so freaked out, I would have made a smart-ass comment about steroids. But I took the opportunity to take another step backward, readying myself to leap up and run.

"We need to leave. Now. Your brother would kill me if anything happened to you. They could come back... and I'm not sure you can go home either. Like I said, they're looking for you."

Really looking at the man for the first time, I took in his appearance. Light blue scrubs adorned his body. Torn, dirty and— I paused my assessment. What was... *Is that blood?* I slowly scooted another step back from the immense man with a body much too large for the blood-splattered scrubs. Arms and shoulders stretched the fabric tight to the point of almost bursting. I wasn't sure how they'd survived the abuse going by the noise I'd heard from the straining material. Shoulder length hair, too dirty to tell the color, maybe a light brown, framed a face smudged with dirt. His face lifted and his unusual leaf green eyes met mine. They were highlighted by high cheekbones and a few days of stubble that traced along his chiseled jaw. Watching me, his lip curled up slightly in one corner as he moved slowly, attempting to limit his threatening appearance.

Standing at his full height, towering over me, he stretched out his hand, "Come, we can't stay here. It isn't safe."

"Who are you? And how do you know my brother?" I asked again, scooting yet another step backward. I was torn. Stay with the potential murderer in the woods and find out what happened to Jax or take my chances on my own. He just stared at me expectantly, hand still outstretched. "Jesus, you expect me to go with you? Really? Do I look fucking crazy?" He blinked, tilting his head as he studied me and remained silent. His face now blank of emotion, he dropped his hand. I glared. *Damn it, Jax. You'd better be alive, cause I'm gonna kill you.* "At least give me your name." I growled.

"Jax said you'd be feisty." He frowned and dragged a hand across the back of his neck, like he had to think of an answer. I felt my eyebrows draw together in frustration. "I'm Garron. Now, we have to leave. Before they come back."

His eyes finally left mine to scan the area and the stretch of road in either direction. Reaching out to me once again, offering to help me up, I hesitantly took hold. He yanked me to my feet with unnatural strength and I stumbled into his chest. His hands clasped my upper arms as he steadied me, and an odd tingle vibrated from his touch. His hands were so warm. Looking up to meet his gaze, I realized just how huge he was. At least a full foot taller than me. I stood there frozen for a moment, my eyes locked on his, my skin buzzing where we touched. I jerked back and blinked, breaking from the strange daze. Could I trust him? He knew something about Jax, and for that reason alone, I had to go. God, I must be crazy. I just hoped it wouldn't get me killed.

Chapter 14

Garron

I was starving; my body craved sustenance more than ever and I hadn't slept in days. But I couldn't stop now. Working with Jax to plan our escape had been no easy feat. And now that I was out, I couldn't wait any longer for him. *Goddammit, Jax. It was supposed to be you! The whole thing went fucking sideways.* We had discussed the needed events if one or both of us made it out of there. The kids were safely at the cabin, with strict instructions to stay inside. I let them get a few hours of sleep, taking first watch. Then I needed to find Maxine, warn the doctor's family and get word to Sierra. Jax had gone over Maxine's basic routine, what she did most days, where she worked, what gym she went to. I couldn't help absorbing any information about her. It was clear they meant a lot to each other—they were all either of them had left. A true family bond. I was envious. With all the stories, I had even begun to feel like I knew her.

I quickly made my way to the doctor's home just before dawn. My short explanation regarding my appearance and the situation had her husband on edge. But that was expected. They must have discussed the possibility of this event because he immediately spurred into action. Emergency bags were already waiting in a closet as he raced around, collecting the children and a few final items. It only took a short time before he was shaking my hand and pulling out of his driveway. I couldn't remember the last time I'd heard a 'thank you', or even shaken someone's hand. Something so simple had felt strange and made me uneasy. I truly hoped the doc would be OK and would meet up with them soon. But a sinking feeling filled me as I watched them pull away. I didn't think they'd ever see her again. At least they weren't in cages... or dead. No one deserved to live in a cage forever.

I headed back northwest toward where I hoped to find Max. It felt nearly impossible.

I wasn't even sure I was in the right area, but hoped this was a road she frequented on her runs. Jax had tried to be as specific as possible with directions. Instinct and monster inside pushed me forward, guiding my search. Surprisingly, it was easier than I'd thought.

I still wasn't sure I'd made the right choice. Then I caught the scent of... something delicious? My beast stirred, and my mouth watered. I shook my head— just friggin' hungry. I'd been tracking my way through the woods for hours in the dim light, the canopy of trees shading everything. It felt so surreal, like a dream. It'd been so long since I'd been outside. The indoor training sessions had forced me to learn combat, tracking and dispatching. But it had nothing on the actual application in real life situations. Breaking out of that underground nightmare had been utter luck. At least I was putting some of the training to use.

Jax had said I should head southeast and find his sister. Now that I'd taken care of business with the doc's family, I had to almost double back. We knew that Maxine was in danger, that the Gregori's wanted her. But she was probably the only one in a position to help us. Neither option for her was safe.

I would have to gain her trust. And Jax had said that since they'd lost their parents, she'd changed. She'd mostly shut herself off from others. Now she'd have no choice but to listen to a stranger. I never thought in a million years I'd be the one to escape, and forced to explain my life to a woman. She knew nothing about the experiments and what was being done in the underground catacombs. I'd barely spoken to anyone other than Jax in decades, now I had to convince some girl I didn't know to help. I mentally cringed. I'd almost rather be tortured.

Between finding Jax's cabin and getting the kids safe, getting to the doc's family and now looking for Maxine, I'd been running for a couple of hours.

My legs pumped under me as I jumped over logs and downed trees. I needed food soon as I was starting to tire. The doc said we'd have to focus on protein— not sure why that was so important now, then again, maybe it had always been. But something to do with the new injections had increased our metabolisms and made it even more of a necessity. I'd worry about that later. I couldn't stop. Not until I found her. Jax's directions were vague despite his best efforts, but I pushed myself forward. I couldn't let those people get to her first. She was in danger and had no idea. I prayed I'd get to her in time and that she would even listen to what I had to say.

Trying to help me, he had described her small frame, golden blonde locks and big, hazel-green eyes. I had put the pieces together like a puzzle in my mind, though nothing had prepared me for the actual thing. I should've known better; she was his sister after all. Familial love had colored his view. Spotting her through the trees, I ran ahead and ducked down, hiding in the brush as my heightened sight drank her in. Damn it, Jax, I mentally cursed him. I should've known a brother's description wouldn't be exactly accurate.

It had to be her. I couldn't explain it, but there was not a single doubt in my mind.

She presented a graceful package as I watched her run the deserted road in the early morning light. Her blonde ponytail flew behind her as her feet pounded at a brisk pace. A peaceful expression was on her face, along with a rosy flush that ran along her cheeks and neck. Sweat glistened on her forehead and chest, her full breasts bouncing with each beat of her feet. Defined arm and leg muscles pumped her body forward. She was a sight I had not expected. I just watched her, transfixed, and unable to avert my gaze.

Her chin lifted slightly, and I tilted my head. It was as if she was scenting something. Suddenly, a rabbit leaped across the road. It spastically darted right and left in front of her. She then dropped her chin, solely focused and picked up her pace. Was she chasing the rabbit?

Halting my thoughts, I could hear the shifting of gears in the distance. As I focused, I could make out the sounds of the Hummer that had been following me. I'd noticed them right after the doctor's family had fled. I didn't think they had seen me as I hid, watching them pull into her driveway. Several men had piled out of the Hummer and kicked in the door. Minutes later they were out, empty-handed. I was so glad I'd made it in time. But now they were here. Fuck. I thought I'd lost them. I had a very few brief minutes before they'd be on top of us. I had to do this now. I sent up a small prayer—not that it had ever worked before. I didn't have a lot of options for a nice sit-down conversation. Ha. I almost laughed out loud at the thought. When had I ever had a sit-down with anyone?

Maxine passed the spot where I was hiding, oblivious to me or the oncoming vehicle. I picked up my pace, running almost parallel to her. As I heard the Hummer getting closer, I pushed myself harder. Launching my body across the road, I grabbed Max around the waist and we tumbled into the woods. Trying to wrap my body around hers to spare her any injury, I immediately had to defend myself. I barely dodged the elbow she threw at my head. Losing my grip, I slammed into the ground, luckily taking the brunt of the fall. She shoved off me and staggered to her feet. Readying herself for battle, she glared at me as she pumped out heavy breaths; she looked glorious. I was momentarily stunned. But recovered by putting my hands up facing out, keeping my stance wide. Her unfocused eyes darted from side to side, and she made her move. Leaping to the side, she quickly darted back in the opposite direction, trying to evade me. My reflexes were too fast though, and I countered her as she tried to dodge around me. Diving sideways, I curled one arm around her waist and one over her mouth as I turned in the air, again taking the brunt of the fall. I immediately flipped on top of her, pinning her to the ground. Not removing my hand from her mouth, afraid she'd scream, I peered down into her wide eyes. For a moment, all I could do was just stare into their depths. Right around the pupils were flecks of yellow and brown, that starburst in the brilliant green. A quick flash of red startled me out of my trance. *What the fuck?!*

She bucked her hips, trying to throw me off, and I pressed harder, pushing her small frame into the ground. I could hear the Hummer even clearer; it was almost on us now.

"Shhh, settle down! Be still!" She must have heard it too because she redoubled her efforts to get loose.

She freed her leg and brought her knee up, making sharp contact with my side. A shallow breath escaped with a grunt as I settled between her thighs. The heat of her body burned through my clothing, threatening to muddle my thoughts. I quickly tried to reassure her that I was there to help, but she wasn't buying it.

"If they see us, we're dead," I growled at her. Her eyes widened again, and she nodded. I could see the calculating thoughts running through her head. She was going to run as soon as I let her up— unless I could convince her that she was in danger. "They are NOT help, Max." She stilled at my use of her name, looking confused. "Your brother sent me." Now I had her attention. She scowled at me, the furrow in her brows making a crease between her beautiful eyes.

My eyes shifted to watch the black Hummer race past us, unaware we were here. A trail of dust followed in its wake. "Please don't scream," I pleaded with her as I removed my hand from her mouth and my weight from her small body. She scurried out from beneath me, panting, demanding my name and answers. I had never heard a woman curse like that before.

Anger flared at her stubbornness, and I felt my beast rising within me. Knowing my eyes would be sparking with red, I dropped my gaze. Putting my hands out in hopes she'd shut the hell up, I ground my teeth, trying to keep control. The heat within me tried to reach out to her. Sucking in a few deep breaths, I felt more in control and looked up, hoping my gaze was normal. She didn't scream when our eyes made contact, so I stood, slowly.

I tried to explain quickly and reached my hand out to help her up. She stared at my hand for a few heartbeats before accepting. I jerked her up too fast, not considering her tiny frame, and she fell against my chest. Her palms pushed lightly against my pecs as she caught herself and leaned her head back to look at my face. Jesus, she was so petite. The opposite of Jax's large frame. Heat prickled along my palms where I steadied her upper arms. After a moment, I stepped back and looked down; her hazel eyes were wide and untrusting.

"Do you know where we can go to talk? I've got a lot to explain, and you're going to want to pay attention. We don't have much time. I'm not sure what they're going to do to your brother... if they've found him. And they're looking for you too. I'd rather not go back to your place. They may be on their way there now."

She cleared her throat, rubbing her hands up and down her arms. Stepping backward to put more space between us, she looked me up and down.

"Umm, you need clothes... and shoes. You can't be seen looking like that. No offense, but you look like a deranged mental patient that just escaped... uh, are you a mental patient?"

I scowled. "I'm not a mental patient." *Fuck, maybe I was. What the hell did I know? I've been stuck in a cage for... I didn't even know how long. God, years...decades maybe?* She was right about the clothes. "But I agree. Where can we get clothes?"

"I'm sure you could find something of Jax's that would fit. We could try there." She paused. "I don't suppose you parked a car near here?"

"Yeah, my car is right around the corner. I left it next to my personal helicopter. We should probably take that. It'll be faster." I frowned, not knowing where the snarky comment came from.

"Wow. You're an ass." She frowned, dropping her hands loosely to her sides. "His place is about nine miles from here." She pointed a thumb over her shoulder. "If I can't get my car, it looks like we're walking."

"I'm not up for a leisurely stroll. We need to make time. We don't have a lot of it."

"I can keep a brisk pace. Think you can keep up?" She cleared her throat. "I'd like to add before you answer that you're not wearing shoes either," her eyes rolled, mocking me. "I can't wait to hear why the hell you don't have shoes."

Good Lord. She was just as snarky as her brother. "I can keep up, just get us there. And stay off the main roads. Like I said, they're looking for you." Without another word, she took off.

I still couldn't believe I was breathing fresh air. It energized me and scared me shitless at the same time. I couldn't even remember the last time I'd seen the sky. It almost seemed like a dream. Maybe it was. The creature running next to me was nothing short of amazing. And people like me, we didn't get amazing.

Hell, I didn't even know if I could be considered a person anymore. The things done to me... they'd decimated the man I once was, turned me into an animal... or worse, a monster.

It was almost unbelievable that I'd made it out. Guilt threatened to tear apart my insides because Jax wasn't with me. The man I'd been able to call a friend. The only friend I'd ever really had. I didn't want to think they'd recaptured him, but the fact was, if he'd escaped, he'd be here. It was clear family meant everything to him, and that's why I was here. I'd made a promise, one that I fully intended to keep.

She was jogging steadily, and I was keeping up without any trouble. Not a total surprise. My energy seemed to have renewed since we'd met. Probably just my adrenaline. There was a part of me that thought I'd never find her, that I'd fail. After getting the kids to the cabin and finding the doctor's residence, it had to have been over twenty-four hours since our escape. I hadn't slept or eaten and was pushing myself on willpower alone. Until I saw her.

The moment I'd tackled her off the road and our bodies tumbled together through the woods; a new energy filled me. I really hadn't anticipated her resistance, but that had been ridiculous. Why wouldn't she retaliate as a stranger attacked her in the woods? I cringed at the thought. Then remembered how I'd seen a flash of red in her eyes as she defended herself. But it had been so quick, I'd probably imagined it. I'd been sleep deprived and starved before— one of the many trials I'd endured. They'd push you to the breaking point. So, it wasn't exactly the first-time reality warped itself for me.

I couldn't help glancing at her as we raced between the trees. I'd never seen anyone so beautiful. *What the fuck was wrong with me?* I needed to stay focused, and we needed to get Jax. But the wind rushing past my ears and the drumming of my heart almost lulled me into a state of calm. The fresh air was amazing. It felt freeing. Free. I was free. I smiled and enjoyed the moment. My mind wandered, unable to stay in the present, while memories of the last few days drifted through my thoughts as we ran silently through the woods.

She startled a little as I moved up next to her.

"Can we get there today?" I asked sarcastically, without looking at her. Jax had mentioned that she was a little competitive, and I hoped she'd take the bait. I needed to get him out; it was eating me from the inside that I was here, and he wasn't. She glanced in my direction with narrowed eyes, then sped up. We ran the rest of the way through the woods and on a couple of dirt roads. It was a quiet morning, and I felt confident we'd hear any approaching car. My muscles felt strong, even with all the running and crawling. I wasn't sure what was happening to my body, but my leg was healed by the time I'd reached the cabin with the kids. I wasn't even winded at this fast pace, and my feet were having no trouble pounding over the terrain. Amazing. I looked over at Max and she glanced back. I shot her a quick smile and put on a burst of speed. She countered my acceleration with some of her own. And I did again. We played our little racing game until we hit a main road and slowed down. An odd feeling stretched in my chest. *Was I happy?* The thought was so strange, I almost stumbled as I came to a stop.

"We've gotta cross. Then we head over that small hill. His house is on the other side." She pointed out the direction as she bent at the waist, resting her hands on her upper thighs, catching her breath.

"OK, be careful. If you hear any vehicles, don't let them see you." She nodded, and we listened for a moment before crossing and making the last steps to Jax's house.

Chapter 15

Maxine

I didn't know what was happening to my body, but I felt strong and wasn't winded at all. As disturbing as that was, what bothered me even more was how well my running partner kept pace with me. *Who the hell was this guy?* We pounded over the various terrain and I tried to stay alert, but my thoughts kept drifting to the last few days. Internally I shook my head. I needed to focus. There was some seriously fucked up shit going on.

I felt eyes on me, bringing me back from my thoughts. Chancing a glance back at the stranger, I hoped he hadn't noticed my preoccupation. I needed to get a grip! I wanted to kick myself for checking out of my head for a second. That was dangerous, and I was an idiot. He shot me a quick smile, flashing the sexiest dimples that almost had me stumbling, and put on another burst of speed. I blinked rapidly, trying to shake off that smile and countered his acceleration with more speed of my own, catching up in seconds. Then he did it again. The competition helped me keep my attention focused, almost as if he'd done it on purpose.

For a short time, I felt light and carefree, my worries drifting away. I felt like I was running with a friend, not a complete stranger. That thought had me scowling. I didn't know this man. But I supposed he could have killed me back when he first tackled me in the woods if he'd wanted to. His muscular body and big hands looked like he'd have no trouble with snapping my neck. I peeked sideways. His arms pumped with power and his large biceps strained against his scrub top as we sped through the forest. We played our little racing game until we hit a main road and slowed, halting at the edge of the wood. "We've gotta cross," I said, hands on my thighs as I panted a little. "Then we head over that small hill, his house is on the other side." I pointed at a small grassy hill, surrounded by more woods across the road.

We stood in the wooded area behind Jax's house for a few minutes. Just watching, listening. I was having trouble standing still. My anxiety was ramping up… I was hiding in the bushes with a total stranger. I had no weapons and kept twitching at every little noise, waiting for him to start hacking my body into little pieces to leave out here. I glanced around and slowly sidestepped a few feet, squatting near the base of a large tree.

Attempting to look like I was just resting, I leaned against the tree. Trying to keep an eye on the house in front of us and one on the stranger, I feigned nonchalance —at least I hoped I did— because I wanted the sharp looking stick just a few inches from my feet, in case I had to stab this guy in the eye.

After about fifteen minutes of nothing, Garron gave a short whistle, startling me. Jerking my head toward him, I gripped the stick at my feet. I met his eyes and noticed a small tilt to his lips as he nodded toward the house.

"I think it's clear."

We trekked across the lawn in swift strides, leaping up the steps of his porch; I grabbed the doorknob and Garron grabbed my arm. Looking from his hand on my arm to his face in warning, I gripped the stick, preparing to strike. He just shook his head at me, lowering his eyebrows in a stern expression. I released the knob and took one step back as he moved forward, pushing me aside, leaving me without any option but to get out of his way.

"I'll go first."

"This is MY brother's house, you ass." I snapped back.

"It may not be safe," he held up his index finger in front of his mouth. "Something is off here."

My breath caught as memories of the last time I was here popped into my head. The fox. But Garron had already opened the door and stepped over the threshold before I had a chance to warn him of the dead animal. I moved quickly up behind him so that I could explain. But instead, I just stood there, speechless.

There was no dead fox. Cabinets and drawers were open, the contents smashed and scattered on the floor. Chairs were overturned, as was the couch. The house had been trashed. I continued to creep deeper into the house, stunned, not paying attention to my partner searching every room in a very military-type pattern.

"Who... who did this?" I whispered. "Why?" I spun around, pointing a finger at Garron. "What the hell is going on?" He walked toward me slowly.

"I'm truly sorry you've been pulled into this. We have a lot to talk about." He continued toward me, and I stiffened, gripping the stick I still held. Brushing past me toward the kitchen, he grabbed one of the few glasses not smashed, poured himself some water from the sink, and gulped it down. He rinsed and refilled the glass, handing it to me. I hadn't thought about my thirst until now and accepted the glass, nodding gratefully. Taking a few greedy gulps, I looked at Garron over the rim.

He was watching me as I swallowed, his eyes following the movement of my throat. Lowering the glass and clearing my throat, his eyes shot back to mine. His jaw flexed as he rubbed the back of his neck and lowered his eyes with a scowl lining his face. My body warmed, and my cheeks flushed in response to his gaze. I cleared my throat again and set down the glass.

"Um," I started, but paused, swallowing a lump as dread tickled the back of my mind. I had a feeling that whatever he was going to tell me was going to be horrible. *Just be blunt, Max. You don't know him from Adam, and you need answers.* "Where's Jax? What the hell is going on? Just tell me."

"So, this is going to seem a little overwhelming and crazy. Maybe I am crazy. I don't know where to start." He sighed and turned, heading toward the living room.

I noticed a slight wobble in his step as I followed him to the living room. Arms crossed over my chest, impatiently waiting, he up righted the couch, which seemed to take very little effort.

"This may take a few minutes, maybe you should have a seat." He sat down and gestured to the spot next to him. I rubbed my hands over my face, and smoothed my fingers across my eyebrows, pressing them into my temples. My head was starting to ache. I put space between us as I sat down and ran my now sweaty palms over my thighs.

"Jax is alive. That's the good news. I guess, just... start at the beginning." I shrugged my shoulders, turning toward him. He looked a little pale and a sheen of sweat broke out on his forehead. I tilted my head a bit. The last time I'd seen someone look like that was at one of Sierra's workout classes. Then about two minutes later, they passed out. Uh oh. His jaw clenched, the muscle ticking beneath his stubble.

Before I had a chance to say anything, he took a breath and launched into an unbelievable story. No, story was the wrong word. Nightmare was more appropriate. He stood about halfway through and began pacing, seemingly unable to contain his nervous energy. I knew he was holding back some of the horror as he told his story. The pacing stopped as he braced a hand against the wall, bowing his head and breathing deeply. I remained silent. I mean, really, what could I say?

After a moment, he continued. I listened as he told of the beatings, brainwashing, unusual physical training and unknown medicines forced upon him. How they would break him down and try to rebuild him as if he were some machine. But not just his mind, his body as well. He'd also been pushed to work, clearing out more tunnels beneath the facility. Much, but not all the work was done by hand, as the mountains were too unstable for large equipment to be burrowing through and beneath them. By the sound of things, there could be tunnels under the entire town.

They'd kept close watch over him during the endless training sessions as they seemingly prepared him to head into battle. And to my shock, there were others, my brother being one of them. Then, just as he'd get familiar with a sparring partner or worker in the tunnels, they'd disappear. Never to be seen again.

"How... I don't understand how all this could be happening. Right here, beneath Second Wind and the medical facility! It's crazy!" I bit my lip, not wanting to offend him. My brain was spinning. "I knew Nico was a psycho, but Elias? We've known him and Jonas since we were kids. Since my mother worked with their dad." I sucked in a breath. "Oh my God... do you think...

was my mom part of this?!" I stood. My knees wobbled, and I sat back down almost immediately. "No, she would've never agreed..." My thoughts took a dark turn, and I had an idea of why she was no longer with us. I felt a hot tear run down my cheek. I swiped at the tear as more followed. Garron crouched down in front of me. Heat radiated from his bulking form, and it felt as though I was facing the sun on a summer day.

"I'm sorry, Max. I had no idea. Being able to talk about all of this out loud has helped put some pieces together, but there are so many still missing. I'm sorry. I'm not good at talking." He put his hand over mine and reached up with the other. His touch was gentle as his thumb stroked away some tears, a strange look of anguish pulling his eyebrows together.

"God, Garron, what you have been through... it's... horrible. I don't even know what to say. I'm so sorry." There is just no way someone could have made up such an elaborate story. This man, and so many others, my brother included, had been subjected to unspeakable horrors. My heart broke for him and all the others.

His big green eyes met mine. They were so beautiful and filled with so much sympathy. His huge hand cupped my face gently, a slight tremor vibrating through his fingers. An unusual heat crackled along our connecting skin, and I was lost in his gaze for a moment. The feel of his hand on mine. His smell was so comforting, like warm spices and musk. The inexplicable heat from our touch spread warmth through my body and I leaned forward slowly, breathing him in deeper. Having an urge to touch him in a completely different way than the friendly gesture he'd offered.

I started to feel a little lightheaded and disconnected from my body. His eyes dropped to my lips, and I nibbled on them, sucking in the bottom one and slowly releasing it from between my teeth. His jaw flexed and his nostrils flared in response. Green eyes shot back to mine, and he stilled. He took a deep pull of air through his nose and shot to his feet. But not before I notice a spark of red flash through his irises.

Chapter 16

Jaxon

Floating in and out of consciousness, I vaguely recognized some of my surroundings. I was being dragged by my arms by who I assumed were two guards. My head lolled backward as I bumped along roughly. My whole body ached, and my heels felt as though they were on fire as they scuffed across the ground. I didn't have enough energy to lift my head as the blackness faded in and out.

"Take him to the lower level. Throw him down there with the others. The doctor down there will direct you where to go," Eddie barked.

"The lower level?" One guard stammered.

"Yes, you fuck wit. Take him down, now. I'll be back to deal with this shit later."

I heard feet stomping away. The swish and ding of the elevator doors opening and closing was familiar, but I still didn't have the energy to open my eyes. One guard adjusted his grip on my arm.

"You ever been down there?" He asked.

"No man," the other replied quietly, "but I've heard some fucked-up shit, though. Like the crazy doctor working down here has been there for like, over twenty years, and he never leaves. Probably just stories. The guards that work in that section are on strict confidentiality clauses. I heard that Mr. Gregori would make them disappear if he found out any info had been leaked. And not in a 'you're fired' kinda way, if you know what I mean."

"Jesus, you serious? Don't tell me that shit! I got kids, man."

Their conversation halted as the doors slid open and they continued dragging me on to my new destination. The temperature was cooler down here, and the air held a musty stench that mingled with some kind of antiseptic smell. I cracked my lids open with effort. The hallways were a little smaller, darker, and a lot less shiny than the upstairs lab. It automatically gave an air of an undesirable location. My shoulders ached as they continued my descent down the hall. My eyes closed, and I wondered where they had taken Paige and if she was OK. Who was I kidding? Neither of us were OK. We were fucking screwed.

We came to a stop at the sound of short, quick steps heading our way.

"Ooh, I heard we had new ones coming. It's been a while since something fresh was brought down. Follow me." The voice sounded like an old man unable to retain the same pitch. His voice rose and fell with each word and gave me a slight feeling of seasickness. The two guards yanked on my arms and my shoulders protested as they pulled me back into motion. I fought to keep my eyes open, and retain what I was seeing, but I was still foggy and weak from the taser. My head lolled from side to side as I watched a few closed doors pass by. There was nothing of significance to remember. I must have blacked out again, because the next thing I was aware of was the grating noise of metal scraping against metal and being tossed roughly onto the floor. A cold cement floor. I groaned as I pulled my arms back to my sides, my hands and fingers numb from the restricted blood flow.

"Hold him still while I get my sample," the pitchy man said. The thought finally occurred to me, it must be the doctor, as a small prick registered in my arm. I tried to pull my arm away from the sensation, but I was just too weak. I had been feeling so much stronger before we tried to escape, I had no idea why the hell I felt so drained now. I hadn't even realized they were finished when the scraping metal noise rang out and the bars to my new prison were slammed closed. I tried to lift my head, but a wave of dizziness claimed me, and I blacked out once again.

I dreamed of Sierra. The two of us together. Doing mundane things like sitting on my porch, drinking coffee, cuddling on the couch, and watching a movie. The scenes kept changing. Days morphing with nights. Oceans and deserts. Nothing made sense, but they all had one common factor, Sierra. We were together and happy. We looked out over a mountainous landscape, and I turned to her, wanting to tell her all the things I'd never been able to. To tell her I loved her. I reached out and cupped her face, turning her head toward me. Bright red irises locked onto my gaze.

I bolted upright, gasping as I pressed a hand to the center of my chest. I glanced around. *Where in the fuck was I?* Gray brick wall surrounded me on three sides with metal bars making the fourth. *Right, we didn't make it.* I let out a long breath and pulled up my knees, resting my elbows on them and running my hands through my hair. *Fuck.* Standing up, I paced the ten-by-ten space. There was a military-type cot against one brick wall and a precisely placed hole in the floor the size of a five-gallon bucket, a couple of steps to the right. I could guess, that was where I was expected to relieve myself. The thought clearly registered with my bladder. Glancing into the hole, I was hoping it could be a way out. No such luck. The bottom of the hole was about two feet down and had what looked like a six-inch opening on two sides. Probably why it didn't smell too much like a sewer down here. It looked like it was purged with water regularly.

After relieving myself, I continued my pacing and tried to get an idea of my surroundings. The only thing I could see through the bars was more brick on the opposing wall. I pushed my face against the bars and grimaced at the sour, tangy scent of the metal. Nothing but an empty hallway in either direction. The overhead fluorescent lights gave everything a greenish hue. A bulb further down flickered. Well, this was definitely not an upgrade to my accommodations.

I sighed and walked back to the cot. Sitting with my elbows on my knees, I rested my head in my hands. My mind ran over the last few days, and I hoped Garron and the kids had made it out. I prayed he got word to my sister, and I fervently hoped she got the hell out of the city. I didn't know exactly how powerful the Gregoris were, but was well aware who was at the top of the food chain in this local area. If anything happened to her, I didn't know what I'd do. Apparently, a whole lot of fucking nothing since I was stuck rotting in this hole. I had to get out, but how?

I thought about Sierra and that horrible dream. God, I wished I'd told her how I felt. Eh, what good would that have done? I was still stuck here. But that dream... Jesus. That was some freaky shit. My stomach growled at that moment, and I started to get the shakes. I tried to remember the last time I'd eaten. God, I didn't even know what time or day it was.

Maybe an hour or so later, a pair of footsteps and squeaking noises sounded down the hall. I got up and gripped the bars with my shaking hands. Pressing my face to the bars once more, I still couldn't see anything, so I listened. Metal grated against itself and there were scuffing noises, as if something was being dragged across the floor. The squeaking stopped and started several times before I could see the doctor and the guard pushing a cart behind him.

"Ah, you're awake. Good. I'm very pleased with your blood samples." That pitchy voice said. "Forgive my manners. I suppose I should introduce myself. It's not often my subjects are brought to me with the cognitive ability to have conversation." His eyes narrowed at me for a moment, the two of us just staring at each other. His brows drew together as if confused. "Ah, yes. My name," he clasped his hands together. "You can call me Dr. Heller. What shall I call you?"

I simply continued to stare at the man in front of me incredulously. His worn, brown loafers brushed the bottom of his navy-blue khakis. The white lab coat hung past his hips and was buttoned all the way up to the furthest button, and just the hint of another white collar peaked out from underneath. He was tall and thin, almost frail, and I was guessing in his early seventies. The skin from his pale cheeks sagged, giving him small jowls. His round glasses sat on a thin, pointy nose, and there were dark circles around hollowed out eyes that watched me shrewdly. He cleared his throat while adjusting his glasses and smoothing down his combed over, silver hair.

"I asked you a question, young man, don't be rude." He said as if he was scolding a child. I scowled at his tone but decided to play along.

"Jaxon," I bit out through gritted teeth.

"Very well, Jaxon. A few hours ago, after I analyzed your blood samples, I found some very interesting things. First, you need to eat. Your body is still mutating. I'm pleased you are here. Your samples are some of the best yet. Not surpassing our missing favorite, of course, but the next best thing." He scowled. "He was very special, our first." He began to mutter to himself as his gaze stared out at something far away. I wasn't sure, but I thought he said something about the beginning. *The beginning of what?* "But you, you will do in his place. Your red blood cells are growing exponentially, but your body is not fighting, it's adapting. Very similar." The doctor muttered the last part to himself, rubbing his chin, then turned back to me. "And it appears you need more. Normally, this would cause low oxygen levels, kidney and or organ failure and a plethora of complex medical complications. Your body, however, is changing, and actually getting stronger. I will be back later; I need to check my other patients." With that, he gestured to the guard. A plate with a large slab of bloody meat was shoved through a perfect sized slot at the bottom of the metal bars on the floor. Two bottles of water followed.

"It's raw," I ground out while trying to absorb the new information. *What did he mean, was Garron the first?*

"Yes, you'll thank me later." The doctor said over his shoulder, as he and the guard continued down the hall, pushing the cart with the squeaking wheels.

I scowled at the food. Picking up the plate, I eyed the meat. I had no idea what type of animal this had been, but once I inhaled the scent, it didn't matter. My stomach growled and my mouth watered. My vision turned red and any reservations I had toward that raw meat disappeared. I gripped the cool, bloody meat with both hands. Biting through the bloody flesh, I tore off a chunk. I closed my eyes as the cool juices burst in my mouth as I chewed. I devoured the meal in record time, licking my fingers clean. My body immediately began to feel better, stronger, and energized. *What the fuck was wrong with me?* I sat down on the cot and started making a mental list of questions for the doctor. I had so many. Ugh. What I really needed was to figure out how to get out of here.

I began pacing in my cage, trying to work through my anxiety and anger. I halted my steps as noise from down the hall began to filter through my preoccupation. Now that I had some energy, my other senses seemed to be working better too. There were moans... at least two others were down here. I moved to the bars, pressing my face against the cold metal. I focused on my sense of smell, as I still couldn't see beyond the bars. Taking deep inhalations, I tried to figure out what each scent was. A cleaning antiseptic, undertones of mold, more raw meat, sweat, dried blood, some kind of animal, sickness... and something... floral? That smell I knew.

"Paige?" I whispered and waited silently, holding my breath for a response. A minute or two ticked by. "Paige? It's Jax," I said a little louder.

"Oh my God, Jax? Is that really you? I thought you were dead." She groaned.

"It's me! I'm not dead. Yet. Are you OK?"

"I don't know. I'm feeling a little better since I ate. But..." When she didn't continue, I started to worry.

"But what? Paige... what's wrong?"

"Jax, I... something is wrong. I– I don't feel right. I think I'm sick."

"Hang in there. We ARE going to get out of here. I'm so sorry my plan didn't work."

"Don't be sorry. I wasn't much help. You should've left me." She started to sob.

"Don't cry." *Goddammit, how the hell was I supposed to console her from here?* "We'll get out of here, Paige. I'll figure out something." I rubbed my hands down my face. *How the fuck were we getting out of here?! Think! Think!!* "I need a little time. I'll come up with something. Save your energy," I pleaded. Several minutes went by and I thought maybe she'd fallen asleep.

"Jax?" she asked quietly.

"Yeah, I'm here."

"I... I think I'm dying." She sucked in a sob. "I feel wrong. My... my skin is turning a gray color and I've got all these red lines showing up. My head is pounding, and I can't stop shaking. The meat helped some, but I'm still wrong." She let out another sob. "I don't want to die, Jax. I'm scared." I hated the way her voice trembled.

"We ARE getting out of here." I didn't know what to say to make her feel better. I didn't think it would matter either way. She was giving up. "Paige, you listen to me. We are in this together. Don't give up. Sierra will kick your ass for being a quitter." She let out a small laugh at that, and I let out a breath I didn't even know I was holding.

"Ok, I'll try." she said in a small voice.

"Hey Paige, I thought I heard other voices. Did you see anyone else when they brought you in?"

"Yes, there are... others. But Jax, some of them are..."

"Yes," a voice cut in, "there are more of us. And she's not sick, she's turning." The deep voice rumbled, and I froze.

It took me a moment to ask, "Who are you?"

The deep voice rumbled back, "Blaine." I gripped the bars.

"Blaine. I'm Jaxon. How — How long have you been down here? And what do you mean, 'turning'?"

"I don't know, forever? I've lost count of the years," he said despairingly. My small feeling of hope plummeted. "And she's turning. The gray skin and red veins. It'll only be a couple of days before it's complete. I've seen a few others like that. They aren't here anymore."

"Before what's complete? What's happening to me?" Paige screeched. I could hear the panic in her voice. "Oh God." She sobbed.

"Paige, we'll get help. I don't know how, but we'll figure something out." I tried to keep my voice strong, reassuring.

"She needs to stay fed. If she gets too hungry, the Red moves faster. For whatever reason, raw meat slows it down. I don't know how or why. It just does." I heard a scraping noise and pressed my face into the bars, still trying to see in vain. A huge, muscled arm slid a plate of meat across the floor. "Hey lady," Blaine called, "take mine. I'm not hungry anyway. It'll help." Paige hiccupped. And after a few seconds I saw the plate slide a little further down the hall. I could barely see her tiny fingers reach out and grab the piece of meat.

"Thank you," she replied through sniffles.

I had so many questions to ask Blaine. But I had to wait. Once Paige fell asleep, I'd try to talk to him again. I had a horrible feeling that all the answers I was going to get would only upset her more. Clearly, I couldn't console her from here. There was nothing I could do right now but wait; I hated being so helpless; it fed my anger. Taking a sip of the bottled water, I laid down on the cot and threw an arm over my eyes and tried to calm myself. I needed to figure out the routine down here... then I could search for weaknesses.

Chapter 17

Maxine

Garron was backing away from me. But I was still moving forward as I placed my hands on his chest. Tilting my head, I ran my nose along his jaw toward the spot right below his ear. Inhaling, the warmth spreading through my body turned into a fire. He smelled absolutely delicious.

I registered a low noise, almost purring that surrounded us. As if seeing from a distance, there was a small realization that the noise was coming from me. Garron jerked back, his body rigid. Grabbing my forearms, holding me at arm's length as he looked into my eyes once more. His eyes went wide, and a few emotions flashed across his face. Shock, anger, and something else... Before I even had time to think about it, a pang of hunger racked through me. It felt like a punch in the gut. I jerked my arms from him and wrapped them around my middle. I held in a breath for a heartbeat, then let it out slow and shaky.

Moaning from the pain, I leaned forward, curling in on myself and let my forehead rest on Garron's shoulder as he stepped forward.

"What's wrong? Talk to me!" His voice filled with alarm.

"I... don't know. I–I think I'm hungry." My stomach clenched at the thought. "Uhhhhghhh, I'm so hungry," I moaned, still bent forward, trying to apply pressure to my twisting stomach. I took another deep breath through my nose. That smell. My mouth watered and my teeth started throbbing. A cold sweat broke over me and a tremor raced through my body.

"Max?" His deep voice vibrated through me and a tingle raced up my spine, tightening the hair on my scalp. I leaned back, putting my hand out, trying to put distance between us. But my body had a different idea.

I had no control. My body took over as if it was being possessed. Fear spiked inside of me, and I struggled to gain control. But it happened so fast, my body moving on its own. I leapt on top of him, screaming in the back of my mind as my body moved like a spider monkey. He stood to his full height just as he started to lose balance and stumbled backward. Before we hit the wall behind him, I had already wrapped my legs around his waist and torn his scrub top. I clawed at the offensive cloth with my left hand, shredding it away from his neck, shoulders, and chest. My legs tightened and my right hand dug into the skin of his back for more leverage. He grunted from the squeeze.

"Max, stop. I don't want to hurt you." His large hands gripped my waist as he tried to dislodge me. I reared my head back and jerked my body forward. Slamming my teeth into the juncture between his neck and shoulder, I bit down. His roar ripped through the room, shaking the house as blood pooled in my mouth. I wrapped my lips tightly over his skin and swallowed. He spun, slamming my back into the wall, making me let go on a gasp. Taking advantage of my momentary release, he grabbed my ponytail, pulling backward harshly. I watched, as if from a distance, as his eyes roamed my face. I could feel the blood dripping from my chin as my tongue darted out to collect what was on my lips. His other hand came up, gripping my jaw as his thumb rubbed over the blood on my chin. A small twitch curled up the corner of his mouth, almost a smile. I met his eyes and watched as red began to fill his irises until there was no more green left.

What the actual fuck? My body tensed, as some part of me recognized it as a threat, but I wasn't scared. Keeping my eyes locked on his, they crackled like a smoldering fire as I lowered my chin. A deep growl rolled out from between his very sharp-looking teeth. *Were they like that before?* I hadn't noticed. But honestly, right now I didn't care. Something else was guiding me. Something primal.

"Don't fucking move, Maxine." His voice was dark and gravelly. I ignored his request, trying to yank my head free by jerking it to the side. His answering growl of disapproval only made my body heat more. I felt like I was burning up.

"I'm still hungry," Another knot twisting in my stomach, making me groan. We were both panting heavily as my eyes kept darting to the wound on his shoulder. I still couldn't move from the grip he had on my hair. The right side of his mouth curled up into a full grin, flashing a dimple and some more teeth. My heart skipped a beat and I swallowed hard. Blood red eyes tracked to my exposed throat.

"Me too," he breathed, leaning forward.

Pausing and squeezing his eyes shut, a pained expression drew his eyebrows down and inward. The next moment, I was tossed onto the couch, bouncing across the worn cushions. By the time I settled, blinking rapidly and gathering my wits, Garron was gone. The door we had entered an hour ago, now ajar. The house was silent, except for my rapid pants.

My body almost instantly cooled, and the hunger had hardly been sated. My stomach twisted with need, and I doubled over, wrapping my hands around my middle once more. What the hell had just happened? The fog in my mind lifted slowly, the wheels finally starting to turn. *Oh. My. God. I had bitten him. Drank him.* My stomach clenched with the thought, and I wasn't sure if it was from disgust or want. And then he just disappeared, faster than anything I'd ever seen before. How the hell did he move that fast? What was he? Shit, what was I for that matter? I was clearly not ok.

I gripped my head in my hands and leaned forward over my knees, taking deep breaths. A small tremor ran through me, slowly turning into an all-body quake. Raising my head, I glanced down at my hands and froze. The veins under my skin were pulsing red. As if a red lightning was flashing beneath my skin. *What was happening to me?* Panic had air sawing in and out of my lungs uncontrollably. Sweat beaded along my skin as I continued to shake. *Oh god. I was going to pass out. No. No. No.*

I rose on unsteady feet, staggering toward the door. The room filled with sparkles and started spinning. Dropping to my hands and knees, too afraid to remain standing, I crawled toward the open door. I needed to get to Jax's old car in the garage. Then I could get help. But who could help me? I couldn't go to the clinic. Not after what I'd just learned. The panic continued to rise as I pulled spastic shallow breaths and sweat now dripped from the tip of my nose, splatting off the linoleum. I had a vague thought that my racing heart would just explode or stutter to a stop and I'd die here. How strange that the last time I'd visited my brother's house, I'd felt similar. Another near death experience.

Black spots grew in my vision as I inched toward the door at a snail's pace. *Please, don't let me die here. I can't leave Jax stuck in that hell.* A small gust of fresh air from the doorway felt cool as it blew past my dampened skin. I had to get to Frank. He's the only one I could trust to help me. To help Jax.

Even with the bone deep worry for my brother, it was the image of green eyes and a set of dimples that flashed through my mind before everything went black.

Chapter 18

Garron

I raced through the woods, my mind swirling with so many mixed emotions. Emotions that were as unfamiliar to me as the outdoors. It was overwhelming. Hate and pain were the only things I'd felt for so long. I needed to get away from here, just keep going. Never look back. I was finally free from that hell. I'd done what I said I'd do. I'd informed the doctor's family and found Jax's sister. She now knew where he was and what was happening in the depths beneath the city. She wasn't my problem.

Move forward with the plan. Destroy that miserable hell and get as far as I could from this place. Getting everyone out on my own wasn't looking great, but at least I'd put an end to their plan. Whatever it was. I had imagined, once they'd figured out how to control us, we'd be sold. Evil across the world would pay top dollar for the skills they'd been forcing us to learn.

Slowing my steps, I crouched down behind some shrubs. I could smell the animal approaching and my mouth watered. Maxine's face flashed through my thoughts, and I swallowed hard. Hunger rode me before I had even laid my eyes on the blonde beauty. But her scent, coupled with the red flashing within her irises, had my control nearly shredded. I wanted to do more than taste her. I wanted to devour her, amongst other things. Something within her was calling to the monster beneath my skin. How? Why? My teeth throbbed and I could feel them lengthening, the monster rising. I could barely control it. And if I'd harmed my only friend's sister, I'd never forgive myself. I owed Jax my life, and that would be far from repayment. Shit. I couldn't run like a selfish coward. I had to go back. We had to do this together, or we'd both fail.

A twig snapped only a few yards from me, refocusing my attention. I had already made sure I was downwind and my steps silent as I closed in. The predator within me knew exactly what to do. I gritted my teeth as my limbs stretched and claws emerged from my fingertips. This was far from the first time my body distorted, allowing reign of the monster they created. But this situation was very different. We were free. And we were hungry.

The animal was just beyond the bush now, its head down as it munched on ferns protruding from the forest floor. I shifted, readying myself and its head shot up, ears twitching. It was trying to decide which way to run. The deer snorted and stomped at the ground. A wide grin pulled my lips over my sharp teeth as my jaw elongated. I sprung over the bush, swiping my clawed hand through the air. I just grazed its hind quarter as it spun to get away. Two more steps and I launched myself forward, grabbing the set of ivory and brown horns atop its head. My legs straddled the deer and squeezed as it tried to buck me off, a sharp keen coming from its throat. A howl ripped from me as I jerked the horns with force, snapping its neck and silencing the noise.

The deer hit the ground with a thud as I jumped off. Towering over the still animal, chest heaving, a brief flash of memory assaulted me. I'd done this before. Not with my bare hands, but with a rifle. It had been my fathers, and we had been hunting for food. Cold ground crunched beneath our feet as we crept through the woods. "Son," my father whispered, and I slowed my steps as I looked back at him. "Aim true, boy. This meat needs to feed the family through the next three weeks. You start the mines with me on Monday." I nodded, even though I didn't need the reminder. I'd moved back here to help my family and the failing mines we owned. His workers had been slowly disappearing and production was low. If things didn't change soon, my father would be forced to sell or just simply close. And he'd sunk every penny into that literal pit. The legacy our forefathers had brought to this country would be lost. And I had promised to help. My only two siblings were sisters, eleven and thirteen, and unable to work in the mines. I was the only male heir, from my father's first marriage. And he made it clear he was depending on me. The memory disappeared too quickly as I froze, slack jawed.

I have a family! Or at least, had? Where were they now? What was my last name? Dammit! Frustration burned through my veins and my stomach took that moment to growl. Without a second thought, I swiped my claws down the length of the deer and tore a section of the now bloodied and matted fur away from the sinew and muscle beneath. The metal tang of blood quickly dwarfed the unpleasant musty scent of the fur. Heat radiated from the body as I sunk my teeth into the tender meat, replenishing the much-needed proteins.

Several moments passed as I took my fill, devouring the entire hind quarter. Finally feeling sated, I stood over the animal, silently thanking it for the nourishment, before turning to head toward the cabin. I needed to make sure the three that made it out with me were ok and were planning to go back. Mason and Trent seemed like they were both on board, but the girl, I wasn't so sure. She had such a hard time during the escape. I had serious doubts she would have been with us when we emerged. The guys wouldn't let her give up though. They wore their feelings for her on their sleeves. I frowned. Why did that make me think of Max? Fuck.

She was in rough shape when I left. And it really didn't seem that she had a clue what was happening to her. I wonder if she knew what she needed. My hand absently rubbed over the now healed bite on my neck and my body warmed for an entirely different reason. I growled and a flock of small birds scattered between the leaves on the trees.

Spinning back around, I used my claws to tear the back strap of meat from the deer and started stomping back towards Jax' home. Back toward the blonde beauty that was stirring unusual things inside me. Things I was not interested in. My only goal was to get Jax and burn that place to ash. But I had to make sure she was ok. Didn't I? I was doing this for Jax. He'd be devastated if anything happened to her.

I approached the cabin with caution. Scenting the air, not noticing anything different from when I'd been here earlier. The door was still open. As I closed in, Maxine's unique fragrance drifted past me. She was still here.

I thought she would have left. Not one thought of why she would stay here came to mind as I bounded up the steps. It didn't make sense.

Oh fuck. Her body was lying on the floor, face down, as if she'd been crawling to the door. She must not have taken enough blood when she bit me. Her body had known what to do, but it just wasn't enough. I tossed the meat on the counter and rushed to her side.

"Maxine! Wake up!" I nudged her shoulder. Nothing. "Max!" I nudged her harder this time, rocking her body a bit with force. A small moan sounded, and I let out a breath. She was alive. Thank God. I rolled her over, but she still didn't open her eyes. What the fuck was I supposed to do? I looked around in a panic.

Deciding I should move her, I slid my hands, now back to normal, under her shoulders and knees. Her small frame was easy to lift, but still limp in my arms as I cradled her against me. Her head rolled to my chest. She looked almost angelic with her face lax, as if she were resting. Scowling, I noticed my body warmed to all the places we touched.

Spinning around, I kicked the door shut and carried her to the room with a bed. She muttered some incoherent nonsense as I gently laid her down. Her body shook with little tremors and goose bumps broke over her flesh as I pulled away. She must be cold. Shifting the blankets to get her under them, I didn't bother removing her shoes. She was lucky to have them. I glanced down at my hands, noticing they were covered in dried blood. I winced, hoping that it hadn't rubbed off on her and was thankful she hadn't opened her eyes. Knowing I must be covered, and would have most likely scared her.

Another moan left her, and she curled onto her side, clutching her stomach. Shit. She was still hungry. I quickly grabbed the meat from the counter, knowing this was what she needed.

"Max, you need to eat." I shoved the now cool meat to her mouth. Her eyes remained shut as her hands flew out, trying to push me and the meat away. Maybe I shouldn't have shoved it at her? But she needed to eat, and I was hoping the smell–– her eyes shot open, red sparking through them as she snatched the meat, greedily sinking her teeth into it. She moaned again, this one sounding very different. It sparked a heat that shot down my spine and my cock twitched, stirring beneath the thin clothing.

After a moment of pure shock at my body's reaction, I snapped my mouth shut and swallowed hard as I turned to leave. I hadn't had a reaction like that for as long as I could remember. At least not without the added drugs the facility forced on me. My teeth ground together as I clenched my fists. I needed to leave, now. That would be the right thing to do. She knew to stay hidden, and now that I'd given her meat, she'd know how to survive. She'd figure it out and be fine. I needed to get back to the others and figure out how we were going to get Jax and destroy that hell.

Chapter 19

Maxine

The creak of the floor had my eyes shooting open. My body's need had overruled anything else that was going on, virtually oblivious to my surroundings. The loss of control was fucking terrifying and very, very confusing. But the panic that bubbled up my chest at seeing Garron leaving trumped it all. He was leaving! Not again. I needed him to find Jax, and if he left, I wasn't sure I could do it on my own. It wouldn't stop me from trying though, even if the odds were not in my favor.

"Wait!" I croaked. He didn't even miss a step. I cleared my throat and tried again. "Garron, please! Wait!" He stopped this time but didn't turn around. There was a beat of silence, then he moved forward without a word. I scrambled out from under the covers, but my sneakers tangled in the sheets, and I fell forward, hitting the ground with a grunt. My shoulder took most of the impact and I was slightly thankful it wasn't my head. Rolling to my hands and knees, I lurched to my feet, all unsteady as I burst through the doorway.

Garron stood, hunched over at the kitchen sink, scrubbing his face, hands and arms. The material covering his back and shoulders strained as his huge muscles flexed beneath the fabric. I was silent as he continued the vigorous scrubbing, watching the water splash over the countertops and onto the floor. My legs shook with effort to remain standing. They felt so weak. As did the rest of my body. A strange heat pulsed through me and even though my body was hot, I still had a shiver. Shit, this felt like fever sweats. I did not have time for this. I did not have time for my body to shut down, not now. Jax needed me and I could barely hold myself up.

Black spots floated back through my vision and I felt as though I were standing on a rocking boat. Blinking rapidly, I focused back on Garron, trying to center my growing vertigo. His body stood straight as he shut off the running water and pushed wet hair back from his face. Reaching over the back of his head, he grabbed the mangled top and peeled it off. Using it to pat his face dry as he turned. My mouth immediately dried. His body was all corded muscle, flexing with his movement. His huge arms and pecs bunched as he continued to dry his face. And I couldn't help staring and tracing the lines of his defined abs down to the V that dipped below his pants. His body was perfection.

The makeshift towel dropped to the floor and my eyes locked on his, creating a moment of stillness. The room stopped spinning. It was just him. I swallowed hard as his brilliant green eyes stayed on mine. His face remained blank as a few rivulets of water dripped to his chin and the ends of his hair. I wished I knew what he was thinking. But I had no time to ponder as my body flushed with heat once more. His nostrils flared just as the pulse of heat sent an almost prickling sensation over my skin. My legs buckled, but before I could hit the floor, strong arms were cradling my body. A small gasp parted my lips. How did he move that fast? I didn't even see him twitch.

"You're still too weak. And you need to rest." He strode back toward the bedroom with me in his arms. The heat that pulsed through my body increased at all the places where we were in contact, and I wondered if he could feel it too.

"What the hell is happening?" My voice was shaky. "I'm scared. Am I dying?"

"You're not dying, but I'm not sure what's happening. Your body is reacting as though you've been given The Red."

He set me down on the bed and turned to leave. My body cooled almost instantly with the loss of his touch, and I shivered. The chill was so unexpected and violent that my teeth clattered together, causing him to turn back. The dizziness swam over me again and I screwed my eyes shut, praying

I wouldn't vomit. I heard a frustrated sigh as I clenched my teeth to keep them from making noise and to hold back the bile.

"Please don't leave." I whispered almost breathlessly. I couldn't explain it, but his closeness made me feel physically better. I just needed to collect myself. Maybe in a few minutes I'd be able to function. I just needed a few minutes. He cursed so quietly; I almost couldn't hear it. The next instant, the bed was dipping, and a warmth settled over the left side of my body. Neither of us uttered a word, and I curled toward the comfort of his heat as my body sank into oblivion.

My eyes blinked into the darkness as I awoke, feeling so comfortable. A sense of peace and warmth enveloped me as the rest of my senses returned slowly. Breathing in deeply through my nose, dark spices filtered in, sparking my stomach to grumble quietly. I blinked harder this time, debating dragging myself out of bed for some coffee.

I froze, eyes now wide. The comfort I'd initially felt was gone as my heart picked up its pace. I remained still, trying to take in the darkened surroundings. A dim light came from a doorway just past the bottom of the bed, but I couldn't see anything other than the top of the doorway and ceiling from my position. This was not my home. Attention jerked to a chest rising and falling under my head and palm. The steady thump of a heartbeat, not my own, in my left ear. Oh my God. I was curled on and around a very large, warm body in a darkened room that was not my own. And his arm was wrapped around my back and waist, a hand resting on my hip. The hand flexed. Panic ripped through me, and I shot up and out of the bed in a flash. Dashing through the dimly lit doorway and into the living room, I only had a moment to realize it was my brother's house before arms wrapped around me, tackling me to the floor.

The body that grabbed me twisted before impact, flipping me on top and taking the brunt of the fall. I let out a scream.

"You shouldn't have run." A deep voice rumbled with warning. The arms immediately loosened, and I rolled off, scrambling back to my feet and darting toward the door. My body jerked to a stop as I reached for the doorknob. Heat crackled through my veins and my sight sharpened in the darkness. As if pulled by an invisible thread, I turned slowly as breaths now heaved from my chest. The darkened silhouette of a man flickered with a rainbow of color, and I stumbled backward, my back hitting the door with a thud. What the fuck? Blinking as another bout of panic raced through me, my vision cleared of the color kaleidoscope, and I recognized Garron as he slowly stalked forward.

His eyes sparked with red bursts in the darkness as he slowly strode across the space, and my body heated again. But this pooling heat settled low in my belly. It curled lower and lower, until my core began to ache with need. I didn't move as he continued to eat up the space between us. I should run. I wanted to run, to escape out the door my back was already pressed against. But I couldn't move.

Both of his hands slammed against the door on either side of my head, causing me to flinch. Chin lowered as his eyes locked with mine, the low growl that rumbled up his throat made my knees tremble, and a wetness flooded my core.

"When you run, the monster wants to chase." Garron dipped his head and ran his nose along my collarbone and up to my ear on a deep inhale. This situation seemed like a replay, but in reverse. I had become the prey. Lips against my ear, he whispered, "We enjoy the chase. Almost as much as the capture."

Placing my palms against his chest, I meant to push him away. To shove hard enough where I could get the door open and escape to the garage. But as soon as my hands pressed against his bare chest, my skin lit with red, the veins crackling beneath. Heat pulsed through me on a wave, settling in my most sensitive areas. Oh god. How was this happening? What was happening?

Another growl curled from him as his lips skimmed my neck.

"Delicious." he murmured in my ear, causing a shiver as my head dropped back, a small thud against the door.

His sharp teeth scraped over my heated flesh and a small moan crested my lips. A need so fierce swept through me and my legs wobbled. Garron's hands were immediately under the curve of my ass, lifting me, my back still pressed against the door. Instinctually, my legs wrapped around his waist and my breath hitched as his hard length pressed against my core. The pressure nearly had me undone as another pulse ripped through me.

My eyes found a faint pink mark at the base of his neck. The spot I had bitten had already healed. Something inside of me bristled at the fading mark. And before I had time to think, my body jerked forward, teeth sinking into his flesh. A renewed burn flashed through me, and a sheen of sweat coated my skin as I swallowed.

The world spun as his blood and heat rippled through me. No, it wasn't the world; it was us. We spun in a large arc, moving back toward the living room and away from the door. I was still firmly wrapped around Garron as I released his neck and pulled back to look at him. His chest heaved, causing a tantalizing friction against my peaked breasts. My lids were heavy, a different need threatening to take over.

Red sparks filled his irises until there wasn't a spec of green left and his lips curled into a feral grin. Dual dimples showed through the dark stubble on his cheeks and my core clenched in response. In this moment, I didn't even care that I had no understanding of what was happening. The most basic of needs were driving me now. And whatever Garron saw on my face must have been the acceptance he was looking for.

The strap of my tank top was yanked out of the way before his teeth sank into the same spot I'd bitten him, but on my shoulder. The pain was sharp and fast; I let out a high-pitched squeak before a gasp burst from my blood-stained lips. Pain quickly receded as Garron began to take deep pulls at my shoulder. The heat I felt before was nothing compared to the burn encompassing my body now. A bead of sweat trickled down my spine and pulled him closer, almost on autopilot. My legs were still wrapped around his waist, and I tightened my thighs, bringing my heated core closer to him.

His hands wrapped around my hips in a rough grip, and he slid my body down until I felt him nudge against my sex. Tingles rushed over my skin and a low moan rumbled up from my chest. I almost came apart right there. His mouth released my shoulder, and he pulled back to look at me, his eyes still red and hooded. Panting, I blinked up at him. My brain was fried. No coherent thoughts were registering. But my body was responding with or without its navigator. A satisfied growl was my only warning before I was spun toward the couch.

I released his waist as he tossed me onto the dark green sofa. I bounced once and righted myself onto my knees, crawling back toward him on the opposite end. In the back of my mind, I knew this was crazy. I didn't even know his last name. But some primal part of me had taken over, and she didn't give a fuck. She wanted him and it looked like he felt the same, if the large erection straining against his scrubs, was any indication.

His animalistic gaze caused the beast inside of me to practically purr as I prowled closer. I grinned as I assessed the wound on his shoulder, letting my eyes travel over his amazing physique and the impressive length straining against his pants. He stood stock still. His bright red eyes locked on me as he waited, a knowing smile just bringing up the corners of his lips.

Reaching the edge of the couch, I climbed up onto the arm, still on my knees. My eyes followed the trail of blood from my bite down his large pecs and chiseled abs, down to where it almost reached his belly button. I looked back at his face, locking my eyes with his as I bent down and traced my tongue over the bright, red line. Part of me was screaming that this was beyond wrong, that this was disgusting, but whatever was inside of me was clearly running the show. Licking all the way back up to his shoulder, my face was almost next to his when his hands grabbed both sides of my head. He pushed me back just far enough for our eyes to clearly meet. His red gaze bounced back and forth between my eyes, his chest heaving with barely contained restraint. He was giving me a chance to stop.

My body refused to move as heat pulsed within me. For a moment, I thought I saw a flash of uncertainty in his eyes. Was he rejecting me? My body was vibrating with the need to touch him. For him to touch me. He waited three long heartbeats, and the anticipation of his next move tightened my chest. I took a breath to speak, but his lips crashed onto mine with a searing kiss. Every inch of me tingled with need as his tongue darted out, caressing my own. His hands traveled slowly down my body, brushing over the curves of my breasts and the small of my waist. Then, firmly grabbing the globes of my ass, he dragged me forward against his bare chest. We were flush against each other as his hands glided back up my body.

Grabbing the hem of my tank top, he pulled it over my head, dropping the cloth. Goosebumps broke over my flesh as he reached for my ponytail, setting the curly waves free.

Keeping his eyes on mine, he unzipped the front of my sports bra at an agonizingly slow pace. Once unlatched, he gently removed my bra from my shoulders as his hands trailed hot, tingling sensations down my arms. My nipples tightened as his fingertips caressed my breasts as light as butterfly kisses. Looking down at the perfect way his large hands cupped me, a heated sigh left my lips. Garron's gaze flashed back to mine and then to my lips.

"Tell me to stop and I will."

I stayed silent, warring with myself. I wanted this stranger and so did whatever had been awakened within me. My body pulsed with a need so raw I couldn't speak, so I just nodded. That small smile curved his lips again; it was my only warning before another searing kiss had me gripping his arms and pressing my body against his. Our tongues slid against each other, dancing for dominance. Rough hands gripped my hips and tugged my shorts and underwear to my knees. Not stopping the kiss, his hand slid between my thighs and covered my sex with a heated palm. Gently rubbing his palm back and forth, he traced a calloused finger lightly over the crack of my cheeks before dipping between my slick folds. A gasp turned to a moan as he tested my channel, sinking in one finger, then two, pumping in and out slowly. I gripped his arms harder as my legs began to shake. Scowling at him as he pulled away, I made a small noise of protest before he shoved me backward onto the couch. I bounced twice before his hands caught my feet, removing my socks and shorts.

I propped myself up on my elbow to watch his eyes roam over my body.

"So perfect," he whispered. I smiled in return.

"I'm enjoying this so far," I purred. "But if you make me wait much longer, I'm going to have to take care of this myself." I said, lifting an eyebrow while running a hand between my thighs. *Holy shit, where did that come from?* A low warning growl rumbled up his chest and he dropped his scrub bottoms, climbing over the edge of the couch.

His thick length bobbed; a corded vein visible as he climbed toward me. Then my view was obstructed as he leaned forward and ran his tongue through my wet slit. I gasped as my head rolled back. He made an approving noise.

"You taste amazing."

Licking and swirling his tongue through my folds, my hips rolled toward him rhythmically. He added two fingers, gliding them in and out to the beat of my hips. I could feel a low pressure gathering, as if it was pulling energies from every place inside of me. My entire body began to tingle as he combined swirling his tongue through my folds with each pump of his fingers. My breath came out in heavy pants and my fingers dug into the cushions. He trailed his tongue over me, swiping upward, and sucked onto my clit. I cried out as my body exploded; red sparks burst behind my eyes and my back arched off the couch.

Garron watched me as I came down from my high, panting. A satisfied smile curved his lips. The sexy dimple in his right cheek peeking out as he sat back on his heels, wiping my juices from his chin.

"Oh God. That was incredible," I breathed.

"I'm not done with you yet."

Chapter 20

Garron

I looked down at Max; a contented smile graced her face. Sweat glistened on her forehead and chest as I watched her breasts heave with each breath. My God, I had never known anything so perfect. The beast inside of me wanted to howl. I couldn't recall a moment of happiness in all my life that could compare to how I was feeling right now. I'd literally made her glow. Red sparkles still crackled under her skin, which should scare me, but somehow comforted me instead. I'd taken cues from each moan and thrust of her body. Our bodies were guiding us through the single most amazing experience of my life. Her pleasure was mine, and the satisfaction radiating between us now made me want to beat my chest and roar to the heavens.

My body was relaxed as I watched her slowly come back to me, but my mind decided to take that moment to flash back to the past—to the disjointed memories that didn't make any sense. Confusing flickers of memories stabbed at my skull, bits and pieces of caves, pain and death. As a teen, being drugged and dragged from my bunk. I'd been abducted. Then I was just stuck in a hell of torture and experiments, and I never thought I'd see the sun again.

A small humming noise brought my attention back to the beautiful creature in front of me. She was incredible. I wanted her. But my brain wasn't ready to let go of the past as it spun with tortured memories, dragging me from the blissful moment. I wasn't sure how long it had been since my last female encounter; the twisted doctor, Dr. Heller, had forced a few of us together for 'testing'. Usually within forty-eight hours of receiving some sort of injections, he'd bring a female to my cell. Sometimes they were so drugged they could barely speak. Others had practically torn my clothes off to have access to my body. I'd never wanted to hurt them. And when I refused to have sex with the unwilling females, I'd been beaten and starved for days, left to rot in the lower-level confinement. When I was too weak to be defiant, the guards would drag me back and the doctor would start anew.

It was obvious to me the females were undergoing their own versions of hell. My stomach rolled at the memory. We weren't allowed to speak. Shock collars prevented conversations. Who they were, where they came from or what was being done to them aside from our forced sexual contact was a mystery. The memory of them watching me, studying me while I was forced to fuck the females until completion had me closing my eyes on a shudder.

I hadn't realized I'd pulled back when soft, warm hands cradled my face. Opening my eyes, hazel green irises, full of concern, stared into mine.

"Are you OK?" Max asked. "You're shaking."

"I-I don't think I can... I'm... Jesus. I don't know what I am, besides just wrong. I could hurt you." I squeezed my eyes closed, pulling back. I shouldn't be here. I could barely keep my thoughts present. One wrong move, one distraction and the beast inside would shred her.

"It's OK. Garron, look at me... please," she begged. "If you were going to hurt me, I think it would've happened already. I don't know how to explain it, but I feel safe with you. And I feel your incredible sadness. So much, it's making my chest ache. I've felt my own pain like this; no one should have to feel this way."

Tears pooled in her eyes, but did not spill.

"I would like to take that away from you. To help you forget, even if it is just for a moment. This moment. If you'll let me." She tilted her head, waiting as I just stood watching her. I was unable to speak, a knot tight in my throat as my jaw clenched and unclenched. I tried to swallow past the lump.

A sad smile curved her beautiful mouth, "I'd like to try."

Compassion poured off her in waves. Taking my hand, she pulled me around the side of the couch and stood to meet me. With my hand in hers, she headed through to the bedroom. Barely pausing to turn on the light, my feet followed hers into the bathroom.

Sliding the glass door to the shower open, she turned on the water. Holding her hand under the spray, she adjusted the temperature. When she turned back around, she shook her blonde curls loose to tumble down her back. Smiling up at me, she stepped under the spray and raised her hand out in invitation.

I stood watching as the water sluiced over her curves. Her body glistened as the water caressed every inch. I felt a moment of jealousy toward the water as I watched her perfect pink nipples tighten. A surge of want raced through me, erasing all other thoughts, and I reached out and took her hand.

Water bounced off my flesh as I stepped in behind her and slid the door closed. I couldn't remember the last time I had had a hot shower. We were permitted showers and personal grooming once a week. The fifteen minutes were given to wash and shave, and used as a form of reward. If we'd behaved. If not, we simply got a hose. Forced to strip and stand against the wall as one of the guards blasted our skin raw. They hadn't even allowed a towel or time to get dressed. Forcing us to walk back to our cells naked, clutching our issued garments.

My eyes closed as the warmth seeped into my skin, helping to remove the cold thoughts that lingered. The warmth from the water was amazing. I had forgotten this. Even with how great it felt, I frowned. Something so simple had been kept from me.

I startled and froze as hands gilded over my shoulders and down my arms, her touch so gentle. She paused, waiting for me to open my eyes.

"May I wash you?" she asked quietly.

I looked down at her and nodded. I hadn't had a kind touch in so long. It almost felt wrong. Reaching for the body wash, Max poured some on a loofa and squished it until suds filled her hands.

Her hands moved slowly over my shoulders, massaging circles of suds that dripped down my back and chest. At first, I had a hard time relaxing, expecting pain, but each slow circle she drew on my skin had the tension washing away. The soap had a masculine smell, and I had to remind myself that it was Jax's house, not another male associated with the sexy woman in front of me.

Her hands trailed down my chest and stomach with the soap and a tingling began to grow, spreading through me. The twin weights between my legs grew heavy and my cock hardened. She knelt to wash down my thighs and calves, urging me to raise one foot, then the other as she cleaned my body. Dirt and filth circled the drain. I'd never had anyone take this kind of care with me; the feeling was almost too much, and I had to focus on keeping my breathing even. The gentle care was so alien, a spike of anger swelled. I needed her to be rough, to be punishing. The tenderness threatened to crack the hardened exterior I'd worked on to keep me alive. Working her way back up my legs, she reached around to massage my ass. A groan left my lips, the dark thoughts leaving once again as my cock bobbed at the sensation. Looking up through her lashes, a smirk graced her lips as she collected the twin weights in her hands, and gently massaged them with suds. A flash of red sparked in her gaze when her hands gripped my cock, stroking the sensitive skin with her slippery hands. The scent of her arousal was delicious. My head rolled back on my shoulders at the feel of her hands on me, lost to the sensations.

A small splat noise came from the loofa hitting the shower floor. The noise bringing my attention back, but I didn't focus on the sponge. Her small hands gripped my cock as she brought her lips to the tip, then slowly sucked it in. I muttered an incoherent curse as she moaned around the head of my cock. I braced my hand against the shower wall as my knees weakened at the sensation. *Holy fuck.* Her now red eyes met mine as she moaned again, sucking me a little deeper, sending sparks of pleasure up my spine. She took more of me, my soft head hitting the back of her throat, but I was too big for her to take it all. Her hand couldn't reach all the way around my girth, so she accommodated with a twisting motion as she pumped her fist in time with her mouth. Red sparks flashed behind my eyes as my breathing sped up and my balls tightened. Placing my hand on her head in warning, she answered with another moan. *Jesus Christ.*

"Stop. Max…" I breathed as I shoved her back, causing a popping sound as she dislodged.

"Garron, I want to. Please, let me finish."

"No."

I grabbed her wrists, roughly pulling her up to a standing position facing me. Releasing her hands, I wrapped one hand around her waist and threaded the other through her wet hair, gripping the back of her head. Pulling her flush against me, she let out a little gasp, right before I claimed her mouth. Our mouths moved against each other in a heated kiss. Her tongue swept over my lips, and I opened them, meeting hers in a fevered dance. Max pressed harder against me, and my hands traced down the curves of her body to cup her ass. Lifting her, she wrapped her arms around my neck and her legs around my waist. I grinned at the familiar position as I pressed her against the tiled wall. My cock nudged at her slick folds. She pulled her head back as much as the wall would allow and looked into my eyes.

"Yes, Garron, please." She said breathily, then began lowering herself onto me. I tried to remain still, to give her time to adjust as she moved up and down. She bit her lip, taking a little more of me inside of her each time. Despite her slick readiness, her channel was tight and hot. So hot. My eyes rolled back in my head as she finally sunk down on my length.

"Oh God, this feels so good," she muttered, with a small moan.

Pulling herself back up, I gripped her hips and started to thrust slowly, guiding her against my movements. Small cries of pleasure left her lips as we worked the slow rhythm together.

"Garron…" she panted between her labored breathing. I met her gaze as the red crackled through them like bolts of lightning.

"Whatever you need, take it." *I'm yours.* The thought echoed in my head. I leaned my forehead against hers, losing myself in our rhythm. Our grunts and moans of pleasure filled the small space. I pulled back to see her eyes trail to my shoulder. The wound there was already healing. She gripped my shoulders hard, pulling herself forward, and bit down. A pleasured growl left my lips and I thrust harder. The sensation of her on my cock while pulling from my shoulder almost had me lose my balance. Her moans drove the fire beneath my skin. My vision sparked with red.

I slid the door of the shower open and stepped out, not bothering shutting off the spray or grabbing a towel. I'm not sure how I made it to the bed, but we never broke contact. All I knew was her. And my carnal instincts were driving me to take this woman. I lifted her hips, withdrawing from her hot sheath. She made a small noise of protest as her lips parted from my flesh and I tossed her onto the bed. She bounced once and flipped her body forward, landing on her knees. Crawling toward me across the bed, she looked like a lioness stalking her prey. Her red eyes fixed on mine as she rose up to her knees once again. Licking the blood from her lips, she watched as I leaned down to claim her mouth. I could taste the coppery tang of my blood as I kissed her swollen lips.

Pulling back, I flashed a grin as I pushed her backward to lie down. Climbing over her body, I pushed up one of her knees and ran my tongue through those perfect folds. She tasted so good. Like something sweet and spicy at the same time. Her cries of pleasure increased at the friction of my tongue stroking over her clit. As I pulled back, she propped up onto her elbows, about to protest again when I grabbed her ankles. Dragging her toward the edge of the bed, I twisted her legs one over the other, flipping her onto her stomach. A small squeak sounded as I grabbed her hips, pulling her backward. Her feet hit the floor and I pushed her head toward the bed.

Before she could speak, I guided my cock to her entrance and sunk in.

"Oh God," she shouted. I released her head, moving my hands to grip her perfect ass. I squeezed and massaged her round cheeks, watching my glistening length slide in and out, reveling in the feel and the sight. Low moans left her lips with each thrust. Taking that as my cue, I began to piston into her, driving her cries of pleasure to screams of ecstasy. Her back arched as she tossed her head, damp tendrils of hair slapping her skin. Red hazed my vision once more, and my body took carnal control. I reached out, grabbing a handful of her hair. Pulling her toward me, I bent forward, wrapping my other hand under her body, grazing her bouncing breasts. Her back arched more as I continued my rhythm. I slid my nose along her shoulder toward her neck, inhaling her sweet scent. God, I wanted more. I wanted all of her. *Mine.*

Without thinking, I bit down, sinking my teeth into her soft flesh. The guttural noise that left her lips was the most erotic sound I'd ever heard. The sweet and spicy tang of her blood coated my mouth, and I swallowed. She tasted of sunshine and citrus. My body was on fire as I drove into her while pulling from her neck. My balls tightened and pressure filled my lower belly. She screamed my name as she spasmed around my cock. Her hot channel gripped me in pulsating waves. I let go of her neck, rearing back, and roared as I burst. Hot jets of my seed pumped out of me as I slowed my thrusts. Her head dropped forward onto the tangled sheets as I moved slowly in and out, my hot cum dripping down her thighs.

I reluctantly withdrew. She collapsed forward, a sigh leaving her lips. I stood there, looking at this amazing creature. I had never known a pleasure like this. A feeling of rightness spread through my body as I stared at Max. *Mine.*

And she was in danger. I couldn't let those men take her. I'd die before I let them treat her as they had me. No one would touch her. Dark rage swirled at the thought. She rolled over, pushing her tangled waves out of her face to look at me. Her once again hazel eyes traveled up my body, a blissful smile on her lips, until she reached my face. She propped herself on her elbows; her smile gone as her eyebrows pulled together.

"What's with the face?"

I tilted my head, not really understanding the question.

"Garron, what's wrong? Was—" She paused. "Was it OK?" She dropped her eyes.

Oh God, she thinks I didn't enjoy her? This amazing woman was perfect... and I had to get her out of here. I was so stupid to spend this time here, leaving us exposed. We were in danger. She was in danger. And this beautiful creature made me forget all of it.

My lack of response as I ran through my thoughts must have pissed her off. She abruptly sat up, pushing past me heading toward the bathroom. The door closed, and I heard the shower door slide shut, the water still running. I ran my hands through my still damp hair and sat on the edge of the bed. Looking around the room, it made me envious at the basic normality. A nightstand with a lamp in the corner next to this huge, soft bed. God, I'd never been on a bed this large or soft. I vowed to have one someday. The tall dresser against the wall had drawers pulled out, the contents thrown about the room. I stood, walking closer to find something to wear. Finding a pair of running pants with three white stripes down the sides and a plain white t-shirt that looked like they would fit, I pulled them on. The pants hung low on my hips and just reached my ankles, and the shirt was too tight across my chest and arms, but the material was soft and kind of stretchy; it would work. I found a pair of socks and wiggled my toes at the softness surrounding my feet. I had missed socks.

Something shiny caught my eye. The sunlight through the window reflected off a smooth surface peeking out from under the scattered clothing. Reaching down, I picked up the object, realizing it was a picture frame. Turning it over, I immediately identified it as a family photo. A very young Jaxon stood smiling a wide grin, right hand on his hip and one foot on a soccer ball. The man smiling behind him, an arm draped over his shoulder, could only be his father. The features were so close to what Jax looked like now; it was incredible. A young Max stood next to Jax with the same huge grin, her left hand on her hip and her foot on a soccer ball as well. I froze when my eyes reached the woman behind her. The smiling face looking back at me had a dark stillness flood my veins. I knew that face. How could I not have put the names together? Doctor Devins. The woman responsible for a large part of my 'treatments'. She was Jaxon and Maxine's mother.

Chapter 21

Maxine

I stood on shaky legs, my hands pressed against the tiled wall and my head bowed under the stream of steaming water. Tears leaked down my cheeks and blended with the spray. *What was I doing?* Confusion and shame for what I'd just done made my chest painfully tight. I had just met this man. How did I know he wasn't a lying psychopath? His story was so elaborate. No one could make that shit up, right? No. I had a feeling in my gut at the truth of his words. He had suffered a lifetime of horrors. But I still didn't know him. Even if every fiber within me called to him, pulled me to him. He. Was. A. Stranger.

The disturbed look on his face, one of torment, and anger was not what I expected to see after the most amazing and fucked-up sex I'd ever had. I thought of our last hour together and my body heated at thoughts of our erotic interlude. Oh my God. I had bitten him... and swallowed his blood. And he had done the same in return. What the hell was happening to me, to us? I froze at the next thought that popped into my head as his still hot seed dripped down the inside of my thighs. He finished... inside me.

I had zero romantic interest since Logan and I split. He had broken my heart, even though he hadn't believed I had one. Apparently, I had trouble getting close to people. Who would have thought? A girl that basically lost both parents and practically raised herself wouldn't have issues? I let out a long sigh as the water sluiced over my face. I'd thought we were close, but my ideas didn't seem to mesh with his. He'd left a little over a year ago, and I hadn't taken my birth control since. I mean, what was the point? My battery-operated boyfriend wouldn't get me pregnant, talk back or underperform. And it's not like my crazed brain would have thought to ask the escaped mental patient for a condom. *God.* I scrubbed my hands over my face.

"Get it together, Max." I whispered the command to myself as I took a deep breath.

OK, decide on a plan. Finish cleaning up, take Jax's old Honda Civic in the garage to town. God, I hoped that POS would start. Make a quick stop at the Rite Aid drug store for some Plan B emergency contraceptive and then go see Frank. He'd have some ideas on what to do next—I hoped. Whatever this was with Garron, it would have to wait, at least for now. I needed to focus and come up with a plan to get Jax out of there. Then what? Run? To where? I tried to slow my breathing, thoughts and the tremors in my hands that were heading toward a panic attack.

Finding my resolve to move, I finished with the shower and wrapped a towel around myself. Running one of Jax's combs through my locks, I looked in the mirror. My shoulder was almost completely healed, just a teeth-shaped, angry red mark adorned my skin. No open wound or even a scab. I ran a finger over the slightly raised skin—amazing. Turning around to get dressed, I glanced at the bare floor. Right, my clothes were in the living room. Rolling my eyes at myself, I opened the door and stepped into the bedroom. What a mess. I'd worry about that later. I continued my trek through the disaster and into the living room. Looking across the space, Garron was standing in front of the living room window, his face turned up and his eyes closed.

The sun streamed through the glass, highlighting some of the golden strands in his light brown hair. He turned toward the sound of my feet padding across the floor. As his gaze shifted to mine, still graced with the sun's rays, his leaf green eyes sparkled in the light. I stopped for a moment, because he was beautiful. His shoulder-length hair was pushed back behind his ears and his face free of dirt. I could clearly see the contours of his high cheekbones and square, masculine jaw. Full lips that turned up slightly in an almost smile were surrounded by dark stubble that had grazed my skin not long ago. A white t-shirt pulled taut over his chiseled muscles and the borrowed pants hung low on his hips. He was the sexiest man I'd ever laid eyes on, and my body flushed with heat. The feeling literally sizzling through my veins. *Fuck!*

I spun around, internally scolding myself and trying to swallow the excessive watering in my mouth. Praying I hadn't drooled, I resumed my search and located my clothing. Bending over to pick up my shorts, I heard a strangled choking sound behind me. Whipping around, my cheeks heated at the look of shock on Garron's face. I had forgotten I was just in a towel. *Really fucking lady-like, Max.* Cringing, I mentally slapped my forehead. Bending at the knee, this time, I grabbed the rest of my clothes and b-lined it for Jax's room. I dressed quickly and threw my towel back into the bathroom.

Meeting Garron in the kitchen, I grabbed a quick glass of water and filled him in on my immediate plans. Aside from the Plan B part, I was not up for having that conversation right now. Wanting to include Frank, he had protested, despite my assurances that Frank was trustworthy. But then relented when I suggested telling someone else about the Gregoris' facility. Frank had military experience and had weapons we may need. After having seen his arsenal in the basement, I had no doubt he was the man to ask. We needed help, and he knew it.

The small, detached garage was more like a shed—the rickety old boards having been hammered together in haste. You could actually see through spaces in the wood, as if it had been an unsupervised boy scout project. Jax always used to laugh and tell me he couldn't care less. As long as it stood stable and had a roof, it was good enough for him. I pulled open the two large entryway doors. The two doors provided plenty of space to fit a car through, and then some. I sent up a silent prayer after grabbing the keys that were hidden under the floor mat. Sliding the key in the ignition, I stepped on the clutch and gave it a twist. The engine sputtered to life.

"Hallelujah!" I whooped. I eased the car forward and out of the garage. Garron shut the garage doors and walked around the back of the car. I gave it a pat on the dash. "Good girl," I cooed as Garron slid into the passenger seat.

"Did you just talk to the car?" he asked, eyebrows lifted.

"Why yes, yes I did. She's always nicer when you tell her how good she is." I smiled.

"And you thought I was the mental patient," he shook his head.

We took the most inconspicuous route to town. I lost my train of thought as I glanced at Garron out of the corner of my eye. He had a look of wonder on his face, much like that of a child. His hand darted up and down like waves of the ocean as his muscled arm moved out the open window. I half expected him to start shouting "wwweeeeeee!" He was just adorable like this. Almost innocent. I had to remember how much he had missed, being locked away for so long. People doing God knows what to him. My focus returned to the road, my mind taking a dark turn as a protective instinct rose inside me. I was going to make them all pay. I didn't know how, but I'd think of something.

"What's wrong?" He interrupted my thoughts, pulling his arm back inside.

"Huh?"

"You look... angry?"

"Do I? Sorry, I'm a little stressed right now." I snapped back. "I feel like the entire world just flipped upside down. And I'm praying Frank can help us. Because if he can't, I may never see my brother again." He just nodded, gave no reply, and rested his hands on his thighs. I refocused on getting to Frank, and we rode in silence the rest of the way.

Reaching the sports store, I did a drive-by to make sure there were no unusual vehicles in the parking lot. All clear. As I went to pull into the parking lot Garron reached out, grabbing my hand on the wheel. Tingles erupted at his touch and I pulled my hand back.

"Don't park here, around back maybe?"

"Right. Good idea," I nodded. I parked my brother's beater next to some overgrown shrubs around the back of the store. The dumpster was the only thing back here and we'd have a straight shot to the back door. Most of us, aside from Frank, only use the side entrance—no one ever parked in the back.

Once inside, a small buzz alerted Frank someone had come in. The old man was much faster than one would expect, and silent too. He stood in the shadows of the storage room we had come in. Garron pivoted in front of me and his low growl barely registered in my ears. Had I not smelled Frank's woodsy scent, I probably wouldn't have known he was there. Garron must have noticed his presence before I did. But by the time we'd noticed we weren't alone, he was already behind us, hand on the butt of his pistol strapped to his hip. Being around him so much, I'd all but forgotten about the accessory he sported daily.

"You're not due in 'til this afternoon. Who's your friend?" he asked in a serious tone, eyes locked on Garron's face.

"Jesus, Frank. You almost gave me a heart attack. I need to talk to you. Got a minute?"

"Yup. Who's your friend? I'm not usually up for askin' twice." He bit out, eyes never leaving Garron.

"Uh, sorry. This is Garron. He's ah..." I was cut off as Garron relaxed his stance and moved forward.

"Hello, sir." Garron put his hand out. "I'm a friend of Jax."

Frank stared him in the eye for a moment that seemed to stretch on and on. It was so quiet, just the ticking of the clock as I waited for Frank's approval. Finally, he reached out and gave Garron's hand a shake. His shrewd eyes bounced to mine.

"I'm sorry to drop in, but I really need to talk to you. It's important. Jax is in trouble." I blurted.

"Mmmhmm. Well, you kids head into the break room and grab a coffee. I'll go tell Cory I need a minute." He headed down the hall toward the front of the store. I turned and practically ran into Garron. He was looking at the picture on the wall of Frank and my dad.

"Jax looks a lot like him," he said quietly. My lips drew into a tight line as I nodded.

"Come on," I replied, motioning him toward the break room. I passed by the coffee pot that looked like it was filled with tar and headed for my small personal locker. Grabbing an old t-shirt that read 'Camping: All fun and games until someone burns their wiener', I pulled it over my sports bra. I was feeling a little less naked now, standing in my place of work with a shirt on. Turning back toward Garron, a small laugh left his lips as he read my shirt. His smile and laugh stunned me. And those sexy twin dimples in his cheeks caused a quick flush of heat. I dropped my eyes.

"That's cute." A sweet amusement in his tone. *Yeah, cute. You keep smiling like that and I'm going to lock us in here together.*

"Thanks." Was my only reply as I tried to make myself busy by tidying the table. A set of footsteps headed back our way, halting my line of thinking. Frank rounded the corner.

"Alright, what d'ya wanna talk about?" Yup, that's Frank, no nonsense. I let out a breath.

"Ok, Jax is in trouble. Like BIG trouble." I held out my arms in a 'huge' gesture. "I don't even know where to start."

"Spit it out, Max. Time's tickin'."

"Well, Mr. Gregori is dead. I may have accidentally killed him. Jax is in some sort of prison lab thing under the school with all these other people. Garron and Jax tried to escape with others and Jax didn't make it. They're doing terrible things to people. The Gregoris' goons are looking for us and something is…" I looked at Garron and back at Frank, "wrong with me." My voice started pitching higher as I rushed through the words. Frank just stared, not saying a word. I began to fidget and chew on my bottom lip as I waited for a response.

I opened my mouth to say something, and Frank blurted out, "Stop." It was a demand. No room for discussion. And I slammed my trap shut. He looked from me to Garron and back again, clearly making decisions in his head.

"You two, come with me." He turned, heading toward the basement door. "Now!" He barked over his shoulder, and I jumped, moving into action with Garron on my heels.

We stomped down the old basement stairs and weaved through the stacks of boxes. The musty smell and dust tickling my nose as we reached Frank's thick, ominous door. He just stood in front of the door for a few heartbeats. Maybe making some sort of decision about helping me. Who knew, and I wasn't about to ask as he finally moved. Unlocking and opening the door, he stepped into the spotless room, and the overhead fluorescent lights turned on. We followed Frank silently past his arsenal. I didn't bother to turn around. Just imagined the shocked look Garron must have on his face. I couldn't blame him. This room was insane. I'd never seen so many weapons.

Frank's boots made heavy footfalls as he made his way past the arsenal.

"I promised your dad I'd watch out for you two." He said, turning to look at me. "Who knew you'd be such a pain in the ass." He huffed. "Your dad and I spent a lot of nights working on intel about the Gregoris. I think we have a few things that can help."

He reached out toward a large map of the local area that was tacked to the wall. I'd never really paid attention to it. Granted, I'd only been down here once before, and I had been a little too distracted to take notice. Looking at it now, I could see it was detailed with large property markers showing the local schools, parks, reservoirs, trails, and permitted hunting areas. Nothing out of the ordinary for a sports shop. Frank ran his hands over the map, as if smoothing the paper to the wall. His left hand stopped on the local reservoir and his right on the Second Wind Children's Home. Palms flat over each location, which happened to be exactly across from each other on either side of Big Bear Mountain, he pushed. Two hard presses in succession and the wall popped open. Not just a closet sized space, but the entire wall. My mouth hung open. *Who was this man?* Walking toward one end of the wall, he grabbed at the crevice of space he'd created. Sliding the wall horizontally in the opposite direction, almost like an oversized patio door, I stared inside. Photos of all the Gregoris and scattered post-its lined a wall to my left. A large table sat below the photos. I didn't even realize I had stepped forward—my feet were on autopilot. Piles of papers and notebooks were heaped on its surface. My fingers trailed over stacks of paper, and a faint growling noise registered in my ears. Spinning around to survey the area, I remembered the squirrel in the other room.

Turning back to the table a little too quickly, I knocked a stack of papers to the floor. The blank papers exposed a map that had been underneath. No, not a map, it was a schematic of Second Wind. Showing entrances, exits, rooms, multiple floors above and below ground, and my mother's handwriting was all over it. My stomach dropped and goosebumps broke over my skin. I swallowed around a lump in my throat as tears threatened to well up.

"What the hell is this, Frank?" I asked shakily.

Chapter 22

Garron

I wasn't sure who this 'Frank' was, but it was clear Max trusted him. And I got the feeling that trust didn't come easy for her. The man had a stockpile of firearms better than the training facility I had been forced to use. I'd attempted to use them to my advantage on multiple occasions, but it always resulted in tranquilizer darts and beatings. Finally, I'd just stopped. I'd given in and done as they asked. Knowing I'd never be free, I'd accepted my fate. Until Jax. I halted my line of thinking and refocused on the now, determined to help my only friend.

I could make sense of some maps Frank had. I recognized several of the tunnels indicated, but there were more not shown. This map must have been quite old.

"Where did you get this?" I asked. "It's old, and there are other areas not shown here." I pointed to a particular tunnel. Frank turned toward me, a shrewd look on his face.

"It has been a long time since we've been able to gather information. Most of this came from Maxine's mother, when she worked for the Gregoris. We were trying to collect enough information to stop them. She discovered some experiments, among other things, that she couldn't stop by herself." His eyes darted to Max and back to me. "So, we were working together to collect information and close it down. But she disappeared and Clint got arrested. So, things have been on hold for quite some time. I've added a few pieces here and there, but I ain't had any solid leads in a long time," he explained. "Until recent events, like the local animals acting funny and being infected with something. We've been getting reports about all sorts of wildlife... 'being not right'. They're larger and more violent. I've been tracking the reports that started about two and a half months ago. Not to mention the uptick in some sort of flu. People are dyin', goin' missing." Frank moved to the wall and pulled down another map from a spring-loaded roll near the ceiling. Max moved forward.

"You never mentioned any of this to me. What the hell, Frank? This is the whole county. What are all these red marks?" she asked.

I moved next to Max, examining the sporadic marks all around the county. They converged into multiple masses around one area.

"Remember that squirrel in the other room?" he asked. She nodded. "These are all similar sightings, all various animals. The masses are converging around this area." He pointed to a condensed area of red marks. "This is Big Bear Mountain. The Gregoris' property. Here is the original mine entrance," he pointed and dragged his hand across the mountain to the opposite side. "Here's Second Wind Childrens School, and right below is the facility. That spans below the mountain and under some of the town itself."

"Frank, what does this have to do with anything?" Max's voice was pitching higher as she slapped her hands against her thighs.

"The reports all talk of stronger, faster, more violent animals with red eyes or with a variety of body mutations." He paused for a moment, letting the information sink in. "Whatever is infecting these animals, I'm afraid the Gregoris already knew about it."

"Why? What makes you think that? And how the hell is that even connected?" Max's voice was bordering on a screech. She hadn't quite connected the dots, but I had.

"They've already started using it, have been using it." I frowned. Both sets of eyes turned toward me. Frank's knowing gaze stayed on my face as he inclined his head for me to continue. "The Red. I guess that's what it's called. Not like they shared any pertinent info. They've already started figuring out how to use it. And have been using variations of it for as long as I can remember. They've been working with the radiation located in the base of the mountain for more years than I've been there. But The Red must have been unearthed recently. They were so excited and the... treatments changed." I stated, quietly. Frank looked back and forth between Max and me.

"They give it to Jax?" he asked. I nodded. No use in keeping the information to myself. What good would it do to keep my mouth shut at this point? "Both of us. And a few others that I know of. We were all kept separated, so it's hard to tell how many of us there were." Max's eyes went wide and her face paled. A look of panic took over her features.

"Oh my God. What the hell is happening? How are we supposed to fight that? Jesus, they killed my mom over this shit!" She dropped her face into her hands, her shoulders trembling.

"Look here, Max. You pull it together right now. That panickin' ain't gonna fix nothin'." Frank barked, and her head shot up. She wiped a tear from her cheek as she answered quietly, "Yes, sir."

"Now, our priority is to get Jax the hell outta there. But we can't leave others behind. I never left no man behind, ain't gonna start now. Garron, I need ya to fill me in on the other tunnels. We need all the information we can get." I moved forward, and the intercom next to the wall buzzed, causing Max to jump. I hadn't even noticed it before now. A young man's voice came over the speaker.

"Frank, uh, Eddie's here to see you. Says you got something he's supposed to pick up." The speaker went quiet. Frank turned toward us.

"Eddie didn't order anything." Frank looked back and forth between Max and me, taking notice of my body tensing.

"Eddie?" I asked, "He's a security guard?" Max and Frank both nodded. A growl rumbled low in my throat and my vision hazed red. Max put her hands on my arms, forcing me to look at her.

"Hey," she whispered, "calm down." Her eyes shifted toward Frank, then back to me as she raised her brows, clearly pleading. She leaned toward my ear. "Your eyes flashed red."

Frank cleared his throat and pressed the intercom button. "Have him hang tight for a second, Cory. I'm just finishin' up and will be right there," he said. Turning back toward us, he ushered us out of the secret room and slid the wall closed. He looked back and forth quickly between Max and me.

"You have any trainin' with handguns?" I nodded. "Good. My gut is tellin' me something's up right now. I don't want either of ya seen." He handed me a Beretta 9mm after checking the clip to make sure it was full, and I tucked it in the waistband of my pants, re-tightening the tie. He handed another to Max after doing the same. She looked at the pistol in her hand.

"I'm not shooting anyone, Frank." Max rolled her eyes, but a tremble was in her hands as she held the weapon.

"You may not have a choice," he replied gravely. Then pinned me with a glare. "Head up the stairs behind me, and to my office at the back. There's another exit door there. Looks like solid wall space, but you'll see the knob on the wall. Meet me at my place later." He started moving toward the door to exit his 'equipment room' and stopped. "Zero-one-two-three-four-five," he looked back at me.

"Are you having a seizure? I know how to count, Frank." Max said, rubbing her hand in a pinching motion over her forehead.

"Such a smart ass." His lips flattened in a humorless smile. "It's the code to get in here if anything should happen to me." Her hand dropped limply to her side.

"Jesus, Frank. It's just Eddie. He's an asshole, but—" Frank held up a hand, stopping her.

"Max. You and an escapee show up for help with news about your brothers kidnappin'. Twenty minutes later one of Gregori's goons is here to pick up an order he didn't make." He paused, giving her a hard stare. "Ya putting the pieces together now?" Her face paled again, and she nodded. "You." He pointed at me. "Keep her safe and we'll figure out how to get Jax outta there." I didn't really know this man, but I liked him. He was a straight shooter and he clearly cared about Max and her brother.

"Yes, sir." I responded.

He eyed me for a moment, and I held his gaze. This seemed to clear up any doubt the man had about me as we all headed out the door, and he locked it behind us. We followed Frank up the stairs. Before opening the door, he turned back to us and whispered, "Give me sixty seconds, then quietly head toward my office. I'll buy you as much time as I can." Max didn't move, but I nodded. Frank opened the door and headed toward the front of the shop. He left the door open, and I kept my hand on Max's shoulder to keep her from moving too soon. Counting down the seconds, I gave Max a push and we crept silently down the hall.

We'd just made it to the threshold of Frank's office when I heard shouting. Max stiffened ahead of me, hearing it too. The voice I'd heard over the intercom was now ranting obscenities as something crashed to the floor, making a loud bang accompanied by the sound of glass shattering.

"What the fuck, asshole?! She's not here. Take yourself and your Paul Blart squad outta here!"

Max spun around to head toward the argument. I grabbed her shoulders, stopping her from moving. I pressed a finger to her lips and shook my head, then stabbed my finger back toward the office. She scowled at me, a muscle ticking in her jaw, and leaned to peer around my frame. I did not like the look on her face.

Another shout from the male. Then Frank yelled, "Cory, no!" More crashing noises of objects being broken and destroyed, then a few grunts of pain registered in my ears. I knew the exact moment they registered with Max, too. The starburst of red that flashed in her irises told me all I needed to know. I'd seen that same flash in some of the sparring partners I'd had. She was new to this, and I wasn't sure she could control herself. Second thought, I was positive, as she shoved me into the wall with more strength than I thought she could have and raced down the hallway. *Fuck.* I turned, and chased after her, too late, as she had a lead on me.

She reached the end of the hallway, skidding to a stop with me close on her heels. Eddie had a guy by the throat, holding him up off the floor by about a foot. Frank had pulled his pistol, had his barrel trained on Eddie, and was ordering him to release his captive. Five other men, two I recognized from the lab, were spread out around the exit, one of which was advancing on Frank. Eddie's head swiveled toward Max, not loosening his grip on the man thrashing for breath.

"Let him go," Max pleaded. "Eddie, let Cory go. Please."

Eddie dropped Cory, never taking his eyes off Max, and Cory scurried backward, gasping for air. Eddie turned his body toward her, an evil smirk on his face, and began stalking forward. I stepped in front of her. He slowed but kept moving forward as he smiled a toothless smile at me.

"Ah, I was wondering when I'd see you again. I had told them to dispose of you years ago. I knew you'd be trouble." He spat on the floor, wiping his mouth with the back of his hand.

"Huh. I've been the one locked up like an animal. And I still have better manners than you."

He smirked, stopping an arm's length away.

"Looks like they're running a special at the sports store today, two for one." He leaned to the side to look at Max behind me. "Hello, Sweets." His grin grew malevolent. I moved back into his line of sight, blocking Max.

"You will not touch her." I growled, as a fierce instinct to protect filled me.

"Where is my brother, you piece of shit?!" She screamed from behind me.

Cory had moved slowly toward the edge of the counter, without notice, as everyone's eyes seemed to track Maxine. She stepped up next to me, and I put my arm out, halting her without looking.

"Don't," I said in a low tone. She glared at me, and I glanced over in time to see red flashing in her irises again.

"Looks like she doesn't like being told what to do. Pity. Cause I'm gonna be bossin' her cute ass around for a bit. Time to go, Max. Elias is waiting." He held his hand out to her, and the other guards started to move forward.

"You keep your fucking hands to yourself, and step on out of my shop. Or I tell the Gregoris they'll have to find their supplies elsewhere. Approximately two counties over's the nearest suppliers. Might be a bit of an inconvenience." Frank stated low and flat, pistol still in his hand. Eddie clucked his tongue at Frank.

"Don't even begin to think you have leverage here, old man. Boys, Maxine comes with us—unharmed. The rest... collateral damage. Time to go." He swirled his finger in the air, making a circling motion. And all hell broke loose.

The group of guards that were fanned out around the perimeter of the shop moved like a single unit. All converging inward, guns out, behind Eddie. Cory popped up from behind the counter, shotgun in hand.

"You're not taking Max anywhere, you creepy fuck!" he shouted.

Two guards turned their guns on Cory, while the others continued to move in behind Eddie. Cory vaulted over the counter, landing in a crouch. Spinning, still in his crouch with one leg out, he knocked both guards down in a heap. Cory took advantage of a downed man by leaping on his chest and smashing the butt of the shotgun into his face. Blood splattered outward like a lawn sprinkler with the impact. Frank moved quicker than I ever thought an old man could. Grabbing the guard closest to Cory, he caught the pistol held in his hands and shoved the weapon skyward. The startled guard pulled the trigger and shots rang out, peppering the ceiling with holes. Frank used the leverage to slam his elbow into the side of the guard's head, knocking him off balance and dropping the gun. The pistol skidded across the floor and Frank and the guard dove toward the weapon, grappling for the prize.

Eddie didn't even spare a glance in their direction as he lunged forward, reaching for Max. My arm snaked out like a whip, knocking her backward and out of his way. My other fist connected with the side of Eddie's jaw, snapping his head to the side. He turned back toward me, wiping a small drop of blood off his lip with his thumb and examining it.

"I've been waiting for this," he growled back at me, grinning with menace.

Eddie made a lightning-fast spin, landing a kick to my gut. I flew backward as all the air left my lungs from the blow, landing on a rack of clothing.

"Garron!" Max shouted.

I tossed tangled clothing out of my way as I regained my breath and balance, climbing to my feet. One of the guards I recognized, I think his name was Jim, ran at me like a freight train. I quickly sidestepped, but his arm caught my waist, dragging me backward once again. We both clamored to our feet, trading blows to the face and ribs. I'd had enough. I quickly grabbed Jim, or whatever the fuck his name was, and twisted his arm behind his back. Spinning his body in front of me, I gripped the back of his head.

Wrapping my foot around his ankle, I simultaneously shoved his head and pulled back his foot, knocking him off balance and riding his body to the ground. Without losing a beat, I slammed his face into the ground. Then I did it again. I rammed his face against the floor until the asshole quit twitching, and a dark puddle of blood surrounded us.

I looked up to see Max backing away from Eddie, hands in front of her, palms out. She looked like a frightened animal being backed into a corner. My blood heated, the monster within me flaring with anger. A shot rang out and a grunt of pain registered, drawing my attention.

"Frank!" Cory yelled.

He was wrestling with one of the guards, clearly unable to assist as they rolled across the floor. Flailing elbows and fists could be seen in their tangled battle, and I could only hope he would be able to hold his own. I glanced back and saw the moment Max's fear changed to anger. Her body stiffened with the knowledge of Frank's injury.

"Frank?" she whispered.

Max straightened to her full height. Not that it was all that imposing, but the way she held herself in that moment spoke volumes. She sidestepped, looking around Eddie, trying to put eyes on Frank. A gasp left her lips as Frank's unmoving feet were visible beyond another rack of clothing. Cory raced across the space, sliding on his knees like he was headed for home plate.

"Frank! Hang on, Frank! Somebody! Help!" Cory screamed. "Frank's been shot! Help!"

Max lunged forward and Eddie countered, jumping in front of her.

Chapter 23

Maxine

Fucking Eddie. The creepy bastard had me backed into a corner, literally. The last thing I wanted was for him to put his hands on me; that thought had me literally shaking. I was freaking out and needed to get away. Every fiber in my body responded to him with revulsion. If I dodged toward the windows at the front of the shop, I might be able to make it out the door using the clothes racks as barriers. And if I could make it outside, maybe they'd follow me and the others could get out of here.

I reached behind my back with my right hand, gripping the butt of the pistol. My dad and Frank had had Jax and me doing small training drills, close quarters combat drills and obstacle courses with firearms included, from a young age. I'd always thought it was for fun, until now. Still, the thought of actually hurting someone made my stomach clench. I wouldn't kill anyone, but it would buy me some time if I shot one or two of those assholes flanking Eddie.

A shot rang out as I was about to spring forward, and the thump of a body hit the floor. I froze. Cory started yelling and my heart dropped in my stomach.

"Frank," left my lips on a whisper. I tried to lean around Eddie to see. My eyes landed on a pair of boots, Frank's boots. I could clearly see the detail in the worn soles as his toes pointed upward.

"No," I gasped. I darted left to get to Frank, and Eddie popped up in my way. "Get out of my way," I growled, as I jerked my hand forward, leveling the barrel of the gun in Eddie's face. He smiled, and quick as lightning sidestepped left, swatting my arm, knocking the gun to the floor. The sharp smack made my hand sting, and I pulled it against my chest. Frank's gasping breaths registered in my ears over the sound of my own heartbeat. "If anything happens to him, I will kill you." I growled, venom lining my voice as it dropped an octave.

"That old bastard had it coming. Boys! Kill that fucking lab rat, and remember, one hair harmed on my little Sweets' head, you'll join him." Eddie grinned.

Rage burned through my veins and my vision began to haze over in a darker shade of red than it already was. The Gregoris and their goons were literally destroying my family. Piece by piece, they were taking everything from me. Something inside of me snapped. Heat ripped through my veins and a darkness within me rose.

Time both slowed and sharpened at the same time. Out of the corner of my eyes, I could see the other two guards advancing. The one to the right of Eddie had angled his body slightly, as if he could coral me toward the center of the room. The one on the left kept taking glances behind me toward Garron. His barrel turned toward him and the guard to the right made the mistake of taking his eyes off of me to watch the movement. I sprang toward the guard on the right. My increased speed was astounding, but I didn't have time to think about it. Using his wide stance, I grabbed his gun with both hands and slammed it into his face as I stepped onto his outstretched thigh. My other foot jammed into the opposite side of his stomach as I used his body like a human ladder. Letting go of his hands, I grabbed both sides of his head as I swung my right leg around the back of his neck to sit on his shoulders. I twisted my hands as hard as I could, and a satisfying pop sounded as I rode his limp body to the ground. I stood and turned toward Frank and Cory at the same time as a fist shot out toward my face. Legs not moving, my back arched backward, I leaned my face toward my shoulder, just missing the blow. I grabbed the arm that was still outstretched over my head and twisted my body. Using all my weight, I tried to pull my assailant down toward the floor with me on top. Eddie was too strong. We both went down, but he managed to roll us, pinning me to the floor. I bucked against him, panicking, and let out a deep, frustrated and half terrified scream. The rage retreated as an ice-cold terror took over. Moving was damn near impossible with Eddie pinning me to the floor. A shriek ripped from my constricted lungs as I tried to thrash below him. My efforts were futile. Then a roar like nothing I had ever heard countered mine.

I twisted my head to see two guards had Garron cornered, their guns raised. But his eyes were not on the guards, they were on me, and they were red. And whoa, he looked pissed. His entire body shook, as the color of his skin faded to a shade of gray.

"Get your fucking hands off her!" he roared.

"You're not looking so good, little lab rat," Eddie taunted. "If he moves, shoot him." He ordered the guards.

Eddie then grabbed my face, squeezing my jaw painfully tight, eliciting a whimper. He held my arm down while his knee pressed into the other, literally pinning me to the ground. I tried to wiggle out of his iron grip but was distracted by the growl emanating from Garron. Eddie wrenched my head back toward Garron, still gripping my face. My eyes widened. Garron's body was growing larger and thicker, red veins now showing beneath his exposed skin. His hands twitched at his sides as they elongated and began forming claws. *What the fuck was I seeing?* I blinked my widened eyes, shock freezing my body. Eddie took advantage of my distraction and ran his tongue from my jaw, over my cheek and up the side of my face to my temple. I winced, squeezing my eyes shut as I whimpered and tried to pull away, disgusted.

"Mmmmm," Eddie purred.

Another roar ripped through the air and the POP, POP, POP of pistols being fired thundered in the small shop.

"No!" My eyes shot open, and I bucked my body with everything I had, knocking Eddie to the side. I scrambled backward, but not fast enough. Eddie grabbed my left leg, pulling me back toward him. I pulled back my right and kicked out, connecting with the left side of his jaw. His head jerked to the side, and he loosened his grip enough for me to break free. Stumbling to my feet, trying to gain balance, I scanned the floor, looking for Garron. Two guards had weapons aimed at something behind one of the clothes racks.

One guard was looking a little wobbly. Blinking for clarity, I realized he was swaying on his feet just slightly. Four large gashes raked across his upper body, starting from his left shoulder running diagonally across his chest to the opposite side of his ribs. The clothing was shredded, as were the Kevlar vest and skin peeking through. The gashes dripped blood steadily from the wounds.

The coppery smell stirred my hunger, and my stomach tightened briefly. But worry for Garron kept my head clear, as I heard unsteady breathing coming from behind the clothes. My chest squeezed as I ran toward him, sliding the last couple of feet on my knees. Tossing clothes out of my way, I found Garron lying half on, half off a pile of the downed sale items. His body and skin were already returning to their natural complexion.

"Garron?" I whispered, my heart stuttering. He rolled his head back toward me, eyes meeting mine.

"Max, get out of here," Garron groaned and then coughed up some blood. I grabbed one of the T-shirts and pressed it to the worst of the wounds leaking blood from his chest. The blood oozed between my fingers. *Oh God, there were too many holes.* Tears welled in my eyes.

"Don't move, we're going to get you help," I said firmly, trying to keep my panic from spilling out.

Pressing harder with both hands on bullet holes, I looked around frantically for help. Cory was holding Frank, half on his lap, while he bent forward, his ear to Frank's face. *Frank was coherent enough to talk, that had to be a good sign, right?* Chaos was still exploding around us. It was clear I was going to have to help myself. Garron coughed again, making a gurgling noise deep in his chest. *No. No. No! Please!*

Closing my eyes briefly, I took a deep breath through my nose and let it out slowly, trying to center myself. Panicking right now wouldn't help anyone. *Think Max! Think! OK, two guards behind me to my right, Eddie to my left.* I'd rather try the two guards than Eddie. If I was fast enough, this could work.

"Garron, please." My voice cracked. "Just... God, don't die! I'm gonna get you help," my voice shook. Garron nodded. His eyes met mine and slid to the side. My brows drew together, and I shook my head. He repeated the movement with his eyes. *Was he trying to tell me something?*

"Garron," I whispered as he squeezed his eyes shut and let out a string of wet coughs again. He rolled a bit to his side to spit blood as it leaked from his mouth, exposing a pistol on the ground beneath his shoulder. Tears welled – even dying, he was still trying to save me. I turned my head toward the guards.

"Please, call 911. He needs help," I begged. Not taking my pleading eyes off the guards, I moved my hand slowly, gripping the pistol. "Please!" I begged louder. The two guards looked at each other, then at Eddie. This was the opening I had hoped for. Whipping my body around as I spun on my knees, I aimed true.

Time slowed as I pulled the trigger. I shot Eddie in the thigh, right above his knee. He fell back howling, gripping his leg. I was up and moving at the two guards before they had time to react. Shooting both guards in the thighs as well, I kept moving. I grabbed the closest guard as he bent forward, using his own momentum to slam my knee into his forehead. His head rocked back on his neck, and he was down for the count. I lunged to the side, ramming my elbow into the side of the second guard's head. He pitched sideways and went down. I ran past them and dove over the counter, sliding across the smooth surface on my stomach. Landing completely ungracefully, I clattered to the ground behind the cash register. *Fuck, that was going to hurt in the morning.* I crawled on my hands and knees, as fast as I could to the phone against the back wall. Grabbing the cordless receiver, I dialed 911 and kept moving.

"Nine-one-one, what's your emergency?" came through in a woman's voice.

Not responding, I peeked around the side of the counter and searched for Cory and Frank. They hadn't moved and I could see Cory's bloody hand pressing onto Frank's side as he wheezed. I drew back behind the counter and whispered, "He's been shot. There are several men with guns and we're being attacked. Please send help!" I was shaking so hard I could barely hold on to the phone, my nerves finally catching up with me.

"What's your location?" the woman asked.

"One-five-seven-seven Old Hollow Road, please hurry, I think he's dying!" My eyes filled with tears as I started gasping for breath at the realization of what I'd just said. Dropping the phone, I crawled back around the counter and headed toward Frank.

"Hello again, Sweets," came from way too close. As I gasped, I turned my head just in time to see Eddie's fist before it slammed into my face and my world went black.

Chapter 24

Eddie

That bitch shot me in the leg! I'd make her pay for that little defiant streak of hers. It was finally my turn. I'd been waiting patiently long enough. She'd rebuffed all of my advances over the last few years. Always hiding behind that counter. And I'd been cock-blocked by that old bastard Frank more times than I could count. Guess I didn't have to worry about that anymore... Thought I'd finally had her last week. Shop was closed, no one was around or in the parking lot. I'd been waiting since dawn for her to show up. What a piss-off when that old fucker interrupted us. I've had dreams about her. My hands on her smooth skin, her whimpers caressing my ears. I longed to hear her voice, begging me for mercy. And I'd give her none. She deserved everything I was going to give her and more. I'd pictured her face every time I'd fucked some slut since I met her.

I let some of them live. Those few knew better than to call the authorities. I'd made it very clear what I was capable of as I delivered their battered bodies to their homes. The unlucky ones ended up as gifts to those abominations in the caves. I'd either gotten carried away with my fun, or couldn't quite make them agreeable enough not to talk. *No skin off my teeth,* I thought, shrugging to myself. Then a smile rose to my lips at the remembrance of their screams. A chill ran down my spine as my dick grew hard, and I let out a satisfied sigh.

Looking around the store, my men were in pretty rough shape. That lab rat piece of shit was peppered with bullet holes, laying in a puddle of his own blood. I walked over, stepping around all the clothing on the ground and kicked the leg of his unmoving body. *Huh, looks like we can kill them. Guess the doc was wrong.* I put two more bullets in his chest for good measure.

"Piece of shit." I growled as I kicked his leg again, then barked at the rest of my team left standing. "Get the others out of here, NOW! We don't want their bodies here when the paramedics or police arrive." The local police wouldn't dare go head-to-head with the Gregoris, but the bodies of our personal security team would be a slight challenge to keep under wraps. "Move it!" I demanded again. "If we get our guys out, they'll have no choice but to place blame on that lab rat. It'll be fucking perfect." I grinned to myself again. Damn, this day was looking up. Finally got my hands on Max, took out that pain-in-the-ass Frank, and that filthy lab rat too! To hell with 'two birds with one stone'. I got three! I felt the smile tug at the muscles in my face.

Moving back over to Max, I hefted her limp body over my shoulder. She smelled amazing, and I breathed deeper, running my hand over her plump ass and down her leg. A growl left my lips as I froze. There was an undercurrent smell... of lab rat. His scent was all over her. Rage lit my veins. *That fucker.* I'd kill him again if I could. I'd fix that smell and make her pay in the process. Hearing my growl, Cory's head swung around to me.

"Put her down!" he yelled from the ground where he was holding Frank. Lowering Frank's coughing, spitting body gently to the ground, he tried to stand as I strode toward him. Reaching him before he had a chance to fully stand, I slammed my boot into his face. His head rocked back on his neck, and he dropped in a heap next to Frank. Frank let out a gurgling cough and turned his head, spitting more blood.

"You'll never get away with this. Ya better hope this is my end, 'cause I'll make it my mission to see you dead," he said with as much venom as his old, battered body could muster. I laughed at the threat and stepped around Cory.

"See ya around, old man," I grinned over my shoulder as I headed out the door with my prize in tow.

I ordered my guys to head back to the labs. The doc could fix them up down there. Well, the ones that weren't dead anyway. They were just kibble now, to be thrown in the caves. It was only since our recent... enhancements, that we were let in on some of the laboratory knowledge. That crazy Frankenstein was going to be pissed that his little lab rat was dead. After all, he'd made me promise to bring him back. His favorite. I scowled. He'd been so proud of that one, even moved him upstairs to work on his procreation experiments. Sick fuck. *What made that piece of shit so special? Whatever, he's dead now.* My scowl turned to a smirk. *I'd been waiting to end him for years.*

I opened the back door of the suburban and gently laid Max across the seat. Reaching into the back, I grabbed a small black tool bag. Pulling out a couple of zip ties, I tightened them around her wrists and ankles. Next, I ripped off a piece of duct tape and slapped it over her pretty little mouth. No reason to listen to her bitching if she woke before I got her to our little love shack. She'd have plenty of time to make noise later. Closing up the back, I almost skipped around the back of the vehicle, but my fucking leg hurt. I pushed the pain aside as excitement filled me. This was better than Christmas morning.

Sliding into the driver's seat, I looked down at my wounded leg. The bleeding had stopped, and the hole was already closing up. I shook off the slight tremble in my hands from the blood loss, and put the Suburban into gear. I'd have to get a booster later. At the very least, some red meat. That freaking Dr. Frankenstein was truly onto something. I'd have to thank him.

A few minutes outside of town, I turned down a seasonal dirt road. The abandoned campground was just ahead. Technology was the downfall of this once beautiful place. No one traveled here, and that was not a complaint from me. Kids didn't want to camp and explore nature anymore. They wanted YouTube and Facebook. Leading their virtual lives, they would never truly experience living. The old forgotten campground was the perfect setting for my fun. Despite being on the top of a mountain, it wasn't the views that brought me here. Though they were spectacular, facing the western portion of the valley as they did. The sunsets were what photographers searched a lifetime for. It was the multiple log cabins scattered throughout the wooded area. No one to see or hear you for miles.

The suburban bounced down the uneven, overgrown trails. The springtime foliage was just thick enough to block out the sun's rays, keeping it damp and dimly lit. As many times as I'd brought my girls here, I'd never worried about upkeep. Just in case someone got nosey, it would still have that abandoned look on the surface. I'd picked a few of the best cabins and worked a little generator magic, stringing a lightbulb here and there; I didn't need much else. A little extra care went into preparing this cabin though; adding a queen-sized mattress, a small bistro table and two chairs. I also added a few pieces of flair, a little something shiny for my sweet. A wide grin spread across my face.

As I opened the door, my flashlight glinted off pulleys and swivels I'd installed on the wall and ceiling. The steel cable almost sparkled where it dangled from the center of the ceiling. Double checking the slack was enough to reach the mattress and the bistro set, I ran around the back of the cabin to start the generator. Pushing the primer button three times, I gave the pull cord a yank. She started like she was waiting just for us, no sputter at all. Jogging back to the vehicle, I saw Max was still out cold. Perfect. Pulling her body toward the door, I got her out far enough to heft her back over my shoulder. By the time we walked over the threshold, the single bulb over the bistro set gave off a low, golden glow that bathed the small space. Laying Max on the mattress, I grabbed her gift out of the small box next to the door. Brushing the hair away from her face, I ran my hand along her small, petite jaw and down her slender neck. Wrapping my hand around her neck, lifting her head slightly, I latched the thick, black leather collar I'd bought just for her. Finishing it off with a small, shiny silver padlock, I sat back a bit and admired how perfect my gift was. Reaching up, I grabbed the cable and attached the locking snap hook to the metal ring on her collar. Perfect. I was practically vibrating with the anticipation of her waking up. Would she scream? Would she cry? Ooh, I hoped she'd fight. My cock throbbed at the thought. Yes, I hoped she'd fight.

Chapter 25

Elias

I supposed it was a nice spring day. The sun was out, the plants and trees were in bloom, and even the birds were singing. Busily fluttering from tree to tree, building nests to soon welcome their offspring into the world. It was a weird cycle, this thing called life, I mused while watching a small robin. Born, live a little, reproduce, then die. I guessed it was all about what you did with the time you had. My eyes moved back to my father's casket being lowered into the ground. I wondered silently about all the things my father had done while alive. Things I was just beginning to learn about. I looked back up and around at the many faces that surrounded me. The number of people who had squeezed into this small cemetery was near staggering. People and tombstones were all I could see. My father had been a well-known power player for decades, and I guessed it had earned the respect of many acquaintances for them to attend such a ceremony. But I couldn't help but notice all the dry eyes. No one looked truly upset. I thought about that for a moment and if it should bother me. It didn't. I was sad, I supposed, even if only because he had been my and Jonas' father in the strictest sense of the word. Father was a term I used loosely. He'd never shown Jonas or me any fatherly affections. His support through the decades had been the tough love kind. Love—that was the wrong word. My mother had shown us love, but my father... my thoughts trailed off as people started moving around. Some came over to offer Jonas and me condolences, others simply left.

The governor of New York stomped his way through the crowd.

"Mr. Gregori, my most sincere condolences for your loss," he said firmly and continued without pause. "My apologies, as this is not the best time, but we have urgent matters to discuss. Some very time sensitive issues your father's death has left... hanging. I'll be meeting with you tomorrow, as I understand your obligations for today. I've had my staff schedule some time for us. I'll meet you at your office," he finally paused, seeing the irritation on my face, "...or anywhere you'd like." He finished while trying to flex an air of authority. He instantly rubbed me the wrong way. What a pompous piece of shit. Jonas stayed silent at my side, and I wondered if he was as irritated as me as the douche never even addressed him. Maybe I should teach him some manners?

"Governor, as you mentioned, this is not a good time. However, I'm aware you and my father had... certain arrangements. And I'd like to take this opportunity to make YOU aware, there have been some changes," I replied coldly, keeping my expression blank. I waited silently as the shades of his face grew increasingly red. Ah yes, there was the agitation I was hoping for. I held back a smirk. "I'd be happy to meet with you. Tomorrow, however, is not going to work for me." His face grew redder by the second.

"But Elias, you—" He halted, his words caught in his throat as I lowered my sunglasses and made eye contact. Narrowing my focus, I pushed my invisible bubble of influence around him.

"It's Mr. Gregori to you, Governor." I lowered my voice. "You know nothing of my business or obligations. And you will not speak of my father or our impending meeting to anyone. Unless I say so. Do you understand?" I paused, watching the muscle tick in his jaw and his pupils dilate as he nodded. "We will meet when I'm ready and no sooner. Call the department heads for National security as well. It's about time you were all brought on to MY team officially." Thinking for a moment, I was curious and amused with how ridiculously easy it was for me to bend his will. A small grin threatened to curve my lips. This was becoming fun. "And you will bring a fresh assortment of scones from that little bakery on State Street in Albany." A dark thought swirled, and my lip curled up. "And your daughter. Bring her to our next visit as well. I think I may have a job for her." His head twitched a bit before he nodded, and I was unable to contain my growing smile.

"Yes, Mr. Gregori, whatever you'd like."

I loved those scones. They were the closest to what my mother used to bake for us as children. And his snobby fucking daughter, who embarrassed me at one of my fathers schmooze gatherings last year, was going to get what she deserved. This fat bastard was going to bring her to me with a smile on his face or I'd have Jonas put his smug ass in a very deep, dark hole.

"I'd like you to kiss my hand now," I said, raising my arm and an eyebrow. Several eyes in the crowd followed him as he immediately bent forward, reached for my hand, and brought his lips to my knuckles. An evil smile finally curved my mouth. Astonishing. So easily influenced, I could get used to this. I wasn't even breaking a sweat. "Gather a list of names of whom you were planning to communicate my father's...dealings to. You will be helping me from here on. Do you understand?"

"Yes, Mr. Gregori." He nodded again from his prostrated position.

"You are excused." I dismissed him with a backhanded wave, done with this arrogant fuck for now. Almost giddy with elation, I still felt energized, something I'd noticed starting after I had received my latest round of treatments. That much focus would have had me completely exhausted previously. Interesting. That took nearly zero effort. I smiled to myself. The newest medicine was working superbly. My mind started spinning at the possibilities. Too bad my father wasn't here anymore. Maybe this would've given him something to be proud of. God, he had been such a bastard.

I sniffed, noticing some wetness coming from my nostril, and wiped a handkerchief under my nose. Looking down at the thin rivulet of blood, I frowned. Guess I could still use a few more treatments; my frown deepened.

Jonas and I finished our small talk, accepting condolences from countless individuals. None of whom actually mattered. What a waste of our time. Afterward, we returned to our father's home. It was time to find out all the things he'd been up to over the last few years. When I started managing the children's home and clinic, he had started divulging some of his secrets. The man had had his filthy paws in everything. It was no surprise to me now why he'd had so much money and power. His several underground facilities had catered to the rich and powerful across the country, and it had all started before I was even born. Everything from anti-aging drugs for high-class celebrities to performance enhancement drugs for professional athletes. And the most recent batch of healing and strengthening enhancements distributed to our military. Some of which Jonas and I had been test subjects for. The thought made me sick. What kind of father did that?

Apparently, it didn't matter if you were his flesh and blood. He hadn't given a shit about us at all. Only that his 'tests' were working. I guess my physical condition had been a bit of a bonus, in a backhanded sort of way. How else would he have shown progress to his backers if it hadn't been for my bones becoming less fragile and my muscle growth improving? At the thought of muscle growth, I immediately had my brother come to mind. I looked across my father's study at Jonas, who was staring out the window in a relaxed military position. Feet shoulder width apart, hands clasped behind his back. His black fatigues tucked into his laced-up boots. His overgrown muscles strained against his t-shirt. He looked lethal. He was lethal. My father had been pumping Jonas and me full of experimental drugs since we were kids. Jonas, now a hulking beast of a man, with a nearly uncontrollable temper, was no doubt his doing. He would never have a normal life, not with his withdrawn and aggressive personality. His beastly stature alone put most people on edge. It looked almost unnatural, the size of him. But I guess it was... unnatural. God, we were both freaks.

As my mind raced and my anger at my father grew, I began to get hot. How had he done this to his children? My temperature continued to rise, and a trickle of sweat ran down my spine. Why hadn't my mother stopped him? Sudden memories of him smacking her face and her falling to the ground in a heap of sobs flashed through my mind. My anger skyrocketed as more once buried memories assaulted my thoughts. Memories of Jonas and me being thrown into small cages and transported to the lab. Of being strapped to a table and injected with drugs before our sessions of electroshock therapy. I recalled the doctor with the accent explaining to my father it would encourage the drugs to remain active within our cells longer.

Were these true memories resurfacing? How had I not remembered such horrors until now? Such pain?

They were only bits and pieces, but I knew in the depth of my soul they were real. I would never forgive him for this. "I'm glad you're dead," I growled out as I slammed my fists down on my father's desk. A pulse of energy burst through the room. The ceiling light popped and sparks rained down as the room shook. The desk's legs creaked as it skidded across the hardwood floor and away from me. Jonas grabbed the wall to steady himself as the open double doors at the entry to the office slammed shut as if a gust of wind had pushed them. Books tumbled from the shaking bookcases that lined much of the wall space. There was an audible click behind me as the last books fell to the floor. Startled and confused, I looked around the space to see Jonas staring wide-eyed at something behind me. Still seated in my father's office chair, I slowly spun to see what had caught his attention.

The bookcase behind me had cracked away from the wall, leaving a gaping hole. I slowly stood, making sure the quake had ceased. As I moved toward the fissure, I realized I was wrong. It wasn't a crack. The vibration must have released a mechanism allowing the bookcase to open. It was a door. It ran a few shelves shy of the eighteen foot ceiling but was wide enough to fit two men of Jonas' stature side by side easily.

"Jonas," I whispered, still unsure about what I was seeing. Jonas was immediately at my side. "Open this," I asked, even though he was already moving. The heavy door was almost silent as it swung open.

Once the door was fully opened, the lights inside automatically turned on. I blinked at the brightness of the overhead fluorescent lights, as my eyes had been working so hard to see into the unknown dark void. A small cement platform extended about twelve feet in front of me to a set of stainless-steel elevator doors.

We stepped forward simultaneously as the elevator doors opened. Entering the small metal box, I turned around, looking for some buttons. There was only one. Pressing the button, the doors silently slid shut, and I could feel the elevator descending. Neither of us spoke as we waited patiently for our destination. After what felt like forever, which in reality was probably only a few seconds, the elevator came to a halt. The doors slid open, and Jonas and I just stayed still, taking in our new surroundings.

The space opened into a large, octagonal reception-type area. Not quaint and cozy, but cold and sterile. A sliding window sat to the left as if to check people in, and there was a closed door just a few feet away. Two more doors sat closed as I peered straight ahead and saw a long hallway jutting out to the right. The cold gray walls added no comfort to my unease as I looked around. Jonas stepped out of the elevator first, heading toward the window. All the overhead lights were on, casting the space in a slightly green luminescence. His booted heels echoed in the empty space as he made his way across the room. I watched as he peered through the window, then walked over and opened the door. I remained still as I listened to his footfalls as he searched the space. After a few moments, he returned to the doorway and motioned for me to move forward.

I moved into the office space to have a look around. A few computers, scanners and printers lined the counter tops. At each one, a high back, rolling office chair was neatly pushed in. Several filing cabinets filled the space, making rows like library bookshelves. There had to be forty to fifty of them. I don't remember ever seeing this place. What the hell had he been doing down here? A dread settled over me, realizing my father had had plenty of secrets. And I was pretty sure I wasn't going to like what I found.

I turned on a computer, and Jonas came up behind me. The main screen came to life with several shortcut tabs littering a black background. Looking over the tabs, a few stood out among the many. Several were labeled with Jonas or my name. Maxine and Jaxon's names appeared too, and I scowled, utterly confused. I assumed I'd find some information here—I never expected to see them. Dr. Devins would never have... I clicked on one of the tabs and it opened a folder with several attachments. No names this time, just numbers. Sliding the mouse over the first one, a loud grinding noise startled me. The grinding noise continued to grow, causing Jonas and me to move swiftly out of the office toward the noise, my investigation forgotten.

Heading down the hallway toward the increasing noise, a blast of cool, musty air hit us. Blowing our hair back a bit as we continued. We both stopped in our tracks as we reached the end of the hall and a small subway-type train pulled to a stop in front of us. The white shuttle doors opened smoothly, and we slowly stepped inside. The gray interior was a step below luxurious, as it was clearly for working purposes. But front cabin had large, plush seating like you'd find on a first-class section of an airplane. Aside from the seating, and the small mini bar, most other things were basic. I made my way toward the back of the shuttle. The next car was very different.

All stainless steel with a few cabinets on the walls and countertops were between them on either side in the front of the cabin. A large space spanned the center, with sliding doors to open on both sides. In the back... was a large, caged area. The cage basically took up the entire rear of the cabin, like a cell. Like the ones in the lab.

I stared at the cell; my brow furrowed. Why would this be needed from my father's home? Something tickled at the back of my mind. I didn't recall ever seeing this before, but a low growl breached Jonas' lips from behind me. As I turned to look at him, my usually stoic brother was shaking with rage. I glanced back and forth between Jonas and the cage he was growling at. There was something trying to surface in my memory, but I couldn't quite grasp it. I opened my mouth to ask why the aggression but was interrupted as the doors automatically slid shut and the shuttle began moving with a jerk. Still not totally solid on my feet, I pitched backward, and Jonas darted forward, grabbing my flailing arm and stopping my descent. With his assistance, I righted myself and moved back into the seating area. Taking a seat, with Jonas sitting across the aisle from me, we barreled down what I could only assume was a tunnel. I had one guess where we'd end up. Now I had even more questions.

As I pondered the new findings, I couldn't shake the feeling that there were pieces missing. I let out a long breath, dropping my head back against the seat. Pinching the bridge of my nose as I closed my eyes, I let my thoughts drift to Max. I'd almost forgotten how excited I was earlier today, anticipating my impending guest. I'd been practically vibrating all day, sure that I would see her soon. The only thing I truly had to smile about on this shit of a day.

Eddie instructions to collect her, unharmed, and return her to my suite. I hadn't heard any recent updates, but then again, I'd been a bit busy—busy burying my father and all. I'd check my tracking surveillance once back at my place if I hadn't heard by then.

The grinding vibrations of the braking system pulled me back to the present. I lifted my head from the seat and opened my eyes as we slowed to a stop. There was no ding of arrival, just the quiet swishing of the doors opening to our destination. We stepped into a hallway that I didn't recognize. But something familiar once again tickled the back of my mind.

"This is the bad place," Jonas said in his deep timbre, tension lining his face as he stared ahead. It put me on edge.

"You've been here?" I questioned, looking at his profile as I drew my eyebrows together. Turning his face toward me, a frown formed on his mouth.

"We both have," he replied. My lips parted to respond, and I froze, a strange sound interrupting me. My eyes went wide as the noise registered in my ears. Screams. They were screams of pain and agony echoing down the hall toward us.

Chapter 26

Garron

I slowly opened my eyes and squinted at the brightness of the sun streaming through the windows. My chest felt like it was on fire. I struggled to take a deep breath and coughed as the air wheezed out of my lungs. Blinking rapidly to gain focus, I realized I was staring at a tiled ceiling. Not the ceiling of the cell I'd called home for so long. I remained still, trying to regain my wits. Where was I? There was a faint sound of engines racing away in the distance. But murmuring close by demanded my focus as I tried to decipher what I was hearing. Voices I vaguely recognized brought recent memories rushing back... Frank. His voice, garbled and raspy now, as he told someone about a map. Another male voice kept telling him to shut up and save his breath. Cory.

I tried to sit up quickly as continued memories of the fight slammed into my brain. I pressed a hand to my aching chest and felt a slippery wetness. Looking down at shredded material, I saw it soaked with blood, and rubbed my hand back and forth, looking for injuries. My bullet wounds had already healed on the outside. The pain must be from the internal tissues still knitting back together. I let out a harsh, barking cough as my chest burned with exertion as I slowly stood. Stumbling out of the pile of clothing I was lying on, my legs felt sluggish, like I was wading through thick mud, as I slowly moved forward, searching for Max.

"Max?" I couldn't see her from where I was standing.

I began slowly staggering toward the voices, then heard Cory call my name as a question.

"Yeah." My voice was rough, and my throat felt like I'd gargled with shattered glass. "Where's Max?" I responded, now clutching the store front countertop for support on my way toward them. Still feeling lightheaded, I stumbled around the debris of the fight; clothes and supplies scattered everywhere. But with each step, my strength was returning.

"I thought you were dead, man! What the fuck? You got shot in the chest! Like six fucking times!" Cory screeched, now standing, and pointing a finger at me. A groan filtered up from the floor and I moved around another rack of clothes to see Frank lying horizontal at Cory's feet.

"Frank!" I kneeled next to the man. This was not good.

"Stop yelling, for fuck's sake," he coughed out. "I'm not deaf or dead, yet. So, listen up, looks like I'm gonna be outta this round of fun boys. But you two got work to do. Garron knows the code to the basement." He paused for a cough. "There's a secret hatch in the floor under the filing cabinet against the wall. Slide the cabinet out and twist the knob counterclockwise while pushing in to open it." Another series of coughs, as he clutched his chest, grimacing. Taking a shallow breath, he continued. "The tunnel runs to my house. There is another supply room. Access code is the exact opposite. Take the C4 explosives and the detonators. The map on the wall will show you where to place them for optimal success. This is not a fail proof plan, however. But it should get you access to the lower level of the labs through the old mining shaft." Coughing again, but this time spitting up blood onto his chest. "Get Jax outta there and then go find that fucker Eddie. He's got Max."

I froze, my shock turning to barely contained rage. Eddie, that sadistic piece of shit, had Max. The image of him licking the side of her face while smiling at me sent a wave rage through me. A tingle ran up the back of my neck as heat flashed through my veins and my vision went red. I could feel sharp black nails pushing their way out from my fingertips. My control over the beast within was slipping.

"Wha-what the fuck!" Cory screeched out, eyes wide as he scrambled backward on his hands and feet like a crab.

Two hands darted out, lifting Cory by his underarms, and spinning him around. A tall, lithe female twisted herself in front of him. Her stance was wide, and her chin lowered as she growled at me, eyes flashing red beneath the dark brown depths. She was stunning. Her slim yet muscular frame was showcased by her form fitting leggings and tank top which hugged each curve. Her coppery brown skin nearly glowed, and thick brown locks bounced down past her breasts as her chest heaved.

"Cory. What the hell is going on here? And why do I smell blood?" A husky voice sounded from her lips.

"Sierra, what the hell are you doing here? What the hell is going on with everyone?" he squeaked, then bristled and stood taller. "I don't need a girl's help," he blurted, trying to sound bold and brushing off imaginary lint from his shirt. She popped a hand on her hip and glanced at him over her shoulder. Only briefly taking her eyes off of me.

"Uh huh," she chided before lasering her gaze once more in my direction.

"Wait, Sierra? Like Jax's Sierra?" I asked, relaxing a little, putting the pieces together. Yes, his description of her was pretty accurate from the stories he'd told. I'd always thought maybe he was embellishing a little. I tilted my head with a small smile. She frowned.

"How do you know Jax? Where is he? And what the hell is... oh my God! Frank?" She looked back at me, her eyes wide before they flashed red again. She began stalking toward me and my body tensed, now readying to defend.

"He didn't do it!" Cory moved forward. "Eddie and the Gregori goons were here. Shot Garron and Frank, took Max. Max called 911 before she was taken, they should be here any minute."

Frank took that moment to let out another wet cough, spitting more blood onto his chest. "Would ya all quit screwin' around." Frank grumbled the demand weakly. "Get outta here before the cops show up. Ya can't help anyone from jail. And believe me, they'll be locking your asses up with what they see here. Even if it's only for a while, time ain't on our side." Another round of coughs. "I wish I had more time to help you kids. All my research and files are in the bunkers. Sierra, go with them. I have a feelin' they're gonna need ya. Now get outta here."

As if on cue, sirens began wailing in the distance, closing in fast. I looked down at my blood-stained chest and torn shirt. I quickly removed the remnants of my old shirt, using the scraps to clean up the best I could. Pulling a new shirt over my head, I heard a giggle from behind me. Sierra was smirking in amusement, and Cory's eyebrows were lifted quizzically.

"Umm, that's a little small for you, buddy," Cory snickered. I growled as I tried to peel off the too tight t-shirt now stuck to my skin like glue.

"It's been a while since I've been shopping." I replied flatly. Sierra reached past me, pulling an XL off the rack.

"Try this, it still might be a little tight over your chest and arms, but at least you'll be able to move and breathe." She laughed quietly through her nose. I pulled the black t-shirt over my head, amazed at the softness and stretch of the fabric.

"Get going. The ambulance and the cops will be here any second." Frank barked.

"I can't leave, what if..." Cory knelt back down next to Frank.

"I'm not dyin' yet, kid. Now get outta here. And go get Max and Jax. I promised their dad I'd watch out for them. Not doin' such a great job from the floor. And I'm gettin' a little grumpy," he huffed.

I squatted down next to Frank across from Cory and placed my hand on his shoulder. "Thank you. I promise, I'll get them out and see that hell destroyed if it's the last thing I do. No one deserves that place." I said, making it a creed. He stretched his arm across his chest, placing his hand on mine.

"I know, son," a sad smile stretched across his lips and my throat tightened. The reaction made me pause. Before I could form a thought, he continued, "When you get through the tunnels, there is more recon information and supplies in my bunker. Take good care of my Max. She's like a daughter to me," he said, looking me in the eye.

"I will," I vowed, nodding my head as I stood and strode toward the basement stairs, not glancing back to see if the others were coming. I was going to get Max, with or without them.

I heard Cory and Sierra saying their goodbyes to Frank as I descended the stairs. Just as I finished punching in the code for the secured bunker,

Cory and Sierra were at my back. We entered as a group, and I closed the door behind us. The locking system made a series of clicks as it re-engaged. I ignored Cory and Sierra's comments of astonishment and awe, making my way through the room. Reaching the device on the wall, I mimicked Frank's previous movements to open a few of the gun cases. Grabbing two pistols and some ammo, I noticed a shoulder harness, much like the ones at the training facility in the lab. I quickly put it on, sliding the pistols into the holsters as memories flashed through my head.

There were only a few of us over the years that had been sent to live-fire training. That I knew of, at least. Military scouts from all over the world attended our underground battles. I'd overheard several languages that I couldn't decipher, making me realize the Gregoris reach extended abroad. How many countries they were involved with, I had no idea. Mostly, our observers commented with astonishment at our speed as we moved around obstacles, and strength as we battled each other in hand-to-hand combat. Or shooting at targets in different lighting extremes, like pitch darkness or post white-out with flash grenades. I could never see their faces behind the glass partitions. But enhanced hearing allowed their excited gasps and cheers to grate in my ears as they watched us heal post battle injuries. It was one reasons I hadn't feared Eddie's creeps shooting at me. It wouldn't have been the first time someone had shot me, or the worst thing I'd endured—and so far, I'd always healed.

We were always garnished with electric shock collars when out of our cells and shot with tranquilizer darts at the end of our training sessions. Guess they were smart enough to assume we would retaliate or make it out, provided there was an opportunity. Sadly, I was always disappointed when I woke up back in my cell. More often than not, I'd simply wished I'd died.

Shaking off the memories, I made my way to the sliding wall at the back of the room. Moving over just enough to step through, I turned back to look for the rest of my group. Cory was right behind me, and Sierra was catching up. Her mouth was wide open and her eyes huge as she took in her surroundings. Finally reaching us, we all stepped beyond the sliding wall, and I closed it back up.

"What is all of this?" Sierra demanded in a whisper.

"I've never seen this room, but I take it Frank's a crazy doomsday prepper!" Was Cory's quiet reply. He slowly turned, taking it all in, then headed toward the table and maps. A low whistle left his lips. "And look at all of this shit!" he whispered, as he pointed to all the maps and information lining the walls.

"Right, the map!" I tore it off the wall, folded it, and grabbed a backpack from a shelf to the left. I slid the map inside the small pocket and zipped it closed as I kept walking toward the filing cabinet.

It took me a minute to figure out the cabinet was on a small track of some sort, making it slide smoothly out of its place. Underneath was the trapdoor in the floor Frank had described. Pushing the knob down and turning counterclockwise, I heard the mechanism disengage. Once completed, it released a small hiss as it popped open, revealing a ladder descending into the ground. Looking at the others' wide eyes and back at the dark hole, I knew I would have to go first. Glancing around the room, I spotted a flashlight on the same shelf I'd just grabbed the backpack from.

"I'll go first, then Sierra. Cory, you'll need to bolt the door closed behind you once you're in." Cory scowled, then rolled his eyes.

"Alright, I'll get eaten last by the creepy trolls in the hole," he said sarcastically as he smiled widely without teeth and a tilt to his head. I briefly wondered if his sarcasm was normal, or maybe he was crazy? Maybe all normal people talked like this now. As I pointed the beam of light down the ladder, I decided maybe I should just leave it alone. I didn't think for a second there were creepy trolls, but I knew of other things that lurked in the dark. And I didn't think now was the time to tell them. The light pooled at the bottom, about twenty-five feet down, onto a dirt floor. I didn't glance back as I descended into the darkness.

Reaching the bottom, I pointed the beam of light toward what appeared to be an endless tunnel. Closing my eyes, I tried to reach out with my other senses. I could hear nothing but Sierra's foot falls descending behind me. The smell of stale air and damp dirt met my nose and an undercurrent of something else. A metal of some sort, and gunpowder. Opening my eyes, I ran the light around the circumference of our space. Light glimmered off a small wire along the ceiling. I followed the path of the wire and found it connected to several small boxes along our path. If I had to take a guess, Frank had a bit of a fail-safe and those were explosives. He was a shrewd man, and I was really beginning to like him. I hoped the emergency team would be able to help him. My sensitive hearing had recognized the wheeze of a punctured lung and the stutter of his heart as we left. Max would be devastated if anything happened to Frank. It was clear that they were a family, of sorts. A small pang of envy thumped in my chest at the thought of having a family.

I moved the beam of light to the ground at Sierra's feet as we waited for Cory to close the hatch. Once he reached the bottom, we started forward, moving in single file. The tunnel was wide enough that if I stretched out both arms, my fingertips would just barely graze the sides. The ceiling was eight or nine feet tall, so I felt comfortable walking upright, not needing to duck. We walked at a fast pace in silence for several minutes, which felt like hours. I wondered how long this tunnel was, and how odd it was that I'd found myself in another dark, underground space within forty-eight hours. It had been a complete whirlwind. A slight ache formed in my chest as I thought about Max. I needed to get her back. The connection I'd felt was unlike anything I'd ever experienced. It was as if I'd been able to breathe for the first time.

A whisper from behind pulled me out of my thoughts.

"Do you think trolls have sharp teeth? I bet they're dull, so it takes longer to chew you apart. And why do they always hide in dark places? Is it because they're grotesque? Like covered in warts or pus bubbles. Ewww, what if the pus bubbles are leaky? Like yellow and green pus that smells like hot garbage?" Cory followed up his musing with a gagging noise.

"Jesus Christ, Cory, you're disgusting," Sierra retorted.

"Look, I'm just sayin'. They could jump out any second. And I'd rather not get eaten. I've got a date with those hot twins from campus. They transferred from South Carolina and have that super cute southern accent." Cory made a 'mmmhmm' humming noise of approval that was just audible over the sound of their shoes crunching the packed earth.

"We've got bigger things than your date night to worry about. And I'm not sure if you've noticed, but there are scarier things than your imaginary trolls running around," Sierra said, and I could hear a tremble in her voice.

"What do you mean?" I asked over my shoulder as I continued my pace.

"People are getting sick. There have been some animal attacks in the area, like weird animal attacks. A squirrel attacked Paige and me in the park a few days ago. Got super sick, but I'm doing better now. Still feel a little weird and wicked hungry, but better. I've overheard some local chatter. People have been hospitalized and aren't getting better after being bitten. My friend James said a rabid deer stomped his buddy to death. His neighbor found the deer eating him in their backyard. The neighbor shot it, and the DEP came to collect the body for testing. I've lived in upstate New York my entire life. Deer don't eat people." her voice started to rise.

"Stop fucking with me, Sierra," Cory ground out.

"I'm not! I don't know why the media hasn't reported anything. There have been at least seven cases of the sickness that I've heard of. The sick people are at the Gregori Medical Center in quarantine. No visitors allowed, not even family. Paige wasn't feeling great, and she checked in at the center... I haven't been able to reach her," she said somberly.

"The Gregori Medical Center? As in, Gregori Labs?" I asked.

"Labs?" Sierra questioned back. "What labs? The Second Wind Children's School is attached, but no lab." *They had no idea of the horror going on below that school.* I grimaced.

Just as I was about to respond, a door appeared in the beam of light.

"Yes!" Cory shouted from behind me. "Let's get out of this fucking troll hole!"

I rolled my eyes and picked up my pace as the door was still quite a way ahead. This tunnel must have been about a mile, if not a little more. As we reached the door, a keypad similar to the one at the store came into view. I punched in the code Frank had given me and the locks disengaged. As we stepped through the door, the floor beneath our feet became solid and the overhead lights automatically turned on.

The space we entered was large, huge even, with two doors to the left, one straight ahead and one to the right. Most of the wall space was lined with metal utility shelving, with camping supplies and cardboard boxes neatly organized. Moving toward the first door on the left, the slam of another door accompanied by a loud whistle had me spinning around. Cory's eyes were wide as he placed his hands on his hips, drawing out the long whistle.

"Damn, ol' Frank IS a doomsday prepper! This shit is legit! Look at it all!"

I turned back toward the door and opened it. More shelves lined the walls of an approximated fifteen by thirty-foot space. Cases of water and other food items filled the shelves. Large bags of rice, boxes of powdered milk and dehydrated fruits and vegetables were stacked among other boxes labeled MREs.

Backing out, I headed into the next room. It was a bedroom area. There were more shelves with cardboard boxes, various camping supplies, and at least a dozen car batteries on one side. A large bed, nightstand, and lamp on the other. I moved back into the central space and walked directly across to an open doorway. Sierra stood just inside. I moved up beside her, looking at the vast space in front of us. There was a large vat of water built into the floor on the right. It almost looked like an indoor pond. On the left was a standing shower and a toilet with a partition between the two. I understood the shower and toilet but was confused about the other. Sierra must have seen my confused look.

"Fishery," she said, and my eyebrows drew together in question. "It's an indoor ecosystem for raising fish. My uncle runs a hatchery for a wildlife preserve, and it's similar. Although his is outside."

"Frank was serious about hiding out, I take it. I wonder what he was planning for?" I mused aloud.

"I'm not sure," Sierra responded. "An apocalypse of some sort? Whatever it is, I hope it never happens. Clearly, he set this place up for years of survival." She took a breath and turned toward me. "So, who ARE you? Where is Jax? And Max? And what the hell happened back there?" she started firing off questions, crossing her arms over her chest. Cory stepped up behind us.

"Agreed. About time we all get caught up on things," he said.

I turned to face them both and nodded my head in agreement as I let out a long sigh.

"I'll fill you in on what I know, but I'm afraid my information may be full of holes. Guess there is no easy way to start..." I paused, looking at their expectant expressions. *Well, they were either going to run screaming or help get their friends back. I seriously hoped for the latter. I couldn't do this on my own. But it wouldn't stop me from trying.* "I've been a captive in the Gregori lab for as long as I can remember. Jax helped me break out, but must have been re-captured. He never met up with me and the kids as we planned." Sierra frowned, worry lining her face. I launched into some vague details of my life while they both stared at me, mouths agape.

I didn't know these people, but I did know I was going to need help. Max trusted Frank and Cory; that was going to have to be enough for me. I just hoped it didn't bite me in the ass later. But really, what were my choices here? Filling these two strangers in about my life and what I knew was so different from my time with Max. The ache I'd felt earlier came back two-fold. I could almost feel my heart kick up, as if in panic. I rubbed my chest, hoping to ease the feeling. Eddie's face popped into my head, and I remembered the look in his eyes as he watched Max. His grin taunting me as he had her pinned to the floor beneath him. I failed to keep her safe. Shame filled me, but also resolve. I'd find her, I vowed to myself. And if that sick fuck laid one hand on her, I'd literally rip chunks of his body away, piece by piece, with my teeth.

I rounded up my vague life story, trying to stick to the basics. They both stared at me, wordless, mouths hanging open.

"So, these sickos that had you, now have Jax?" Sierra asked, barely containing her panic and the tremble in her voice.

"Yes. And possibly Max. If Eddie took her, it was probably on one of the Gregoris' orders." *Maybe not.* I frowned and rubbed my chest again. "I've gotta get these supplies and get to the cabin. I left the kids there. They'll help. I can't ask you to be a part of this." I looked them both in the eye. "We may not make it, and I'm going to make sure that lab is leveled. They are doing horrible things to people. I won't let it happen to anyone else." I vowed. Sierra and Cory looked at each other.

"I'm helping. I can't let Jax stay there... I-I love him," Sierra admitted with tear-filled eyes.

"Max is family. We've always had each other's backs. I'm not leaving either." Cory straightened his back. "I'm not all... I don't know what the hell you guys are," he waved his hand back and forth between Sierra and me. "Super? But I'm a damn good shot. I've got a few moves, and I'm fast. I can run like a scared bitch. So, I'll do whatever I can to help."

I nodded. Well, this was my team, and they'd chosen to be here and were committed. I'd take it.

"OK. Let's grab supplies and get going. Can you guys get us out of town without us being seen?" They nodded. "Great, let's move. I don't want to waste any time." I rubbed the ache in the center of my chest again. *Hang on Max, I'm coming.*

Chapter 27

Jax

My throat was dry and raw. I'd held off screaming for so long... until I just couldn't take the pain anymore. It tore from my lungs until I couldn't scream any longer. I tried to swallow, but had no saliva left. I wasn't sure how long I'd been there. The doctor seemed a little agitated and very determined to get some answers. It really pissed him off that Garron had made it out. From his constant grumbling, it sounded like he put most of his eggs in the wrong basket. *Too bad, so sad.* I tried to laugh at my own joke but barked a cough instead. My head lolled to the side. I had no energy left to lift it. But even if I did, the straps across my neck, chest, arms, and legs prevented me from moving. The metal table they strapped me to was cold, but that offered no relief to my pain.

The doctor had stepped out of the room a moment ago—without a word to me, of course. *Apparently, his guest didn't deserve a farewell. How rude.* I managed to wheeze out a small laugh. Fuck, that hurt.

"Stop being funny, you idiot, and get control of yourself!" I rasped out loud to myself. I closed my eyes for a minute, trying to regain a small semblance of sanity. Slowing my breathing, I tried to focus on each breath. In... and out... The drip, drip, drip of sweat sliding off my hair onto the floor drew my attention. At least I thought it was sweat. Maybe it was blood?

I was lucky enough today to get a brand-new strain of Red from our friendly, neighborhood evil scientist. After the injection and hours of convulsions, he decided I was ready for some new tests. I'd briefly wondered where Dr. Brindle had gone. She had been so much nicer than this asshole. Even if she had still done what they told her to. I wondered if anyone had figured out it was her who'd helped us. I hoped they never found out... for her sake.

I noticed my pain lessening; it seemed like the new strain caused accelerated tissue regeneration. Since I was still alive, I guess it worked. The slicing started small and shallow, growing larger and deeper with each test. The healing did nothing for pain. That, I learned way too quickly. After cutting bits and pieces of me away, I'd periodically blacked out from the pain. He was kind enough to wait for me to wake between tests. Thinking back through my day, I concluded that I'd rather be cut than burned. The pain was literally searing. I barked another long cough, almost gagging this time from the dryness of my throat. I really needed to stop that. It hurt.

Voices drifted from down the hall. I recognized one; doctor fuckwad had been bitching at me all day and that accent was hard to miss. Maybe he was just muttering to himself? The conversation continued, growing a little louder...maybe they were getting closer. The second voice, clearer now, held a familiarity that I just couldn't place. Cracking noises filled the room, drowning out the murmurs down the hall. It was a brief moment before I realized those noises were the bones in my hands. They were fusing back together after being broken, smashed, and yanked out of joint. I gritted my teeth against another howl as the white lightning of pain flashed through my body. Dizziness followed, making the room do a really fun little spin. I wanted to put a foot on the floor; it always helped when I was drunk, but I couldn't move my legs.

Turning my head, my eyes squeezed shut as I fought off the wave of nausea. The pain seemed to drag on forever.

"Hi there, handsome." Came from a husky, yet melodic voice.

"Sierra?" I opened my eyes to see her gliding across the room toward me. I knew it wasn't real, but I sunk into the hallucination, escaping the now. A gold silk nightgown clung to her luscious curves. The slit in the gown showed her long slender legs with each step. Her light brown skin, nearly glowing, as her hips swayed. The deep V in the neckline drew my attention to her pert nipples as she closed the space between us. Sierra was the most beautiful woman I'd ever laid eyes on.

"God, I missed you," I whispered to her. She leaned over me, a smile gracing her plump lips. Her pink tongue slid out and across her lips, giving them a very kissable shine, and my gaze locked on them. I wanted to suck that plump bottom lip into my mouth. The gold nightgown made the little gold flecks in her eyes glimmer, as she looked into mine. My heart skipped a beat as she ran a gentle hand across my eyebrow and down the side of my face. A tender move she'd been pulling on me for years. Dark brown locks tickled the side of my face, and I sighed her name as my eyes closed briefly.

"Let me touch you," I begged, not understanding why my hands weren't all over her already.

"Jax, I need you," she whispered in my ear. "Jax, I need you to be strong for me. Hold on, baby. It's almost time for you to leave." Leave? I wanted to stay here with her forever.

I'd never told her how I felt about her. Always trying to keep her at arm's length after seeing what my father went through losing my mother. That was a pain I could avoid. He was the strongest man I'd ever known, but that had brought him to his knees. It nearly destroyed him. As much as I didn't want to admit, Sierra had found a way through my constructed walls and into my heart. It was terrifying.

"I want to stay here with you. I've missed you so much. I'm sorry. So sorry I never told you." I tried to swallow past the lump in my throat that formed with my confession. She'd forgive me, she had to. Right?

"I love you, Jax. But you already knew that. Now, wake up! Jax, wake up," she said sternly. I stared at her, blinking in confusion.

"What the hell are you talking about?" I retorted.

"Wake up, Jax! I said, WAKE UP!" She slapped me across the face.

"What the fuck!" I scowled at her. She reared back and slapped me again, harder this time.

I blinked hard as my eyes watered. As my blurry view cleared, it wasn't Sierra that was standing in front of me. It was Grant, the Alpha team security guard that worked with Eddie. His second in command. The bastard that had been breaking my bones and smiling at my pain filled grunts and shouts for the last several hours. He smacked me across the face, and it took me a moment to figure out what was happening. I had been hallucinating. Shit.

"Wake up, you stupid fuck. Dr. Heller has a guest and they're coming to see you," he growled.

"Thanks for babysitting," I ground out flatly after spitting out the blood that was pooling in my mouth. He backhanded me this time, splitting my lip.

"Because I had to 'babysit' your stupid ass, I missed getting a chance at your sister this morning," he smirked at me.

"What?" I asked, as my eyes unfocused, darkness swamping my peripheral and another wave of dizziness hit. I blinked slowly, refocusing on my surroundings, hoping I didn't just pass out again. I squinted, settling my gaze on Grant. His smile widened as I tried to collect my thoughts.

"Thought I lost ya for a sec." He snorted. "And I thought you knew about your sister." He brought his fingertips to his mouth, making an 'O' shape in an 'I said too much' gesture. "Guess you have been a little preoccupied. Elias sent Eddie and a small team to pick her up. Sure hope she gets here in one piece." He followed up with a small snicker.

"You motherfucker!" I howled, back bowing as I thrashed against my restraints. "You touch her and I'll—" he interrupted me as I tried to pant out my threat.

"You'll what?" he mocked. "You aren't going to do shit, but lie there like a good boy and take what you're given." Rage boiled inside of me, and my vision hazed over in a shade of red. Hate and thoughts of violence took over my body, and it was almost as if I was pushed behind a wall inside my head. I felt my body heating as the groan and strain of the leather straps holding me down began to stretch and give. My muscles began to swell painfully, and my appendages lengthened. My hands stretched and flexed, attempting to grab and squeeze. And I heard the shrill sound of metal tearing as my nails bit into the metal table I was lying on. Chin lifting, a roar ripped from my body. The restraint popped loose from my neck, and I lifted my head toward the guard.

"Holy fuck!" Grant shouted, his eyes like saucers as he stumbled backward, reaching for his belt. I looked down the table at my body... which stunned me for a second. My body had taken on a slightly gray hue and red veins were visible underneath my skin. My arms and legs were longer, and my muscles had doubled in size, and appeared to still be growing. I channeled some energy, focusing on my right arm and popped the leather restraint loose. Reaching up, my hand came into view. Long fingers, tipped with dark gray claws, briefly passed my line of sight before they were slicing through the restraint across my chest. Too freaked out to think about what I was becoming, I focused on getting loose. As I sat up and leaned over to break my left hand free, a sharp pain stabbed my chest. Shock waves radiated through me, briefly stunning me with the pain.

I followed the wired electrodes stuck in my chest to the asshole holding the stun gun pointed at me. A deep, feral growl rumbled up my throat, as I pulled the electrodes free, tossing them to the floor, never taking my eyes off Grant. The man was white as a sheet and continued stumbling backward as I reached over to release my left hand. Just as I sliced through the restraint, I felt another sharp pain. The initial stab immediately sent an icy feeling into my neck that quickly spread down my body. My pulse rate slowed drastically as I fell backward onto the table. A feeling of paralysis took over, and I rolled my head to the side just as a figure came into view.

Dr. Heller rounded the table, shaking his head. "I told you to watch him!" he shouted at Grant. "You idiot! Do you know what kind of mess you would've created by letting him go? We've already lost my prize specimen! Have you idiots been able to collect him yet?" He threw the empty syringe to the floor. "Nevermind. Clean up this mess, now." His accent thick with anger as he waved his hand over the area and turned, dismissing the guard. "I will speak to Mr. Blasco when he returns. And I'll deal with your mistakes later," he said with a dark promise. "Apparently you are useless. Had I not returned when I did, things would have been... unsavory, I'm sure. Now, re-secure him! Mr. Gregori has just arrived and wishes to see what we are working on. He should be returning from the holding cells any minute. And if you don't want to be placed in one, I suggest you move with haste!" The doctor turned on his heels and headed for the exit.

Stopping in the doorway, he turned back, letting out a deep sigh and addressed me.

"Mr. Devins, you are quite exceptional. Not as exciting as your predecessor, a true loss that one, but intriguing, nonetheless. I should've expected it given my previous notes. Your mother was quite sly. Now, if you'll excuse me, there are a few individuals I'd like the Gregoris to meet first. I think they will be most pleased with our recent results." Smiling and full of pride, the doctor turned back toward the door and exited the room. As I lay on the cold table, listening to the grumbling guard as he attached new restraints, I seethed, unable to move. I was going to fucking kill that man and all the motherfuckers in this place... after I got the others out of here.

I could just make out the voices floating down the hallway as another wave of dizziness hit. The doctor was discussing another patient.

"She's not responding to the treatments the way we had hoped. But she is progressing in a different direction. I'm quite sure we will be able to utilize her... mutations. She's still lucid and able to follow directions, most of the time. However, her need to consume large quantities of raw flesh inhibits her ability to rationalize at times. It's quite interesting. When she was brought in with the others, I had anticipated a similar decomposition of sorts. The Red, as we've called it, does not bond with everyone the same. Paige has had a unique mutation. Her body regenerates from the decomposition phase upon consumption of raw meat or blood, making her appear almost normal. The others either mutate physically, unable to return to their normal physique, or transition in and out of the mutation with emotion. Mr. Devins has shown exceptional progress in this." I groaned, trying to fight against the darkness clouding my mind and pay attention to the doctor's ramblings.

"I will need to see the results from the compliance portion of our research. I'm aware of the program. My father had been funding its research for well over two decades. The radiation that originally closed the local mines has been quite lucrative on many fronts. I'm also aware of our progress with Red over the last few months. I've read some intriguing reports from our southern lab." Even though the voice dropped an octave, it was one I recognized. "I've seen results, personally. And I wish for the new strain to be put to use immediately. I have Eddie collecting the perfect subject." I could hear the smile in Elias' voice from here. "And Dr. Heller, there will be no mistakes with this one. Do you understand? You will treat her with the utmost care. She is mine."

My mind was so foggy as I fought the darkness. My last thoughts were of Max. And praying to God that Garron had gotten her to safety.

Chapter 28

Max

The pain in my cheek throbbed, and I reached up, tracing my fingers over a lump. I groaned and rolled onto my back, holding my aching face. A jingling noise brought my attention to my surroundings and my eyes popped open. I froze, not even a breath escaped my lungs. Lying as still as possible, I tried not to panic, as I had no idea where I was. Slowly exhaling, I tried to keep my breathing quiet as my eyes came into focus. Stagnant air filled with scents of mold, wood smoke and fuel invaded my nose. My stomach rolled as a thread of terror began to take root.

The ceiling overhead was made up of old beams of wood and there was a single lightbulb hanging to my left. Its low glow gave the room dim light, and I blinked my eyes. I could hear a motor running in the distance—a lawn tractor? A small glimmer drew my attention to one of several hooks secured to the ceiling. My eyes followed the thin, shiny cable through the hooks. It seemed to drop from the center of the room, like the end of a spider's web, directly to me. I jerked up to a sitting position and the jingle at my neck had me gripping at some sort of collar. I sucked in rapid pants and dropped my hands to the floor. Scurrying backward on my hands and feet until my back hit a wall, I slid downward and dropped onto my ass.

My pulse kicked up as panic rose inside of me. I frantically looked around, realizing it was a small cabin-type space. The walls appeared to be made of thick, round logs stacked on top of each other. There was a closed door straight ahead and a small bistro set to the left. The single light bulb hung above the bistro set without any fixtures, as if lighting had been an afterthought. A small stone step to the right of the door was a platform for the wood stove perched on it. The black wood stove, as well as the stove pipe running from the center to the wall behind it, had a layer of dust. Someone had clearly not used it in a while. There was a single window just to the right. The light coming through was barely there, as if it was just past dusk, or possibly pre-dawn. *How long have I been here? How did I get here? Where the hell was HERE?*

My breathing was escalating into a panic attack, and I dropped my head between my knees. Just breathe, just breathe. I laced my hands behind my head and tried to focus. After I got my breathing under control, I picked my head back up. As I pushed my hair back from my face, my hand grazed the lump I'd already forgotten. I gingerly touched the sore, swollen area as memories assaulted me.

Eddie. That motherfucker. I reached for the collar around my neck, feeling a small padlock at the back. A small sob left my lips and tears pricked at my eyes. Reaching backward, I wrapped my hands around the thin cable. As I tugged, it made a zipper-like noise running through the eyelets across the ceiling. My emotions warred within me, anger and terror rising to the surface. It must have been him who had brought me here.

I pushed to my feet, slightly unsteady. Looking down, I realized I was standing on a mattress and my shoes had been removed. A soft, light blue fitted sheet was over the queen-size mattress lying on the floor, and a darker blue blanket laid in a heap next to me. One pillow was next to the blanket, with the same shade as the sheet for a case. How nice of him to coordinate, I thought dryly. Stumbling ungracefully, I got to the floor. The cable pulled taut, and I reached up and tugged again. I began choking as the collar strained against my forward movement, the cable not allowing me to go much further. I reached for the door, grasping at air, still several feet away.

Not able to get my fingers between the collar and my neck, my eyes welled with tears. I had to get this thing off. Blinking hard, I looked around, noticing the cable ran through a series of hooks along the ceiling and down the wall toward the door. It reached the bottom of the doorway and exited through a small hole in the wall. I tried to swallow, not sure if the lump in my throat was from the pressure of the collar or the situation. Probably both. Trying to clear my throat, I realized how parched my mouth was. I began coughing, clutching the collar. I wasn't sure if the coughing was a direct result of thinking about my thirst, or if there truly was a tickle—or maybe the fucking collar was just putting too much pressure on my neck. Either way, my noises must have alerted my captor.

My heart rate kicked up at the sound of footsteps coming across what sounded like a small porch. The noise of a lock clicking free had me backing away. The door slowly opened, almost too dramatically, and my heart pounded in my chest. A shrill squeak from the old hinges had me jerk, then a hand came into view as it slowly pushed the door open with a flat palm.

As the door fully opened, my eyes widened at the silhouette of a man framed in the doorway.

"Hello, Sweets," a voice rumbled from the shadows. I was frozen in place, but my eyes darted around, looking for something to defend myself with. I reached to my back, just remembering the gun I had there earlier. A small snicker sounded from the darkness.

"Looking for something, Sweets?" he asked, then continued without waiting for a response. "Do you really think I wouldn't have taken the pistol at your back? Now, now," he chided. "Is that really a way to greet me home? I'm more partial to a 'Hello Master', since I DO get to choose." Eddie said with a smile as he stepped into the room. Ignoring me as I stared wide-eyed, he walked to the small wood stove, dropping a pile of chopped logs onto the stone pedestal. "It's going to be a little chilly tonight, not that you're going to notice." He started to make a fire, not turning to look at me while he got to work.

"Wha—" I coughed and tried to clear my throat. "What are you doing, Eddie?" I finally asked, my voice shaking. He glanced over his shoulder toward me, a smile curving his lips.

"Well, isn't it obvious, Sweets?" His overly pleasant tone made my stomach twist. "Keeping you. Oh, I've been trying to gain your attention for far too long." Shaking his head, he turned back to his task of starting the woodstove.

"The police, my friends and family, they'll find me. And you'll go to jail forever. Just, let me go. Please, Eddie. I won't tell anyone, promise." I pleaded. His deep laugh echoed through the small space, and I flinched.

"Silly little Sweets. You have no family. Your parents are gone, Jax..." he snorted, "won't be more than a puddle by the time they're done with him. And your friends..." He let out a *tsk*ing noise. "Who? Frank? Dead. That kid you worked with? Worthless. And that lab rat that put his scent all over you?" His voice began to rise, and my body trembled. "Yeah, that piece of shit. I put a few extra bullets in his chest for old times' sake. I'm afraid he won't be coming." A small breath left my lips. *No.* What he was saying couldn't be true.

"You're lying," I said weakly. Another small laugh rumbled from his chest.

"Am I?" he retorted, as the fire he'd been working on flared to life.

I was silent as tears now dripped down my cheeks. A great sadness enveloped me, and tremors coursed through my body. I couldn't help the sobs that burst forth with my racing thoughts. If Frank and Garron were dead, there would be no one left to get Jax. Oh, God. Frank had been like a second father to me. And Garron, even in the short time we'd known each other, the connection I'd felt was unlike anything I'd ever experienced. Something about him had called to me on a soul-shattering level. I don't know how I knew, but we were meant to be together. We hadn't had any time. Pieces of me began to fracture inside and the ache I felt in my chest made me crumple to the ground. I braced myself on my hands and knees, gagging and trying to breathe.

"Well, I can't say I didn't expect some tears. But you're being a bit ridiculous," Eddie chirped. "Now get up. Wipe your fucking face off and sit down at the table. I'll be right back." He stomped out the door without a second glance. I sat back on my heels and covered my face with my hands, unable to stop the sobs. I wasn't sure how long Eddie was gone, but his scowl spoke volumes when he stood in the doorway again. He had a plastic grocery bag in his hand that he tossed to the table as he simultaneously slammed the door shut. The small cabin rattled as dust plumed from between the logs.

"I said, get your ass to the table. We are going to have a bite to eat while we discuss our ground rules." He barked in a demanding tone. I looked up from my place on the floor, still unmoving, as my body hiccupped in response to trying to quiet my emotions.

Eddie moved with staggering speed to my side. Grabbing under my arm, he wrenched my body to a standing position and shoved me toward the table. The cable at my neck tugged me backward just as I reached the table's edge. I stumbled back as an involuntary choking noise broke out of my mouth.

"Hmm, guess I didn't judge the length quite right. It was a little difficult to gauge while you were sleeping," Eddie grumbled. He walked back outside, and I heard a tiny whirring noise as the cable attached to my collar began to slacken. I reached behind my head, pulling the wire with slight relief. Eddie returned, shutting the door behind him, and pointed to the chair next to the table. "You should be able to sit now." I cautiously moved to the chair and lowered myself down, still holding onto the collar, waiting for the tugging sensation. When none came, I placed my hands in my lap and stared down at them.

The rustle of the plastic bag had me looking up through my lashes without moving my head. Eddie placed a paper plate and a bottle of water in front of me. I quickly grabbed the water, twisting the cap, and began swallowing. The cool liquid felt great in my mouth but swallowing it down was hard with the tightness of the collar pushing on my throat. I managed to get half of the bottle down before I heard Eddie clear his throat, demanding my attention. I lowered the bottle to the table.

"I have something for you to eat," he said.

"I'm not hungry."

"I didn't ask if you were hungry. I saw the flash in your eyes before you took down one of my men at the sports store. You need to eat. It will help with the healing." He pointed to the lump on my cheek. "It must have been a while since you've eaten?" he asked, but I didn't answer. "Clearly you're infected." I just scowled at him, angry and confused. "The Red," he sighed, and rolled his eyes like I was an idiot. "You need meat. Most of us do now." He dug out a package and tore it open, slapping a raw, bloody steak on the paper plate in front of me. A frown pulled down my features and my eyebrows drew together right before its smell permeated my nose.

The tangy, metallic smell hit my nose, and my mouth watered. Instinct took over and I snatched the piece of meat from the plate. Bringing it to my mouth, I tore into it with my teeth. Closing my eyes, the flavor and blood burst over my tongue and I almost groaned. My body was more than pleased. Trying to swallow my first bite, I choked —the collar way too tight. I gagged and coughed, spitting the meat onto the floor while grabbing at the obstruction.

"A little too tight, Sweets?" I lifted my head, seeing Eddie grinning from across the table. He stood without another word and came around the table toward me. I flinched. Harshly grabbing my head with both hands, he tilted my face upward. Smiling down at me, he relaxed his hold, and rubbed a thumb across my lips. I flinched again at his touch, and my stomach rolled as he lifted the thumb to his mouth and sucked off the blood that he had wiped away. Still smiling and not having taken his eyes off mine, he reached into his front pocket.

"Turn around and don't move. This will be your only warning. Do you understand?" he said sternly, not blinking. I nodded as much as I could with his hand gripping one side of my face. "Good. Now turn." I did as he asked, turning slowly. He gripped my neck from behind and I heard the pop of a latch right before my collar loosened. Clicking from the lock snapping back into place made me flinch again. "Now, turn around and eat," he demanded.

I'm not sure I could've stopped myself from devouring the raw meat if I had wanted. Now that I could swallow, I consumed the huge steak as if I'd been starving. The wave of nausea that had been present since I'd woken slowly dissipated within minutes of me finishing my meal.

"Feeling better?" Eddie purred as he watched me from across the table. He was sitting back, one leg across the other, completely relaxed. I had almost forgotten him as I'd eaten. "Even your face looks better. Seems I was right. It helped your healing, just like with us." He smiled as I reached up, touching my face to find the lump was gone. "Oh, Sweets, we're going to have soooo much fun."

Chapter 29

Max

"Don't you fucking touch me." I growled, moving backward as far away from Eddie as I could. He stalked toward me, unbuttoning his flannel shirt. My eyes darted around looking for a weapon—the fucker didn't even have silverware on the table!

"Relax, Sweets, we're going to have fun together, you and I. I've been waiting for you for a looong time. Since the first day I met you behind that counter, I made sure I was on call for any pickups at your store. That cock-blocking old man is finally out of the picture, and I've got you here, all to myself." His head tilted sideways in thought for a moment. "I haven't thought about what I'm going to tell Elias though. You were supposed to be delivered to the lab by tonight. Hmmm. Well, maybe he can just have you when I'm done," he shrugged. "I could always blame your condition on that lab rat. Poor, fucked up little freak. No telling what state of mind he was in after finally escaping a life of torture."

"Garron would never hurt me!" I yelled as I pressed my back against the wall.

"Is that so? Huh. Too bad he's dead and there'll be no way to prove that theory." He gave me a broad, mocking, tight-lipped smile. A lump formed in my throat and an ache in my chest.

"I fucking hate you," I seethed.

Draping his shirt over a chair, he pulled a large hunting knife from the holster on his belt. The dim light glinted off the blade as my pulse started hammering in my chest and sweat beaded on my forehead and upper lip. My too wide eyes tracked the blade as he twisted it back and forth and I trembled. It had grown dark since our dinner, and I hadn't heard any cars driving past. I had a fleeting thought that I wished I knew where we were, but it wouldn't have made any difference unless I could get out that door. I was against the wall next to the mattress. The door was on the other side of Eddie. I would either have to go around him or through him.

He smiled as he slowly stalked toward me. His blade twirling in his hand. He stopped about three feet from me.

"Take off your clothes. I'd like to see what you've been hiding," he demanded in a dark tone.

"Fuck you!" I screamed and darted right. He reached for me and missed as I faked the step and tucked into a sideways roll to the left. The cable tangled in my hair and pulled the collar painfully as the leather bit into my neck. Gritting my teeth and hopping to my feet, I darted to the door. My arms reached out across the distance for the knob as Eddie's hand wrapped around my collared neck. The quick move halted my breathing for a moment as I flew backward through the air. My back slammed to the floor, knocking what air I had out of my lungs in a whoosh. Eddie's hand was around my throat as he pinned me to the wooden planks. I rolled my body backward as much as possible in his grip and wrapped my legs around his neck. He lifted up, pulling my lower half with him. He didn't let go of my neck, and I tried to squeeze my legs, but he jumped and slammed my upper half back to the floor, knocking the wind out of me again. My legs fell loose, my slight advantage gone.

"Not smart, Sweets. Not smart." He began dragging me backward across the floor by my neck. My hands latched around his, attempting to loosen his grip, and my legs and feet flailed and twisted as I tried breaking free.

He lifted me briefly, still holding my neck land slammed my body back down onto the mattress, seemingly unaffected by my nails digging into his skin. My legs thrashed, attempting to kick him or jolt my body out of his grip, but nothing was working, and I needed to breathe. Black spots started moving into my vision as I fought to draw in air.

"Looking a little blue, Sweets," he grunted with effort. "Let me give you some help there," he said while changing his position, never removing the hand from my neck.

He moved, placing a knee in the center of my chest, and pressed some weight into it. My struggle was slowing with the lack of oxygen and more of my vision filled with darkness. Terror at the face above me was my last thought as the darkness fully took over.

Green eyes smiled at me, and I looked down at our intertwined hands. Smiling, my gaze moved to the beautiful sunset. The sun looked as though it was descending into the reservoir itself. Blues, purples, pinks, oranges, and yellows of the sky were so vibrant it looked unreal. The stillness of the water resting between the two green mountains echoed the reflection perfectly.

"This is my favorite spot," I told Garron. "You can only get this view from this mountainside. The hills here have too many cliffs where the trees can't overgrow the view. I just wanted to share this with you. I've never brought anyone here before." The last part I whispered, a little unsure how he'd take it.

"You are more beautiful than a thousand sunsets." he said as he turned my face toward him.

I never knew you could see love shine through the eyes of another; but in that moment, it was clear. I felt like chocolate melting in a tropical sun. A sweet, warm puddle. He leaned forward slowly, our eyes locked on each other. Tingles of heat spread under my skin. The warmth of his breath fanned over my lips right before his lips took mine in a soft, sensual kiss. His tongue teasing the seam of my mouth as I let out a small moan of pleasure. The tingles of heat began to pool low in my belly and I leaned in, silently begging for more. But he pulled back, his hooded eyes glimmering with sparks of red.

"Garron," I whispered. His hands curled around my arms, sliding down, and squeezed when they reached my thighs. The squeeze grew more firm. I furrowed my brows at him as it became painful.

"Stop," I demanded. He shook his head, sorrow lining his features.

"It's not me."

"Stop!" I shouted as the pain grew, now sharp and stinging.

My eyes flew open on a gasp. I blinked rapidly as my eyes had been tearing from the pain. The logs connecting the walls and ceiling came back into view. As well as the clarity of where I was. I tried to move but couldn't, finding my arms and legs tied down. My heart picked up a jack rabbit staccato and sweat beaded my lip almost instantly. As I lifted my head, looking down the line of my body, Eddie came into sight.

"Ah, there you are. I was wondering when you'd make it to the party." His smile grew wide. "This is really no fun with you unconscious."

He picked up his hand, twisting something back and forth to glint in the light. I blinked, trying to make sense of what I was seeing as my eyes struggled to focus. The blade he was waving gracefully back and forth was dripping with blood. My blood. As awareness and horror took over my features, Eddie let out a manic laugh.

"Yes! There it is!" he howled toward the ceiling in triumph, holding his arms out wide. "I told you we were going to have fun!" He said, almost as if he was scolding a child. "Now, feel free to scream."

Bringing the knife down, it pierced my skin as he dragged it down the length of my thigh. A shrill scream left my lips as pain seared through me. The sharp sting was unlike anything I'd ever felt.

"Ah, yes!" Eddie howled again with glee. "There is no one around for miles! And your screams are the most beautiful ones I've ever heard." He climbed over my body, straddling my waist as I panted, trying to catch my breath. "I'm so glad we took time to eat. You're healing remarkably well. We'll be able to keep this up all night!"

A sob bubbled up my throat as I turned my head away from him. He gripped my face, securing it to the side as he bent down and licked up the column of my throat. I whimpered. "You smell sooo gooood," he crooned in my ear. "I'm going to taste every inch of your body, inside and out." He nipped back down the side of my neck and over my clavicle. Sitting back up, he pulled my face back to the center. Tapping the flat of the blade under my chin, he slid the tip down my neck. Reaching the hollow of my throat, he twirled the blade, the sharp pricking sensation trumped by the searing burn radiating from my leg.

Moving the tip further down, he pressed it into my skin. The sharp instrument split the skin between my breasts and blood pooled, following his map to my navel. I tried to control the sobs as the involuntary jerking motions associated with them caused the blade to go deeper. Tears dripped into my ears as I lay there in pain, trying not to move.

"This just won't do!" Eddie said with a pout. I blinked rapidly, trying to clear my tear-filled eyes. "You're healing much too quickly," he said as he sat back, one arm across his chest, the other hand cupping his chin. I lifted my head to look down at my chest, just now realizing I was only in my bra and panties. The slice in my chest was already closing.

"Please Eddie, don't," I begged. He waved his hand dismissively.

"I have some ideas to remedy that," he said with a grin as he bent forward, running the knife back down my chest, following the same trail as the last. Another scream ripped from my lips as white-hot pain threatened to steal my vision. This time he didn't pause the blade at my bra but cut straight through it. My skin had fileted open slightly and my bra slid off my chest, exposing my breasts.

"Mmmmm" came his hum of approval. Eddie leaned forward, cupping my breasts and pinching my nipples as he ran his tongue up the length of my fresh wound. Lapping up the pooling blood, he sat back, hands still on my breasts. Angling his blood-soaked chin toward the ceiling, a roar ripped from his chest, shaking the small cabin. I tried to pull my arms in to cover my ears and found the briefest of give.

"Fuck!" he growled loudly. Looking back down at me, the air in my lungs froze. His gaze flickered red as he stared down at me. "You taste incredible."

He bent forward again, lapping up the remaining blood pooled at my navel. I shook from the sobs wracking my body. When it was gone, an angry look took over his features, and he hopped off me backwards. With the weight of his body gone, I began to struggle and pulled at the restraints. His heavy breathing pulled my eyes back to him and a cold dread swept through me.

His body began pulsing with his breaths and red veins sparked beneath his skin as his muscles grew. His chest and arms, every inch of skin I could see, was growing larger. Terror froze me for a second before I started struggling again.

"Oh, Sweets, I had no idea. What ARE you?" His voice was low and gravelly now. "I feel incredible!" He paused, head tilted sideways, a predator watching its prey. "Now, where do you think you're going? We are far from done. I'm going to enjoy every inch of you."

Adrenaline kicked in and my blood started to heat. A red haze shaded my vision as I gritted my teeth and pulled a hand free from my restraints. Using the burst of strength and energy I still didn't understand, I reached over and pulled the other arm free as well. As I sat up, a sinister chuckle sounded from near my feet, and I briefly realized he hadn't stopped me.

"Don't stop on my account. I like it better when they fight," he said, his now fully red eyes locked on me. He was still breathing heavily; a wicked grin curved his lips and his hands flexed at his sides. His skin had a slightly gray color as the red veins rippled beneath the surface. Another shiver of terror trickled down my spine and I began pulling at my legs. Frantically trying to free them, I didn't see the backside of his hand as it connected with my face. My head careened backward with the impact and my body followed. I bounced on the mattress and sparkles twinkled around my darkening vision.

I lay stunned, clutching my face, wondering if my head was still attached to my neck. The world was spinning as rough hands gripped my hips and tugged my body down the mattress. I tried to shake loose from the fog wrapped around my head, but everything was spinning. I barely registered the body that wedged itself between my legs. A hand wrapped around my throat, giving it a squeeze, and my eyes rolled back as I attempted to focus. Two light slaps tapped my cheek.

"No passing out this time. You're gonna wanna stick around for the fun we're going to have," Eddie's malicious voice said in my ear. I groaned and weakly tried to grab the hand constricting my neck.

A firm hand roughly grabbed my breast and trailed down the still sensitive wound to my belly. A whimper left my lips as my head lolled to the side and was quickly wrenched back to center again. The firm pressure continued down to my pelvis, gripping me through my underwear. I began to thrash, and a garbled scream bubbled up my throat as awareness trickled back to me.

I tried to buck him off as he licked down my chest, still holding my head down with pressure on my neck. Gripping his arm, my nails sunk into his skin as I tried to peel off the pressure to my throat. His other hand ripped away the fabric that had been keeping him from my most sensitive flesh. My whimpers increased as tears leaked from my eyes. His fingers roughly roamed over my pussy, breaching the access, and sliding inside. A sharp sting registered in the plump tissue above my nipple as he bit down hard enough to draw blood, and another scream left my lips. I could feel the sucking pull as he drank from the fresh wound in my chest. His head reared back as another roar shook the room. Trapped under his weight, I continued to thrash as much as I was able, which wasn't much at all.

"You taste so fucking good!" His bellowed words followed his roar. "This is the most addicting high I've ever had," he breathed out and panted with excitement. As he straddled me, he let go for a brief second to free himself, before his hand tightened on my throat once more. My nails clawed at his arm as the pressure was now stopping my voice and drastically reducing oxygen to my brain. My body weakened, and he took full advantage.

Tears streamed from my eyes as I lay helpless to his assault. Dizzy from the lack of oxygen, my efforts to rebel were weak. I was fucking helpless and utterly destroyed. I wished I'd just died when he sunk the knife into my flesh. His hands moved to my shoulders, allowing a harsh gasp of cool air to enter my lungs. The returning oxygen gave me a small reprieve, and I sank my nails into his chest, dragging them downward as I pushed at his body with renewed effort. Trails of blood dripped down the path my nails scored and splashed onto my chest and stomach as he lifted one hand and smacked my face. Stunned, I felt blood seep into my mouth from my split lip as I pressed my hand over my cheek and mouth.

"So fucking smart, my Sweet. Don't worry, I'll take care of that." He panted.

Eddie moved with speed, and the glint of the knife caught my attention as it descended toward my legs. There was a moment where my legs snapped back toward my body like a rubber band as my restraints were severed, and then I was being dragged downward again. His harsh grip on my ankles increased painfully as he twisted my legs one over the other and forced my body to flip onto my stomach.

Large gray hands gripped me with bruising pressure from behind and my hips were immediately lifted, placing me on my hands and knees. I tried to scramble forward, only to be yanked backward. He leaned over my back, pressing his sweaty chest onto me. Harsh breaths were in my ear as he snaked his hand around my neck. Before his grip could tighten, I dropped my head forward and brought it back with as much force as I could. A loud crunch echoed around us quickly followed by a howl of pain. He jerked away from me, his hands covering his very broken nose as blood gushed between his fingertips. I took the fleeting moment and put all my effort into swinging my body around and landed a solid elbow to his temple. His naked body dropped to the ground in an unmoving heap.

I frantically looked around for anything usable as a weapon. The poker he had been using to stoke the fire was lying on the stone slab. I ran toward the object, only to be yanked backward and off my feet by the collar around my neck. Standing back up, I moved as swiftly as I could, testing the length. Borderline hyperventilating, I reached the end and stretched my arm, missing the poker by a few feet. A disheartening sob broke free, and I looked around frantically. My eyes darted over every surface. Eddie was still unmoving, but not for long.

I stretched my leg out, holding onto the cable attached to the ceiling for balance. My toes just grazed the end of the handle, sliding it a little further away. "Fuck!" I whispered in a frustrated panic. Re-checking my balance, I stretched my leg out again. The cable at my neck had no more give, and the collar began to cut off my air as I stretched. I continued to reach, and the pressure on my neck was painful enough to make my eyes water. My toes finally found purchase, and I carefully slid the poker across the floor to within reaching distance. A groan sounded from behind me, and my pulse nearly jack-rabbeted out of my chest as I lowered myself and picked up the poker.

Turning around, I hurried back toward Eddie. He rolled onto his back, holding his face, and groaned. His eyes popped open and met mine.

"Don't ever fucking touch me again!" I screamed as I raised the poker over my head. Gathering every bit of energy I could, I let out a battle cry as I swung like I was chopping a block of wood. I smashed the poker into his fucking skull hard enough to hear bone crack. I stumbled backward as I pulled back and did it again. "Fucker!!!" I screamed shrilly.

Pulling the poker out of his skull, the blood dripped freely to the floor as I used it to reach for his pants and dragged them close enough to grab. I quickly dug through the pockets, looking for the key. Having found what I needed, I unlocked my restraint and stumbled over to my pants hanging over the bistro chair. Sliding them on, I rubbed at my sore neck as I looked for my shirt. I finally found it, cut in half next to the mattress. Guess he couldn't figure out how to get it over my head with the cable attached. Asshole.

I spotted his flannel on the floor next to the bistro. It would have to work for now. I pulled it on and buttoned it. Grabbing the poker, I headed for the door. I had no idea where the fuck my shoes were, but I couldn't stay here a second longer. I ran out of the cabin, spastically looking around, and spotted his Tahoe around the back. Pulling on the handles, I couldn't get into the vehicle and there was no fucking way I was going back into the cabin. So, I took off on foot, moving as fast as I could. Me and my poker were getting the fuck outta here.

Tears leaked down my cheeks at the loss of so much in the last twenty-four hours. I wiped my face, still shaking from adrenaline, reeling from the day's events. God, had it only been a day? I stayed to the side of the graveled road as the ground was softer on my feet. Not sure where I was, but the faint light over the mountain from the already set sun glowed straight ahead. West it was. It had to end up somewhere. A dull ache formed in my chest as Garron's face flashed through my mind. I rubbed mindlessly at the ache as another tear leaked down my cheek. I hoped he was resting peacefully. He deserved it. More tears trickled from my eyes and my gut twisted at the memories. What a horrific life he'd had. Garron had been a whirlwind in my life, but I'd truly thought we'd have more time. I'd never felt a connection like the one I'd felt with him. I still felt like a part of him was with me somehow. I wished I had a chance to show him happiness. He truly deserved a chance at a normal life. One filled with love, laughter, and smiles. I frowned. I guess we were both broken now. He'd probably never have wanted me after... Eddie... I hiccupped and held back a sob. I felt disgusting. I could smell him all over the shirt I was wearing, and it was making me sick. But it was getting cold, and I grimaced as the only other choice I had was to freeze naked, so I picked up my pace. Maybe I should just give up here. I could slowly drift off to sleep. Hypothermia would kick in, and if I was lucky, I'd just not wake up. Wiping the sleeve under my running nose, I pulled the shirt tighter around me.

"Fuck, it's getting cold!" I growled. With my luck, I'd just lose my fingers and toes.

Chapter 30

Maxine

I had been walking for hours, and my feet were cold and aching. I stopped and leaned against a large maple tree to take a short break. The moon offered little light, with the clouds constantly drifting in the way. But my vision was surprisingly good. I was amazed by what I could see as I made my way through the woods. I'd veered off the path of the road some time ago, trying to keep heading westward. Now, I was second guessing that idea. Everything had been such a whirlwind over the last few days. Trying to focus on anything but saving Jax was making my head throb. I had no answers to any of the questions my mind was fabricating, and it was frustrating. I leaned back against the tree, trying to slow my breathing and my thoughts.

Tilting my head back, looking up at the branches; the lowest one looked close enough for me to reach if I jumped. Maybe if I climbed a ways up, I could get a better bearing on where I was? This bullshit of wandering through the woods wasn't getting me anywhere... at least, I didn't think so. I closed my eyes, trying to expand my senses, looking for any noise or smell that might lead me in a direction... but I was coming up blank. Well, up it was.

I jumped up, grabbing the lowest branch. I wrapped both hands around the branch like a hug, facing the trunk of the tree. Swinging my body forward, I pushed off with my arms and used the momentum as I ran up the trunk of the tree. Twisting my body back toward the branch, I swung one leg over to straddle the limb. A dull pain registered in my pelvis, and I leaned back against the tree, taking a deep breath. Tears welled in my eyes as a flash of recent events invaded my thoughts. I pressed the palms of my hands against my eyes, attempting to push back the emotions and sobs threatening to leak out. *I will not break. I will not break. I will not break.* I repeated the mantra in a whisper... at least not right now. Focus. First, figure out where I was, so I could get the fuck out of here.

Bracing my hands against the trunk of the tree at my back, I stood slowly. Leaning to the side, I reached out and grabbed the adjacent branch, and lept. A small gust of air escaped as my stomach collided while my legs swung freely underneath. Hoisting myself up, I continued to climb the uneven branches until they were too thin for me to continue. Looking down and a slight wave of dizziness hit as I realized how far up I was. Holding on, I turned my body as I looked for a view through the leaves. Squinting in the darkness, my vision sharpened as I concentrated on the surrounding landscape. As I searched for anything recognizable, my spirits started sliding until I spotted a familiar rock formation jutting out from a mountainside. My heart rate picked up as I realized it was a place Jax and I used to hike to and meet my dad during hunting trips. The rendezvous spot was about one mile from my dad's hunting cabin. I nearly jumped up and down with glee, but I was in a tree, so I settled for a fist pump to myself. Climbing down as quickly as I could, I swung from the last limb and landed in a crouch.

As I turned to take off toward the cabin, a series of yips and howls ripped through the air. A chill rippled down my spine and I grabbed the poker I'd left leaning against the base of the tree. I was certain a pack of coyotes were hunting not far from here, but was unsure how close they were. Thank goodness their excited howls were in the opposite direction I was headed. I took off at a fast clip, not interested to see if they got any closer. Only able to move at a slow jog, I tried to keep a decent pace. My feet and hands were so cold, a prickling sensation was running through them.

A good twenty minutes passed, and the ground started becoming rockier, indicating the cliffs should be close. My heightened night vision made navigating the forest easier. At least I wasn't running into trees or stubbing my feet on any of the large rocks protruding from the ground. It was too bad my newfound strengths didn't include manifesting shoes. The bottoms of my feet were throbbing, and I was sure they were covered in cuts. Another howl sounded in the distance behind me. They were clearly getting closer, and now that I'd thought about the cuts on my feet, it reinforced the thought that they were probably tracking me. *Fuck.* I tried to pick up my pace, but my feet were so cold and sore, it was hard. My energy level was waning, and if I didn't make it to the cabin soon, I might end up as their dinner guest. And not in a good way.

I reached the base of the cliff just as a loud series of yips started. They were much closer than I'd hoped. The eerie sound raised the hair on my neck and a shiver vibrated through my body. Even if I wasn't being hunted, I'd never liked that noise. They sounded like a group of little children screaming from their short distance away. Truly unnerving. My heart raced, there was no way I was going to fight off a pack of coyotes. And I highly doubted I'd outrun them to the cabin at this point. My only option seemed to be up.

Quickly surveying the cliff side, I tried to map out the easiest route. Just like the climbing wall at the gym... yeah, right. Except there was no safety rope and a pack of hungry coyotes waited for me to slip. *I was so going to die.* But I hadn't made it this far just to quit. Swallowing down my negative thoughts, I closed my eyes briefly. *I would not die here. I was getting my brother and making the Gregoris pay for destroying my family.* My eyes popped open with a new resolve. I headed toward the left of the cliff face. If I could climb the first twelve feet, there was a small ledge that ran along this side of the mountain. Another howl rent the air—much too close. I reached out and started pulling myself up. Finding footholds without shoes fucking sucked. My toenails scratched into the stone painfully as I tried to find purchase. I'd be lucky to have any left by the time I reached the top.

My hands reached the first ledge, and a small smile curved my lips. Just as I slid one leg onto the ledge, I gasped as a sharp pain registered in my opposite foot and panic had my body tightening in fear. The weight of the coyote dangling with my foot in its mouth was dragging me down. A high-pitched scream left my lips as I fought to hold on to the ledge. The coyote was growling fiercely as it tried to shake its head back and forth, using its weight to gain a meal. White hot pain seared through me as my skin shredded from the jagged teeth embedded in my foot. The rest of the pack had reached the area below me and the howls, growls, and yips were nearly deafening.

Gripping the edge of the ledge, I held on with one hand and wrenched myself toward the rock face. The pulling and tearing sensation were so painful, it caused my vision to darken as little black spots started floating around the periphery. Sharp pants burst from my lungs as I fought the urge to pass out. Grabbing for the poker I'd hung from my belt loop; I yanked it free. Reaching back as far as the rock wall would allow, I swung as I bellowed a warrior cry. But that motherfucker would not quit. I repeatedly bashed the coyote for an unknown amount of time until it finally let go, falling to the ground. Weakly pulling my leg up, I grabbed my foot as the blood seeped through my fingers. A whimper leaked out, then I was gulping back a sob as my body shook with a mixture of fear, pain, and adrenaline. The smell of my blood oozing down the rocks sent the rest of the pack into a frenzy. They continued jumping while screeching their ungodly noises, trying to reach me. At least I'd made it high enough where I'd be safe for now. With my blood loss and the night's events, my energy was waning drastically, and I shivered uncontrollably.

I had to make the bleeding stop before I could go any further. Tearing off a strip of cloth from the flannel shirt I was wearing, I wrapped it around my foot and tied a knot on the top. The pressure initially caused another sharp pain that had more tears streaming down my cheeks, but it was now fading to a dull throb. My body wasn't healing as it had been earlier tonight, probably due to copious blood loss. Sweat beaded my brow as a wave of dizziness hit. Great timing for my newfound strength and ability to quit. I briefly wondered about what was wrong with me and wished I knew. Snapping my thoughts back to the present, I mentally scolded myself. I needed to focus. This was going to have to work until I could get to the cabin. Dad always kept a fully stocked first aid kit there. I only hoped I could make it.

After a few deep breaths, the spinning slowed, and I found my resolve. I stood on shaky legs. If I stayed here, I'd die. Holding onto the rock face, trying to steady myself, I searched for the footholds I'd originally planned out. Finding what I was looking for, I reached down and grabbed the poker I'd left lying at my feet. Probably better to take this. There was no telling if I'd need it again. After sliding the poker back through the loophole in my jeans, I began slowly making my way upward. My body shook with exertion as I tried to block out the frantic coyotes below. Each time my feet or fingers slipped, causing pebbles to fall, they resumed their cheers, hoping to see me plummet. I briefly thought of the gladiator shows that used to play on TV. Only there were no cheers of encouragement and no mat to catch my fall. Just cheers of demise and death. Jerks.

My body and limbs ached with effort as I closed in the distance to the top. I was so close now, only a few feet to go. Reaching out to my right, my fingertips just brushed past the next handhold. I quickly pulled my hand back to its starting position and tried to steady myself. I exhaled and reached out again, trying to stretch my arm just a little more. My fingertips just reached, and I curled them to increase my hold, but my nails barely scratched the stone surface before the rock started breaking apart, crumbling out of my grasp. A small squeak left my lips as my body swung backward, my left hand and foot still holding. With all my effort, I pushed my muscles to move back against the stone. Once I'd stilled, I sent up a small prayer of thanks that I hadn't fallen. I chanced a glance down and saw the coyotes circling and jumping wildly at the base of the cliff far below.

The sun hadn't fully risen yet, but the pre-dawn light was making things clearer. I saw another small crevice in the stone a little bit above me. I'd have to swing out and push upward with my legs at the same time if I was going to reach it. And if I could make it, I'd literally be less than two feet from the top. A small glimmer of hope bloomed inside me. Almost there, I was going to make it.

Now or never. Pushing out and up simultaneously, I grunted as my eyes locked on my target. My arms stretched out achingly as my body arced through the air. A moment of weightlessness was my only peace as I slammed painfully into the rock. A gust of air burst from my lungs as I scrambled to grip... anything. I'd overshot my target, giving myself nowhere to place my feet. My fingers dug into the small shards of shale sticking out from the cliff. As my lower body swung forward, bouncing off the stone, the momentum jerked my arms, causing my fingertips to slip.

"No!" I squeaked out as my right hand lost its grip. My feet were scratching at the stone, and I ignored the feeling of a toenail ripping painfully away as I tried desperately not to fall.

Holding on for dear life, quite literally, I reached up with my right hand. My body was shaking violently with effort, and sweat dripped into my eyes and down my back. Just as I found a ridge with the fingertips of my right hand, the stone beneath my left crumbled. An audible gasp ripped up my throat and my body slid down the sharp stones and off of the cliff. For the second time tonight, I was airborne. Not being able to accept my fate, I pinwheeled my arms, mainly out of reflex. A strong hand darted out from the top of the cliff, grabbing mine in midair. The hand gripped mine firmly, and my shoulder protested from the sudden stop in trajectory as my body crashed into the unforgiving rocks. I was so shocked and exhausted I just hung there, dangling over my dinner companions.

As I was slowly lifted, I stretched up and gripped the hand, holding on with every last drop of energy I had. I reached the top of the cliff and kept going. Tan work boots came into view first. As I continued to rise, my eyes tracked up a pair of thick thighs covered in old jeans. Then a white, ribbed tank top, marred with dirt and grime that was stretched over a broad chest. A strained neck, and the handsome face attached had a square jaw covered in a light brown scruff. The matching hair had a messy look; almost like an overgrown buzz cut, which was in total disarray. I stared straight ahead into a pair of kind brown eyes, and it took me a moment to realize my feet had yet to hit the ground. He was literally holding me by one arm suspended in front of him.

Starting to squirm, a puzzled look took over his features before his eyes widened in realization and he set me down. I winced and let out a hiss as my feet touched the ground, immediately sitting down. Sparkles fluttered in my vision, and I tried taking deep breaths. The young man bent his knees and squatted in front of me, lightly gripping my shoulders.

"Miss? You OK? You don't look so good." He glanced around as if looking for help. "Shit," he muttered. "Uh, what's your name?" he asked, turning back toward me. I scowled at him, wondering why his face was doing the Scooby-Do wave and black spots were now closing in around him. "Hey, Miss! What's your name?" he shouted as he gently shook me.

"I'm not fucking deaf," I slurred out as the world spun a little. A grin curved his lips, and he repeated his question once more, adding "I'm Mason." I reached out with both hands, trying to hold him still. I wished he'd stop moving back and forth like that. "Max," I muttered, just before everything faded to black.

Chapter 31

Elias

I was almost giddy with all the new information and possibilities before me. My mind was spinning as we continued to tour the underground facility. Dr. Heller, along with a few other scientists in our western facilities, had been working on tissue manipulation and regeneration for over twenty years. I was finding out about so many amazing accomplishments as we wandered through the corridors. Some of the most advanced experiments were happening within the catacombs below my home! Astonishing. The majority of successful cases were with the individuals kept below my father's mountain. My mountain now. My father had had no conscience, pushing everything to its limits. Clearly, even using his own flesh and blood hadn't stopped his desire for results. My hatred for the man still festered, even with my newfound strengths—which I clearly owed to him. And the direct introduction of Red over the last month had boosted my results even further. But looking over the data from our multiple locations, it was clear most of the success was here. But why?

Dr. Heller filled me in on our contract with the military as we continued down, yet another hallway lined with cells. I had no idea how many people were being experimented on down here. I'd had theories, but until today, it was clear I had underestimated them.

"The direct introduction of Red has increased our results substantially," Heller continued. "The subject you'll see next successfully bonded with multiple strands of animal DNA. Our military has requested an advancement in human defenses. Cam, as we like to call him, has just recently had success with chameleon DNA. This allows him to blend in with the surrounding environment, masking his appearance. Our previous attempts also included splicing porcupine DNA. It would have provided him with the obvious defensive quills, but we've yet to see results with those endeavors." He stopped us in front of a ten-by-ten brick cell with a sliding metal cage door. I moved forward as I peered into the empty cell, confused as I searched for its occupant.

Jonas stepped up to my side and shoved me a step backward. As I scowled up at him, the corner of my eye caught movement. An arm stretched through the bars but stopped just shy of reaching us. My eyebrows shot up as the rest of the man came into view. He was tall and thin, but muscular. The sinew was visible in his arm as it stretched through the bars. His hair was deep brown and shaggy around his almost gaunt and angular face. His brown eyes bulged just slightly, but it was the feral look in them that caught my attention. They should have disturbed me, but they didn't. I tilted my head, studying them for a moment. I could feel my mind reaching out to touch his. His hate for this place, for the doctor and for me radiated loud and clear. A sliver of worry touched my mind and an image of children behind bars fluttered behind my eyes. Exhaling sharply, my own eyes widened.

"I should've warned you not to get too close," Dr. Heller chuckled. "Like I said, we've recently begun seeing, and I use that term lightly here, more successful cases." The doctor smirked at his witty remark. "Cam's been with us for some time and apparently needs a reminder of guest etiquette." he said, scowling as Cam growled at him. "Please follow me. We have much more to show you."

The doctor had clearly missed our little interaction. Had anyone noticed? I looked around at the two guards flanking us and up to Jonas. No one seemed to have noticed our strange exchange. My eyebrows drew together, and I looked back over at the man behind the bars. A shimmer of fear flitted across his features before his scowl darkened as he backed away, fading into his surroundings. He was aware of the exchange, but no one else. Incredible.

A strange sense of power filled me from that quick look of fear, and I liked it. I wasn't certain what had happened back there, and my mind twirled with ideas. It wasn't until we rounded a corner and advanced down yet another hallway that I realized I must have read his thoughts.

This new corridor of cells was slightly different. There were two large rooms, one on either side of the hall. They had solid metal doors with windows lined with mesh to peer through. Looking inside, each room had three sets of bunk beds. In one room, six children, with ages varying from three to around ten, peered back from a central gathering on the floor. It looked as though they were playing a game or participating in a learning lesson. The room across the hall was similar, but with only four children. The children that peered back from the second room rang with familiarity. Although I'd never seen these children before, images of their faces flashed through my mind as I recalled the memory from just moments ago. Someone else's memory, Cam's memory. Well, how interesting. I grinned and a shiver of pleasure trickled down my spine. I stood a little taller.

I was so lost in my thoughts that I only just caught the end of what Dr. Heller was saying. I tried to follow up with what I'd retained from his little speech.

"So, some of these children were born here?" My voice rose with curiosity.

"Yes, we've had several fertility and embryonic projects in past years. Few were successful. Some of the children we... acquired. Our cellular bonding seems to work better with children. Perhaps because their bodies are still growing and are more receptive to changes. Also, the longer our patients are retained at the core of this facility, the better our results. We have found that this location produces extraordinary results due to unusual terrestrial radiation. Thus, the discovery of Red encased in the mountain has opened many new doorways as well as an explanation for the radiation, to an extent. Where or why the Red is specific to this location, we're still learning. We've added another team that is actively exploring the caves, and this mountain. We halted previous exploration due to some––

complications." He frowned as he rubbed his chin. "Unfortunately, we've lost communication with new team as well. The tunnels are intricate and vast, over 1000 feet below us, and radio frequency is not optimal." Interesting. "However," he waved his hand in the air, "progress in the maternity ward here has slowed due to infertility. We have found as women progress with the experiments, or the longer their stay here, the less fertile they become." He paused for a few moments. "Also, conception seems to require a more natural method for success. And our participants are, how do I say? Somewhat reluctant. Certain medications have been required to assist in this matter. The mothers rarely survive the birth of the child. But we have had some successful cases. The children to your left were all born here, as well as a handful of others that were in the original trials." My brows furrowed with thought.

"How long ago were the original trials?" I asked.

The doctor took a deep breath and let it out through his nose. "The embryonic manipulation program, or EMP, if you will, started approximately thirty years ago."

My eyebrows shot into my hairline. "Thirty years ago?"

"Yes, Mr. Gregori. Your father had already established the facility under more acceptable pretenses. Gearing our scientific research toward the rich and powerful in the event of a cataclysmic disaster. It was through our findings and manipulation of plant cells that we discovered...other avenues. Quite honestly, I believe it was the birth of you and your brother that drove your father to seek more aggressive advancements in cell and tissue manipulation." I stood stunned. I hadn't considered that all this was because of us. The doctor made eye contact with me, and my senses flared as I locked onto his stare.

Visions–no, memories–flashed through my mind. My father, at the head of a table, every seat surrounding the table filled. I only found a few faces familiar. One face I recognized was Maxine's mother. Mrs. Devins sat stoically in her white lab coat as my father's face turned beat red as he yelled and slammed his fist on the table.

"There will be no limitations." He jabbed a finger at each person in the room. "You will explore ALL avenues. I will not have my own flesh and blood be an embarrassment to the Gregori name!" Spittle flew from his mouth as he ranted.

"The government has laws against what you are suggesting, Mr. Gregori." Mrs. Devins replied. My father's dark gaze flew to hers and his voice lowered an octave.

"I'm fully aware of the laws, Mrs. Devins. I've spoken with the joint chiefs of staff and the head of defense for this great country—we will have no barriers. The laws will no longer apply to us. I've garnered a contract to provide our military with advancements that are unprecedented. I've offered my own children for cell regeneration research to assure them we are serious. They are discreetly allotting us a great deal of money. The government is aiding us in any and all requirements, including an unlimited number of children and medications from anywhere in the world. You are all now privy to, and responsible for, the best advancements known to man. But make no mistake, this and our sister facility are secure as well as your access. Any breach of security or leak of information will not only result in your death, but your family's as well." Mrs. Devins' face paled at the threat, as did the rest of the table's occupants. "Dr. Heller," my father boomed, turning his gaze toward me, and it took me a moment to remember this was not my memory. "Whatever you need, you will get it. I expect a list of requests on my desk by Friday. Now, I suggest you address your staff accordingly. We may have to split your team to provide the best results and use of our southern facility."

My vision came back to my own, and I shook with adrenaline. No one seemed to have noticed the exchange that had just happened, except Jonas. He stepped forward, placing a hand on my shoulder. I was positive he just caught my body language, but I'd have to discuss what had truly transpired with him later. I wondered if he'd ever had a similar experience. The doctor was completely unaware, he'd just shown me a glimpse of the past. *So, apparently, I could see memories? What the fuck?* Questions and possibilities flooded my mind.

I followed Dr. Heller and the guards down the hallway on autopilot. I could not wrap my head around my newest ability or what had transpired below my home all these years. All the secrets were unraveling before me.

Secrets that were now mine. There was so much to learn, and I had so many questions. But my personal experience was at the forefront, and I was very curious.

"Dr. Heller, have any of your experiments produced abilities? Other than regeneration, of course," I asked. He reached up and tapped his chin while pursing his lips for a moment.

"It's funny you should ask. We've seen a few unexplained phenomena resulting from certain... modifications." His shrewd gaze scanned my body up and down. "We became aware of them about eight to ten years after the initiation of the program. Most of these resulted in terminations. They were uncontrollable. Your father had an issue a while back with... a project. So, after that, all subjects showing signs of such were terminated." I scowled, meeting the man's eyes once more and an image of a young woman popped into my head, but disappeared just as fast. Her features were vaguely familiar, but I didn't have time right now. I'd have to remember to revisit that later. As my mind raced with questions and possibilities, a wave of dizziness overcame me. I wobbled on my feet for a moment and Jonas grabbed my arm, keeping me vertical.

The doctor's keen gaze looked over my face and then to the arm holding me up.

"Have you eaten today, Sir? When was your last treatment?" he asked quietly.

I tried to focus on his face to answer his questions, but I was suddenly so weak I had trouble forming words. He nodded his head in understanding.

"Come with me." He left no room for argument as he turned on his heel and headed down the hall. Jonas practically carried me down the hall, following the doctor. This was fucking humiliating. All my progress and now my brother was back to carrying me. I was so weak; I barely had the energy to hate myself. He paused in a doorway when we heard a moan. My eyes were having trouble focusing, but there was clearly a body strapped to a table.

"Whaaa sss thaa?" I slurred out. Jonas looked down at me.

"Jax."

My legs nearly rubber and shaking so badly, Jonas held all my weight. I could barely put a coherent thought together, let alone the pieces of this puzzle.

"Bring him here, now," the doctor ordered from the doorway of the next room. Jonas immediately started walking, holding up my limp body. I collapsed onto a bed and Jonas lifted my legs, straightening me out to a slightly more comfortable position. The doctor's face appeared above me.

"Have you been experiencing these lulls frequently?" I shook my head... at least I thought I did. Fantastic, now I was having trouble simply moving my head? I lie there seething, unable to even utter a simple response.

The doctor sighed. "Your specific treatments were modified throughout your childhood. The newest doses containing the concentrated Red were only recently. It was your father's request, before he passed. Unfortunately, this may require more frequent doses than the previously researched formulas; it's more potent but will not last as long." He pulled out two separate vials from a small refrigerator built into the counter. One had a blue liquid, and the other a bright red liquid that almost glowed. It was so bright. Hell, maybe it was glowing.

He unwrapped a sterile syringe from the drawer beneath the counter and withdrew his specific doses from each bottle. As he neared the table, Jonas let out a low growl. I patted his hand the best I could, never taking my eyes off the Doc. He pushed up the sleeve on my left arm and wiped the spot above the crook of my elbow with an alcohol wipe. The cool sensation registered as the syringe neared my arm. I noticed how the mixture of blue and red made a strange combination. The color had turned a vivid purple that also seemed to glow, just like the red substance.

I watched as the plunger depressed the liquid into my vein. Within minutes, the fog in my brain began to lift. My body, however, was taking its sweet time. As I laid there, my brain ran a hundred miles a minute. A renewed anger grew inside of me. Anger at my father, at this program, and at myself for being so weak. The anger swirled and turned to rage as it boiled inside as I waited for my body to respond. I needed a permanent fix. And Dr. Heller would give it to me. No more waiting.

With a permanent fix, I wouldn't need constant treatments. I could have a life without weakness. I could have all this power and strength, and I'd know everyone's deepest secrets. I would be invincible. And I would have Max at my side. Warmth spread through my body, thinking about all the things I could do with her, to her. There were so many possibilities running through my head. She would grow to love me. She'd never be able to hide any secrets or lie to me like my family had done my entire life. I would make her perfect, and Dr. Heller was going to help me.

Now thinking of Max, where the fuck was she? I couldn't stand how slowly time ticked by. I wanted to run my hands over her perfect body, to smell her skin, to drag my fingers through her blonde curls, to have her love me forever. A frustrated growl rolled up my chest. *Where was she?* Eddie was supposed to have brought her in already. My fists clenched and I scowled. What time was it? No matter. I was done waiting, if only my body would cooperate.

"Jonas, get a hold of Eddie and find out where the hell he is with my delivery." I barked, my voice getting stronger by the minute. I was sure she would love me now that the doctor had changed me. I wanted her almost more than air itself. She would be my happiness. A happiness that had been missing since my mother died.

As soon as I could get vertical, I would take my life to the next level. I refused to be a victim any longer. I refused to be weak any longer. This world would be mine, and Max would be at my side to rule it with me.

"Doctor Heller! Get your staff together. Come to a solution for my situation. NOW. I am done waiting." I would accomplish what my father couldn't. This facility and everything in it was mine now. And things were going to change.

Chapter 32

Maxine

My whole body ached, but pain wasn't the only thing I felt as I slowly came awake. My stomach cramped with a stabbing sensation and a hunger unlike anything I'd felt before. It was as if I could feel myself dying. I couldn't make sense of it, but I needed to eat—now. I remained still and fought through the pain. Focusing on my breaths to stay as slow as possible, and not alert anyone that may be near, I panicked... where the hell was I now?

Without opening my eyes, I reached out with my other senses. I no longer felt the collar around my neck or the shackles around my wrists and ankles. A familiar scent invaded my nose, reminding me of family, of home. It calmed me slightly, then I realized I was lying on something soft and that I was warm. The crackling noise of a fire filled my ears before I heard the scrape of a chair sliding across the floor. Still, I remained unmoving, even if my heart was jack hammering in my chest. The cramping in my stomach was almost too much to bear as I laid there, and sweat was beading on my upper lip. If it was Eddie, I might only have one chance to get away, and I didn't want to blow it. My rising anxiety made my heart feel like it was going to beat out of my chest as my brain screamed for me to run.

Footsteps slowly made their way toward me. I tried not to twitch, not to make a move, as my flight instincts flared and fear gripped my thoughts.

"I know you're awake, your breathing has changed." A smooth, male voice said, interrupting the silence. Stiffening, I realized his nearness. "I'm not going to hurt you. I'm not sure if you remember me, but I helped you up the cliff. You were pretty banged up, so I brought you back here to rest."

His steps paused, keeping his distance. My mind raced. His words sounded calm and true. I wasn't sure how I could tell, but I was confident he wasn't lying to me. I searched my memories, but they were blurry. A kind face popped into my head, and I opened my eyes.

"Mason?" I whispered, my voice raspy and my throat dry.

"You remember." I could hear a smile in his voice, even though he still didn't move closer. I sat up, realizing I was on a couch. Pulling the blanket that was over me up to my chin with a tight fist, I looked at the stranger. He stood just on the other side of the couch, arms down at his sides, palms up in a non-threatening gesture. He looked to be about six feet tall and was built like a football player. Big shoulders and biceps stuck out of his white wife-beater tank. The tank was tucked into a pair of old, worn jeans and some basic tan work boots covered his feet. His light brown hair was messy, as if he'd been running his hands through the short length. A crease of worry ran between kind, brown eyes and a small reassuring smile curved his lips just above the dimple in his chin.

I didn't feel any threat radiating from him, so I chanced taking my eyes off him and glanced around for a door or windows. Knowing where the exits were made me feel like I had options. I needed options. The room was lit by the soft glow of sunlight coming through the windows. I must have been out a few hours, tops. Unless it was the next day. Fuck.

Really looking at my surroundings now, and not just the exits, I took in the familiar cabin and gasped. My father's cabin.

"Who are you? And how did you end up here?" I asked, slightly panicked as I scowled. *Maybe he's a squatter? But how the hell did he end up out here? Our cabin is remote, and only a handful of people know where it is.*

"Like I said, my name is Mason. What were you doing in the woods alone? And climbing without gear? You were nearly dinner for the coyotes," he retorted, evading my questions. My blood started to heat with my annoyance and the slight bit of gratitude I had for him saving me waned. Why was he avoiding my questions? I wasn't sure I had the energy to fight if this situation turned on me. At that thought, I recalled my father had a few weapons stashed here. There was a pistol on the top shelf in the closet and a hunting rifle under the floorboard in the back bedroom. Since he was standing in front of the closet, bedroom it was.

"I need to use the bathroom." I stood, dropping the blanket, and started backing slowly toward the hall. His eyebrows lowered in suspicion, and he took a step forward. I stiffened at his movement and we both froze, our eyes locked on each other. I watched his body tighten to spring in the event of my continued movement and bristled at the almost imperceptible threat. My heart rate picked up to a building staccato, I could feel my pulse in my eardrums. My mind raced; I refused to be locked in another cabin, even if it was mine. He would not lay a hand on me without one hell of a fight. He would have to kill me if he thought he was going to keep me here. A red haze began clouding my vision.

He must have seen something on my face during our standoff and raised his hands up slowly, palms out. But I was too far into my own thoughts, and instinct was taking over. I dropped my chin and a growl rumbled up my chest. His eyes widened at my threat.

"Wait…" It was the only thing he managed to get out before I launched myself into the air. I dove, arms out, over the back of the couch, tucking into a summersault, and popped up to his right. I swung my fist out toward his head, but he was fast. He caught my wrist before I could make contact and yanked me forward. I stumbled and threw my other hand out to shove him, but he grabbed that too. His hands were like vices as they clamped down on my wrists and a wave of panic rushed up my neck. I did the only thing I could think of and used the momentum to leap forward. Wrapping my legs around his waist, I twisted my ankles together behind his back and squeezed. The air whooshed out of his mouth with a grunt and an audible crack sounded. He dropped to his knees, but I didn't let go. Adrenaline was running my body now, and my instincts were fully in control. My head reared back, and a roar ripped up my throat. I jerked forward and sank my teeth into his shoulder. A short howl of pain burst from Mason's mouth, and I tightened my legs. I closed my eyes and swallowed down his blood as it pooled in my mouth, warmth spreading through my body. I took greedy pulls at the wound, my hunger driving me. Tingling sensations swept over my skin, the cuts and bruises beginning to heal.

My strength wasn't returning like last time, though. And the taste differed from Garron's blood—diluted somehow. I whimpered as thoughts of him flickered through my mind. Missing the richness, the power, and the warmth that he had seeped into my soul.

A deep moan sounded in my ear as I swallowed another mouthful. I just now realized the hands that had held my wrists were on both sides of my waist now and evidence of his pleasure was pressing against my core. *No. No. No!!* I tore my mouth away from his shoulder, simultaneously releasing my legs and pushed him away. He fell forward onto his hands, head bowed forward, sucking in deep pants of air. I scrambled backward, only stopping when my back slammed into the back of the couch.

"I... oh God. I'm sorry..." I choked out. Head still bowed; Mason raised his hand up in a waiting gesture. He tried to speak, but coughed instead, wrapping his hand and arm around his waist. "I'm so sorry," I repeated as I covered my mouth, mortified by what had just happened. He tried again to choke out words, but I could barely make out what he was saying.

"Garron," he rasped out. My eyes grew wide, and I sucked in a breath. *How did he know I was thinking about Garron??*

"Wh-what?" I stuttered out, shocked at his words. His voice was so raspy, I wasn't sure I'd heard correctly. Maybe I was wrong, but I thought he said Garron. But how? Why? He coughed a few times, arm still around his waist, and raised his head. Brown eyes met mine and a sparkle of red flashed through his irises. *Holy Shit.* I stared as I started connecting the dots.

"You're one of the kids," I squeaked out in a high-pitched whisper.

"Garron got us out, told us to stay here. We're not kids you know, we're legal adults. We can take care of ourselves. Well, I thought we could, til you showed up," he answered, a bit winded and with a small grin.

"Oh my God, and I... Jesus Christmas! I attacked and bit you. I'm sorry," I repeated, horrified. There was no way I could excuse what I'd done.

"I'm OK. I think you may have cracked a rib and ruptured one of my kidneys, but I'm OK." He said with a snort, then grimaced. "We heal faster now," he said while still sucking in short breaths of air. He sat back, still on his knees, pulling his shoulders back to stretch. His eyes closed, and a grimace lined his face. My gaze flicked to his shoulder and the wound I'd created. Shame filled me as I watched rivulets of blood drip down his arm.

As I watched the blood slowly seep from the wound and merge into little pathways, it rolled down his arm like tiny tidal waves. Heat tingled through my veins. His taste still lingered... and I was still hungry. I couldn't help licking my lips.

Mason's head was bowed, with his hands resting on his knees as he tried to take deeper breaths. It almost looked like he was offering himself to me... maybe he was. A part of me was screaming for me to go, to leave this man and back away. But the hunger, and the new monster inside me, was dominating my body. I leaned forward slowly, to not attract attention. Like a predator, I stalked my prey, my eyes never leaving the wound as I inched forward silently.

As I closed the distance, now mere inches from my meal, the door to the cabin burst open. Mason's head shot up at the noise, and I twisted toward the intrusion.

"What the fuck? Mase! You get away from him!" a young woman shouted as she ground to a halt just two steps into the room.

A feral growl left my lips as I assessed the new threat. She was about five foot six with red hair that glittered copper as the sun shimmered in the open doorway. She was wearing a black t-shirt that read 'Disturbed' over black leggings and a pair of old Puma sneakers. The almond-shaped eyes that sat above her freckled cheeks flicked from me to Mason and back, and she widened her stance. Red flickered through the light golden brown in her eyes as she returned my growl with one of her own.

"Get away from Mason, now," she ground out, fists clenched.

"Bell, don't..." Mason coughed out.

But it was too late. She moved. I jumped up as she started sprinting forward. Her hands darted out to grab me as she lunged, but I was too fast. Mason's blood had renewed some of my energy, strength, and speed. I spun to her right as if I was pirouetting and landed a kick to the center of her back as she passed by. She hit the floor stomach first and slid as if she was on a slip-n-slide. Mason staggered to his feet and stepped between us. The girl sprang to her feet and spun back toward me, a sneer curling her lip. She lunged forward again, but this time Mason blocked her forward motion with an outstretched arm.

"I'll kill her for hurting you," she growled out, thrashing against his hold now that he'd curled her into his chest.

"Bell, I'm OK. Just calm down. I'm OK, seriously," Mason spoke pacifyingly in her ear, trying to calm her.

I'd just straightened my stance and started to relax when two arms wrapped around my torso, pinning my hands to my side. A shriek left me from the surprise attack, and I immediately bent forward, pulling my assailant over my back. I tossed my body to the side and threw all my weight on top of whomever had grabbed me. Just as we landed, me on top, I slammed the back of my head into the person's face.

A pained "Fuck!" left a man's mouth as he let go. I rolled to the side and scrambled to my feet, crouching in defense. The young man rolled to his knees with his hands covering his nose.

"Crazy bitch, you broke my nose!" he blurted out, a muffled complaint through his cupped hands.

"Easy, everybody! Easy!" Mason yelled, and he moved between the girl and me again. "Guys, this is Jax's sister. The one Garron went to look for," he explained.

"Then where is Garron?" the girl asked, confusion and worry lining her face.

"I don't know. Haven't gotten that far yet. Everything kind of... exploded before I could really ask," Mason replied. "Let's start simple." he turned back to face me. "You already know I'm Mason. This is Bella," he said, turning and pulling her under his arm. "And that," he pointed to the young man on the floor, "is Trent." He moved toward the kitchen table and seated Bella, before plopping down into a chair himself. I shifted my body to keep Trent in my line of sight and sidestepped toward the table. "You can trust us; we're not going to hurt you." Mason said as he rubbed his hand up and down Bella's arm as if to make sure she understood.

Trent stood and slowly plodded toward the kitchen. He was tall, maybe an inch or so taller than Mason, but with a leaner build. His black hair was buzzed tight on the sides and seemed just a bit longer than skull trim on top. His dark, almost black eyes were framed with thick eyebrows that were drawn together. He glanced back at me as he made his way around the kitchen, clearly unhappy. The goatee framing his angular jaw and his narrow nose gave him a mischievous appearance. Droplets of blood stood out on his pale, defined chest and abs as the flannel shirt he wore was unbuttoned. The black, military style pants hung loose above his hips, tightened with a belt, as if he was trying to keep them from falling off his slender frame. His feet were adorned with filthy, used-to-be-white slip ons.

My gaze traveled over all of them as Trent grabbed a towel from the kitchen drawer and started cleaning himself up at the sink. All their clothes looked so familiar.

"How long have you been here?" I asked.

Mason spoke up first. "A few days. And I see your curiosity as you're looking us over. We borrowed some toiletries to clean up a bit, and the clothes from the dressers and closet here. We plan on replacing them when..."

"You don't need to replace them." I smiled, waving my hand in the air, hoping it helped make peace. The two now seated at the table seemed calm enough, but I was keeping an eye on Trent. "They're here in case we ever got stuck out here or lengthened our stay. I'm glad they were useful."

Trent brought the percolator to the table, and set a steaming mug of coffee in front of Bella. The smell of coffee wafted through the cabin. It smelled wonderful. She smiled up at him, love shining in her features.

"Thanks," she said quietly, and he smiled back.

They looked so sweet and young with their smiles briefly showing. I found myself grinning, enjoying their momentary happiness. I kept my body still and moved my eyes. Mason had been quiet through their exchange, and I was a bit curious about their relationship. Mason didn't smile as our eyes met. He was watching me, watching them.

"Maxine, right?" he asked, but continued talking before I could answer. "Can we offer you a cup? Please," he gestured to an empty chair. "I think we have a lot to talk about." Trent walked out to the porch and brought back two skinned rabbits.

"We thought you might be hungry when you woke up, and I didn't want you eating us." He scowled at me, then looked over at Mason's shoulder that was already healing, with an 'I told you so' smirk. He set the rabbits in the sink and started cleaning them. My cheeks heated with embarrassment.

"I'm so sorry about that. I really don't know what's wrong with me. I thought I was sick until Garron explained a few things. I'm still not sure what's going on. I mean, it's crazy, right?"

"It's OK. We've been struggling with the same thing. Your case is a bit different; I imagine. I don't know how you became infected, but you smell different than we do." I cocked my head in question as he continued. "We were exposed, along with your brother, when we tried to save some idiot who wrecked his truck while trespassing," Mason scowled.

Bella picked up where he stopped. "Jax helped us get the guy to the emergency room, then we all got locked up. They said they had to quarantine us. But it was their way of fucking us up even more. I don't think they were giving us medicine to make us better. We think it was the opposite. They've been locking kids up, doing horrible things to people for a really long time."

I shook my head. These poor kids. I couldn't imagine the horrors they'd gone through. Even if it was only a fraction of what Garron had told me about, it was too much.

"I'm so glad you guys made it out. Did you see my brother? Was he OK?" Hope bubbled in my question.

Trent spoke up this time, his tone somber, "We split up in the tunnels. He was trying to bait the guards to lead them away from us. We didn't see him again after that." He paused, then looked in my eyes as he sat down next to Bella. "Why isn't Garron with you?" Worry lined his face—worry lined all their faces as they stared at me, anxiously waiting for my response.

Tears filled my eyes as his handsome face flickered across my mind. The lump in my throat threatened to choke me. He had been going to help these three get away from there. Now they had no one. They couldn't go back to that school. What the hell were they supposed to do? I rested my elbows on the table and dropped my face into my hands. I let out a shaky breath and pushed my hair back from my face. Clearing my throat, I shook my head.

"They shot him. He was trying to protect me." A sob escaped me.

Bella clasped her hands over her mouth. Mason wrapped an arm around her shoulders, pulling her closer to him. Trent scooted closer to them both and rested his hand on Bella's arm, rubbing comforting circles with his thumb. I wiped the tears that leaked down my cheeks and massaged the ache in the center of my chest.

"He—He didn't make it." I choked back a sob. I could barely talk around the lump that had formed in my throat, and I swallowed hard. "But I swear on my life, I will do everything in my power to destroy those bastards. I'll bring that entire mountain down if I have to." Their tormented gazes flicked to mine, and I saw resolve forming. "I've gotta get my brother out first." I said, looking each one of them in the eye. "Will you guys help me?" I asked, knowing I shouldn't. They were just kids. No, they were adults. And they deserved their own retribution.

Bella's glare looked like cold steel as she reached down, taking each of her guys' hands. They took a second to look back and forth between each other in wordless conversation. Mason looked up from her eyes to meet mine. "We'll help you. But we need to get them all out."

Chapter 33

Maxine

After a quick, cold, but very needed shower, I grabbed an old pair of leggings and a long-sleeved T-shirt from the dresser in the back bedroom. We all sat at the table, discussing the lab and what transpired there for hours. The kids filled me in on the experiments they had been subjected to, as well as some other things they'd seen. Horrendous didn't even begin to touch on what was happening below the school and that mountain—Garron had shielded me from so many things. Nonetheless, his story had been terrifying and would haunt me for the rest of my days. But where his filter must have been an attempt to keep us both human, I was now filled with rage. These three kids' story had lifted the blinds. They took turns speaking about things they'd endured, seen and heard. So many people and children had been and still were, being subjected to unthinkable horrors. The Gregoris were playing God, and clearly making a profit from it, for well over twenty to thirty years; we guessed.

To think that my own mother had most likely been a part of their experiments. I felt like tearing my hair out. I felt like screaming until I had no voice. I felt... betrayed. All these years, I thought they'd killed her. She probably killed herself, knowing we'd never forgive her for what she'd done. For the first time in my life, I was thankful she was dead, and that my father had not found out what she had been doing. I hoped Jax hadn't found out either, but I knew that was just wishful thinking. God, what were they doing to him right now?

"We need a plan." I said with determination. "Can you three try to draw a map showing me how you all got out?" They looked at each other and nodded their heads in agreement. "We'll need weapons. You said the guards have tasers and guns. We'll need to be prepared to defend ourselves... and..." I looked at each of their faces. They weren't kids anymore. Not after all they'd been through—their innocence was gone. "Kill them if necessary," I finished. I rubbed my temples as the stress was causing a dull throb in my head. "We'll try to get as many out as we can. Then we'll destroy the lab." I thought about our options for a moment. "Frank has a small arsenal at the shop and most likely in his house." *Great, how are we going to get there?* I frowned. "Shit. I won't be able to show my face near there. Not only are the cops probably looking for me, but Eddie's crew will be too." They knew I'd try to go back there. It felt like acid was rolling in my stomach, just saying his name.

I swallowed against the lump in my throat and the small tremble in my hands, thinking about what happened to me, Garron, Cory, and Frank. *Keep it together.* I knotted my hands under the table, hoping I was concealing my nerves, and looked back up at the kids. "Aside from Eddie, the locals don't know you. You'll have to go to the shop, pretend like you're just stopping to buy hiking equipment. No one will suspect you." I waited for their collective nods. *Good.* "I'll give you directions to the shop and house, as well as the info I have on his supply rooms. I don't know much about the house, but I'm sure if you look hard enough, you'll find something useful, or explosive. If you meet a guy named Cory, tell him you're helping me and that I'm OK."

"What are you going to do?" Mason asked.

"Well, we only have two weapons here. What was that guy doing on the mountain that got you into this mess?" I pondered out loud.

"No clue. He was completely out of it. Kept rambling about helping his friend. I'm guessing the Gregoris sent someone to check it out?" Trent answered with a shrug.

"OK, well, I'll hike up and see if I can find anything useful. Only two reasons someone would be up there—logging or quarrying. Sometimes they have a few sticks of dynamite or maybe some equipment to help clear areas, maybe we'll get lucky. Then I'll scout the cave entrance in the old mining shaft."

"Don't go in without us," Trent said with a serious face. "There are... other things down there... things besides the guards to worry about."

I looked at Trent quizzically, my brows furrowed. "What do you mean?"

"I'm not sure. We could hear things scratching and groaning. And the smell..." they all wrinkled their noses.

"Something bad is down there," Mason concurred. "Please, just wait for us. We don't know what it was. We couldn't see anything. But whatever is down there smells wrong—or sick. It makes all the hair on my body stand up. I think we were being followed or hunted. Whatever it is, it's dangerous." They all looked at me wide-eyed. Bella's hands wrapped around her middle as if she was trying to fight off a chill.

"It's death," she whispered. Jesus, these kids were creeping me out.

"OK. Deal. I won't go in without you. Now, it's going to take several hours for you to get there and back with supplies. We'd better get a move on. I don't want my brother or those other people down there any longer if we can help it."

I grabbed a small cinch sack from the closet along with my dad's hunting knife. The knife had its own sheath, and I strapped it to my leg over my leggings. My old hiking boots were still in there, and I took them outside to shake out the leaves and dust them off. I rolled my eyes at myself for not taking better care before I put them away as I smacked them together, loosening the mud from the tread. Sliding my feet in and lacing them up, I headed back inside. My feet, scrapes and bruises had healed thanks to Mason's blood. Grabbing a water canteen, I filled it with spring water from the tap and threw it in the sack, along with a small flashlight.

We all wished each other luck and headed out in separate directions. I sent up a small prayer that they would make it back safely, and hopefully with something useful.

I paced myself as I hiked through the semi-familiar woods. It had been years since I'd been here, but most landmarks remained. My mind wandered back to my now healed body, amazed that my feet no longer hurt.

Apparently ingesting another infected person's blood accelerated the regeneration of tissue. It was interesting, and totally fucking crazy. Garron had mentioned a few things during his story that raised so many questions. We just hadn't had the time to dive that deep into discussions. And now, I guess we never would. The dull ache in my chest throbbed at the thought of him and a tear slipped down my cheek. I swiped it away harshly. Something deep inside told me I'd never be the same, never be whole again, body and heart. Pausing for a moment, I took a deep, shaky breath, and let it out slowly. I needed to stay focused, stay angry. I'd have time to mourn him after I got my brother out and destroyed that evil place for what they'd done. How could people have such disregard for human life?

But they weren't people. They were the Gregoris. And they employed filthy creeps like Eddie. I shivered as my stomach twisted at the thought of him. I had a slight feeling of satisfaction, thinking about him lying on the floor of that cabin as the blood leaked from his head. He'd deserved a worse death. But it's not like I'd ever want to see him for a redo. I hoped he enjoyed his special seat in hell. Filthy bastard.

I'd always thought it was just Nico. That Elias and Jonas were different. We'd been friends after all. Practically growing up together, I thought I knew them. We'd all played together as kids, at least when my mom had worked for their dad... before she died. Maybe they didn't know. But that couldn't be. They would have found out when Nico died, right? Of course, they would have. They would have been informed of all of Nico's business ventures. And they'd chosen to continue. To keep Jax prisoner. I hoped I was wrong. But if I was right, I wasn't sure how, but I'd make them pay.

I picked up my pace a little as I'd slowed with my trailing thoughts. The mountain range was turning rocky again. More cliffs would be up ahead. If I could reach that portion of the mountain range, the area where the men had been trying to quarry, or whatever they were doing, wouldn't be far. Hopefully, I could find something useful and scout out the cave entrance as well.

I made my way over fallen trees, my thighs burned with the uphill climb. I clearly needed more rest and a good meal. The rabbit had sated my appetite for now, but I needed more. But more what? My stomach felt full, but my body still ached with hunger. I pushed the need down, as I continued forward. A few small rock formations were ahead, and I made my way around them instead of climbing straight up. I had to be getting closer to the top by now.

A noise ahead had me slowing my steps. Growls and hissing started to drown out the other noises of the forest. Fierce howls grew louder the closer I got, but I couldn't make out what type of animal was causing the ruckus. I debated turning and finding another way around this portion of rock, but my curiosity got the better of me. As I climbed up a large boulder, I gripped the ledge that jutted out behind it. Holding on tight, I leaned around the rock formation. Cool air froze in my lungs as I tried to comprehend what I was seeing.

Chunks of hair and blood were scattered all over the flat surface of dirt and rock. The conjoined noises of the battling animals had fallen quiet as the victor sat on its prey. A large raccoon had its back to me—its fur was matted with dirt and blood. Bald patches showed sickly gray skin beneath as its body heaved with exertion. Smacking noises as it ate, and an odd type of purring emanated from where it perched on top of the mountain lion. *Jesus, that raccoon just killed a mountain lion? What the hell?* My cinch sack shifted with my lean and began slowly sliding off my back. I gasped and scurried to grab the bag. The pack never hit the ground, but the contents inside made a clanking noise, which drew the attention of the raccoon, and its chewing and purring noises abruptly stopped.

The mangy animal lifted its nose in the air, sniffing deeply as its head and gaze swiveled toward me. I stayed stock still; one half of me hoping those red eyes attached to the blood-covered face wouldn't see me. The other half was frozen in fear. I briefly wondered how many times a person could feel terror before having a heart attack. A chittering noise pierced the air, and my eyes zeroed in on the blood covered mouth. Pulling myself back behind the rock ledge I was peeking around, I hoisted myself up. Climbing as quickly as I could, my nails scratched at the rocks as I headed straight up the ledge, not looking back.

Mid-way up, I found a large, flat space that extended the length of the small cliff. I ran the short length and chanced a look over my shoulder. The chittering noise had turned to a growl, and I saw the raccoon's head pop up at the other end. *Shit!* I frantically looked around. If I jumped down from this height, I'd surely break something—it was just too high. Looking up, it was about nine feet to my next hand hold. I wasn't sure I could jump that high... but it was my only option. Trying not to panic, I stupidly looked back at my stalker again. A chill swept through me. It was completely on the ledge now, its snarling lips peeled back from its bloodstained face. Jagged teeth snapped open and closed as blood and saliva spewed everywhere with its jerky movements.

I stepped backward toward the edge, shaking my hands out. I had one shot at this. Blowing out a breath, I sprinted toward the rock wall. I could only take three steps for my running jump, but I used the momentum to launch myself upward. I pushed off with my legs as hard as I could and continued running up the wall, scrambling and pushing my booted toes into the rock, propelling myself up. Reaching with both arms extended as far as I could, my fingertips gripped the ledge. My legs swung underneath me as I shook with the effort to pull myself up. With my forearms bent, I rested my chin on the ledge. I swung my legs side to side like a pendulum and threw my knee over the edge, pulling my body up. Rolling onto my side, I panted as I looked up at the late afternoon sky. That was crazy, and way too close. I took a minute just lying there to catch my breath.

Wiping some sweat off my forehead, a new noise reached my ears and my brows furrowed as I tried to figure it out. It was almost like a scratching noise. I rolled to my knees and crawled toward the noise. Before I reached the edge, a little black paw shot up in front of me and I jerked back. In almost slow motion, I watched as the clawed paw curled each one of its digits over the rock. The tips of the raccoon's ears appeared next, then its little masked face came into view. I let out a small shriek as the beady, red eyes met mine, my body already scrambling backward.

I was on my feet an instant later, bolting through the woods as fast as I could. Normally those fat little shits would just lumber about, looking for garbage to eat. But not today and I refused to be on the menu. I didn't look back again as I ran uphill toward the quarry, hoping I could gain some distance or simply lose the freaky, trash panda.

Zig zagging through the woods, I continued. No unfamiliar noises reached my ears, and I was hoping I'd lost my disturbing pursuer. It was dusk when I reached the quarry. I looked around at the useless, scattered equipment. Large holes were dug into the land, and a bright red dust covered everything. Walking up to a hole, I peered into the darkness. I couldn't tell how deep the holes were, but they seemed endless. There were two more holes just like this one that I inspected, and they were all lined with red. No quarry equipment could do this. There had to have been some sort of mining equipment used here. If the kids had told the Gregoris what that man was doing on this mountain, there was no doubt in my mind that they would have had a team here immediately. Looked like they got what they needed, but what was it?

It was still light enough to see, and it was eerily silent as I continued to look around. All my senses were on alert, fear hanging in the back of my mind. That racoon had been terrifying. Spotting a duffle bag peeking out beneath some rubble, I grunted with effort as I pulled it loose. Falling back onto my butt with the duffle in my lap, I dusted it off. The wind took that moment to pick up, swirling around me. Red dusty clouds plumed around me as an updraft from the drilled holes helped stir the air and I coughed, waving my hand to clear it away. My lungs burned from the invasion, the thick dust cloud just hovered around me, stealing my oxygen. I twisted onto my hands and knees, coughing and gagging. A tingling sensation, almost a chill, ran through my body as I tried to catch my breath. My stomach twisted and all my muscles spasmed. Falling to the ground on my side, I shook uncontrollably. I curled in on myself, my fists holding my knees to my chest. Sweat drenched my clothes as my body burned. It was like flames were licking beneath my skin. My eyes squeezed tight as flashes of red burst like fireworks in the dark behind my lids. I had a fleeting thought that I was going to die here as I continued to spasm and twitch. Briefly, I wondered why I didn't just quit. Just give up. The nightmare that the last twenty-four hours had held... it was unbelievable. Maybe it wasn't real, and I'd wake up and this nightmare would just be over.

The dirt and rock bit into my skin as I shook. The physical pain reminded me I was truly alive. This wasn't a dream. The horror was real and Jax was still there; I was the only one left to get him out. I couldn't, wouldn't, let him down. *Just. Get. Up.*

I tried to crawl, to move away from the dust filling the air. My limbs just wouldn't function as my body continued to seize.

Unaware of how much time had passed, I was thankful when my body slowly started to relax. Finally able to sit up, I ran my fingers under my eyes as they were still watering from all the dust and convulsing. I sat there, unmoving for a moment, just catching my breath.

Reaching back down to unzip the bag, I startled at the sight of blood across my fingers. Hoping it was just the red dust mixed with my tears, but knowing better, I wiped them on my pants and opened the bag. I pulled out a smooshed granola bar and a pack of cigarettes; setting them aside, I kept digging, hoping there would be something useful. There was a half empty bottle of water and a t-shirt that read 'Theory of a Deadman'. *Hmm, at least they had good taste in music.* I dumped a little water on the t-shirt and wiped off my face, not caring that the shirt smelled a little funky. Seeing a little clearer with the dust out of my eyes, I kept exploring the bag. I pulled out a lighter, then a moldy sandwich in a Ziplock bag and tossed it to the side, trying not to retch. Reaching back in, I grabbed another Ziplock bag. I held it up toward the darkening sky, trying to see what it was. My eyebrows shot up when I realized it was six quarter sticks of dynamite... in a Ziplock bag? Really? These guys were morons. But who was I to balk at good luck— finally, I'd take it! It was definitely better than nothing and would surely be useful.

I grabbed the dynamite and lighter, put them in my cinch sack and stood. I took a moment to stretch my limbs. Oddly, they were feeling good. Really good. A strength filled me that I hadn't had moments ago, and I tried not to analyze what was happening. I probably couldn't if I wanted to. Turning toward the only road I could see coming into or going out of this place, I started walking. The sky was almost completely dark by the time I reached the wrecked pickup truck. The tracks were covered with new growth and leaves, and had I not been walking, I wouldn't have seen where they'd spun off through the woods. There was a rifle, still partially attached to the back window of the truck; I had to climb through the passenger side window and slide carefully past the broken shards of glass, The doors had been smashed too badly to open.

Pulling the clip from the rifle, I counted six bullets. Again, I'd take what I could get, and felt grateful to have found anything at all. After grabbing my flashlight out of my bag, I slid the shoulder strap over my back and across my chest and headed back toward the road. Surprised I could still see well enough as the darkness of night had taken over, I found the road without use of my light.

Making my way back through the woods, I remembered the directions the kids had guesstimated and hoped they were right. A prickly feeling kept running up and down my neck, and I couldn't help feeling like I was being followed—I was constantly looking over my shoulder. My vision was amazing, even better than before, but I didn't see anything that would cause alarm. I couldn't tell why I felt this way as nothing stuck out as strange. It was just a feeling. At that thought, a twig snapped in the distance. I stiffened a little but didn't slow down. Pulling the rifle over my head without missing a step, I kept a steady pace, keeping the business end pointed down but ready. The side of the mountain dished out a bit, and a chilly breeze blew past my face. If I hadn't felt the breeze from the caves, I would have missed the entrance. No one had used the mines in so long, there were no longer any signs in the landscape. Trees and brush had grown over this side of the mountain, making the dark and dilapidated entrance unrecognizable.

As I stood in front of the entrance, the breeze coming out of the cave was constant, but faint. The cool, damp air was musty and had a disturbing underlying odor. I had never smelled anything like it, and it made my stomach twist and my skin crawl. I rested my hand over my stomach as I scowled, trying to guess what it could possibly be. Distracted by nausea and confusion as I tried to peer into the entrance, a gurgling growl sounded behind me and I stiffened, realizing my stalker had caught up. Crap.

Spinning around, I pulled my rifle up in front of me and spun it horizontal, as the oversized raccoon launched itself at my face. Its teeth clamped onto the stock of the rifle I held out, the force knocking me backward. I hit the ground, flat on my back, and the wind rushed from my lungs.

Swinging the rifle out to the side and smacking the animal into the ground, I rolled to my knees. I yanked the rifle back, but the raccoon wouldn't let go. It snarled and shook its head, like a dog playing tug of war.

"Let go, you filthy little freak!" I ground out as I tried to stand. The raccoon seemed content gnawing on the stock of the rifle. Hoping it wouldn't notice, I decided to let go and slowly back toward the cave. The raccoon paused, seeing I was no longer attached. Shit. My eyes widened as it spun toward me, spittle flying from its mouth as it chittered loudly. The mangey creature's red eyes followed me as I continued backing away slowly.

Warmth bloomed in the center of my chest, making me stand up straight in surprise. Heat rushed through my body, and I glanced down at my hands. I could see the veins running under my skin, a red glow beginning to show through. The chitter turned to a growl and my attention snapped back. I raised my hands outward and resumed moving backward at an agonizingly slow pace. The stop gesture I made with my hands struck me as ridiculous. *Like the raccoon gives a shit that I want it to stop.* I almost rolled my eyes at the thought, but I didn't dare take them off the animal in front of me.

I wasn't sure if it was the glow or my movement that excited the raccoon, but it took the opportunity to spring toward me. I dodged out of its way, but not before its claws slashed through my t-shirt and arm. The startling pain in my arm caused me to stumble, and I dropped into a roll to prevent myself from face planting. Popping up, I spun, keeping the raccoon in my sight as I tried to move toward the woods, readying myself to run. The heat in my body was rising with each second, causing me to break out in a light sweat. But I didn't have time to think about it. The animal hissed and spit, shaking as it stalked toward me. I slowly crouched down, reaching for the knife I just remembered was sheathed above my boot. The crazed beast lunged at me while I was trying to open the release to free the knife. My breath caught in my throat; eyes wide as it stopped just an inch from my face in midair. I followed the arm that held the creature as it was pulled away from me. A sharp flick of the wrist snapped the raccoon's neck, and the animal went limp.

I staggered backward in shock, landing on my ass. A hand appeared before me, reaching out, and I stared for a second before I shakily took it to stand. Strong hands cupped my face as my blood nearly boiled in my veins. Gorgeous green eyes with sparks of red flickering through them met mine.

Chapter 34

Maxine

"Garron," I whispered as my throat constricted on a sob. This wasn't real. My mind was playing another trick on me. A cocky smile spread across his lips just before he leaned forward to claim mine in a searing kiss. I returned the kiss with passion as heat flooded my veins with his nearness, and I moaned as I wrapped my arms tight around him. *Please don't let this be a dream.* I squeezed my eyes tight, wishing it was real. Another part of me thought I must be dead. That dirty trash panda had finally killed me. A tear leaked out of the corner of my closed eyes as he pulled back, hands still cupping my face. He wiped the tear away with his thumb as I took shuddering breaths.

"Don't cry, Max. Look at me," he said quietly. I shook my head, and a small sob left my lips, eyes still closed. I couldn't. If I opened my eyes, he'd be gone, and I'd be dead or worse. Every time I'd woken up lately, it had been just another version of hell. I was OK with staying in the dream. "Max, please. Look at me," he begged.

I shook my head in protest, but slowly opened them anyway. If this was a dream, I wanted my eyes on him just one more time. Brushing my hands lightly over his features, I tried to savor the moment. God, he was beautiful. I looked back and forth between his bright green eyes. Even in the darkness, they sparkled. This couldn't be. He couldn't be. I saw the gunshot wounds. I heard him choking on his own blood as I tried to stop the bleeding. Sucking in another shuddering breath, I tried to talk as thoughts and ideas flooded my brain and poured from my mouth.

"You're dead. Am I dead? Oh my God, I'm really dead!" I always thought I'd see my mom again when I died. Maybe that part will come later? At least my death was virtually painless. "That fucking raccoon actually killed me. Oh God! Who is going to help Jax now?" I buried my face in my hands, trying to slow the mounting hysteria.

A chuckle left his mouth, and it was one of the most beautiful sounds I'd ever heard.

"I am definitely not dead, and neither are you. Although you were pretty close a minute ago." He frowned. "It takes quite a bit to kill me, I regenerate too quickly. I probably should have told you. The experiments... well, let's just say it's not the first time I'd been shot."

"But I couldn't hear your heartbeat, and there was so much blood. You were DEAD! Are you sure we're not dead?" I asked again, confused. "And, how... how did you get out of there? How did you find me?" My eyes darted around the darkness. I was in the middle of nowhere. Even if we weren't dead, Garron finding me in the dark woods was impossible.

"We're not dead," he smiled sadly, "I'm so sorry you thought I was. And I'm not entirely sure how I found you. I... I could feel you. I can't explain it." He rubbed at the center of his chest with his palm. "And when I got close enough, I could smell you." The corner of his lip curled into a half smile before he leaned in and inhaled, running his nose up the side of my neck. A shiver of pleasure tingled up my spine and I moaned, leaning into him. "God, you smell amazing. I could just eat you up." His voice dropped an octave. My core tightened as heat blazed through my body; I could feel his hardened length pressed against my stomach. I almost couldn't think. An image of Garron pressing me against a tree as I moaned his name flashed through my thoughts. Mine.

Two strong hands cradled my face as he slowly pulled back to look at me. Red blazed in his eyes, but I wasn't afraid.

"Your eyes, Max," his voice rumbled. "Your irises are completely red, and they're glowing. God, you are so fucking sexy," he growled the last part, the timbre causing my most sensitive parts to ignite, and I almost climbed up his mountainous body. The heat between us almost crackled where we touched. But a noise behind him drew my attention. Actually, several noises.

Sticks snapped under booted feet, closing in on us. His eyes grew wide with the realization that we were no longer alone. But before he could move, I'd pushed him to the side and slightly behind me and dropped into a crouch as a snarl ripped from my lips. My limbs burned as my veins lit up, sparking beneath my skin. My arms and legs grew larger, and dark claws sprouted from my fingertips—a monster unleashing itself.

"Max, no!" he shouted. But it was too late. I wouldn't let anyone hurt him again, separate us again. Mine. Primal rage burned in my veins, and I tore through the woods with one purpose. Destroy.

Red hazed my vision, making the night so clear I could see in amazing detail. Leaves falling from the trees were almost falling in slow motion as I ran toward the threat. Thoughts of Eddie and his men attacking us flashed through my mind, fueling more rage. I would tear them apart before they hurt anyone else I cared about.

Flashlight beams shone from in between the trees, and I slowed my steps, trying to be as quiet as possible. I made a wide circle around the two beams of light, stalking my unsuspecting prey. *Why were there only two?* No matter, they'd be dead within minutes. The beast inside ruled my thoughts and movements. I didn't care anymore. They all deserved what was coming for them.

Just as I rounded a shrub, ready to pounce, a silhouette stiffened and swung a beam of light right at me. The gasp sounded loud in the quiet night as I ran full bore at the light shining directly into my eyes. I leapt into the air, claws out, as I reached the person holding the flashlight. They tried to dodge, but I gripped their shoulders, my momentum pulling us to the ground. We slammed to the ground, rolling through the dirt and leaves, grappling each other for the top. The flashlight bounced across the ground, spinning like a top and making the trees look like we were at a disco.

We continued to roll, finally coming to a halt as I braced my legs over the shadowed figure, knees pressing them down. Spots filled my vision from the light that blinded me moments ago, but I didn't let it slow me down. Hand raised back, ready to slash a throat, I froze in mid swing. The flashlight beam landed on the face I had pinned to the ground, and recognition stalled my movement.

"Sierra?" I squeaked out on high pitch. Just as realization hit, a freight train plowed into my body, and we rolled through the woods. Arms wrapped around me like a protective cage and my body never even touched the ground.

Air sawing in and out of my lungs, I looked up as Garron brushed some strands of hair from my face.

"You are fucking incredible," he exhaled, "but you almost just killed your friend." A sheepish smile formed on his face. "I didn't have a chance to tell you they were coming. As soon as I felt you, I took off. I couldn't wait for them. It took them some time to catch up." Coherent thoughts came back to me, and I realized what he'd said.

"They?" I asked.

"Cory, too. They're going to help us get Jax." I sat up with Garron's arms still wrapped around me, and a shaky sob left my chest. I was so glad they were here and OK. A small weight lifted off me; I hadn't realized how worried I'd been for them. I turned away from him and dropped my head into my hands. Lifting my eyes, I looked at my hands and the receding claws. Normal color bled back into my vision and my body trembled with the fading adrenaline.

"I almost hurt my friends," I mumbled. "I don't know what the hell is happening to me." I covered my face with my hands in shame.

"I wish I knew what to tell you. We're experiencing a lot of the same things. But whatever is going on, it's changing us. You reacted similarly at the shop, only this time you were much more aggressive. And your body changed, it didn't do that before. You were... I think... you were protecting me."

It was my turn to look sheepish and I could feel a blush coloring my cheeks. I turned my face away and moved to stand up.

"Don't hide that beautiful face from me. Ever. I never thought I'd meet anyone like you. I don't plan on letting you disappear from my sight ever again." Before I could say another word, he moved around me with lightning speed to claim my lips once more. I never pegged myself to be a romantic, but damn, I just melted. Returning the kiss, I matched his desperation and need. Unable to comprehend what was happening, I sank into the feeling. And I felt whole. Like all my shattered pieces were being put back together.

I reluctantly pulled back and opened my eyes. His glowed a deep red now, and the veins coursing beneath my skin were pulsing with the same glow. Panting, my chest heated. Part in shock, part in arousal. A throat clearing drew my attention, and I stepped back, breaking our contact. My eyes tracked where the noise came from, and an embarrassed smile broke over my face.

"Sierra, Cory! I-I'm so sorry I attacked you! I didn't realize it was you, that you weren't a threat. God, I'm so glad you're OK." I ran up and gave them each a hug. It felt so good to see them, I almost sobbed again.

"Damn girl, that was some serious crazy!" Cory blurted, and I cringed.

"It's OK. We're OK. And it looks like you're doing better now," Sierra said with a sly smile and a raised eyebrow. "Not to ruin the joyous reunion, but what now? We need to get Jax. Soon. I have a horrible feeling in my gut, and I don't want to waste more time," she continued. Thoughts of my brother had me immediately sober, and I nodded.

"I met the kids." I said, turning to Garron. "I sent them with directions to get supplies that could help. We were going to meet back at the cabin. I planned to scout out the cave, but now that you're here, we can come up with something more solid."

"Great, let's go," Sierra said as she moved forward, passing me. I totally understood that she wanted to get moving, but damn. She was basically running blind.

"Um, do you know where you're going?" I asked. She stopped and turned toward me, crossing her arms over her chest and rubbed her hands up and down her biceps.

"No," she grimaced, "my turn to be sorry. I just... I can't stand still. I'm having a hard time concentrating, and I've got this bad feeling like we're running out of time." I nodded, understanding.

"It's OK. I get it. Follow me, I'll try to hurry." I turned and started walking into the darkness.

"Great, more dark, creepy woods. I wonder if we'll run into the Blair Witch? Maybe a sasquatch?" Cory muttered, and I rolled my eyes. He had always been dramatic, but it was nice having him here.

A small snicker came from Sierra. "I think we already saw the sasquatch... it's Max." I cringed for a second before a laugh burst from my lips. Everyone joined in on the brief levity, and I soaked in the sound of laughter from my friends, hoping this wouldn't be the last time I heard it.

. . .

Garron

I couldn't believe I'd found her. After Cory told me Eddie took her, I almost went berserk. It felt like there was a hole in my chest, a constant ache. It had been hard to suppress the rage that had boiled within me without her at my side. I wasn't sure how, but I was able to feel her the closer I got. Like there was some sort of magnet drawing me to her. I'd thought I'd have to burn that lab to the ground to find her, and I would have done it. The monster within me more than pleased to kill them all.

Eddie was a psycho. The worst one of our guards. He'd been helping torture us for years. He'd reveled in our pain, and I was looking forward to ripping off his limbs. But that could wait. I had Maxine back. But how did she escape? I'd have to discuss this with her later. Plotting how to peel the skin from his retched bones and bask in his screams of pain could wait. I'd found her. The ache in my chest disappeared the moment I saw her. Her blood called to me in an almost literal sense. Her veins had lit up like a beacon, drawing me in. She was so beautiful and fierce. And she had no idea.

Max was quiet on the way back to the cabin. A sort of sadness radiated from her. I could only guess at the thoughts running through that pretty head of hers. I wanted to reach out and touch her, to run my hands over her body, to taste her. Her body and blood were like nothing I could have imagined in my wildest dreams. But she kept her distance, giving me a wide berth as we walked. It confused me. Our reunion had been brief, but passionate. I felt in my soul that she wanted me as much as I wanted her, yet she put distance between us... I frowned, thinking how it was probably for the best. How could someone like her want to be with a monster like me? The things I'd done, and the things done to me... I was far from worthy of her affection.

We'd been walking for over an hour, moving at a fast pace through the woods. My sight, even in the dark, was amazingly clear, and I continuously scanned the area for any threats. After a few miles of silence and a cold shoulder, I dropped back behind Cory. I figured I'd watch their backs and give her some space.

I watched the group ahead, and my mind wandered. Sierra smelled like one of us. But sort of diluted? She stomped through the woods with a confident and strong stride; it matched her personality. I'd keep an eye on her, keep her safe. I owed Jax that. He would be so happy to see her again. He'd often said her name in his sleep and had included her in so many of the stories he'd shared. I felt envious of the time they'd had. I wished I'd had the same with Max. History and stories, and a life to share...

Max was clearly transitioning. I'd never seen another one of us change so gracefully. It was usually violent and painful, and sometimes the infected wouldn't be able to come back to themselves at all. I hadn't seen Jax turn, but I'd heard him. The monster inside him had taken control, wanting to destroy. But he'd always returned, unlike most of the others.

Cory, on the other hand, was completely human. Normal. And just a few days ago, I would have envied that so much; to have a normal life, full of friends and laughter—but meeting Max had changed me. I never thought I'd want anything more than to be normal. Now I just wanted her. She took that moment to glance at Cory and gave him a warm smile; my chest tightened. I silently watched as he returned the smile and gave a wink. I ground my molars together, keeping my growl from rumbling out. If he looked at her like that again...a picture of my teeth tearing out his throat flashed through my mind. Taking a deep breath through my nose, I pushed back the monster wanting out. She clearly felt a kinship with the sarcastic man, so I would do my best to keep him safe as well. She didn't need anymore loss and tragedy. She deserved to be happy. I'd do everything I could to free her brother and demolish that lab. Maybe she could go, start over, and make a life. I wasn't going to delude myself that it might include me. I knew what I was. A monster. And this world had no place for someone like me.

The faint smell of smoke filtered through the breeze. The cabin had to be close. Ten more minutes of walking and it came into view. We all let out small sighs of relief at the prospect of a place to rest.

Walking up the steps of the porch, Max stumbled. I darted forward, catching her arm before she landed on her face. I turned her toward me.

"What are you…" my words stuck in my throat. Her pupils were pinpricks, her skin pale with a gray tint and slick with sweat. Her body went limp in my arms, and I lifted her. Cradling her gently, I shoved through the door and headed straight for the bedroom. I didn't answer Sierra or Cory as they called out to me, worried for their friend.

I gently laid her down and sat next to her, cupping her face. She was cold and her eyes fluttered closed.

"Max!" I tapped her cheek. "Max! Look at me!" Her eyes fluttered back open, and they rolled around, unfocused. I slapped her cheek a little harder as I panicked, calling her name. Opening her eyes again, she whispered something I couldn't understand. I leaned over her, placing my ear next to her mouth.

"Sssso c-cold, ssssooo weak…" she stuttered. It dawned on me then that she must have overexerted herself and was in withdrawal. She needed fresh meat or blood, or her body was going to go into shock. I should have recognized the signs, but I had been too lost in my own thoughts. The last person I'd seen at the lab like this—I closed my eyes and swallowed––had ended up in the caves. Rejected. I stopped that line of thought immediately. She needed one of the doctor's injections or a massive dose of protein. I ground my teeth; I could help with this.

"You need blood, Max."

Cory and Sierra were in the doorway.

"Max? Is she OK? What the hell is going on? What do you need us to do?" Cory asked, all in one breath. Max shivered violently. "Dude, don't let her die! Fuck! I can't handle all this crazy shit! Max! Don't you dare leave me!" he shouted and gripped her legs. Cory's shake on her legs caused her to groan. I whipped my head in his direction and let out a growl, low in my throat, as I eyed where his hands were. His eyes widened at my warning, and he let go, holding his hands up in surrender. I swallowed, trying to control my monster, wanting to break free and tear off his limbs.

"She's going to be OK. She needs…"

"Blood," Sierra finished, solemnly. I looked at her and red flickered in her irises. *Shit. She is going to need some soon too.* "I'm grabbing something from the kitchen. Cory, come with me," she grabbed his arm, dragging him from the bedroom.

"But—" he argued, but quickly stopped with the glare she shot him. He looked back at Max, torment written on his face. If I was a better man, I'd have let him stay. But the beast beneath my skin wanted to tear him to shreds just for looking at her. And I wasn't sure if I could control myself, not with Max lying here damn near helpless. His decision made, he nodded, dropping his worried eyes, and let Sierra lead him from the room.

My attention back on Max, I removed my shirt, tossing it on the bed next to her. I closed my eyes, focusing on my hand, forcing my claws forward. I'd only done this a few times, having learned from some of the more extreme experiments. They came forth with ease for the first time and I wasted no time, quickly slashing open an artery in my neck. Gritting my teeth at the sharp pain, I lifted her torso and angled her head at my throat.

"Drink," I demanded. She didn't move, a dead weight in my arms. I pulled her back to look at her face and her head lolled to the side. "Damn it, Max!" Swiping a finger through the blood steadily leaking from my throat, I rubbed it across her lips. Nothing. Doing this a second time, I followed with a kiss, pushing my blood into her mouth with my tongue. The moment it registered, her hands flew to my biceps, her grip painful, nails digging into my skin. A low moan rolled up her chest and her eyes popped open; her bright red irises locked on the blood trickling from my wound. I didn't even see her move as she buried her face against my neck in the next instant and started taking greedy pulls. I closed my eyes, listening to her swallow as she held me in an iron grip. A small, protesting noise emanated right before she sank her teeth into my flesh. The wound must have been healing, slowing the flow she so desperately needed. I stiffened for a brief second before a blissful heat rolled through my body, starting at my neck and spreading.

I felt almost euphoric as she continued sucking at my neck. There were only two other times I could recall feeling this way. The last time we shared each other, and when the doctors had drugged me to attempt procreation with the other captives. I scowled and tried to push those thoughts away. This was nothing like that. I actually wanted this female. She called to something within me. There was a connection unlike anything I could've imagined. I had no idea what this was... but the ache I had felt at our separation had made it hard to breathe. Then, as I sensed her in the woods, it had begun to lift. And when we touched, it felt as though lightning flashed through my veins. Heat had boiled through me... like now. I groaned as my body hardened, and I fought the urge to rip her clothes off, to bury myself inside her.

Hearing my groan, she stiffened just before jerking away. Scrambling backward until she hit the headboard against the wall, hard, she leapt to her feet. Her chest heaved as red eyes looked at me, unseeing, and red veins beneath her skin sizzled in the dim light. Both her hands shot out in front of her, palms up, and she screamed. A shockwave blew out from her body, and I flew backward off the bed and slammed into the adjacent wall. I bounced off the wall and landed in a crouch. My right hand and knee braced on the ground as my head snapped up to look up at her, stunned. *What the fuck was that?!*

Chapter 35

Maxine

I was jolted back to reality by the sound of a high-pitched scream and a loud bang. *Where the fuck am I now?* I immediately panicked as my life had been fading in and out of the darkness too many times to count over the last few days. Most of my time awake and aware was filled with a series of disturbing events. Trying to focus and get my pounding heart under control, I looked around and realized the scream had come from me. I was practically wallpaper. Plastered against a wall and standing on a bed in a log-lined room. The cabin scene sent my heart jack rabbiting. *No! I can't be back here.* Now hyperventilating, my eyes darted around. The familiarity of the furniture surprised me, and I realized it was my dad's bedroom.

Heavy breaths drew my attention to the floor across from me.

"Garron?" I whispered in momentary confusion. He slowly stood, palms out in a gesture of surrender.

"I'm not going to hurt you Max," he replied softly. Scowling at his remark, my eyes zeroed in on the blood trickling down his chest from a wound on his neck. *Did I do that?*

I jerked in alarm and jumped from the bed as I heard footsteps running down the hall toward us. I spun and began clawing at the floorboard, tearing it out of my way with almost zero effort. Reaching into the opening, I felt around blindly until my fingertips brushed over my father's shotgun. I was already spinning back around, cocking the pump action as the door burst open. My father had always kept his weapons at the ready, so I knew it was loaded. He had taught us, at a young age, not to even think about touching them without permission. A quick flash of my ass getting spanked so hard I couldn't sit for two days zipped through my memory. We were, however, taught to respect firearms and how to use them.

I was a fraction of a second from squeezing that trigger at the on-coming threat, when I realized it was Cory and Sierra in the doorway. I exhaled and pointed the weapon at the floor.

"Jesus, you guys! I almost shot you!" I admitted shakily.

"Wouldn't be the first time you tried to kill us tonight," Sierra said flatly, crossing her arms over her chest. "Maybe we can work on this not becoming a recurring issue?" She lifted her shoulder and one corner of her mouth, pressing her lips together.

"Max, you OK? We heard you scream." Cory pushed past her and wrapped me in a hug. I hugged back with the arm not holding the rifle and let out a sigh, relaxing into his embrace. A low, warning growl echoed in the space and my eyes darted over Cory's shoulder. Garron was standing, fists clenched at his side, chin lowered, and his eyes were shimmering with red as they locked onto mine. Red lightning pulsed under his flesh, tracing the veins under his taut skin. I moved slowly forward and wrapped my now free arm around Cory, pushing him behind me, never removing my eyes from Garron's. I tilted my head sideways and lifted an eyebrow in a silent question. Several seconds ticked by as he watched me; no one moved an inch. Relaxing his stance as he gained control, he gave me a slight nod. The tension in the room waned to a more tolerable level, and we all began to breathe normally.

"You look better," Sierra stated, breaking the silence. "How are you feeling? And what the hell was that screaming about?"

I looked down, staring at the wooden floor planks. What was I supposed to tell them? *I think I have PTSD, and was having flashbacks from Eddie taking me? Doing unspeakable things to me?* They didn't even know—and I didn't want to tell them. I didn't want to talk about it and most definitely didn't want their looks of pity... or disgust. I wrapped an arm around myself and bit my lip.

"I'm sorry, just ah, a... hallucination... I guess." My reply was weak, and I didn't even want to look at their faces to see if they believed me. "How long have we been here?" I asked, changing the subject.

"About an hour, maybe a little more." Cory responded from behind me.

"The kids aren't back yet?" I asked and reluctantly peeked at Sierra as she shook her head. I stepped aside so I could see everyone as she started talking.

"They left some food, and I... may have eaten it." She looked sheepish. "I just can't seem to sate my hunger. I've never been hungrier in my life. Garron explained what he could, but I'm still so confused." She rubbed a hand across her forehead. "Some of the local wildlife are getting...sick. They're violent, changing, and..." she paused, worry lining her face, "attacking people. The people that are bitten, they're changing too, like me. Well, the ones that don't die, anyway." she shook her head, as her face creased into a frown. "Paige got sick. Like REAL sick. She went to the medical center, and I haven't been able to reach her. I don't know how, but we have to stop this. And from what I can piece together, that lab... I think it's all stemming from there. I mean, I could be wrong. Hell, I really have no idea. But we need to get Jax and shut that place down."

"I agree," I stated, finally looking up and meeting their eyes. Cory just watched me, a worried look on his face. He knew me too well, and from the stare he was giving me, he knew I was hiding something. I tried to ignore his look as I continued. "We've gotta shut it down. I don't care if the entire mountain comes down. But we've gotta get everyone out first. Those people down there, they didn't have a choice. They deserve to be freed. No one deserves to live in a cage, tortured and beaten." I saw Garron stiffen out of the corner of my eye as I cleared my throat and spoke with conviction. "We're getting Jax and everyone out. Then that place is dust." I looked over and gave Garron a small smile.

"We brought Frank's map, and your dad had another one in the cabinet. And there is some paper too. If Garron can give us descriptions, we can combine it with the map the kids drew... I know it won't be totally accurate, but it should be good enough to get us in," Cory said as he moved around me. One corner of his mouth quirked up as he met my eyes. I almost thought

I saw a bit of sadness in his gaze as he headed for the door, but the glance was too quick. "Sierra, help me get some of this stuff together." He patted her shoulder as he passed her. She shot a last glance at Garron, then one my way, and nodded as she turned to follow Cory out, shutting the door behind her.

I walked over to the bed, setting the shotgun gently across my lap and paused, letting my hands rest flatly over the weapon.

"What just happened, Max?" Garron asked, not making a move to come closer. I closed my eyes and shook my head, a frown marring my lips. I really didn't want to have this conversation. My body was not my own. I'd never felt so...unhinged. I'd dealt with depression and anxiety for years since my mother's death. But this, this was... I had no words. And I was terrified.

"I don't know what's wrong with me." My voice sounded small and weak.

"Wrong with you? You just tossed me across the room and never even touched me," he stated quietly. "Not that I'm anything close to normal anymore. But I'm pretty sure that was beyond 'not normal'." Silence filled the space between us, but I kept my eyes on my hands, not wanting to see his face. There was something really wrong with me and the rejection I felt coming might just send me over the edge. "And you lied to your friends." My chest tightened at his words. He was right. I'd lied, and it made my stomach roll with nausea. I didn't turn to look at him, afraid I'd see 'monster' written all over his face. Reaching up with both hands, I ran them over my face and pushed back the curls that had fallen forward. He continued talking, letting his last statement slide, and I was grateful. "I've overheard stories while in the lab. That this sort of thing may have been possible, a child early on had developed certain... abilities. She was terminated. No one ever saw her again. The doctor was moved... maybe she was terminated too. I don't know for certain. But I never saw her again either." He sounded sad, but I didn't want to look at the disappointment I could picture on his face. "Max, look at me, please. I swear I'm not–I won't ever hurt you. You know that, right?" He moved slowly toward me as if I were a skittish cat that would bolt at any second. Hell, I kind of felt like it.

I watched him out of the corner of my eye, not ready to turn and fully face him. I was afraid. Afraid of what I would see on his face. Or maybe it was what I wouldn't see. I didn't know what I wanted or if I had anything left of myself to give him. An 'I'm sorry' didn't seem appropriate here. He needed a chance at a better life. He truly deserved it. And I... I was just broken. No mother to guide me, my father incarcerated, my brother... God, who knew what he'd be like once we found him. The lump that formed in my throat kept me from swallowing. The things they were probably doing to him—I didn't even want to imagine. Eddie had been kind enough to throw some horror stories at me while he had me locked in that cabin. All the things they were doing to Jax–things they were going to do to me. We were running out of time. Elias was in a hurry to outshine his father, and it sounded like it would be starting with me and my brother. Bile rose up my throat, making my chest burn, and I closed my eyes, willing it back down.

My body warmed even before his hands gently rested on my shoulders. Soft pressure followed, gently turning me toward him. I allowed myself to be guided, but kept my eyes downcast. Shame filled me. I wanted to sob. I could have hurt him. And I didn't even know how I'd done it. What the hell was happening to me? My mind stopped its racing questions as his hand slowly moved over my shoulder and up the side of my neck. My skin almost sizzled under the direct contact, and my pulse picked up. His hand stilled over my racing pulse, no doubt feeling it pound beneath his hand.

"Max," he whispered pleadingly. When I didn't respond, his hand continued its slow glide along my neck, gently lifting my chin, forcing me to look at him. Despite what Eddie had done to me, heat pulsed through my body at his nearness. I felt like climbing up his enormous frame, wrapping my body around his and just hanging on, never letting go.

The need for his comfort was overwhelming. I wasn't sure, but I'd imagine this feeling being similar to how a magnet might feel... if one could. I'd never felt a pull like this in my life. His thumb brushed across my cheek, leaving a sizzling warmth as I opened my eyes. Green eyes sparkled with miniature red explosions. *Wow. My own personal fireworks.* The tenderness held in that gaze made me feel so raw. His thumb brushed over my cheek once again, this time wiping away the tear that managed to spill over.

"Please don't cry. I really have no idea what to do when you cry. But I know, whatever this is," he motioned, waving his finger back and forth between us, "it's undeniable. Our bodies, our blood... they call to each other. I can see the red lightning beneath your skin when we're near. When we touch, I feel everything inside of me come alive. I feel you," he rubbed the center of his chest, "I feel you here. Even when I can't see you. I can't explain it, but You. Are. Mine." His deep timbre and words vibrated through my body. I blinked at him; eyes wide with the truth he spoke. He wasn't rejecting me. My heart kicked in my chest, so hard he probably heard it. "You are mine, Maxine, as much as I am yours." His lips brushed mine with the lightest kiss and my eyes fluttered shut. My body melted against his as my hands cupped his face, and I returned the gentle, sweet kiss. Our lips moved together slowly, sensually, unhurried. Little red sparkles lit up behind my closed eyelids and my body heated, tingling everywhere we touched. My God. I felt the truth in his statement to my bones. I was his and he was mine.

Pulling back, I looked up. His eyes held so much emotion, shimmering with red sparks.

"Garron, I..." I didn't know what I was going to say. I was so scared. Everything had been tumbling down around me. I had to tell him what happened. He had a right to know, to know that I was... what? Broken? Damaged? Dirty? I felt all those things. I knew deep down that it wasn't my fault. That Eddie had been the true monster. But what if it changed the way he looked at me? I felt like I was hanging by a thread. Garron was making me feel whole again. But what if he couldn't handle it or worse, didn't want me after I told him? That last thread holding me together would break. I didn't think I would survive losing someone else I cared about. But I couldn't blame him either. I was touched, used by a man he hated most. A man that had helped keep him imprisoned and tortured for years. A man that HAD tortured him for years. Maybe he'd always see that when he looked at me. That story could never be unheard. I swallowed hard as another tear slipped down my cheek.

"Hey..." he wiped the tear away, "I can feel your sadness. It's making my chest ache. Everything is going to be alright. I'm here for you, Max, always." His statement was so quiet, so gentle, so sincere. A sob broke from my lips.

"I don't want to think anymore," my voice wobbled. "Make me forget, please, for just a little while." I looked back and forth between his now brilliant green eyes. He closed them and leaned his forehead against mine.

For a moment I thought we'd just stay like that, wrapped in each other for comfort—but he pulled back. A small bubble of panic rose in my chest as he stepped backward. He lifted the gun from my lap and rested it against the wall next to the headboard. Grabbing the comforter, he pulled it back and motioned for me to crawl in. I stood frozen for a moment, not sure what to do, staring at the bed. I'd asked for this, but I wasn't sure I was ready. Oh God. Panic crept in, and my hands shook. He lifted my chin, drawing my attention.

"I can just hold you, if you'd like. No pressure, just comfort," he gave a small smile. God, we were both just hanging on. The vulnerability on his face almost ripped another sob from my chest. I leaned into him this time, my hands on his chest as I reached up on tiptoes to place a kiss on his lips. He was too tall to reach and bent forward to meet my lips. The kiss was gentle and sensual, awakening a heat throughout my body. His hands trailed down my sides and grasped my shirt, raising it slowly. He paused briefly, then continued, moving slowly enough for me to stop him, as he could still sense my nervousness. This man was truly incredible. He was trying to do as I'd asked but giving me the opportunity to change my mind. I mimicked his movement, sliding my hands over his chiseled chest and the ridges of his abs, lifting the sides of his shirt. He smiled into the kiss, never breaking contact. Once both our shirts were as high as they could go, we parted just long enough to get them out of the way. I held him close, my arms wrapped around him, my hands flat on his shoulder blades. With our chests pressed together, the skin-on-skin contact had my temperature rising higher and my mind solely focused.

Wrapping his hands under my ass, he lifted me up and placed me on the bed. I made a small noise of protest as we separated to remove the rest of our clothing, and a quiet chuckle left his lips. My eyes traveled to his amazing physique and lingered on the evidence of his arousal. I swallowed.

"Hitch over." He lifted the rest of the blankets and we both slid beneath them, facing each other. "We can just rest," he smiled, brushing some stray curls back from my face. I cupped his cheek, rubbing my thumb back and forth over his cheekbone as I met his gaze. I could have stared at those beautiful eyes for an eternity. But my body had a mind of its own and continued to heat with his tenderness. He would never hurt me, and I needed... him. Just him.

"Make love to me," I whispered, the words almost a question. His brows pulled together as a worried look crossed his face. Understandable, since I had been giving him mixed signals. If I kept up this game of whiplash, he was going to run. God, I was a mess.

"Max, I..." he was rejecting me. I held my breath and my body tensed as a bubble of panic crawled up my chest once more. "Stop," he sighed, closing his eyes, and shaking his head gently. "I'm not sure I know how. I'm so broken and fucked up. Maybe this is... a bad idea."

My eyes shot wide. "You are NOT broken." I dared him to challenge me as I stared into his eyes.

"Anger, hatred, and rage is all I have felt, been allowed to feel. Until you. I don't know how. I don't know how to be gentle. I'm not sure I won't... I can't hurt you." He admitted. God, we were both so vulnerable.

"You won't hurt me." I shook my head. A small, sad smile pulled at my mouth. "Not ever. I feel that to my soul. I trust you, Garron. Now, don't think."

I raised my chin and kissed him. Silencing any more words. I closed out the world around us, focusing on this man, here and now. We melted into each other, our soft, heated kisses guiding our bodies. We moved together like the perfect slow dance, gliding and sliding. Our unhurried rhythm lit my veins on fire. The passion we shared was filled with so much unsaid emotion. Our lips broke apart as he rocked slowly into me, my hips meeting each one of his thrusts. Panting breaths mingled together as our eyes locked on each other. I'd never felt so in tune, so connected to anyone. It was almost overwhelming. Pressure began to build, and my entire body tingled. My hands gripped his shoulders, and I could see red lighting up my veins. Red glowed around his pupils, expanding until his irises were completely engulfed. My body responded to the sight, heating even more as he continued his slow, deep thrusts.

"Oh God, don't stop," I begged.

A sexy smile curved his mouth as a deep growl rumbled up his chest. The sound went straight to my clit, my back bowed off the bed and an orgasm ripped through my body. He tilted back, angling himself to find the perfect spot, keeping my orgasm pulsing. His hands gripped my hips as he picked up his pace. I was lost to the incredible sensations. Looking back at his face, his beautiful, glowing eyes flicked to my throat. I knew what he needed; I could feel it echoing through our bond.

"Yes," I breathed out.

It was all he needed to hear. He pulled me up, still connected, and held me tight to his body, still moving inside of me. Cupping the back of my head, he tilted it for better access to my neck. He kissed me deeply, pulling back to look into my eyes once more before burying his face in my neck. The bite was a quick, sharp sting, making me gasp. Then euphoric pleasure coursed through me. He groaned as he took deep pulls at my neck and increased his speed. He came on a roar, sending me over the edge for a second time.

We collapsed together, exhausted. I nuzzled into his chest with his arm wrapped around me and my leg draped over his. He pulled the sheet over us, and I made a small hum of pleasure.

"Get some rest," Garron said quietly.

"But—" He cut me off.

"You won't be able to help if you're strung out and exhausted. I'll get you up in a few hours. As soon as the kids get back. Then we'll go. Now rest."

"OK, but just a few hours. We can't afford to wait much longer." I yawned. I felt him nod. Then drifted off to the beat of his heart under my ear, lulling me to sleep. I felt the light pressure of a kiss on my head as the darkness of sleep took me. And I couldn't be sure, but I almost thought I heard him whisper 'I love you'. Probably just wishful thinking.

Chapter 36

Maxine

The murmur of voices carried down the hall. Keeping my eyes closed, appreciating the comfort and warmth of the bed, I stretched out like a cat. A small hum of approval had my eyes shooting open, and I jerked backward.

"Hey, you're OK." Bright green eyes met mine and a sad smile curved his lips. I relaxed as I took in his features. Circles were under his beautiful eyes and the stubble was growing into a thick, short beard.

"Hey," I smiled back. "Did you sleep at all?" I asked, already knowing the answer.

"Nah, wanted to make sure you were OK. Besides, you were twitching and whimpering a little. I was going to wake you if it got any worse." I sat up, pulling the sheet over my naked chest and almost laughed at the small pout that formed on his face.

"I heard voices. Are the kids back? How long have they been here? How long have I been asleep? Do you think they have any information about Frank?" I scooted toward the bottom of the bed.

"Slow down. They're not here yet. You were out for about two or three hours. You definitely needed it." I dropped the sheet, deciding modesty would have been more useful a few days ago, and started searching for my scattered clothes. Garron sat up, swinging his legs to the floor, and tossed the blankets aside as he stood. Clutching my clothes to my chest, I eyed his naked body and my mouth watered. He was built like some sort of God; tall, broad, chiseled muscle and a package that clearly functioned perfectly. My body tingled with the thought of how we'd spent our time just a few short hours ago.

"Darlin', I can smell your body heating. If you don't stop that soon, we may never make it out of this room." He slid his pants up his legs and paused to look at me before buttoning them. A cocky grin curved his lips, causing a dimple to show, and he raised an eyebrow in question. *Holy fuck, he's sexy.* I cleared my throat and dropped my eyes as a blush stained my cheeks. If he kept looking at me like that, I'd never be able to control the awakening hunger. I tried to focus. Quickly sliding my clothes on, I sat on the bed and laced up my shoes. By the time I was done, Garron was waiting for me before opening the door. I threw my hair into a quick ponytail and grabbed the shotgun leaning against the wall.

"Time for some plans. We can fill in the kids when they get here. Let's go get my brother."

· · ·

Jaxon

Days and hours all blurred together from the pain, from the experiments, and from the fire burning in my veins. God, maybe I was dead. Maybe this was hell. To be poked, prodded and pulled apart piece by piece, only to heal and have it done again. The pain was too much to bear. I just wanted to drift off into the darkness. I just wanted to give up, to have it all end. The few times darkness claimed me for its own, it had seemed almost blissful. That few seconds within the nothingness where I was at peace. No pain or worry. My body and mind—just blank. What I would give for that now. But no, I wasn't so lucky.

My jaw clenched against the spasms threatening to shake my body apart. My teeth nearly shattered under the force of my pain. "Just tell me where I can find her, and I'll end your suffering." A smooth voice echoed through the small, sterile room.

"F-fuuck y-y-yoouu," I gritted out between one of my spasms.

"You know, this would go so much easier if you'd just help me find her." Elias turned to Dr. Heller. "Clearly, this approach isn't working. Can you excuse us for a moment? I'd like to talk to Jaxon alone."

"Mr. Gregori, since the loss of my most prized subject, Mr. Devins is the best I have and has shown spectacular results. If possible, I'd like to continue my research with him... when you are finished, of course. Sir." The 'sir' was added just a second too late. Elias did not respond to the doctor, and I waited for the backlash. A few seconds ticked by and there was only the soft click of the door closing. I assumed there was an unspoken conversation, but I wasn't privy, being strapped down and such.

A icy finger trailed up my arm and over my bicep.

"Such a shame. This wasted body. What have you truly done, Jax? All this time, all this... strength and health," he spit out the last three words as if they were dirty. "What have you done? You've never accomplished anything. Stayed in this nowhere city, hopping from job to job." He huffed. "You can't even keep a girlfriend." I stiffened with that statement. How the hell had he known about Sierra? A small laugh echoed through the room. "Didn't realize I knew so much about you? The stiffening of your body tells me I hit a nerve." *Dammit!* I gritted my teeth again, trying not to scream with my frustration. "She's quite the beauty. Not really my type. But maybe I could make an exception. A secondary, perhaps, after your sister, of course."

I growled, straining against the straps holding me down. "I'll fucking kill you if you touch either one of them," I tried to muster my deadly intentions, to be intimidating, but I was so weak. How scary could I be strapped to a table? They hadn't fed me in what felt like forever. My body and mind were becoming sluggish.

"You. You who had everything. A beautiful and smart mother, and a father who loved you." I wasn't sure if I'd heard his voice crack slightly on that last statement until he cleared his throat. "And that sister of yours. She'd do anything for you, for her family." I growled again at the smile I could hear as he continued. A humorless laugh echoed through the small room. "Oh, don't worry, you're going to find Max. And YOU are going to bring her to me. I am going to give her everything she didn't even know she needed." I struggled against the restraints, the straps cutting into my skin.

"You're just another Gregori monster, like your father. I'd rather die than deliver my sister to you!" I gritted out with more disgust than I thought I could.

"Well, well, a Gregori monster, huh? Ah, you have no idea." He grabbed my lower jaw, twisting my face toward him. My eyes widened. *When did he get so strong? And is he bigger?* An evil smile spread across his face, and his eyes lit with amusement. Then they started to swirl. *What the fuck?* I couldn't look away. Black and bits of brilliant red swirled like a whirlpool, and I was being sucked down into its depths. Flashes of my memories burst through my mind. My mom holding me when I fell off my bicycle; my dad hugging me for getting my first buck when we went bow hunting together; when I stood proudly, cheering as my sister graduated high school with honors; my first date with Sierra after harassing her for weeks; sneaking photos of the underground labs, before I knew how horrific it truly was. All these memories were mine, and I was being forced to share all of it.

"No!" I shouted, closing my eyes. "Get out of my head!!"

Elias laughed maniacally. "I must admit, this is the most resistance I've gotten so far. I'm kind of enjoying the challenge. But enough with the playtime. You ARE going to help me, whether you like it or not." There was a sharp crack as he struck me across the face. My eyes popped open with shock, and I was met with the swirling blackness. There was a brief second of regret because I knew better. Then, nothing. No pain, no worries, no fear. I just felt relaxed, refreshed. I laid still, my body enjoying the respite. There were some quiet noises, a jingling of buckles being released, and pressure being lifted off of all my extremities. I flexed my hands and stretched my limbs. Turning my head, a man came into view. A spark of familiarity vibrated through my body and a nagging sensation itched at the base of my skull.

"Hello there, Jaxon. How are you feeling?"

Jaxon, right. That was me. I nodded with a small smile.

"I'm well, thank you." A wide smile broadened his face. Elias. Yes, his name was Elias. I couldn't recall how I knew this, though. He wiped away a small trickle of blood from his left nostril. But I didn't care to try to understand. I sat up slowly, looking around. I shrugged internally, not really caring where I was.

"We have some work to do today, Jaxon." He handed me a fresh set of scrubs he pulled out of the cabinet across from us. "Please get dressed. I'd like you to do a few things for me." I quickly changed into the new scrubs, leaving my stained and tattered ones on the table. "Dispose of those in the trash. They will no longer be of use." I did as he asked immediately, hoping for some praise. I just wanted to make him happy. "Now, follow me." He led us into the hallway and past several doors. Finally reaching our destination, we entered what appeared to be some type of large office. I didn't recall ever being here before, but again, I didn't care. "I have some things to go over with you. I'll be sending you out with some tasks to complete today." I felt eager to please.

"Yes, I'd like that. What did you have in mind?" I asked. He looked at me briefly, a smile widened his face, and he turned back around. He opened a filing cabinet and leafed through, pulling out a yellow, tabbed folder.

"Well, I'd like you to kill someone for me and retrieve another." He pulled a photograph of a man out of the folder, handing it to me. I knew this man. That nagging sensation tingled at the base of my skull again.

"Garron?" I asked.

"That's correct," he smiled at me, waiting for something.

"What would you like done with him?" I was confused and not sure what he wanted. His smile broadened. He appeared very pleased. I liked that.

"I'd like you to find and kill him. Eddie seems to think he's dead. But after reading his file, and watching our experimental footage, I'm quite positive he's incorrect." I nodded. I could do that.

"Would you like me to go now?" I wanted to get started. That would please Elias.

"Not quite." His hands continued to dig through the filing cabinet. A large folder was extracted and set on the counter.

"My team was kind enough to make physical copies to go with all our digital files. It appears you and Maxine have been in the system as long as

Jonas and I." He paused, seeming to be in thought. "If you complete my tasks as requested, I may just provide you with some of the knowledge I've recently acquired." He continued leafing through the file and shrugged. "Not that you'll be able to do anything with the information. Now that you're mine."

He pulled out a photo of a beautiful young lady. Familiarity rang through me, and my body twitched. Maxine.

"Ah, yes. Maxine. Such a beauty. I can barely contain my excitement to have her by my side." He turned to face me, and I looked directly into those swirling eyes.

"Bring her to me, unharmed." That feeling returned to the base of my skull and my head pulsed with increasing pressure. I shook my head. Max. My sister. Heat rose up my spine and spiked a sharp pain through my head. A memory crashed into my thoughts. Of my father giving me one last hug. He was wearing an orange jumpsuit and being pulled away by guards. My sister sat at a small, round table with her knees pulled to her chest as she sobbed.

"Promise me, Jax, take care of your sister. I love you both so much. You are both so special, so important. Take care of her. Promise me!" Dad demanded as he was pulled backward.

"I promise, Dad, I won't let anything happen to her." I looked back at her petite frame, huddled in a ball as tears tracked down her face.

"Do whatever it takes, son. And don't ever forget how much your mother and I love you both." The heavy metal door slammed closed between us, locks immediately clicking into place. I pulled Max up into a hug, holding her trembling body.

"We'll be OK, Max. I promise. I won't ever let anything happen to you. We'll do this together, OK?" She sniffled, wiping her sleeve under her nose.

"OK, you and me," she said quietly, nodding and wiping tears from her cheeks. I squeezed her tight one more time, and we left the prison together, ready to face our new future alone.

The memory faded, leaving a scowl lining my face.

"I won't give her to you," I growled. I'd never let this monster get his hands on Max. I surged forward, reaching for his neck. I was going to rip his twisted little head from his body. An invisible wave of power burst through the room. I was flung backward, and my body bounced off the closed door at my back. Catching myself on my hands and knees, I looked up in shock. The walls shook, papers and photographs fluttered through the air, falling to the ground like snowflakes.

"What the—" were the only words to leave my mouth before Elias was kneeling in front of me. He gripped my chin so tightly, a sharp pain radiated through my teeth. I tried to move but seemed to be frozen as his eyes locked on mine. The black and bits of red swirled as I tried to fight against the hold. A heavy pressure built in my mind. I howled inside my head as I fought against control, against the pain that made my head feel as though it would explode. My arms shook from resistance as I reached up, gripping the sides of my head. Surely remnants of my brain were leaking from my ears as I pressed against my skull, trying to keep it together. Still on my knees, the howl I'd been holding back ripped from my lips. This pain was the worst I'd endured here yet. I wasn't sure how much longer I could hold on. Breath panted out of my body in shallow bursts. Elias' eyebrows drew together as his eyes continued to swirl. His jaw clenched and another trickle of blood leaked from his nose.

"You... will... do... as... I... wish," he gritted out between his teeth.

Murderous thoughts of this asshole flickered through my mind. An image of Max. Then Sierra, as she smiled up at me with love, even though I'd never told her how much I truly cared. Regret. It was my last thought as my mind went utterly blank.

I blinked at the discomfort that radiated from the back of my head and down my neck as I found myself staring at the ceiling. What the hell was I doing on the floor? Elias was standing in front of me, wiping his nose with a Kleenex. His eyes tracked me as I stood.

"Are you ready to get started?" His voice was thick with irritation. I nodded. "Good. You've proven to be quite the pain in the ass. It would almost be worth disposing of you now... if I didn't need you to get that sister of yours. I'll probably just let Dr. Heller piece you apart when I'm done. Maybe I'll watch," he finished the last thought on a mumble. The words were only that to me, words. I felt no anger, no worry. Just a need to make Elias happy.

"What would you like me to do now, sir?" He finished picking up the scattered papers, stuffing them haphazardly into the file folder.

"Bring Maxine to me. And, if by chance you run across Garron... dispose of him." I nodded. Turning on my heel, I reached for the door handle, but just as I stepped through the threshold, an explosion shook the facility. Small bits of dirt and cement poured out of the new cracks from the ceiling and walls. Red lights began flashing through the hallways and the power flickered. A few guards rounded a corner, running to the opposite end of the corridor and disappeared down another hallway.

I turned toward Elias. His eyes were wide.

"Elias!" a voice bellowed from down the hall. I spun around, tracking where the voice had come from. Jonas ran at full speed toward us, barreling down the hall like a freight train. "Elias!" he yelled again.

"I'm here! What's going on?"

"There has been a breach. The explosion was near the children's ward. And the monitors showed cell doors ajar in the military and splicing experiments hall. Garron and the other escapees have been visually confirmed." Jonas reported through heaving breaths. Swallowing thickly, he continued, "We must get to the shuttle tunnel now, brother. This is not going to be good." I looked back and forth between the brothers. Elias' face filled with rage.

"God Dammit!!!" he roared. "I will not lose this! I've waited too long for things to go my way! I'll be damned if I'll let it all be destroyed by some insignificant lab rats!" His eyes swirled with more red and the surrounding air vibrated.

"There's something else," Jonas said reluctantly, his deep voice dropping an octave. The muscle in his jaw ticked as if he was debating on continuing.

"What?" Elias barked impatiently.

Jonas cleared his throat and looked at me. "Maxine is with them."

Chapter 37

Maxine

Anxiety permeated the air. It felt like time was dragging as I paced around, waiting for the kids to return. Sierra and Cory sat at the table, studying the map and praying for accuracy with the labyrinth of tunnels. Cory's knee bobbed as a dull thumping noise from his foot sounded like a bass drum in my skull. Garron was stoic and unnervingly still, patiently waiting. Thoughts race through my head with reasons he could look so relaxed. The pressure of what we were about to take on threatened to crush me—clearly this wasn't the most tension-filled day of his life. Sadness swept over me, thinking of what he'd most likely endured over the last... God, probably fifteen or more years. I knew he'd kept the horrific accounts of his past to a minimum. Trying to shield me from the nightmares... or maybe he just didn't want to talk about it. And I didn't blame him. Sometimes it was easier to bury the pain. I didn't want to recount certain events in my life, either. My stomach twisted with nausea, and I pushed the thoughts back. Focus. Breathe. Focus. We had to get Jax and release the others. If we failed, people would die. And my brother would probably be among them. My head throbbed with pressure, and I rubbed my temples. Dark thoughts swirled within me at the thought of losing my only sibling. I gritted my teeth and clenched my fists as my body heated. Small sparks lit up under my skin and I held my breath, hoping no one had noticed, and stealthily moved toward the door.

"I'm going to grab some fresh air," I blurted from the threshold. I swiftly fled out of the cabin and down the small steps of the porch, not even sparing my friends a glance. I could pace out here without everyone giving me the side eye, waiting for me to lose my shit, and then hopefully get a grip on myself.

Peering down the rocky hillside behind my family's cabin, I leaned my shoulder against a tree. I was having trouble gaining control of my emotions. I felt so scattered and on the verge of losing my mind. Trying to push negative thoughts to the back of my head without success, I closed my eyes. The lightning flared under my skin and crackled within me, intensifying my anxiety. Trying to control it, I focused on the heat. It suddenly changed, and I held my breath. Furrowing my brows, I tried to concentrate—the heat felt like it was gathering, moving from all-encompassing to just behind me, leaving my front chilled. As if the heat itself was reaching for something.

"Focus on the moment, not the future and not the past. Focus on not giving up. Don't let it break you, use it... use it to make yourself stronger." Garron's deep timbre didn't startle me but seeped into me instead. I let the deep rumble of his voice and his words soak into each bone in my body, each cell of my being. I would stay strong. I would not break. And I would get my brother out of that place. Then I'd burn it to the ground.

Hands gently brushed down my shoulders, trailing heat down my arms, and his fingers twined with mine. I sighed at the touch, leaning back against the strong wall of muscle behind me, my head resting on his chest. Heat wrapped around me. Whatever was happening to me, it gravitated toward him. Drawing us together.

"What is happening to me... to us? I... I don't understand," I whispered. He leaned his head forward, wrapping his hands still twined with mine to crisscross my middle. In a tender move, he nuzzled the top of my head. This sudden...thing... between us. It was so surprising and terrifying. It made my head spin and yet felt so right. But how? How could we have become so connected in such a brief time? My emotions were a hurricane, and this man was standing in the eye of the storm. Unmovable, like a beacon of strength that was meant only for me.

"I'm the last person to have answers." he paused, sighing, and I thought he'd finished. "I feel you. I felt you before I even laid eyes on you. I would have found you, even if I wasn't looking. Your body lights up for me in the darkness and I am pulled to you like a magnet. What this is or what it means, God only knows. But deep in my soul, my body calls for you. You are a missing piece returned, making me feel more whole than I've ever felt in my life."

Holding back the tears, I closed my eyes and stayed silent. The tightening of my throat made a response impossible, even if I knew what to say. I just stayed wrapped in his amazing warmth, letting him hold me. My thoughts echoed his almost word for word. I wanted to stay in this moment, with him, forever. And that scared the shit out of me.

. . .

When the kids finally returned, we took stock of what they had managed to bring back. Our supplies were sparse, but between the C4 Garron had brought back from Frank's bunker and the firearms the kids had gathered, we hoped it would be enough. We were quite a mismatched group and had no clue what we were getting into. The plans were all pieced together with vague directions and an incomplete layout of the facility. As we all grabbed whatever we could carry and headed toward the caves, I sent up a small prayer that we'd get everyone out safely.

We accessed the old mining entrance and squeezed our way through. It was slow going and the cool, damp air did nothing to hamper the sweat created from my nerves. Everything inside me was screaming to go the opposite way we were headed, away from the danger. I wrinkled my nose at the smell as we made our way through the unfinished caves. Something else was down here... and from the strength of the increasing stench, it was probably a lot of somethings. No one object could reek that much. And I couldn't shake the feeling we were being followed, watched, as I constantly glanced over my shoulder.

Garron incapacitated the few guards scattered around and near the access of the main corridors where we found entrance. We moved as swiftly and silently as we could. The lower level was cold, but the walls lined with metal bars and people in various stages of illness were what chilled me to the bone. The glazed and haunted looks from the captives would be burned in my memories forever. Most of them didn't even react to us running by! They were either too weak or too sick, perhaps too drugged? Garron tugged me past as I slowed my steps.

"We'll come back this way. We won't leave them," he whispered. But I couldn't help glancing back at the poor souls trapped here. Disgust and rage simmered at the atrocities being committed here.

We reached another level of hell and found more scattered cells. Some people behind the bars were either mutating or had purposely been altered. I had to consciously remember to blink and close my mouth as it jacked open with shock as Garron continued dragging me down the corridor. A hiss broke my shocked haze, and I stumbled. Garron ignored my pause, focused on our task. He kept moving, as if a man with scales like a snake for skin wasn't standing there and staring at me. Taking in his features as we creeped past, I noticed his eyes were also snake-like; vertical slits down the center, but instead of the normal brown or yellow most snakes had, this man's eyes were red. He said nothing as we passed, just watched us with those eerie eyes. The next cell appeared empty, until a slight movement caught my attention. I leapt back as a man seemingly materialized out of nowhere right next to the bars.

"Hey!" he whispered. And I paused, the rest of the group slowing to a halt behind me. "Get us outta here!" he demanded.

I nodded a little spastically, "We will, I promise."

Garron turned back, rushing to my side.

"Cam? I thought you—"

"Good to see you, man. You thought what? That I went for a stroll? Got a new job?" the man snickered. "Been down here since the last combat training we had. Guess they weren't so happy you kicked my ass again," he grimaced. Garron shook his head and rested his hand over the other mans through the bars.

"I'm so sorry, Cam. I had hoped maybe you got out."

"Nah, they didn't even upgrade my accommodations, bastards." He snickered again, clearly trying to make light of the subject.

"We're getting everyone out of here. Be ready. It's gonna be fucking chaos. When the alarms go off, grab whomever you can and head west through the unfinished tunnels. There's an exit; we'll find you," Garron turned.

Cam reached through the bars. "Get the kids, Garron. Don't let them stay in this hell another minute."

We reached the end of the corridor. It split into two directions with a windowed door directly ahead. Garron headed toward the left. I paused, staring at the door. Grabbing the handle and twisting, I was surprised when it opened. It was a small control room, but only one computer and a switchboard with several buttons lined the main desk area. The monitor showed the hallway and cells we'd just passed. Two rows of boxes were all lit up; the red squares blinking 'secure' had me clenching my jaw. *What would happen if I'd turned them all green?* I stared down at the control panel. Uncertainty warred within me. What would I release? Cam seemed coherent at least, but the others? Thoughts of the snake-like man sent a shiver through me. Cory poked his head in.

"What the hell are you doing? We're kinda on a time crunch here!" He looked around at the small filing cabinets and basic office paraphernalia. His eyes grew wide as he saw where my hand was; on the switchboard.

"Cory." His name was a plea. He responded with a shake of his head. Not deterred, I argued my case in a hushed tone. "There must be another control room. This one only shows the cells we've passed. What if we don't make it back here? I can't leave them." I turned back to the control panel.

"Max, you don't know what that does. Or even worse, what it will open and what you'll let out. Don't fucking do it, Max." I swallowed. "Maaaxx?" I looked over my shoulder at Cory's stern yet worried face.

"They're all going to die down here if we don't get them out." I blinked hard and swallowed; decision made and pulled all the switches down. One after another, the cells opened. The metal grating across the floor echoed down the hall, and my heart lurched. *Please God, let this be the right thing.*

Cory cursed and grabbed my hand, pulling me down the hall and into a sprint to catch the rest of our group. Not waiting to see the captives emerge.

We rounded another corner and Garron was grouping children into the hallway as they came out of two doors opposite each other.

"Mason, you and the others need to get these kids out of here. Head back the way we came, the rest will follow." Bella had a little girl holding each of her hands and was already moving. They were all dressed in dingy hospital gowns with generic, canvas-like slip on shoes. Nothing separating the boys from the girls.

"You'll need our help, and we owe it to Jax," Trent spoke up.

"We'll get Jax. You guys get the kids and the others to safety." Garron commanded, leaving no room to argue. His eyes furrowed as he tracked one of the kids, then turned and kept moving. Pausing momentarily to do a double take of the children. Probably making a mental note of how many there were.

Sierra and Cory picked up their pace to keep up with Garron as I stood watching the children run out of the rooms and into the hall. They were so little. My chest tightened, thinking of all they'd endured already. Small, chilled fingers grabbed my hand, jerking me out of my stupor. A small electric pulse rippled through me. A girl, no more than six, with long golden-brown hair, tugged for attention. Squatting down, I startled at her familiar, bright green eyes as she met my stare with a serious expression.

"Don't go down to the caves," her tiny voice murmured. I just looked at her, confusion lining my features. "Underneath is where the nightmares live." She let go and ran after the others. *Was I even supposed to respond to that?* I stood, staring after her, when a loud explosion shook around me. I clapped my hands over my ears and stumbled as they rang from the blast.

The lights flickered on and off and alarms blared from multiple locations. I caught up with the group after a series of bends and uphill hallways. A few bodies, or should I say body parts, littered the hall. I hung close to the wall, avoiding the appendages and bloody puddles, having clearly missed a small battle and the explosion making a rather large hole in a wall.

"Come on!" Garron shouted over the alarms. Sierra and Cory climbed over the rubble to enter the now gaping hole. And that was where we split; with Garron and me heading in the opposite direction. I glanced back at my friends; Cory shot me a smile over his shoulder before they disappeared around another corner. I swallowed hard past the lump in my throat.

"They're heading to where I think Paige and Jax are being held. We have to get to the main control room and release the door locks or find someone with a key card," Garron answered my unasked question. I was getting confused the further we went. All the hallways looked the same. And if I was honest with myself, I've always been shit with directions. I just hoped he knew where we were.

Garron had managed to incapacitate three guards on our route with his lethal skill, taking them down silently. I should have been frightened at the ease with which he decimated our threat, but a feeling of pride and thanks filled me instead. I would never have made it this far without him. We skidded to a halt and Garron kicked open a door, not even checking the knob. He grabbed me so fast; I didn't even see him move. He had us inside and the door closed behind us before I could even blink. The room was dark, aside from the light coming from the crack along the floor. I sucked in a breath to ask what the hell he was doing, but his hand shot up to cover my mouth. He pressed me against the wall, holding me immobile, both of our chests heaving from running and the adrenaline flooding our bodies. His breath fanned over my ear.

"Shhh, don't make a sound." I complied, not moving a muscle. Not two seconds later, the pounding of several booted feet ran past us.

We both let out an exhale and relaxed slightly. He stepped back, and I looked around the space now that my eyes were adjusting to the darkness. There was a sliver of light coming from another door on the opposite side of the room. I crept silently across the floor toward the door, my curiosity moving me. As I got closer, I could hear voices coming from the other side. I leaned forward, pressing my ear to the door, trying to listen. A male voice was talking in a fast, agitated tone.

"We'll be evacuating to the southern facility immediately. Our back up plan is in effect, there has been a breach." A low growl rumbled in Garron's chest.

"Heller," he bit out between clenched teeth.

A woman's voice answered back, the tone so low I couldn't make out her actual words. Then Heller continued, "We have the files downloading now. The tier one subjects, and treatment applications are already in the transport for pick up." There was a pause. The woman must have been asking questions. "No, subject one is a loss. And I believe the children are forfeit. The initial breach occurred in containment on level three." Heller continued. Another pause and the woman's voice cut in and out. "I understand, we will send a retrieval team. Backup power is not sustaining coms We will be in contact once in route."

Another explosion sounded, this one sounded like it was directly below us. Everything shook and bits of ceiling started to break apart and fall. We were running out of time. I put my hand on Garron's arm, signaling I was ready to move. Without missing a beat, he kicked the door open, and we burst into the room. An old man in a lab coat was sitting in front of a monitor. It must have been Dr. Heller. The screen was brightly lit, frozen and flickering on a woman in her late fifties. Garron rushed forward, grabbing the man and lifting him into the air by his throat. My stomach clenched as if I had been punched in the gut and my heart stuttered. I couldn't move, couldn't breathe, couldn't think. I vaguely registered Garron growling questions and demands while shaking the elderly man in the air. Dr. Heller was shoved forward by the back of his neck toward some type of control panel, but I watched as if from a distance. Alarms that I hadn't noticed had stopped previously, began blaring again as multiple lights lit up the panels along the wide counter space.

Dr. Heller flew past my line of sight, slamming into the wall and sliding down in a heap. I felt frozen. My heart skipped beats; its erratic rhythm coupled with the tightness squeezing my chest was making it hard to breathe. I still couldn't move. My ears were ringing, and I fought to suck gasping breaths into my constricted lungs. Garron's face appeared before me and he gently cupped my cheeks as the edges of my vision blurred and darkened.

"Max! The doors are all open! We've gotta go!" He shook my shoulders. "Now!" His voice sounded so far away, I blinked; tiny white sparkles surrounded him. Red began to fill his irises right before he scooped me up. Cradling me to his chest, he took off running for the door.

Just as we reached the door, it burst open. It slammed into us forcefully, knocking us backward. Garron spun, setting me on my feet and stepped between me and the threat.

"Jax," Garron growled in warning. I tried to move, to stumble around Garron, my wits slowly coming back to me upon hearing my brother's name. Garron's arm reached back and knocked me further behind him. I staggered backward, losing my footing, and landed on my ass. The next few moments were a blur as Jax launched himself forward. Fists and bodies slammed around the room, too fast to track, followed by grunts of pain. A loud roar ripped through the room and Jax flew backward against a wall. His body stilled long enough for my brain to comprehend his distorted features.

"Oh my God! Jax!" A sob burst out. *What have they done to him?*

His body was larger, his skin now gray, and his jaw looked elongated somehow. Red eyes shot to mine as I moved forward on my hands and knees, then stretched out my hand.

"Jax, please! It's me. It's Max." I choked, sitting back on my feet as his stare looked devoid of recognition. My chest throbbed like someone was trying to rip out my sternum. This couldn't be happening. "Don't you fucking dare, Jaxon! You know me." My voice shook as tears streamed down my cheeks. I inched closer.

Garron gave a warning growl.

"That's not Jax. Something's wrong. Back away, Max. NOW." My brother's red eyes swiveled back to Garron and a feral howl ripped from his mouth.

"You must die." The words were dark and slightly garbled. His voice sounded nothing like my brother. Garron jumped to his feet in a blur of movement and attacked.

"Stop!" I begged, another sob breaking out of my fractured chest.

They continued to trade blows as they rolled around the room. Another violent vibration shook through the lab. Jax slammed Garron into a wall of cabinets just as the ceiling cracked above them. Jax jumped back out of the way just as huge chunks of cement and debris poured from the ceiling, burying Garron below.

Chapter 38

Maxine

"Noooo!" My agonized wail had Jax turn his icy glare in my direction. I moved backward, scooting across the floor on my ass.

"I'm taking you to Elias." The flat voice attached to the blank, red stare coming from the beast in front of me was not my brother, it was a monster.

"What did they do to you?" I whispered as tears leaked from the corners of my eyes. This was all too much; my heart was breaking into a million pieces—my whole world was imploding. I'd failed. Oh my God, I failed.

Jax's head leaned back, the elongated jaw stretching wide, showing a mouth full of razor-sharp fangs as he roared so loud the walls shook. More pieces of ceiling crumbled around us as terror flooded me. The vicious noise made my body jerk and spurred me into action. I couldn't stand here and watch him like this. I'd have to find another way to help him. And I wouldn't be able to do that if I was dead. I turned, scrambling onto my hands and knees. Propelling myself forward, I staggered to my feet and back through the door we had entered, slamming it shut behind me.

Bursting through the second door and out into the hall, my heart thundered in my chest as I frantically ran down the corridor as fast as my feet would move. I grabbed the knobs on various doors, praying one would be unlocked. Finally, a handle twisted and shoved my way inside. The lights still flashed on and off, and the alarms continued to wail shrilly. I was alone and had no fucking clue where I was. Icy dread seeped its way into my body as I heard footsteps pounding down the hall toward me. I backed further into the room, a hand over my mouth and the other clutching my chest to keep my heart from bursting out. The cinch sack on my back shifted as I knocked into something in the darkness. I had forgotten I'd even had it on. I ripped the bag off and opened it with trembling fingers. Cool metal touched my fingertips, and I wrapped my hand around my father's pistol.

Another roar echoed down the hall as I backed further into the space, the pistol aimed at the door. The footsteps stopped just outside of my hiding space. I held my breath, trying to stay still but my body and hands shook. Deep inhalations sounded from the opposite side, as if something was scenting the air. *Fuck!* The gun loosened in my grip from my sweaty palms, and I shakily wiped them on my pants one at a time, not losing aim toward the noise. Just as I tightened my grip, the door burst open. A hulking frame was sucking deep breaths in and out, its body heaving. The silhouette sent another wave of chills up my spine; even my scalp tightened with fear. It was as wide as the doorway itself and just as tall. The elongated arms hung at its sides, with claws extending almost to its knees. I swallowed back a terrified sob.

"Jax? Please, Jax. I know you can hear me. Please," I whimpered as I lowered the weapon. The clawed hands raised to its ears, clutching its head as an agonized howl tore from its chest.

The ground vibrated again, shaking loose more bits of the ceiling and walls. This must have brought Jax's attention back to the present, because he advanced. I raised the pistol with shaking hands.

"Jax, please." He didn't even flinch, just kept coming. "Don't— Don't make me—" My finger quivered over the trigger as I tightened my grip. Could I do it? Could I shoot him? My brother. Even if it were to save my own life? Sweat dripped between my tightened shoulder blades. "I— Can't—" A sob hiccupped out. I dropped the weapon and my shoulders hunched forward in defeat. I couldn't shoot him. I'd never do a thing to harm him, even if he wanted me dead. He lunged forward and lifted me effortlessly. I didn't fight as I was carried out of the room, tears steadily streaming down my face.

The flickering lights had dimmed significantly; the backup power had been failing. Brief flashes of light illuminated the hallways, causing an almost strobe-like effect. Guards rushed in and out of rooms, carrying boxes and small cages filled with animals. They disappeared down the corridor without even bothering to look in our direction. Like they were single mindedly carrying out their mission. Jax turned us in the opposite direction.

"Where are…" was all I managed to get out, when what felt like a Mack truck plowed into us. I was tossed into the air, out of my brother's grasp. My body sailed sideways, and I braced myself for the pain from the impact. Heat wrapped around me, and I was righted in the next instant and set on my feet. A second hulking form stepped in front of me, pushing me gently behind him, and let out a menacing growl.

"Garron," I breathed.

Red veins crackled up his gray, muscular arms like lightning in the dark as his towering body stood ready to defend me. My heart skipped a beat; he was here and OK. I really had to stop underestimating him. And I had to do something, or they'd kill each other. I grabbed Garron's arm; heat flared between us, and the veins under my skin lit up with the contact. Energy filled my body with the touch, renewing my sense of purpose and I sidestepped.

"Jax! It's me! Please listen, you can't do this! I need you!" Garron flinched slightly at my words.

"You're. Coming. With. Us." He gritted out between teeth as he lowered his head and began stalking forward. Blood trickled from a gash on his cheek and from the corner of his mouth, coating his lips and teeth, making him look even more terrifying. Almost out of thin air, Sierra materialized in front of him and stepped between us.

She punched her palms out flat, contacting Jax's chest, sending him sliding backward. Her body heaved with labored breaths, her slightly larger frame showed tense muscles rippling down her arms as her stance readied for battle.

"Jaxon Devins! I'm going to kick your ass!" she howled. Sierra looked back over her shoulder, her red eyes glowing in the flickering darkness. "You OK?" Her head swiveled back toward my brother, not waiting for an answer. I was speechless, my mouth hanging open as she stalked forward. "What the fuck do you think you are doing? You leave me without a word. Go missing for weeks. And when I find you, you're trying to hurt your little sister!" Confusion and anger took over Jax's features as he clutched the sides of his head, shaking it back and forth. A small rivulet of blood began to leak steadily from his nose.

"Sssierrra," he ground out.

He dropped his hands to his sides, his chest heaving as his jaw and monstrous features began morphing until his normal facial features returned. The gash on his forehead was now more noticeable and blood dripped freely down his now recognizable face. His body had yet to change back, remaining huge and gray as he took a step toward her.

"Hey, you," she whispered with tenderness, taking a step forward to meet him.

I choked on a sob; seeing my brother come back to us was beyond words. My chest throbbed with emotion, a small smile automatically tugging at my mouth as I stepped forward. Jax's eyes darted toward the movement, toward me.

"Jax?" I tilted my head in question as his body started shaking.

"Max... don't. Stay b-bback. Arrrhhhaaa!" He slammed a palm to his forehead and more blood poured from his nose. Garron's hand shot out to grip my arm, and we both froze.

"Jax, what's happening?" Sierra demanded, stepping in front of him, blocking me from view.

"I... they... Elias... wants her," he gritted out. She reached out and slapped his face, hard. His head twisted with the impact, then his eyes shot to her, glowing with malice.

"Don't you even! I'm exhausted. I dragged myself down here through dirt and crevices. I've fought, been chased, scratched, bit, cut up and bled to get to you. You are staying with me, Jaxon Devins." His nostrils flared. The noise of long, deep inhales seemed to echo in the hallway. Head tilting to the side, he stepped toward her and whatever she saw made her step back.

She tripped over debris that had fallen from the ceiling and Jax launched himself at her. Her body was caught, mid-flight, but instead of righting her,

Jax pushed her flat below him as he caged her in, hovering above. A deep rumble emanated up his chest and she turned her head, eyes squeezed shut. The small rivulets of blood dripped from the wounds on his face and onto hers. She squirmed, her movements panicked, trying to escape from under him, but to no avail. Twisting her head from side to side, drops of blood splashed on her face and lips. Her tongue darted out instinctively, and her body went visibly ridged. Her eyes popped open, and the red sparks flared brighter. Hand darting out between them, she reached up and grabbed his throat. I wasn't sure if it was to push him away or pull him toward her. He grabbed her arm, stopping her movement and ran his nose over the cuts and scrapes from her elbow to her palm. Then he sank his teeth into the flesh above her wrist as a high-pitched noise of surprise burst from her lips.

Their eyes locked in an intimate moment, and I looked away. I felt like I was intruding on something that was for them alone. I squeezed Garron's hand, noticing the scowl on his face as he watched. Turning toward me, I smiled sheepishly, recalling our first moments. I shrugged innocently, eliciting a small, lopsided grin. Even in his beastly state, the dimple from his grin caused a pleasant flutter in my stomach.

"We've gotta go," I whispered, my body still shaking with adrenaline, and he nodded. I cleared my throat, rather obnoxiously, to get their attention and both their gazes shot my way. "Let's get out of here!" As soon as the words left my mouth, another rumble shook the mountain. Jax picked Sierra up from the floor and we all took off at a run. I was so turned around and confused by this labyrinth, I just followed Jax and Garron, trusting they knew how to get us out. I was the last one in line, so they didn't notice when I fell behind.

A hand darted out of a darkened doorway, clotheslining me. I flew through the air from the force of the rebound; the wind rushing from my lungs on impact. I scrambled backward, unable to catch my breath. Time slowed and the scream of terror caught in my throat as my nightmares' ghost stalked toward me.

"Hello again, Sweets." The voice seemed to echo around me, breaching the ringing in my ears. I squeezed my eyes shut and shook my head back and forth. This couldn't be happening. I cracked my lids back open. My nightmare was strolling almost lazily toward me with a huge grin on his face. Plumbs of dust swirled in his wake as bits and pieces of the ceiling continued to break apart.

"You— You're dead. I-I killed you." I stammered, still not believing my eyes. A chuckle filled the air.

"Awe, Sweets, a perfect name for you I might add. You thought you did. But your blood, your sweet, sweet blood…" He licked his lips. "It was a gift, you see. But it wasn't your only gift." He rubbed himself through his pants, grinning menacingly. I forced the stomach acid burning up my throat back down. "I paid a heavy price for that piece, and I didn't even have a chance to finish our fun." He brought up a handless arm and rubbed the stump, scowling. My mouth hung open in shock as he continued. "I still want another taste." The last statement came out low and husky. He was towering over me now as terror and rage warred within. There was no way I was letting that man ever touch me again.

My vision hazed, and my body heated to the point of burning. My heartbeat pounded so hard I thought my eardrums would burst. I took in a breath and the heat burning through me centered in my chest, as if the energy pulsing through me pooled there. The visceral scream burned, as it tore up through my chest and lungs. A shock wave blasted out of my body with my scream, blowing Eddie backward through the air. The walls vibrated and cracked further, blowing bits and pieces inward as the blast radiated like a sonic boom in succession down the hall.

Chapter 39

Maxine

I wasn't sure how long I laid there, totally dazed and drained. Shouts and rumbling from the ground echoed through what was left of the halls. I sat up slowly, my body sluggish. I blinked into the darkness. My vision was as if a red light had been turned on; everything in various shades of red. Bits and pieces of the ceiling and walls floated around like snowflakes. I struggled to my feet, using the crumbling wall to help me stand, knowing time was running out. I had to get out of here and catch up with the others. Stumbling forward, I stopped as a large figure stomped in slow and unsteady movements toward me. A handless arm reached out. Eddie balanced himself against the wall with his stump as he continued to move toward me.

I squinted, focusing on Eddie as he came closer, my vision sharpening. His clothes and skin beneath were shredded. There were chunks of flesh missing and his wounds were bleeding and oozing freely. His skin looked as though it had been peeled away in layers, like a burn victim. A stench of seared flesh and hair burned my nose, making my eyes tear. Swiping the moisture and dust away with the back of my hand, I refocused. His eyes widened as he looked up, red orbs locking on me as he continued to stagger forward, his mouth pulled into a slow smile. It was more disturbing now as his lips had been peeled away, making his mouth look larger, showing every single tooth. Some of his skin was starting to slowly knit back together through the openings of his mangled clothes. As he advanced, each step became stronger. Even with my waning strength, panic made my body shake. Maybe it was my adrenaline, as my flight instinct was kicking in. I snapped my head around, looking behind me for an exit, seeing only darkness and rubble. I swallowed hard. I had to get past him. It was the only way out.

If I was going to make it, I had to act now—while he was still weakened. It would be my only chance. I reached down and grabbed the knife from my boot. Gripping the handle like it was a lifeline, I took off toward my walking nightmare. Pumping my legs with everything I had, I barreled down the hall. Just as I reached Eddie, I threw my body into a slide, feet first, between his legs. I slashed out as I slid through, slicing along his ankle and through his Achilles tendon. He roared with pain. I popped up behind him, leapt onto his back and sank the blade into the juncture between his neck and shoulder. He reared back with another howl, reaching back and grabbing my hair. Spinning wildly, he threw himself backward into the wall; my body slammed between the two. All the air whooshed out of my lungs and dizziness swamped me, but I hung on. Yanking the blade from his neck was harder than I thought, and I had to wiggle it back and forth spastically before I could draw back to strike again. He slammed back against the wall a second time, and my arm flailed wildly, my grip loosened, and the knife clattered across the floor. A third smash against the wall, and black dots speckled my vision from the force of the impact and lack of oxygen. My body slid limply to the ground as I struggled to catch my breath. Forcing my limbs to move, I crawled down the hall, trying with everything I had left to get away. One arm over another, I used my forearms to drag myself forward. I didn't look back as I could finally lift myself onto my hands and knees and tried climbing over and around debris. I was only focused on a few inches ahead, so when two booted feet appeared directly in front of my face, it startled me, and I quickly sat back with a shriek. Looking up, a large male figure towered over me, scowling. Jonas.

I didn't have time to even utter a word. His massive arm swung out, connecting with Eddie, who had apparently been right behind me. Eddie smashed off the wall and slid down to the floor in a heap, unmoving. Jonas stepped over me and kicked Eddie's head like a football for a field goal. His head rocked backward and lay at an odd angle.

"He won't hurt you again. You OK?"

I stared, not used to so many words in his gravely timbre. He'd never really spoken, even when we'd play as children. Still in shock, I didn't protest when Jonas bent down, lifted me into his arms and turned, jogging down the hall at a quick pace. I knew Jonas wouldn't hurt me, I wasn't sure how I knew that, but I felt sure to my soul. We moved through the halls and doorways, taking twists and turns. Nothing looking familiar. The halls were still dark, and the smell of smoke was thickening in the air. I wondered briefly if Jonas could see as I could, red lighting up our way. A dim light shone in the dark, getting brighter the closer we got. As if the area we were headed toward still had power. With that thought, the lights flickered and dimmed, but remained on. Well, guess this area was on its way out, too. We reached what looked like a small transit terminal where a small white shuttle waited.

Jonas gently set me down on my feet. His hands lingered on my arms for an extra second before he took a step back. The fridged chill of shock was taking over my muscles at the loss of his body heat. Looking into his ever-stoic face, a quiet "Thank you" was all I could manage. He nodded, and it looked like a smile ghosted across his face. I blinked. It was so quick; I wasn't sure if I had just imagined it. His face hardened as his gaze darted behind me at the same time I heard movement. Turning, I saw Elias step into view, exiting the shuttle. My eyes widened as I took in his appearance. He was bigger. Not as big as Garron or Jonas, but definitely bigger than he used to be. His thin and frail limbs were thicker, muscle showing beneath a now tight suit. He walked toward me, unassisted, with an air of confidence he'd never had. His once pale, gaunt face and dull hair now shone with a healthy glow. His features were fuller and more masculine, giving him a strong yet still sharp jawline. A smile lit up his face and there was warmth in his icy blue eyes. He looked happy and healthy, handsome even.

After a moment of shock, my brain came back online, and my brows drew together; he was happy? Amongst all the chaos and death and his father's mountain crumbling around us? Yes, he definitely looked happy and excited. Why?

"Maxine, what a pleasure to see you. I've been waiting." His voice was smooth.

"Elias," I breathed. "What's going on?! Please tell me..." I shook my head. "Please tell me this wasn't you. These people, and Jax... the things happening here..." I trailed off, rubbing my hands up and down my chilled arms.

"Oh, Max. Now, you know fair and well my father started all of this." He stretched his arms out wide, twisting back and forth, indicating all around him. "But he isn't here anymore, is he?" His voice dropped as he leaned forward, a dark look directed at me. My eyes widened.

"You know that was an accident! I never—" he put up his hand with a stop gesture.

"Hey, easy, I know it was an accident," he said in a soothing tone as he stepped forward. "But regardless, you took that from me. I was supposed to be the last face he looked at before his pain-filled death." His hand curled into a fist and all the dots started to slowly connect. He had wanted to kill his own father. Fear seeped into me, and I trembled.

"I'm so sorry, Elias." He closed his eyes and let out a small sigh.

"I love the sound of my name on your lips. And you needn't worry, you'll have all the time in the world to make it up to me." He smiled at my confusion. "You're coming with me." My mouth gaped open. "Our southern facility has everything we need to continue. I'll be the most powerful man in the world. And you, Max, will be at my side. We'll be unstoppable. I can give you anything your heart desires. We're going to change the world. Together." Excitement poured from him. He truly thought I was just going to go. He was delusional.

"I can't go with you," I blurted out in disgust. "You knew Jax was here! That they were doing horrible things to him, to Garron and other people. I have to find Jax. And the others." I shook my head and began to turn. Anger welled up with thoughts of everything that had happened over the last few days. I knew I should just keep my mouth shut, but my emotions were getting the best of me. I spun back, deciding to finish some of my tirade.

"Frank was hurt! He is like a father to me; he may even be dead! And because of you... Eddie..." I bit back a sob, covered my mouth and dropped my eyes.

"Now, that will never happen again." His voice was firm, and my shocked gaze shot back to his. He knew? "I'm truly sorry Eddie had ulterior motives. I didn't know he was capable—But I made him pay—with flesh and blood." He was angry now and a sinister tone entered his voice, his mouth pulling down into a scowl. Rage began to fill his eyes as they swirled manically, and it was terrifying. My body stiffened, realization ringing with the memory of Eddie's missing hand. Had he cut off Eddie's hand? I trembled, fear replacing the anger, and backed away slowly.

"Don't be afraid of me, Max." Our eyes connected and I felt like I was falling. Sliding down into an abyss. The room narrowed down to Elias. Everything else tumbled away. "That's it," he spoke in a soothing tone, smiling. I felt my lips pull up, mirroring his. "Now, let's go. We have lots to do...together." He stretched his hand out toward me and I stepped forward. Calm swept over me; Elias was going to take care of me.

Heat pulsed through my body, so hot it drew my attention, and I paused just before my hand touched his. I looked down quizzically at my outstretched hand and saw red lightning crackling under my skin. My vision suddenly changed, and I blinked rapidly. Elias' eyes met mine, his brows drawn together in confusion. My head swiveled from his gaze, as if I was being forced to redirect my attention by some intrinsic instinct. I recognized the figure immediately. Heat pulsed from Garron as his body glowed with a brightness that drew me like a moth to a flame. He wasn't even in the room, and I could still see him. Heat brightened to vivid colors. It was as if I was seeing infrared, and right through a wall! A small surge of panic made me aware that it shouldn't have even been a possibility, that maybe I was just crazy. Perhaps this was a dream...or was it a nightmare?

A primal roar ripped through the air, stopping all thought as a door exploded from its hinges, blowing inward, and I blinked against the new gust of debris. Garron burst through the opening, chest heaving. His gray skin lit up like mine, and his red eyes glowed like flame as he stalked forward, anger pulsing off him in waves. He was huge. Almost everything about him had nearly doubled in size. Jax and Sierra surged in behind him just moments later. I turned the rest of my body toward Garron, gravitating toward him like a magnet without even thinking. Our eyes met and my thoughts cleared as my pulse quickened.

Shots rang out and a guard sprang forward; his gun pointed at Garron's chest. Garron zig-zagged with unbelievable speed, ending behind the guard and tearing his head from his body with a vicious grunt.

I didn't even flinch as I lunged forward, but almost immediately ricocheted backward and onto my ass. Stumbling, I reached out and was abruptly halted by an invisible wall. With energy pulsing around me, and my vision still registering heat signatures, I traced the outline of a bubble around me. *What the fuck?* I spun around, my back pressed against the invisible wall, my vision returning to normal as I panicked. Elias' arm was stretched toward me, his fingers splayed outward as if he was trying to catch a ball, and a small trickle of blood dripped from his nose. He gritted his teeth as he spoke.

"You. Are. Leaving. With. Me. Now!"

His other hand came up, propelling out what I could only describe as a shock wave. Garron flew backward through the air. Jax rushed forward, but was stopped by another invisible wall, just like me. Sierra charged toward Elias, only to have Jonas backhand her through the doorway they came from. Additional guards piled out of nowhere and surrounded us, their weapons drawn.

The energy holding us flickered, and Elias stumbled. Jonas was at his side in a microsecond. I took the opportunity to dive forward and slid on my knees to Garron, who was groaning as he regained consciousness. He rolled to his side and struggled to his feet as I helped him up. I turned to see rage on Elias' face as he watched me helping Garron, and I wished I hadn't. The very air around his body pulsed. I redoubled my effort to get Garron moving as another chill of terror seeped into my body. Elias was going to kill us.

"You would choose that abomination over me?" Elias growled. Sierra regained her footing and raced back toward us, freezing mid-way.

"Let him go!!" she screamed.

I turned, almost in slow motion, dread filling me. Oh God. Elias had Jax levitated off the ground. His back was arched, and his mouth was open in a silent scream. I let go of Garron, lifting my hands in surrender.

"Please, Elias. Don't hurt him." I begged, as hot tears streamed down my face.

"Ah, now I have your attention, don't I? Hmm... I have a proposal. A trade perhaps." He smiled sadistically.

"Wh-what trade?" I asked, my stomach sinking.

"Well, you, silly. I'll trade Jax for you. If you come with me now." Tingles ran the length of my spine, tightening the hair on my scalp and my heart thundered within my chest. *Oh God! How can I fix this? He'll have all of my friends killed, my brother...* My breath came out in rapid pants, sweat beading my brow.

"Tick tock, my dear, your time is running out." He twisted his hand and my brother's arm bent at an awkward angle, making a crunching sound. Jax's deep grunts of pain echoed in the space. Sierra cried out for Elias to stop. My heart squeezed.

"Please, Elias, stop! Don't do this!" He ignored me. He lifted his other hand and Sierra flew across the space, slamming into the wall and dropped to the ground, unmoving. Please, just let her be unconscious, I prayed.

"Guards! Take the brunette, throw her into one of the cages. If that mutant tries to move, shoot him." He dropped Jax to the ground. I went to move forward, but my movement stuttered. "Jaxon, get up," Elias demanded, and I felt a pulse of energy. Jax's body twitched for a brief second, then he complied, standing with his back to us, facing Elias. Another crunching noise drew my eyes to Jax's arm as it righted itself. He didn't move otherwise. "Well, looks like you're both coming with me." He let out a humorous laugh and flashed me a grin.

"No, please. Elias... I..." Garron's hand reached out and grabbed my arm.

"Don't, Max," his whisper was so quiet I almost didn't hear it. Our eyes met, and I saw a flicker of panic. My heart gave a painful thump as a tear slipped from the corner of my eye. I gritted my teeth and pulled my arm from his grip as I lunged forward. The invisible wall reconstructed at my back, and Garron slammed into it trying to stop me.

"Elias, I'll go. I won't fight. Leave them. Leave Jax and the others, and I'll go. Please, let Jax go," I begged. He rolled his eyes at me.

"So dramatic." Another explosion somewhere in the mountain shook the ground and an alarm from the shuttle blared. "Time to go. Get in and I'll let them go. They'll just die down here in a matter of minutes anyway." He shrugged. He flicked his hand toward Jax, and his body sagged. I swallowed past the lump in my throat.

"Jax, you OK?" Concern and panic laced through my words. He spun toward me, an expression of alarm on his face.

"What have you done?" he asked, eyes wide. I ran to him, hugging him as tightly as I could.

"Saving your ass for a change." I pulled back and smiled sadly, trying to hold back the floodgate of tears.

"Time to go, Max!" Elias' voice rose with irritation. I looked back; Garron howled from the opposite side of the invisible wall, bloody smears from his fists pounding against it, blurring the space between us. Or maybe it was my tears threatening to spill. I mouthed 'I'm sorry' and his eyes blazed. I couldn't look anymore. Denying the visceral need to run to him felt like someone was trying to rip out my sternum. If I didn't go with Elias, they were all going to die. I turned back, hugging my brother one last time and leaned against his ear.

"Mom's alive. Go get Dad." I whispered to him only. His body stiffened, so I knew he heard me as I stepped away.

The ground shook and horrible noises of destruction sounded in the distance. I reached out and took Elias Gregori's waiting hand and stepped onto the shuttle. I didn't glance back as the doors closed behind me, too afraid my heart would burst into pieces if I saw the anguish I could hear.

The End... for now.

Acknowledgements

This work of fiction is my very first completed book baby. I truly had no idea what I was getting into... and neither did my husband. Had he known how my crazy mind worked sooner, we may not have been married. In all seriousness, a huge thank you to my husband Carl. Your support and tolerance for unmatched socks, late dinners and extremely odd questions was impressive. I know you'll never read this, and oddly, I find that hysterical and strangely comforting.

To My Little Sunshine, who watched me tote my computer to every sporting event like it was a normal extension of me. Who offered the strangest ideas to aid my stories, leaving me in awe of her imagination. And who showed as much excitement as I felt, when I announced I finally had a publisher.

To my very first editor, Natasja Smith, for cleaning up a chaotic rough draft, pointing me in the right direction and not making me feel crazy in the least. Your help will forever be remembered with the utmost gratitude.

To Stephanie Adam, for showing up at the last minute to take author photos and not making me look like the hot mess that I was.
And to Black Rose Writing, for encouraging my manuscript revision and seeing something worthy in my story. I will be forever grateful.

About the Author

Trinity is a marginalized writer, wife, full-time working mom and serious foodie with a caffeine addiction. Also, an avid reader of all things dark, fantastical, and sometimes scary. A lover of all animals and ironically allergic to everything with fur, don't tell her cat and dog. Determined or stupid? You decide. She loves cooking beautiful meals for her family but finds pizza to be a regular standard, as running to a multitude of sport events with her little takes up most evenings. In free time, she's usually found working on her next new world or reading, surrounded by her cat, dog, and boxes of tissues. Trinity has written *Burning Red*, its two subsequent and a few short stories.

Note from Trinity Slain

Word-of-mouth is crucial for any author to succeed. If you enjoyed *Burning Red*, please leave a review online—anywhere you are able. Even if it's just a sentence or two. It would make all the difference and would be very much appreciated.

You can follow me on FaceBook, Instagram and TikTok. Or visit my website and sign up for my newsletter for updates on new releases and links to fantastic reads.

Trinityslainauthor.com
trinityslainauthor@gmail.com

Thanks!
Trinity Slain

We hope you enjoyed reading this title from:

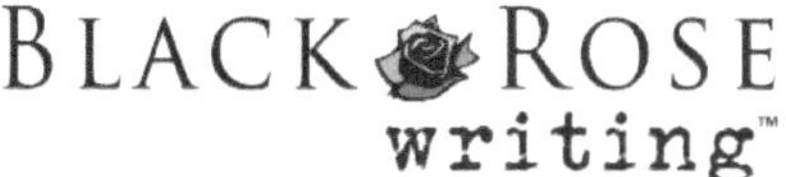

www.blackrosewriting.com

Subscribe to our mailing list – *The Rosevine* – and receive **FREE** books, daily
deals, and stay current with news about upcoming
releases and our hottest authors.
Scan the QR code below to sign up.

Already a subscriber? Please accept a sincere thank you for being a fan of
Black Rose Writing authors.

View other Black Rose Writing titles at
www.blackrosewriting.com/books and use promo code
PRINT to receive a **20% discount** when purchasing.